Advance

Reader

Copy

FRENCH LETTERS

BOOK THREE

CHILDREN OF A GOOD WAR

Jack Woodville London

Vire Press, LLC, Austin, Texas

Published by
Vire Press, L.L.C., Austin, Texas
www.virepress.com

Cataloging-in Publication Data
London, Jack w. 1947–
French Letters, Children of a Good War/Jack Woodville London
p.   cm.

ISBN: 978-0-9906121-8-6
I. Vietnam War   II. Texas—Family Life   III. Historical Fiction
Fic Lon   PS642 L86 2018

CHILDREN OF A
GOOD WAR

An Epiphany

There was a minor commotion in the street and she realized that she had no choice but to follow him outside. It was a relief, she felt, although she knew it was only a postponement.

Miss Herald had gone to Faversham to tell Eldred Potts that she would no longer walk out with him, as it then was called. Her roommate had told her to "just go chuck him." Miss Herald, however, had been raised in a more diplomatic home and, while she had known from the first day when he came up to sit with her on the Commons that Potts was not for her, she also had not told him so quickly enough. He had misread her signs and now, three months later, it was time to get rid of him. She had waited until this day at the end of term, then ridden the double deck bus from Canterbury to Faversham to say that he must discontinue the favor of courting her.

She had practiced her words: "Eldred, it's over." "Eldred, you're a very nice man, but...." "Eldred, I've decided that when term is over I shall go to Australia, (or, perhaps, India), and never come back." None seemed just right when all she wanted to say was she didn't want to date him any longer—no more cinemas, no more walks in the cathedral close, no more fending off his pleas for a snog in the corner.

The difficulty was that Eldred Potts was a very nice young man. Like her, he was interested in archeology. Worse, he lived within a mile of the prime dig on offer, a ruined twelfth-century abbey not more than ten miles from Canterbury itself. She thrilled at the idea of unearthing the tombs of King Stephen and Queen Maude and dusting them off with a toothbrush, of digging up a chalice or the remnants of a scriptorium. She also quailed at the image of Eldred Potts hovering over her in the process. The fact was that she found him boring and, worse, he was deeply attached to his mother, so much so that he lived at home during university term.

In short, Miss Herald couldn't stand him. It was time to say goodbye. Now, but for the commotion outside his parents' home, she already would have said her piece and been on her way back to the bus. She stood on his porch and observed.

"It's one of Mr. Barkus' dairy cows," Potts called back to her from the street. "She's got loose! Let's get her." Before she could ask who Mr. Barkus was or say 'Right, then, I'm off—see you,' or anything else, Potts had run after Bossie. Unfortunately, the cow was headed in the direction of the new motorway instead of back to Mr. Barkus' pasture. "Come on!" Miss Herald was stuck.

Bossie made it almost to the *Maison Dieu*, a lovely old half-timbered inn where Chaucer's pilgrims had passed a last night on the way to Becket's shrine at Canterbury Cathedral. There she found a patch of lawn from which Potts shooed her to get her away from a not-lovely stanchion of high-tension wires. He caught her bell rope and turned her back toward the town.

Miss Herald tried to make a run for the bus but there was none due for a half-hour. She accepted her detour and concluded that the farewell perhaps would be a softer message if spoken on the grounds of the ruined abbey.

The way back lay along the high street. Potts alternated between pointing out the new Sainsbury's on the one hand and the medieval spire of St. Mary of Charity on the other, then clucking "Easy, Bossie," and steering the cow away from the window boxes of the homes that lined Abbey Road. When they neared the playing fields of Queen Elizabeth Grammar, the cow bolted for the lush grass. Miss Herald wanted a reprieve.

"Might you get one of the men to help, Eldred? I should like to catch the 3:18."

"Not many men you'd find hereabout," he answered. "Not at this hour. Into London, most of 'em. There's Lillian Foster." Potts reclaimed Bossie's rope and pointed to a girl, wearing pants, who was kicking a soccer football to a scrum of ten-year-olds. "Her da' is a mechanic, over to Gatwick." He also pointed out the new National Health clinic, a line of women queued in waiting. "Here's like a tide," he said in his wisest voice. "The rail washes all the men away in the morning, washes 'em back here in the evening." Miss Herald assumed that the women left behind were the sand on the beach of such a tide. "The brewery's about the only thing here that's still run the way it always was. That's what my ma says, anyway."

Eldred Potts had known everyone in Faversham since he was out of nappies. From his point of view, he was killing two birds with one stone. Mr. Barkus would be grateful for the return of the cow and, at the same time, Potts could take Miss Herald right up to the archeology dig at the abbey and tell her what he saw for their future. *She surely will like that*, he thought.

They led Bossie to her meadow. She stopped to nip at fresh shoots and to chew, swinging her head lazily from side to side. Eldred Potts fumbled for Miss Herald's hand while the cow ate her way along for a hundred yards, ignored the archeologist's ditch and the perimeter wall foundation stones of Faversham Abbey, and stepped without pause past the black-and-white surveyor flags. Nothing, not a fence or hedgerow, separated the abbey's stone footings, the outlines of its chapel and kitchens, perhaps its gate, from the Barkus Dairy. Potts and Miss Herald followed the cow.

The laborers on site who worked their transits, shovels, and brushes had paid little attention to the cow, or the couple, when they walked onto the abbey grounds. "She done it before," the workers would later report. "Lots of 'em cows wanders over here to graze. Ground's a bit soft, especially over there."

They pointed to an ancient fosse by way of explanation. Indeed, the only one watching carefully was Bossie's owner, Mr. Barkus himself, when, in his words:

"The fokin' cow exploded! As Christ is my witness, she blew up! Just like that."

The noise was deafening. The workers knew only that their ears burst from percussion and pain while brown and white dairy cow rained down on them, hoofs here, tail there, Bossie's pitiful head landing on a wooden tool shed. An entire stomach with intact bag and teats fell nearby.

The *Daily Courier*, the first newspaper on the scene, reported in the morning edition of May 6, 1976:

> "Ain't seen nothing like it," according to Nicholas Ortmore, 30, of Dunkirk, who had been pushing a barrow thirty yards away. Ortmore added, "She was just grazing, like, and 'BOOM!' I looked up to see this cow what was up in the air and then it was coming down. Them young people didn't have a chance."

'It' was the rest of Bossie's torso, which had landed in a single heap on Eldred Potts just as he had begun to tell Miss Herald that he had been saving up to buy her a set of matching picks and hammers. His neck was broken; he died in hospital later that afternoon before his parents could be fetched back from a roofing products sales meeting in Dover.

The vicar, in his sermon for Eldred Potts, delivered a soothing message that he had composed from a blend of the Psalms and the Book of Revelation. "We all walk through the valley of the shadow of death but should fear no evil. Young Eldred Potts surely feared none as he walked through God's meadow. Why?" With a wounded, knowing sigh, the vicar gazed over his parish and continued right into Ecclesiastes: "Because for every thing there is a season, a time to sow and a time to reap. A time to live and, as painful as we find it to be, a time to die. The beast that thou sawest was, and is not; and shall ascend out of the bottomless pit, and go into perdition. The end is coming for us all."

The beast had come for Eldred Potts. The congregation nodded and wiped at their tears.

Most agreed with Mr. Ortmore, especially those in Faversham itself, that young Potts had not had a chance. "It was all them changes that caused this." They could have meant that Sainsbury's should not have forced the greengrocer and the baker out of business, that Lillian should not have been racing about with the boys, that her father and the rest of Faversham's men should have been satisfied with jobs in the town, that Mr. and Mrs. Potts should have been right there at home.

What they really meant was that Eldred Potts should not have been trying to court Miss Herald in the first place. "He should have stayed with his own kind," they whispered. "She didn't even come to the funeral." "Just who does she think she is?"

Others, however, disagreed. The cause was obvious and should have been clear to all. The cow had stepped on a soft, wet patch of lovely meadow and, beneath it, a high explosive bomb that the Luftwaffe had dropped during the Blitz. Buried beneath the surface, it had waited decades before blowing anything up.

"Nobody thinks how things keep blowing up years and years after the War's over," they said, "but it happens all the time. We just don't look for it."

It was small consolation to anyone that Eldred Potts was buried in sight of the abbey ruins. His mourners shook their heads and said to one another that it made them wonder, then buttoned themselves up against an unseasonably cold wind.

Children of A Good War

Part One

Chapter One

i.

A young man who was in the transportation section of a National Guard unit that had been doing its summer training at Fort Carson was in the process of driving a two-and-a-half-ton army truck filled with two squads of National Guard infantry soldiers when something fell downward in front of his windshield, bounced once, rolled underneath the truck, and landed on I-25 just inside the Colorado Springs city limits. Because the unit was traveling in convoy, at least two and perhaps three more trucks struck the body before they could get off the road and come to a complete stop. By the time the highway patrol and city police arrived the driver was so shaken up as to be incoherent. A lieutenant who had been riding in the following vehicle told them that it happened so quickly that the first he knew that something had gone wrong, really wrong, was when he felt the front wheels roll over the body.

Several hours passed while the police tried to find out who Woodrow Wilson Hastings was and where he lived. According to his driver's license he was sixty-seven years old and was a resident of Del Sur, a small town about one hundred miles to the west, across the Front Range. Police also found his wallet with a Visa card and seven one-dollar bills, thirty-eight cents in change, and an envelope sent by a person named Fondren at the Enumclaw, Washington, Public Utility Commission that contained a pamphlet describing the events of a planned reunion in France for the 54th Civil Affairs battalion at the 1984 D-Day Ceremonies, paper-clipped to a crumpled handwritten note:

> "5/30/1983 – Doc, I can't believe it's been forty years. I
> hope you'll join us – Bring Geraldine."

17

There were also two keys, a receipt from the post office for $12.62, a discount coupon for Folgers Coffee, an unused 3" x 5" spiral pad, and one Bic fine point pen.

Several more hours went by before a deputy sheriff in Del Sur went to Will's house out by the river; it was completely empty. He made a few calls that led him to Davy at the fishing tackle shop, where he learned that Doc and his wife had just recently sold their cottage and moved to Colorado Springs.

In Colorado Springs, the police found a listing for Peter Hastings but not for Woodrow Wilson Hastings. Before unduly alarming anyone at that house, they began to make discreet calls to the local hospitals and, given the age of the man who had died on the highway, more calls to the local nursing homes.

The duty clerk at Loving Arms Home for Seniors said that yes, indeed, Dr. Hastings and his wife had lived there for about two weeks and asked if anything was wrong. She added that she was sorry but Mrs. Hastings probably wouldn't be much help, "...as she is a woman who might have dementia in that she hasn't said a word since I first met her back on New Residents Night." Doctor Hastings himself usually left for an hour or so in the morning, she added, to get the newspaper, and then stayed in their room until noon, when "he would walk with his wife down to the dining hall and have a bite of lunch." The clerk had come on duty after lunch that particular day so didn't know anything herself.

The detective wrote in his report that he was escorted to the subject's quarters, where he met a white female, identified as Virginia Hastings, age estimated mid-sixties, blue dress with dark shoes, graying hair, brushed and groomed appropriately, who politely stared at him while he asked her where her husband was, but never said a word. There was an empty coffee cup in the sink and a full cup of cold coffee on the small table in the front room. The detective made the decision to not show the subject's driver's license to the white female, who smiled at him and nodded her head when he said goodbye.

By the time the police decided to go to the home of Peter Hastings, identified by Loving Arms as the next of kin, others working the case had discovered that Doctor Hastings probably had walked that morning from the retirement home to a branch post office, where a clerk remembered telling him that he needed to add more postage to the brown clasp envelope because it was being mailed overseas. It was only a short walk from there to the frontage road of I-25. Two blocks further on there was an overpass with a walkway that crossed directly above the point where the subject had landed on the hood of the army truck.

Peter Hastings was not at home. In fact, at that moment, Peter was thirty-five thousand feet above Cape Cod, Massachusetts, advising Boston air traffic controllers that he was ready to initiate his descent into the New York area. Peter's wife answered the door. The policeman explained why he had come.

"It's not true!" said Peter's wife, Candace. She gasped, put her hand to her mouth, and sat down hard on the sofa in their living room. Her children heard the voices, stopped doing their homework, and ran to the living room to jump into Peter's arms and wrestle with him, only to discover that Peter wasn't home and that a policeman and a middle-aged man in faded slacks and a gray shirt were sitting with their mother on the sofa, holding her hand, and saying, "There, there." Candace was crying so hard that Jeff began to cry as well, without knowing what he was crying about. Tiffany figured out that she should call her grandmother.

Candace's parents arrived in a few minutes and it was from them that the police learned that Peter was Doctor Hastings' son. It was Candace's parents, the Barnetts, who along with the police provided the basic facts for the obituary that the funeral home placed in the Colorado Springs newspaper the following morning:

> Doctor Hastings is survived by his wife, Geraldine, and by his son Peter, Peter's wife Candace, and their children Jeff and Tiffany, of Colorado Springs. Peter is a graduate of the Air Force Academy and a pilot for Pan American World Airways. Doctor Hastings was born in Texas and, before retiring to Del Sur, Colorado, had been the doctor in Bridle, Texas, where he moved after the war. He also is survived by another son, Frank, and wife, Eleanor.

The police had already left before Peter called home from JFK airport to say that his flight had been absolutely perfect. They passed the receiver to Candace.

"Brace yourself," Candace had whispered back to him. "Your father died this morning." She gulped into the phone but was stable enough by then to tell him the basic facts.

"Oh, my God," Peter said. The phone was silent for a few moments, then Peter went on, "Poor Mother. Is she all right? Does she know what happened?"

Candace told him that she had gone to Loving Arms and told Virginia what had happened, but whether Virginia really understood, Candace could not say.

"I think she knows," Candace answered. "Her eyes kind of closed, I don't know how to say it, and she seemed to be looking over my shoulder, at the empty doorway, like she was waiting for Will to come walking in. They gave her something and then she just went into the bedroom and lay down. I don't really understand what happened," she added.

Peter called the funeral home and told them that he would be back home in about six hours. When he landed in Denver he drove to Colorado Springs and went home to see if his wife was holding up. She was holding up fine, so he then proceeded to Loving Arms, where Virginia did indeed look sad but still said not a word. Peter made the decision to go alone to the funeral home, but after meeting with the Director of Caring, he found himself overwhelmed by the decisions, made harder by the fact that it was strongly urged that the service be conducted with the casket closed. They explained to him more of the circumstances of Will's death and gave him Will's personal effects. They also provided a draft of the obituary which, in a dazed silence, he read over.

"We need to add some things," he said. He told them that Will had grown up as an orphan in a little town named Tierra. "It's somewhere between Lubbock and the New Mexico line. That's where he met Mother. And this is a mistake—her name is Virginia, not Geraldine. Where'd they get that?"

"Probably from the police," the Director of Caring responded. "They make mistakes like that all the time."

"I was born during the war and after he came back we moved to Bridle. That was really home. They retired a couple of years ago, to Del Sur, and then they sold the house there. They settled in at Loving Arms right before I flew this last bid." Peter was pretty shaken up about it. "We just got the closing papers filed."

Peter then realized the best thing to do was to have the funeral in Bridle.

"All their friends are there. They don't really know anybody here. They even still have the house I grew up in, never sold it. We were going to put it on the market and then..."

ii.

Will's and Virginia's friends were in Bridle.

Since Will delivered most of the people in town under the age of forty, the news of his death struck them as it would have if he had been their own family. He had set their broken bones and plugged their leaks. He had held their dying hands as their cancers grew and their organs failed. Bridle had been sorry to see him retire and leave and now took it very hard that he had passed away so soon after. No one took it harder, though, than George Grumman.

George was eating a baloney sandwich in the break room of the PanTex nuclear bomb factory when the security guards at the entrance called him on the loudspeaker to come up to the front. His wife, Lucille, had taken the call from Candace and drove all the way to the factory to tell George for fear he would hear about it some other way and have to drive home by himself. "They knew each other during the war," Lucille told the guards. On the drive home she tried to make small talk, about how Will had taken the appendixes out of their older sons and how their younger son, Tog ('The Other George') had been inseparable from Will's and Virginia's son Frank almost until they graduated.

Virginia also had been well liked in Bridle, the perfect mother to help with football banquets, drive boys to swimming lessons, and chaperone school outings. She had had a knack for printing up little things, school and church bulletins, announcements, the sort of thing that people needed without thinking about it. The news that they were moving to Colorado had sparked some comments at the time: "She's moving off to be next to Peter and her grandchildren." "Not really, I just think Doc wants to go fishing." "What about the other boy?" No one remembered as much about the other boy as about Peter. In any event, a Bridle that was saddened by Will's death also was a Bridle that worried about what would become of Virginia, a subject of much discussion over coffee at The Corral before the funeral.

iii.

In Tierra, however, news of his death was not a subject of discussion. No one there even knew Will had died until after the funeral when Butch Fleming called his sister Shirley to say that someone was on his way out to the farm to ask her about some people she used to know. Shirley would later tell people that when it happened, "I didn't know what it meant, but after I put two and two together I knew that the other day, when I felt a deep, strange chill come over me, it was exactly at the moment that Will passed away." She did not mention this, then or later, to Hoyt or Sonny, who had been working in the barn at the time.

Sandy Clayton was asked about it at the VA clinic in Lubbock, by a doctor who had read the announcement in a newsletter from the medical school where he had trained and noticed that Dr. Hastings had gone to high school in Tierra. It was just a matter of circumstance that his next patient was from Tierra and he asked Sandy whether he had known Dr. Hastings. It was not until late in the medical examination that Sandy realized that his doctor was talking about Virginia's husband. He answered that it had been a long time ago. "I'm not sure if I ever met him or not. He was mostly away in the army and when he got out, they moved away. I was just a boy then."

iv.

In Austin, Will's son Frank was at home, trying to focus on writing *An Khe*. He had finally gotten his novel past the chapters where Private Robert Hood had been drafted, made it through boot camp, and been sent to Vietnam. But Frank's mind kept wandering to the title of the book.

"What do you think about *Ambush at An Khe?*" he called out. Previous iterations had been named *Road to An Khe* and *Rescue at An Khe*. *Road to An Khe* was more accurate, since none of the story was actually in An Khe, but the other possible titles seemed boring, or disingenuous, or, in the case of *Rescue at An Khe*, not entirely correct. He wanted something with a bit of punch to it, something an agent would like from the first line. "*Ambush at*

An Khe is closer, don't you think?"

Eleanor called back to him from the next room, saying that he shouldn't worry about the title until the book was finished. "*An Khe* is fine for now."

Frank decided to send Private Hood to The Hairpin, where the Vietcong mortared the American pipeline every day. He began to type:

```
The rifle squad stood guard over Hood while he
probed the jagged metal to see how much damage
the mortar strike had done to the fuel pipe-
line. He peeled away the punctures and patched
up the hole until a real engineer unit could
come fix it repair it.
```

He looked at the keys again and began to worry about the setting. An Khe was up in the mountains but most of the story was down on the coast. There had been a lot of beaches on the coast, long, sandy stretches and soothing blue water. The truth is that mostly they went swimming and drank a lot of beer on the beaches, wading in and out between the fishing boats and the drying nets, giving kids cans of Miller beer to make them go away. Frank sat before the typewriter for a few minutes, trying to figure out how to get Hood from repairing the pipeline to the point where the helicopter exploded. He thought again about the beaches and his mind wandered back two weeks, to the day he had sat on another beach and watched Peter swimming in the ocean.

Peter had walked calmly across the sand, nonchalantly dropping the hotel's towel, then knifed into the water with a perfect dive. Frank remembered it clearly: with perfect strokes, Peter had swum out a hundred yards, flipped, backstroked his way parallel to the beach, then turned and swam back to shore, walking out of the water, trim and infuriating. "Beer?" Peter had suggested. Frank had floundered around to find a beer for him, eager to please. His mind then wandered to...

ring

...the memory of the dinner they'd had. The hotel dining room was open to the sea, overlooking a garden and the pool. Somehow the waitress had known what to bring Peter to drink, a rum punch with shaved ice, and Frank had felt like a...

ring

...fool, not knowing much about cocktails or wines and just ordering a beer. He remembered noticing that, even after the flight and two days of living out of a suitcase, Peter's shirt was perfectly pressed, his leather sandals fashionably perfect for the Bahamas. Peter was accustomed to spending for such things.

I felt like a bumpkin, sitting there in my jeans and tee shirt at the....

The telephone rang again, five times, six, then stopped. Frank lifted his fingers from the keys and waited. He heard Eleanor's muffled voice answering the call and then speaking to someone. He looked back at the typewriter.

Where was I? he wondered. *Yeah, getting the helicopter to the Hairpin.* He typed a couple of keystrokes.

"Frank?" Eleanor called from the next room. "Stop. It's Will."

Frank grudgingly lifted his hands from the keys, turned, and looked at her as she stepped quietly into the room. Eleanor held the telephone in both hands.

"Is Mother all right? Is Dad still on the telephone?" He reached for the receiver.

Frank had known this was going to happen. *It's not my fault. It's Peter's fault. I told Peter not to put them into a nursing home.* He had told Peter that Mother wouldn't like it. He had said they wouldn't take care of her there, either, not the way Dad had been taking care of her. He had even told Peter that Dad wouldn't be able to take care of her in Loving Arms, not the way he took care of her back at the cottage. *Peter should have left them alone...*

Eleanor didn't give the phone to him. Instead, she shook her head.

"No, Frank," she said. Her voice was soft and slow as she tried to say the right thing. "No, it's not Will calling about Virginia. It's Candace calling... about Will."

Chapter Two

Will's funeral was a disaster only if viewed from the point of view of immediate family and one or two others. For most of his friends the tragedy of Will Hastings had taken place back in 1983, when he retired, an unexpected blow to the town of Bridle that was roughly equal to the assassination of President Kennedy, the Iranians taking hostage America's embassy employees, and the Dallas Cowboys firing Tom Landry, all events that proved the world had changed—and not for the better. Even as a disaster, however, it began well.

Virginia rode in the car, all the way from Colorado, with Peter and Candace, and looked suitably bereaved, if lost. Peter, in his Pan Am captain's uniform, and Candace, in a black suit, were perfect, their children models of behavior. Frank and Eleanor came early and spoke quietly.

Frank did not disagree with Peter's choice of a solid pecan casket. It was acknowledged without debate that Peter had had to make some kind of decision and "pecan was fine." Peter, in his turn, nodded when Candace whispered in his ear that there was nothing wrong with Frank saying that he would like to give a eulogy. The arrangements director at the Bivins-Marsh Funeral Home confirmed the plans for flowers and pamphlets, helped choose a guest book and, upon inquiry, learned that interment would be simple to arrange in that Doctor and Mrs. Hastings had purchased four burial plots in the Bridle Protestant Cemetery back in 1968. It was decided that there would be a visitation on Thursday evening and the funeral itself on Friday morning. They left the funeral home, went to a coffee shop, and told stories about Will. Frank asked if Peter had learned anything more about what happened, and Peter said no. He gave the bag of personal effects to Frank with the invitation to see if he could make anything out of it. Frank put them in the trunk of his old Volvo.

Nearly everyone in the congregation had seen Virginia the evening before at the visitation, where Candace and Eleanor had sat with her in one of the pews. Virginia had smiled but, it was whispered, "She didn't really seem to know anyone, poor thing."

The same was not true of Peter. It hadn't hurt the town's affection for Doc that, in the words of Coach Lancaster, "That boy Peter Hastings was solid gold." At the visitation they had shaken Peter's hand, admired his wife and children, and said, "We're sure sorry for your loss."

A lot of people who had stood around the closed casket and flower stands claimed that Peter still looked like a television star and said that when he was a boy he had been friendly with everyone and charmed everyone. Peter had indeed studied very hard in school and also became the best football player in Bridle history. "Nobody could tackle you, not by himself," somebody said to him. "I figured you'd go on to play college ball,"—generally considered to be the highest compliment to be given in Bridle.

Someone at the visitation had asked Candace where she met Peter. "At the Air Force Academy," she answered, smiling but not elaborating. That was enough for another classmate, name not caught, to tell Candace, "Bridle High was especially proud of him for getting in there." Most of them knew Peter had gone on to fly gunships in Vietnam and then become an airline pilot.

"Who are you?" was a more frequent question to Frank. About half of Bridle had been born after Frank had graduated. Unlike Peter, he hadn't left many legends in his wake, nor had Frank given the other half of Bridle much to remember about him, certainly not compared to Peter. Even his old classmates hadn't heard much about him after graduation. "So, what have you been up to since then?"

"Oh, not much. I made it through Tech, got a degree, journalism, then they drafted me." When asked about Vietnam, he always said, "I spent a year trying not to get shot at."

"What are you doing with yourself these days?" someone asked.

"Not much. I'm in Austin now. Working for the paper." Frank wasn't willing to let anyone know about *An Khe*, not yet. Writing for a newspaper was one thing; posing as a real writer seemed to be quite a different thing. Bridle wasn't much of a town for posing, or so he thought.

Becky Grey did bring up the dark, dry, and cloudless night in their senior year when a mysterious sheet of ice coated Main Street. "I don't know anything about it," Frank had smiled, obviously pleased that she remembered. "Okay, what about the curious incident of the letter 'S' that somebody burned onto the football field? Do you know anything about that?" Becky's husband, Marshall, asked. That particular blaze had been fueled by a particularly pungent accelerant later determined to be a mixture of diesel fuel and chicken poop, after which Frank was nicknamed 'Nitro.' Frank weakly denied all knowledge of the events, and they blithely called him a fibber. Except for Tog, Frank did see everyone at the visitation he had hoped to see. It helped him to prepare to give the eulogy.

At the funeral next morning Reverend Antsley, speaking from the Book of Isaiah, said, "Doctor Will Hastings was a healer who took on all of our infirmities and all of our sorrows, yet from his tragic death everyone knew that he was himself stricken and afflicted." No one gave that phrase much thought at the time, nor did Virginia attempt to fling herself on the open casket, in no small part because it was closed but also in part because Peter kept a firm grip on her. A choir sang "Onward Christian Soldiers" and "Amazing Grace." Everyone in the church cried.

Frank spoke after Reverend Antsley sat down.

"My father, Woodrow Wilson Hastings, grew up in Tierra, Texas, and graduated from high school there in 1937. He went to Texas Western College in El Paso and then Texas Medical College in Galveston. He graduated just in time to elope with my mother, Virginia, and get drafted into the army. He was in D-Day in France. I'm not sure a lot of you knew this, but he was wounded pretty badly. I can't imagine a worse patient than a doctor in an army hospital. He recovered and went on to Belgium and Germany and was on his way to Japan when the war ended. The army sent him back to France until 1946, when he and Mother moved here." Frank paused to catch his breath. "So, Dad was a father, a healer, and a hero of the war. But you knew him better than I did, because I was just a son. He delivered most of you as babies, he took out your tonsils and gave you shots and set your broken arms. For you, he was a friend. During the last year that they lived here Dad asked every one of you men and all your families to go up to Colorado and go fishing with him. How many of you remember that?"

They all did.

Frank then reached under the lectern and brought out an ancient wicker fishing creel. He placed it in full view of the audience and stroked it with his right hand, then resumed.

"I last saw Dad about two weeks ago. I made it to Del Sur in time to help them move to the nursing home in Colorado Springs but, to tell the truth, I didn't do much because Dad wanted to go fishing." Frank looked up to see if Peter was scowling; he wasn't. "I'll be honest, I'm not sure that everyone who was there to help with the moving was real happy to see us go off up to the meadow, but that was what Dad wanted to do. I watched him pull on a set of rubber boots and take this old creel," Frank said, holding it up for the congregation to see. "He waded off into a stream toward a pond, then turned around and yelled back at me, 'You don't catch anything, you don't eat.'

"From where I was standing I could see his rod and the fishing line whip back and forth a few times and then touch down on the water. There, at the stream's edge, grass grew under an aspen grove. Pine trees ran all the way to a cliff. Beyond that cliff there wasn't anything but sky and in the distance more mountains, the quiet beauty of a place that was known only to God, to God and to Dad, who that one day was happier than I had ever seen him in his entire life."

Muffled sobs emerged from the pews. Men had brought hankies, and used them.

"We fished all day, or at least Dad did. He cooked a couple of trout over a grill and a fire pit, then made me put out the fire and cover it up and not leave a trace of anything. He said nobody ought to know we had ever been there. He smiled and I cleaned up and it was time to go.

"When we got home the packing was already done. Dad said it was time, and I wondered, *Time for what?* He disappeared inside the cottage, then came back out and gave me this old creel. I said no, but he told me to take it, his fishing days were over, and it was for me." Tears began to stream down Frank's face. "He used to say that in life everybody's just fishing for something. I believe that Dad fished to stay alive."

Frank then opened the creel, reached inside, and produced a printed sheet of silk that he held high for the mourners to see.

"When I got it home and opened it, I found this map inside. Dad used to tell me that maps were the most important things you could ever read.

28

'After the Bible, maps. You have to know where you are before you can figure out where you want to go.' The army used to give these maps to pilots so if they got shot down they could escape and find their way back to England. If you look at this map, you'll see little red ink lines and pin holes that told my dad where he was, and where he wanted to go."

It was just possible that Virginia looked up at that point, and listened.

Frank then brought out five small, leather-bound books, still in their wrapping.

"Then there were these books. They used to sit on a bookshelf in our living room. I don't remember if it was something Dad said, or Mother, or if we just knew, but we were not allowed to ever touch these books. They were off limits, period. Two weeks ago, I learned that Dad had met a man named Beckett back in the war who was just a hospital driver there in France. That driver went on to win the Nobel Prize for literature, and these are the books he wrote. I don't think Dad ever read a word in any of them, but what he told me was that he kept them right there because they reminded him that the least of us harbors greatness."

Most of the mourners nodded in complete agreement. A lot of them looked at Peter, proof of greatness right there in Bridle.

Frank went on. "'You don't have to do this,' I told Dad up in the mountains. He said 'No, it's time.' When he said it was time, he didn't mean it was five o'clock, or suppertime, or anything like that. He meant it was time to finish what he started, to come down off the mountain, to take care of Mother in that nursing home as best he could until death parted them, and that's what he did."

Boxes of tissues moved up and down the aisles. Many sobbed openly.

That, in the words of Tog's mother, Lucille, is when Frank's theater took a bad turn. As she later described it to the ladies who had been preparing the meal for after the cemetery:

"And then Frank plucked that picture out of that fishing creel. How'd he say it? Let me get it right. Here's what he said: 'And this snapshot! This is the only old picture I have of my parents, how they looked before Dad went off to the war.'"

It was just a grainy black-and-white Kodak; Frank held it high overhead to show everybody in the pews.

It was a nice picture, Will in his army uniform, Virginia in a dress and her hair all bundled up in a shingle, the two of them standing on the front porch of Poppy Sullivan's old house in Tierra. As he took out the photograph Frank nodded to one of the funeral home employees, who stepped forward to remove a drape from an easel that stood beside the casket. It revealed the same picture, enlarged to the size of a window.

Virginia saw it and shrieked.

What a closed casket couldn't do the photograph accomplished. Virginia bolted upright in the pew and sobbed loudly, shaking off Peter's and Candace's hands so that she could get to the picture on the easel. She rushed forward, crying, touched the faces on the photograph, and sank to her knees before an astonished congregation. Frank looked on in disbelief. Peter came forward to help her to her feet. Every person in the auditorium cried as one.

It was a wonderful end to the funeral, not diminished by Virginia's continuing to stare at the huge picture even as the men from the funeral home rolled Will down the aisle and out to the waiting hearse. The drive to Will's final resting place was delayed some minutes until it occurred to Frank that the only way to get Virginia to leave the easel and go out to the cars was to give her the snapshot he had in his hand so that she could stare at it on the way to the cemetery, which he did.

The entire town lined the sidewalk that led from the church door to the hearse, mourners sympathetically touching Virginia on the shoulder, stepping forward to give her a kiss on the cheek, to shake Peter's hand. Some, troubled by what they had heard about the actual manner of Will's death, whispered that Virginia looked much better than they had expected. "I don't believe it," more than one of them said as she walked past them. They also took note of how dignified Peter, Candace, and the children looked.

Frank and Eleanor walked just behind them, arm in arm. Most avoided looking directly at them so it wouldn't seem like they were staring.

The hearse turned on its lights for the procession toward the Bridle cemetery and the families moved toward the black limousines, parked side by side, that would drive them. It was at that instant that Peter assaulted Frank.

Blocked from view by the side of one car and by the opened door of the other, Peter grabbed Frank by the shoulder, spun him around, shoved him up against the car, and hissed at him:

"You bastard! You had to hurt Mother with your goddamned pictures and your stories, didn't you! You want a story? How about the one about the French woman Dad knocked up? It's a true one – he brought you back from the war for Mother to raise. You are an actual bastard! And trust me, I'll get you."

Peter's face was wild with anger, eyes flashing, jaw clenched. Then, in less than five seconds, it was over. Peter turned loose of Frank and slipped into the limousine beside Candace, patted her hand, straightened out his uniform, his face already masked with an expression both solicitous and grieving. No one had seen a thing.

Frank just stood there. The doors closed and the limousines drove the three miles into the country to the Bridle Protestant Cemetery.

The graveside service was a kind one. A row of chairs had been placed on a strip of Astroturf in front of the grave. Virginia turned around in her folding chair from time to time, as if she was looking for someone, but finally settled down when Candace found the snapshot and gave it back to her, like a pacifier.

Reverend Antsley inveighed Will's dust-to-dust transition. Will's pecan coffin was lowered into the grave while the choir hummed, "Nearer my God to Thee." Mr. Bivins himself closed the service by reminding everyone that the family would receive visitors at the community room of the church, where the ladies of the congregation had prepared fried chicken and iced tea for refreshment.

Back at the church community hall, dozens lined up to shake Peter's hand. "My goodness, you look just as good now as you did when you were a Bronco." "That uniform looks like the one you wore to Homecoming that time." "You still flying?" one asked. Peter pointed to his wings and said the magic words: "Pan Am."

As for Frank, even those who had listened to his eulogy seemed mildly confused about just who he was. He stayed close to Virginia. Lucille Grumman walked over to hug her, and George shook Frank's hand. Frank asked about Tog. "I didn't see him at the funeral. Is he still working at the bomb factory?" They were embarrassed to admit that Tog was not, but did not say where he was. Others merely congregated in the room and, when they saw Frank looking at them, nodded at him and he nodded back. Eleanor sat with Tiffany and Jeff while they ate cake and drank Welch's grape juice.

Eventually the visitors all drifted away. It was time to leave.

Lucille wanted to say something but George took her firmly by the elbow and led her outside to their car. It had been a good funeral, a satisfying funeral for all but a few, but Will Hastings' time on earth was over.

Chapter Three

i.

Peter had forgotten how much he enjoyed the drive from Bridle to Colorado Springs. It was not particularly scenic, not before arriving in New Mexico anyway, but it was historic. Given the absence of bends in the road, or even curves of any particular interest, he could put Candace's new Voyager on autopilot and let the minivan drive itself. In the meantime, Peter daydreamed about other times he had been exactly there.

His earliest memory of that stretch of road was from boyhood camping trips. He and Frank would be in the backyard with Hercules or with Tog, playing touch football or war or helping Virginia hang the laundry. Will's ancient Chevrolet would roar into the driveway in the middle of the day, and within an hour they would be stuffed into the backseat with an army surplus tent, some fishing gear, worn-out clothes and moth-eaten sweaters, off for a seven- or eight-hour adventure that passed through foothills and rock outcrops, a drive past Capulin and dozens of unnamed volcanic cinder cones. Somewhere between Raton ("Mouse tone") and Trinidad the road followed a canyon where Indians had painted petroglyphs on the cliff walls. The final legs over aspen-filled mountain passes were so unlike the barren flatland of Bridle and, (he was sure he remembered it) Tierra, that Peter thought it was a wonderland. They would camp for two or three nights, starving, eating cornbread (which Mother could whip up from nothing) and trout (if they caught any) cooked over an open fire. Peter didn't fish much himself and more or less ignored Frank's claims of doing so. He did hop back and forth on rocks in the streambed and lie on his back in green meadows. He played hide-and-seek (mostly 'hide') with Frank. Peter was very good at hide-and-seek.

"License plates," he heard Jeff say from the backseat. "States," Tiffany's voice answered. "States are too hard, just letters." His children began their road game by spotting a letter on a license plate, a billboard, a highway sign. "A, there's a B, C." "It wasn't a C, it was a G!" It seemed to Peter that he had played license plates or billboards all his life. It was a good thing, a family thing to do in the car. Mother had been very good at it when they were boys.

Candace reached across the open space between the front seats and took his hand. He looked in the rearview mirror and saw his mother in the backseat. Virginia smiled, vacantly, and gazed across the arid land as they crept along toward Colorado. By the time they had reached the midway point, and everyone wanted restrooms and cokes and chips and the car needed gasoline, Peter had let the black cloud of the funeral recede from memory. He knew he was a lucky man.

Capulin was only a mile or two off the highway. It was a perfectly shaped volcano, a spot to look out for on a long car trip. When they were boys, he and Frank had stared out the windshield, competing to be the first to see it. Will had stopped at Capulin once or twice and, to be honest, the view from the car was about as good as the view on the ground. Even so, they invariably got out and peered over the rim to see if, finally, there was any brimstone and lava bubbling up. (There never was.) Peter could always outrun Frank from the car to the rim, and back, to claim the best seat and get first dibs on whatever comic books they had brought.

Still, Peter's best memory of Capulin was not of boyhood trips, nor of the drive to Colorado Springs for his Air Force Academy interview, nor even the time he passed it on the train home that one glorious year of the goat. His best memory of Capulin was of the first time that he had taken Candace to Bridle to meet his parents.

They had dated, furtively, until he graduated and was commissioned. Afterward, Peter proceeded to spend every penny of his lieutenant's pay, his TDY money, and some of his housing allowance to buy a used split-window Stingray. In one frantic weekend, Peter had driven from Holloman Air Force Base back to Colorado Springs, gathered Candace up, then drove all the way to Bridle to show Virginia and Will the girl he had been writing them about.

He had been nervous; Candace had been a wreck. She had fretted for eight hours: "They'll hate me. They'll think I'm after you because you're an officer. They'll think I look like Goldie." (Goldie would in the future

34

become Goldie Hawn, but then she still was just a ditzy go-go dancing weather girl on *Laugh-In.*) Candace lamented that all she had brought to wear were bellbottom jeans, sandals, tie-dyed shirts, and some beads. She had taken off her headband and let her long, thick hair flow freely and, with no air conditioner and the windows down, it had blown around inside the Stingray in a way that made her almond-shaped face even more lovely.

Virginia was so pleased that Peter's girlfriend seemed not to care what anyone thought about her that Virginia approved of Candace on the spot. Frank was away at Tech and didn't come home for the weekend. Tog was working the night shift at the nuclear bomb assembly plant. Will took Candace around town to show her the high school ("He was a pretty good football player") and the church ("He was one of those boys who sits still all the way through the sermon"). They went to The Corral for a Coke and a hamburger where they ran into Marshall and Rebecca ("Just Becky, really").

Marshall insisted on walking them over to see the grain elevator where he and Peter had shoveled wheat during high school summers. Candace rode with Becky out to the old Collins farm to check on the irrigation motors, where it came out that Peter had been her escort at Homecoming one year when Peter made a quick trip home from the academy. Candace didn't seem the least jealous; indeed, she liked Becky very much and felt a sense of personal loss when Virginia later confided that, "Becky and Marshall lost a baby about three years ago, right after they married. She'd rather have the baby than that big old farm." Candace found that she was falling in love, not just with Peter but also with his parents and his hometown.

They had stopped at Capulin on the way back to Colorado Springs. The Corvette was a bit cramped—the car was full of whatever clothes and bags and food Virginia had pushed off on them for the road trip—and, by the time Capulin came into view, they'd needed to stretch and walk around. Now, as the Voyager full of Hastingses drove by Capulin, Peter remembered every detail of that drive-by, of their getting out of the Stingray, of walking to the edge of the volcano rim and sitting down, of him putting an arm around her. Of her braless chest that brushed against him as they kissed and the jolt of electricity that made erect every blood-gorged part of his body. Without the least regard for whether it was daylight or dark, whether another car might drive up beside them, or for any other thing, she had simply pulled her blouse off. It took less than thirty seconds for them to get the rest of her clothes off, and all of his, and use them as a blanket against the flinty ground.

He had been frenzied at the sight and touch of her; she'd intuitively figured out what she needed to do to settle him down long enough to get him all the way in. It was the first time they made love, or even come close.

Although their intimate life from that point forward was loving and satisfying, both of them would remember for the rest of their lives the rapture of their having made love on the rock-hard ground not two miles from where the Voyager now passed. Peter saw her smile and flush red, and she touched his leg as they continued to drive toward Colorado Springs with their children and Virginia in the backseat of the minivan.

Peter wanted to feel good about more than just the drive home.

"I'm going to write to Frank," he said. "I need to apologize."

Candace had learned that letting Peter talk through whatever was on his mind was the best way for him to unburden himself. She listened for the letters 'M' and 'N' from the backseat, or the plea to go see the volcano or just to stop at a gas station, but the kids were as quiet as Virginia.

She looked at Peter and he continued.

"We had another argument at the funeral. I tried to keep it under wraps." He paused to see if by expression or word Candace seemed to know anything about it, but she gave no hint. He continued: "I guess it started when he showed up late to Del Sur when we were moving Mother to Loving Arms. Mother and Dad," he corrected himself. "All he did was take Dad fishing, but he sure wasn't going to have anything to do with the hard parts. Then he bolted."

That much was true. Frank had been in the Bahamas, of all places, when the time came to move Will and Virginia to Colorado Springs. Peter had taken the burden of getting Will to sign the papers to sell the house and of finding a nursing home. He and Candace had had to rent the U-Haul and drive over the mountain pass to Del Sur, then worked hard to pack up everything in Will and Virginia's cabin. Some of it had to be put in storage and decisions made about what had to be thrown away and what could be taken to Loving Arms. Then they had had to pack the trailer and clean the house one last time.

When Frank did finally show up, all he did was take Will fishing. It was true that he did go back with them to Colorado Springs. Then he took one look at the nursing home and practically disappeared. Frank stayed just long enough to listen to the talk about visiting days and use of the laundry room and how to arrange for the van to go to church, but he was visibly unwilling to be helpful with any of it. Frank hadn't carried more than a box of pictures into Will and Virginia's unit before he declared that he was through and left.

"Then he shows up at the funeral, all crocodile tears over Dad dying and his preachy eulogy. I couldn't take it anymore and when he pulled out that picture and upset Mother so much, I just kind of lost it. I should have had better self-control."

He paused and checked the Voyager's speed and the gas tank. It was another half-hour to Raton. Candace still looked as beautiful as the first time they had driven to Capulin in the Corvette. "I'm going to write and apologize."

Candace wanted to know where his next trip was.

"Back to London. I've got to get up to Stapleton tomorrow to dead-head to JFK and then to London. Better than Dallas and back, Dallas-New York, Dallas and back." Dallas and back wouldn't make the new house payments, but that was his problem, not hers, and he didn't say it. As much as anything, Peter liked the London flights because a couple of the other pilots had let him in on a secret. Sometimes there was a seam in the schedule that let him make some extra money. If the layover was long enough, he could make another deadhead out of London or Frankfurt to pick up a leg back that needed a return pilot before his scheduled return to JFK. "Four days out and back, home Sunday."

The drive began to seem long by the time they left Raton, where the gas station attendant had refused Peter's credit card. "No sir, it will be $12.41 *in cash.*"

Peter had challenged him on the credit card being void. "Can I see the list? Look, it's 691, not 961. You got the numbers wrong. My card is fine."

"Sorry, sir."

It had been a close call, given the state of Peter's Visa account. It aggravated him enough that he decided to not spend another cent in Raton. By the time they reached Trinidad everyone was hungry. Then Jeff wandered away from the café; he was found staring in the window of a hobby store a block away.

"What on earth are you doing here? You know you're in trouble!"

"I was just looking at the model airplanes. Tiffany has her stuff."

It was true; Tiffany had brought her Cabbage Patch doll. Jeff, however, had broken a wing on his F-16 fighter and there hadn't been anything he could do about it. The shop window had an F-16 and a half-dozen other really good planes, some fighters and gunships and P-51s. Peter let Jeff off with a warning.

When they finally did get to Colorado Springs he was sure that he saw a grimace on Virginia's face as they parked in front of Loving Arms. *That's the last thing I need today,* he thought. He then felt a twinge of guilt for thinking that it was a good thing that Virginia couldn't actually talk to them. *Mother griping about going home.* It was after midnight when they finally pulled into the driveway of the new home and got the kids to bed.

ii.

Peter did not forget to write to Frank. The flight crew stayed overnight at the Paddington House in London and, rather than go straight to the pub with them, Peter went first to the hotel guest reading room. On hotel stationery he wrote:

> Dear Frank: I apologize for my outburst there between the cars outside the church. In the grief of the occasion, especially with Mother reacting to the photograph and us arguing two weeks ago, I lost my temper. I'm sorry. Let's say no more about it.
>
> Peter

He signed it, put it in a Paddington House envelope, and slipped it into the top of his flight bag. He intended to mail it to Frank when he got back to JFK, but the jet stream between Greenland and Iceland slowed the return flight so much that he barely made it to the deadhead flight back to Denver. It was the middle of the night when he parked the new Corvette in his driveway and opened the door of their new home.

Peter checked on Tiffany and Jeff and then climbed into bed next to Candace. She woke up long enough to say she was glad he was home and to hold him for a few minutes. He tossed and turned as he always did after crossing six time zones twice in four days, but at last he settled down and went to sleep.

It was late the next morning, long after the kids had gone to school and Candace had left to teach yoga, that he found a letter from Frank. The letter had been mailed in a cheap white envelope. His name and address were scribbled in a barely legible mess. Worse, the postage stamp depicted a B-17 bomber.

That bastard!

Frank must have scoured post offices and stationery stores to find a stamp with a B-17. It looked exactly like the one that Peter had spent almost three July weeks of 1958 in cutting, trimming, assembling, gluing, painting, and hanging above his bed. It was by far the most difficult model plane Peter had ever built, much more complicated than the P-51, more tightly fitted than the Horsa glider or the DC-3. It had vastly more parts than any of them and, in addition to the complicated wing root and vertical stabilizer, it had thirteen machine guns, functional bomb doors, and glass turrets on the belly, the tail, and in the nose. Peter had spent almost twenty hours on the paint alone and had chosen the name "Bronco" in honor of the Bridle high school football team that he hoped to make as a freshman. The plane had been so much larger than the others that it was the first thing anyone saw when Peter opened the door to his bedroom. It was the first thing Frank had seen the day that he barged in, and the first thing that Frank had smashed to bits. The postage stamp reminded him why he detested Frank so much.

Peter took out his letter from Paddington House and ripped it to shreds.

It took Peter a half-day to write the new letter. He composed three drafts, crumpling them up because they said too much, too little, were too harsh, or were too lenient. In the end, he decided that pointing out some features of Frank's own birth certificate would say all that needed to be said, and he replied with his comments. He folded them, stuffed them in an envelope, and took them straight to the post office. He paid no attention whatsoever to the picture on the stamp that he bought and dropped the reply in the outgoing mail box. From the moment the letter disappeared in the mail slot Peter felt as if a weight had been lifted from his shoulders, a weight he had carried all his life.

Peter walked back to his new Corvette and lowered the roof, pleased that there was not a single storm cloud anywhere in the sky. *If that was wrong, God would have sent me a sign,* he concluded, pausing to gaze toward Pikes Peak and the heavens beyond. *God always sends signs.*

Chapter Four

i.

August crept toward September. America celebrated Labor Day. Jeff wanted a pair of Air Jordans, which he did not get. Tiffany wanted a credit card, which she also did not get. Peter thought Candace wanted a microwave oven and bought one. Candace wanted to know why the Challenger space shuttle blew up, and wished, to herself, that Peter would quit flying. Peter instead flew to London.

England did not celebrate Labor Day but, due to a clause in the union contract, Pan American pilots did; their labor agreement produced for 747 pilots an extra thirty-six hours in the London layover. Peter found a jump seat on a leg to Frankfurt where he could pick up a deadhead to Karachi and co-pilot a very profitable return leg before flying home.

Peter loved being a pilot. He loved the freedom of flight, the view from thirty thousand feet, the intricacy of control, and the mysteries of navigating not just between cities but also between lands and civilizations. He loved the look people gave him when they saw his uniform. He listened to his seatmate.

"Yes," the man said. "I return from Frankfurt. I was for a conference." Peter's seatmate offered him his hand. "I am Shuja. Are you a pilot?"

"I am. I'm Peter." Peter shook Shuja's hand, wondering if 'Shuja' was the man's first name or his last. "But not on this leg." Peter handed his dinner tray back to the flight attendant and chatted with Shuja for a few moments, just passenger chat. "I'm deadheading to Karachi so we'll have a fresh crew to bring the plane back to London."

"Dead head?"

"To fly in one direction without duties. To just sit and let others fly the plane. I'll fly the return leg, back to Frankfurt." Peter noticed without

41

looking that Shuja had eaten his vegetables but avoided even touching the meat on his dinner tray. "The meat's always kind of dodgy on flights. Sometimes a steak, sometimes just the leather."

"Dodgy?" Shuja spoke with the lilting English of an educated Middle Eastern businessman. His dark eyes and blue blazer set off no alarms in Peter's mind.

"Dodgy. Of uncertain origin, better steer clear," Peter explained. Peter wondered whether lunch might have been pork, then realized almost before he had said it that not even the purveyors at Pan Am would be dumb enough to serve pork on a flight to Pakistan.

"I think, Peter, that we will find that it is goat. I also do not eat goat as well you imagine." Shuja smiled and patted his belly.

It was goat. Peter liked goat.

"Certainly it is not beef," a concession to the rather large group of passengers onward bound to Bombay. "Mumbai, my friend," the man said, "as they call it now." He winked and declined the attendant's offer of an after-dinner *digestif*. It was not hard to see that Shuja was devout. "Have you traveled to Bombay?"

Peter had not. Shuja had had the opportunity but his superiors thought it dirty and unnecessary; he preferred Bangkok. "Do you know Bangkok?"

"Yeah, went there once. During the war. That's probably not the best way to see the place." Peter thought that there was no good way to see Bangkok. For him it had been a nasty, crowded mess of dirty hotel rooms and noisy, smoky bars where the whores had staked him out with the other American soldiers who were there for rest and relaxation. He had hated it.

For fifteen or twenty minutes Peter and Shuja compared cities they knew: London, Frankfurt, Berlin. Both expressed a wish to see Singapore. Both had eaten pasta in the Piazza Nuvona in Rome and *dolmas* in Athens. Shuja had skipped the Parthenon and Peter had avoided Syntagma Square. Peter had never put a toe in the Mediterranean. Shuja said that, even though he was interested in the United States, he had not been there, and was very sure that there was more to the Middle East than Peter might suspect. Peter told him that he should go anyway, and that the best cities in the United States were New Orleans and San Francisco, not New York. Shuja was suitably intrigued.

"Ah, and Cyprus! You must go there, Peter." Shuja kissed his fingers and waxed poetic about lovely beaches and gentle farmlands overlooking the barbed wire of a civil war that separated Turks and Greeks and Christians and Islamists. "And it has a very nice airport. I am certain you could make a plane such as this land there without any problem. Is it difficult to fly this airplane?"

Peter said that a 747 was just like any other airplane to fly, that the difficulty really was in managing all its systems. "The most critical thing during flight is to maintain weight and balance. There's a delicate system of pumps that transfer fuel from the center tanks to the wings and from fore to aft. The plane itself is a pilot's dream."

"But to land such an enormous machine. It must require rather a huge airport?"

"Not really. Seventy-five hundred feet. Six thousand in an emergency if the plane is empty. You could land it nearly anywhere."

The flight attendants made the cabin dark and Peter hinted tactfully that part of his pilot's duty was to rest for the next leg. Shuja said, "Of course, forgive me," and left for the lavatory.

Peter put on a sleeping mask and, to the thrum of jet engines and the arid, antiseptic atmosphere of a jetliner cabin, he drifted off, his mind's eye swaying gently from image to image, foreign lands and cities, exotic plates and cheap pubs, runways known and antiquities seen, oceans crossed and mountains topped, exactly the life he had wanted. At the last, with goat kabobs in his belly, Peter drifted into a nap, his mind's eye recalling one image in particular, the image of a goat he had known.

He still was not at liberty to talk about the goat, Billy XV to be specific, but the goat had been one of Peter's most satisfying accomplishments.

ii.

"They know about the record player," Rocky hissed. Rocky Hillyard had just marched down the front steps to his place in the line, then done an about-face and stepped into the formation. It wasn't really a formation, just a front rank with no rows behind it. The other Air Force cadets remained at attention, eyes front, focused as best as possible on Pike's Peak in the distance. There was the hint of a storm.

"Yours?" Peter hissed back.

"Quiet in the ranks," roared the cadet commander in chief. "Shut the fuck up!"

It was Rocky's record player, but he had been ordered to shut the fuck up, so he gave Peter an almost-imperceptible nod instead.

Rocky, Peter, and the others stood at attention until the air officer in charge came out through the same doors from which Rocky had emerged, marched down the same steps, and stopped directly in front of the six cadets who were lined up in front of the building. Major Hawkins stepped up to the first man in the row, stiffened to a more formal position, made a right face, and stood before the student as if he were conducting an inspection, which, in a sense, he was. He glared into Peter's eyes, then the others, as he marched down the line.

"Hastings! Two steps forward!"

Peter marched two steps forward, halted, and stood at attention. Pike's Peak had the beginnings of a late autumn dusting of snow, brilliant white on the ridge high above the gentle roll of forest below, the aspens and evergreen trees glowing in the clouded evening sun. A breeze flowed from the Front Range toward the prairie. He wished that Rocky had answered him before O'Malley had barked. CICs were pricks by nature; O'Malley was an exceptional prick.

"Left face, march! Follow me." Major Hawkins led the way as Peter marched up the steps and into Fairchild Hall. The linoleum echoed from their boots as they made their way inward, past offices and doorways that Peter had never seen before. The click of typewriters leaked into the hallway; the abrupt ring of cheap telephones broke the rhythm. They passed the elevator doors and walked to a set of stairs, Peter one step to the side and one step behind the air officer. Without a word, they proceeded up the stairs. Two women, civilians, descending, saw them, tried to keep straight faces, giggled, passed them by and disappeared. An airman, a janitor, and a man delivering boxes of office supplies stood aside to let them step onto the second floor. They, too, smiled, and watched the pair walk to the double doors nearby. "Halt!"

Peter followed Major Hawkins, waited briefly in an outer office, and then was summoned into the conference room. He marched forward, faced the presiding officer, stood smartly to attention, and waited.

"At ease, Cadet." Peter did not recognize the man but, since he sat at the head of the table and the plate on the wall outside the door stated 'Dean of Students,' it was clear that the prank had reached higher up in the school than he had expected. Hawkins stood at attention by the door. A military science instructor was seated closer to where Peter stood. Another man across the table was, to his surprise, an athletic trainer. "Do you know why you're here?"

Peter said, "Well, all the second years on my floor were told to be ready to fall out to the administration building, but no, sir, I don't know why I'm here."

No one believed him.

"We've been looking at your record, Cadet." The dean, if he was the dean, was polite, particularly in contrast to the other iron-jawed faces in the room. "High school football, eh? Ever think about playing here?"

"Yes, sir. Yes, sir, I played high school football. But no, sir, I haven't gone out for the Falcons."

"Any particular reason? Seems you were pretty good in high school. All state, some records."

"Yes, sir. But there are more men just on my floor of the hall than there were students in my entire high school. Sir."

"Coach here might ask you about it, not the size of the dog in the fight, that sort of thing. I was interested in something else. Your school have a rival?"

"Yes, sir." Peter sucked in his breath when he saw where the questions were going. He had learned to not lock his knees and to take even breaths, but he knew that he was outnumbered in the room. "Sunset, sir. Mortal rivals, football, basketball, track. If there had been tiddlywinks we would have moved heaven and earth to crush Sunset's tiddlywink team."

The coach asked permission to raise a point and was allowed.

"What's the worst thing Sunset ever did, Cadet? To your school. Pranks, that sort of thing."

The worst thing that Sunset had done while Peter was in high school was to paint shoe polish rattlesnakes on some Bridle car windshields during the last game his senior year. Sunset High teams were the Rattlers, but when they played Bridle they didn't rattle very much. Even the shoe polish rinsed off the windshields with the first sprinkle.

"And the worst thing your team did to Sunset, Hastings? Anything we should know?"

"We beat them, sir. Four straight years. Like cheap tin drums, if I may."

The men laughed. This was good sport and they appreciated a good bull. Hastings would take some work from the picadors before they closed in on him for the kill. The military science instructor was next.

"Do you have a nickname, Cadet?"

Peter said that he did not.

"Remember Sergeant Blackwood? CST?"

Peter's mind raced back to the summer camp, combat escape training.

"He told me you were known in the camp as Poncho Pete. Does that ring a bell?"

"Yes, sir. I had forgotten that."

"Pretty good man with a poncho, that's what he wrote on your CER." The instructor glanced at a sheet of paper in his hand. "'Cadet Hastings exhibited exceptional skill in the evasion component of the course, going completely undetected for two days by use of his poncho to disappear in the forest, despite staff efforts to capture him.' Know your way around a poncho, Hastings. That's good."

"Thank you, sir." Peter had read of cadets who had lost control of their bowel and bladder functions during Honor Code hearings. The men seemed polite enough, but they had established that it was Rocky's record player, he knew that much. Something bad was coming.

"Haven't had photo recon yet, have you Cadet?" Peter began instinctively to clamp his sacral nerves. "Third year course, if you get that far. But you might recognize something from pictures anyway. We want to show you some pictures."

The first picture was a black-and-white photograph taken at the parking lot of the academy's football stadium. He looked at it and said that he recognized it without any problem. The second picture was a bit more of a challenge.

"Take your time, Cadet. Not the usual scene, so study it as much as you like."

The parking lot was bounded by a reservoir on the east and a golf course on the north. A dirt service road on the west led through a stand of evergreen trees and brush to a VIP parking lot beside the stadium itself. Peter studied it and shook his head noncommittally. The sacral nerve is the most critical nerve to prevent urinary leakage, and he concentrated as hard as possible on the parking lot stripes to get his mind off the urge to pee.

The third picture was, he knew, the reason he had been brought to the kangaroo court. Billy XV was plainly visible through the bars of a luxurious livestock trailer on which were painted the letters USNA. The goat stuck his head through the bars and appeared to be waiting for someone to bring him a carrot. The carrot keepers, however, were occupied in erecting a pen from aluminum tubes and wire mesh panels.

"Yes, sir. The Navy's goat, sir. This was in the newspaper."

He looked at them. They looked at him. No one blinked.

"Where's the goat, Hastings?" The kindly dean, the neutral coach, and the suddenly menacing instructor of military science rose as one and leaned across the table. Their eyes locked on his eyes as if they had dreamed of the day when they could peer out through helmet visors and streaking cockpits to lock on the enemy one split-second before unleashing a Sidewinder missile right up his ass. "Where's the goddamned goat?"

"Right there, sir. It's in the trailer." Peter expected physical torment; that was the second phase of hostile captivity, the inevitable consequence of frustrated interrogation. His name, rank, and serial number were summed up in the rest of his answer: "His head is sticking through the bars."

The room was deathly quiet. Peter's ears experienced the same crushing squeeze that he had felt when the escape team was forced to hold its breath beneath twelve feet of water. The military instructor was beginning to behave as the CST trainers had said that captors did—with a burst of fury that was a prelude to physical harm. The coach was hyperventilating. The dean, however, realized his mistake and rapidly defused the room.

"Billy the Goat is missing, Cadet. Billy in the trailer and Billy in the pen are the story of yesterday, when the Naval Academy rolled in and set up their football cheerleading bandwagon in front of our stadium. The midshipmen brushed their goat, put down a bed of Colorado alfalfa, and set up a vigil over their mascot. The story of today, Cadet, is that as of this morning Billy's pen is empty."

Peter knew that. Peter put his masque of inquisitive curiosity on display, a feint of surprise and ignorance at the visiting team's mascot misfortune.

"Bridle is in ranch country, Cadet. Am I right?"

"I would say wheat, sir. But there are cattle and horses."

"And rodeos, no doubt."

"Yes, sir. Bridle doesn't have a rodeo itself, but there are rodeos. In fact, the best one is over at Sunset." In fact, a Sunset cheerleader had introduced Peter to the sport of bareback riding in the backseat of Virginia's car during a rodeo.

"Ever ride a bronco, Cadet? Rope a cow, that sort of thing?"

"No, sir. Not in a rodeo. But everybody learns how to ride a horse. It's that kind of town."

"Of course. And work around livestock. You did that, didn't you?"

"Not really, sir. My summer job was at the grain elevator." Peter didn't mention the school fat stock shows where he learned about makeshift livestock pens. "I was mostly a town boy, sir."

"Look real closely at this picture, will you, son?" The dean handed the last picture back to Peter. "Right about there. See that?" He used a pencil to point to something inside the trees, fifteen or twenty feet from the makeshift goat pen and the stuff-shirted midshipmen who were strutting around the parking lot. Air Force had never beaten Navy, not in football. "What do you think that is, son?"

It was, of course, a poncho. It was all but invisible, a dark green lump curled up inside a dark green growth of golden currant and cliff jamesia. Where the poncho's hood might have been was impossible to tell, nor were there telltale signs of hands or boots. The men inside the room had themselves not seen it until it was pointed out to them by an instructor who had specialized in photo reconnaissance. It was ingenious camouflage.

"Shrubs, sir?" Peter took the photograph in his hands, held it up to his face and studied the poncho carefully, shaking his head. There was no disturbance of bush, branch, or leaves, no sign of human involvement at all. Only the most unfortunate of lens selections would have succeeded in catching it at all, and then only because of a slight glare on the rubberized material.

"I am told, Cadet, that it looks like a poncho." He paused to let it sink in. "I would like to put a few facts together for you. Your record here indicates that you were a broken-field runner in a high school where the boys also ride horses and work around livestock. You were a hurdler. It is conceivable, and this is not an accusation, but it is conceivable that such a talent might be able to get into a stock pen and steal something, such as ... a goat.

It would take stealth and a disguise, someone quite good at such a thing, perhaps someone who could disappear in the forest in the camouflage of a green poncho. And someone who knows something about sports rivalries might be motivated to do such a thing. Do you get my drift, Cadet?"

"Yes, sir."

"If you have any hope whatsoever of still being a cadet in this academy next week, Hastings, you better tell us where the Navy's goat is. Is that clear enough?"

It was. However, such information was a part of the planning that made the goat disappear in the first place. Everyone involved knew something, but no one knew everything; Peter did not know where Billy XV was hidden.

"I'm sorry, sir. I don't see how a well-guarded goat could disappear from its pen in the parking lot. Could the middies have let it get out and blamed us?"

It was at that moment that the dean recognized just how good Peter was. He was athletic. He was smart and clever, both. He was dedicated. He undoubtedly would be a leader; anyone who could make his peers stick their necks out under the noses of not just the midshipmen but also the assorted noses of Naval Academy bigwigs, the smart-mouthed squids who had wangled a trip to Colorado to watch their revered successors trash the pretentious new Air Force country club cousins and, it was obvious, of his own chain of command—that man was a leader. There was no doubt in the dean's mind that this kid not only had led the kidnapping but also had not expected his co-conspirators to do the worst of the dirty work. And he was devious, even in the face of torment. This young man was everything the Air Force wanted in its officers except, unfortunately, he might have to kick the boy out of school.

"Let me be straight with you, Hastings. First, one of the middies is in deep shit because he ran afoul of the Navy's first rule: when you're on watch, don't look at tits. Some girl wandered up to the pen after dark and flashed herself around at the middie long enough to get his mind off his duty. It might have been two minutes, it might have been an hour; nobody lies more than a beached sailor. But however long it was, Billy disappeared. That middie turned his watch over to another poor sucker who listened to Billy bleat for about a half-hour before it occurred to him that Billy sounded like a broken record, the same goat song every twenty seconds, to the dot.

He climbed into Billy's pen to check and discovered that it really was a broken record. Whoever stole the Navy's goat left a portable record player in the straw with a broken forty-five that bleated out whatever goats sing about, over and over." He paused to gather his thoughts. "Next, there is at this minute in our visiting officer quarters one furious lieutenant commander who has two disgraced midshipmen under house arrest. There also is one livid football coach, and one Naval Academy commandant yelling for his head. And your head. Conclusion: Hastings? You better come up with their goat in the next half-hour or get your bags packed. That's about as straight as I can get it. Understand?"

Peter knew the game was up, except that it wasn't. Being stealthy in a poncho in the woods is one thing; going about the business of finding the goat in daylight without implicating the others was a different thing.

"Yes, sir. I'll see what—"

"Twenty-nine minutes and counting. Take that mess of co-conspirators away from the front lawn and get out of my sight. Dismissed. Go!"

The only thing more volatile at a service academy than an angry commandant is two angry commandants. Admiral Paul, USNA, was the dinner guest of General Packard, USAFA, the proud head of an undeniably junior academy that as yet had no particular history or traditions. Each agreed, privately, that the only thing to make rustling the Navy's goat worse would be if the rear area flyboys had the bad judgment to defeat the in-harm's-way sailors on the gridiron. They were angry, very angry.

Candace thus found herself in the position of having to serve them in the VIP dining room when they were on their worst behavior rather than their best. She listened to them as she brought salads, "with local flavors, sirs. The onions and lettuce are from the San Luis Valley. The carrots, cucumbers, and tomatoes are from Pueblo. May I?"

The two flag officers, their juniors, and their athletic directors jerked their heads up while she intruded with serving spoons and bowls, then resumed their threats and entreaties. "Have your head on a platter," was the theme echoed most by the sailors. A rather lame, "...get to the bottom of it," seemed to be the dominant phrase of the aviators. At approximately the moment that Peter was staring at a picture of the stadium parking lot, Candace was clearing away salad plates. Peter was leaving the administration building, on the double, when she served the cauliflower, squash, and green beans.

"I don't care where they're from, little lady," one of the navy men barked at her. "Where's the meat?" She promised him that she would bring it right up. She returned shortly and began to fork out generous portions of something that had been grilled to a crisp perfection.

"Barbequed? Or as a chop, sir?" she held the tray before them so that they could each choose as much of either as they wished. "The barbeque goes nicely with the red sauce, if you like. If you prefer chops you might like a bit of peach mustard." They didn't care.

She succeeded in getting all of them to take some of each before she retreated to the kitchen, pulled off her apron, and disappeared. Candace was on her way out the academy's north gate before someone at the table stopped eating in silence and demanded to know what it was they were having.

"Is this venison? Not as gamey as I thought it would be. We never get deer back east."

"Not venison, Admiral. This is brisket. It's a kind of barbeque. They raise some damned good cattle here. Have some more." The commandant passed the tray to the commandant.

"This isn't brisket. It's more like, mutton. You got sheep out here, General?"

"No, Admiral. This isn't mutton. You get a texture with mutton. Pork?"

"Not like any pork I ever had. We're thirty miles from Washington. I know all about pork."

"Where's the girl? Let's ask her."

The girl was nowhere to be found, but the head of VIP services was. He came out to have a look.

"What's this?" he gulped. "These aren't steaks. What happened to your steaks?" The leaders of the free world glared at him. "My apologies, Gentlemen. I'll be right back." He returned to the kitchen where he threat-ened to terminate, and personally kill, the head cook and the chief waiter, both of whom insisted that the steaks had been grilled to perfection and sent out to the tables. The steaks were, in fact, grilled to perfection and hidden under a metal cover on the back of the steam table. The two men worked together to bring them to the largest number of uniformed stars either of them had ever seen in their dining room.

"If these are the steaks, then what the hell is this?" The commandant knew what it was the moment he asked the question which, unfortunately, was one millisecond too late to shut his own mouth. He frantically waved at the chef to get the tray out of sight, a futile gesture since the chef himself was already extracting a serving fork from behind his apron. The chef took a bite.

"*Cabrito*, sir. Well cooked, but not steaks. My apologies." The bigwigs looked puzzled. "Goat."

The head of VIP services was in the process of snapping his fingers at two young enlisted men standing at the ready when the host commandant exploded.

"Get this out of here, God damn you. Who the hell do you think you are?" He took a menacing step toward the perplexed chef who, to his credit, stood his ground. He did, after all, have a fork and a tray full of hot goat.

"Admiral," the commandant groveled, "this is... I promise you that by God we'll hang every one of the sons of bitches. They aren't going to be dis-enrolled; those little fuckers are going to be drafted and shipped out to boot camp on the first train out of here."

The sailors rose as a body, their admiral at attention. He looked at his aides and staff and coaches, then spun on his heel. His men followed suit.

A college without traditions gives its commandant no history from which to take comfort, no memory of the game of '38 or of uniformed parades down enemy streets. The general had hoped for a friendly wager on the game, maybe a 'boys will be boys' wink and nod with the admiral when, inevitably, the MPs would bring a few of each of their students in drunk after midnight on the eve of the big one. He could have laughed those off.

This was different. There was no precedent for kidnapping and eating the opposing team's mascot. His mind filled with images of Congressional hearings, boards of inquiry, the very public crash of a career that had begun in a B-17 over the fields and factories of Germany. He jumped to his feet and raced after the angriest man he had ever seen.

In the Air Force Academy, all roads lead to the chapel—the road from the VIP dining hall, the road from the administration building, the road to penance, the road to prayer. The chapel was the one landmark that even the naval commandant recognized, and his road led, if not there, at least in that direction. The chapel lay on the other side of a slab of concrete between two uninspiring buildings, an area known as the Terrazo. The flood of flag officers all arrived at the Terrazo at roughly the same moment, those in navy blue huffing across the plaza in full fury, those in sky blue chasing along behind in apoplectic supplication. They were not alone.

Billy XV was tethered by a rope to the landing gear of a P-51 airplane that had been hauled onto the Terrazo specifically for the Navy football game. The lawn of the Terrazo was holding its own against the dry autumn, a soothing touch of green marred only by the fiercely ravaged strip that had been eaten down to the bare dirt within the radius of Billy's rope.

Apart from Billy, the Terrazo was empty. No firsties moved back and forth from Fairchild to the dormitory, nor did any doolies tread upon the marble strips that defined their walking boundaries. The Terrazo was empty, apart from the Navy's mascot.

The officers circled the beast, who showed no more interest in them than it had in the carrot feeders who had lost him the night before. It ate grass. A lieutenant, junior grade, was dispatched to the visiting officers' quarters with the order to retrieve the miserable lieutenant commander and his two detained and disgraced midshipmen. They, upon their return, confirmed Billy's identity and well-being. ("Yes, sir. It's got balls and everything. Billy seems okay.")

Admiral Paul laughed. "I'll be goddamned. I thought I ate the fucker." And he slapped General Packard on the back.

Packard laughed. *Me too*, he thought, and called for MPs.

"Call 'em if you want, Packard," his suddenly relieved guest declared. "Guarantee you, no one saw a thing. Whichever of your little shits was slick enough to pull this off in the parking lot was slick enough to put Billy back in broad daylight. If no one in your whole goddamned academy saw that, none of your goddamned MPs will fix it." Admiral Paul laughed so hard he nearly choked. The admiral knew a thing or two about inter-service rivalries. "Tell you another thing. You ever bring your boys out to play at Annapolis, you'll find out pretty quick that we sailors have a long memory."

He laughed again and, in an about-face, led the troupe away from the chapel and straight to the one other building on the new campus that he had made sure to locate. "Officer's Club, Packard. You're one up, so first drink's on me." He did pause long enough to order two midshipmen and one lieutenant commander to get their asses back to the goat pen and not leave until they drove the creature back to Annapolis.

iii.

The Colorado and Southern passenger service left Colorado Springs at 7:15 that evening. Major Hawkins had taken the handwritten orders to Peter in his dormitory room and stayed to supervise his packing. Dean Baily himself had driven Peter to the station and put him on the train.

"Do not get off this train, Hastings." The train to Trinidad and on to Amarillo and points east would take ten hours to get Peter home. "That's an order."

"Yes, sir."

"Do not lose this travel voucher, either. That's both an order and good advice. Understand?" The dean glared at him, then turned his head away to sneeze and suppress a laugh. He hoped no one from the Navy had followed them.

"I do, sir. I will stay on the train and I will keep this in my hands at all times."

"See that you do. Good luck."

He watched Peter mount the steps, disappear into the passenger car, and reappear in the second window. He was the only passenger getting on the train; everyone else was getting off. The Navy game was the biggest draw in Air Force Academy history. The dean waved goodbye. Peter waved back.

Peter tried to read as the rails clicked off between Colorado Springs and Pueblo but he found the emotion of the event too strong for concentration. The mountains to the west were dark sentinels, the prairie to the east a blank slate. Alone in the passenger car, he wondered whether he could have done anything differently and, if he could have, whether he would have.

Rocky Hillyard was being sent in the opposite direction, the result of having listed the incriminating phonograph on his private property inventory. Coxie was never implicated. No one else was sent anywhere. There had been no time to get word to Candace.

"Sir," he asked the conductor. "How long do we have in Pueblo?"

"Fifteen minutes, sir. Hungry?"

"No. I don't have much money anyway. Just need to get off the train for a minute, if I can."

"You'll have to hurry," he said.

Peter decided to take one more chance on a day of taking chances. The train pulled into Pueblo station and Peter jumped from the car. The station was still open, to his relief, and he found the Western Union window.

"Can you send this?" he asked as he shoved the form to the operator on duty. "How much?" He waited for the answer, fished out a dollar and fifteen cents, and handed the money through the grille. "Has to get there tonight." The operator said it would go out immediately.

At 8:45, the train left the station. Peter sat back in the empty car and gazed across the vast dark prairie on his left, the disappearing peaks on his right, and smiled. He tucked his barracks bag into the corner of the seat and the window and lay back against it. The last thing he read before he went to sleep was the telegram he had sent:

> Mother. Meet me six a.m. Amarillo station.
> Three day pass. I'm a hero. Peter.

He wished Rocky was there to celebrate with him, Rocky and Candace, or even his roomies. It didn't matter, though, because he was about to do some of the things he loved best. He was going to see his mother. He was going to be in Bridle. He was going to wear his academy uniform and be welcomed as the most successful alumnus any little town could ever want.

And, it was Bridle's Homecoming weekend.

It couldn't have gone any better.

iii.

Peter woke up an hour from Karachi. He was content and rested, apart from the nagging sense that perhaps he hadn't been very clear with Candace that this particular bid would take an extra thirty-six hours before he got home. It was complicated; adding the pre-flight, check in, flight planning, and other bits to the leg back to Frankfurt and on to London would make his total duty day just more than was permitted. The nagging sense of whether Candace understood that he was sneaking in extra work was a bit tangled up with the gnawing worry that even the extra pay might not get them back over the hump of the new house payments.

Peter went forward to the front of the cabin a half-hour before landing to beat the crowd to the lavatory and was enjoying a good pee when the plane bucked up and down in a bout of clear air turbulence. A coffee urn in the galley adjacent to the lavatory bounced off the cooktop and soaked one of the flight attendants. A cart rolled loose. The 'fasten seat belts' sign was turned on and the lead attendant announced that the captain had ordered the passengers to return to their seats. Peter decided to abandon both his seatmate and his seat.

He stepped out of the lavatory. "Miss? I'm the return pilot, deadheading to fly the plane back to Frankfurt on the turnaround." The flight attendant looked at him with the familiar mixed gaze that meant she thought he wanted special treatment or that he was going to make a pass at her. Peter did neither. "Ask the deck if they want some help getting in through the turbulence. I'm glad to help." He smiled and braced himself against the cabin wall.

She rolled her eyes, said, "Sure," and called the first officer. A few moments later she put the phone down and answered Peter.

"He says the jump seat is open if you want to come up."

Peter gathered his flight bag from under his seat and made his way forward to the flight deck stairs, then knocked on the crew door. The engineer opened it and waved him in. Peter opened the jump seat and buckled in, gazing almost automatically at the endless banks of dials and meters on the engineering board, then at the navigation and communication instruments and switches that faced the pilots. They were a good crew and he left them entirely alone as they passed checkpoints, received descent and vector instructions, and prepared the aircraft for landing. Not until the runway was in sight did a random thought occur to Peter, that Shuja had not been in his seat when Peter had come forward.

Airsick. Glad he didn't puke on me, he mused.

It also occurred to him that he hadn't actually seen Shuja since they had finished the dinner trays and Peter had closed his eyes. *Some people just aren't meant to fly* was the last thought that flitted through his mind. He heard the co-pilot call off altitudes and felt the airplane descend toward the runway, and Peter smiled with the thought that he was about to add another new country to his log book.

Peter Hastings loved being a pilot.

Chapter Five

i.

"Pan Am 73, report Kajal."

"Kajal, 6000 feet, Pan Am 73."

Kajal was an imaginary dot in the air, a navigation checkpoint located a few minutes from the Karachi runway. Peter listened with a detached ear to the pilot and first officer as they coordinated with the air traffic control tower. Sitting in a jump seat behind the navigation station, he could see only about half the dials and controls. He still found when he was a passenger that the size of a 747 was disorienting, higher above the ground than Bridle's grain elevators had been when he and Frank and Tog had climbed to the top to pee off the roof. The most Peter could do was take a deep breath and leave the landing to the pilots who were actually doing it.

He wondered if Karachi was anything like Bangkok. He could only remember a couple of things after almost fifteen years. He had gone to Bangkok on R & R with the intention of erecting a monument to hedonism, fueled by his buddies' stories. In fact, he spent the first day in a stupor. He tried to remember the name of the road where all the bars were, couldn't, tried to remember the name of the hotel near the military exchange in Bangkok, couldn't. It turned out to be a fogged-in day of drinking a great number of whiskey sours and wobbling across a packed dance floor, of mushing the word "Candace" into the ear of a dark, chubby prostitute who had worked on him for three hours to earn her pay before he gave in and tottered off to a filthy room for a hugely embarrassing four minutes of regret. When he woke up on the second day, Peter had taken stock of himself and decided that he didn't really want R & R, not in Bangkok or anywhere else, and was relieved that he had lied to Frank about being sent off on some top secret mission so that Frank had not come with him.

He had spent most of the next six days on a rooftop bar overlooking the Bangkok airport where he gazed lovingly at planes arriving and departing, then got on the first transport back to Ubon. Within twelve hours of getting back to his unit, he was happily flying a gunship to the Vietnam border, where he made three passes over a convoy of trucks and administered a Gatling-speed destruction of twenty of them and the hundred North Vietnamese soldiers inside them as well. He made a fourth pass over the chaos, waggled his wings at the fury of SAM missiles being fired at his gunship, then flew back to Ubon, dismissing Bangkok from memory for fifteen years. Judging now from the women on the Karachi flight, all baggy clothes and hiding under scarves, Peter concluded that Karachi probably would be even worse than Bangkok.

"Localizer alive."

"Check. Set heading 027."

"Check."

"Glideslope capture."

"Check."

"Outer marker."

Peter forgot about Bangkok again. Seeing what little he could from the jump seat, he felt the lurch of the main landing gear on the runway and the rapid deceleration of the airplane. From the crew windows, Karachi looked a lot like El Paso—rocks, dead earth and dry streambeds, a desert with no place for a plane to go if it didn't stop when it should. Even so, and vividly conscious that it wasn't as exciting as flying a gunship, he truly enjoyed thinking that in just an hour or so he would fly this same airplane and hundreds of passengers away from here, high above almost a quarter of the planet, from the edge of Asia to the heart of Europe. It was that simple.

"Pan Am 73 turn left taxiway C and follow the service vehicle to your station."

The plane turned left off the runway and angled toward a large empty ramp and parking area.

"Auxiliary power unit start." A caution light blinked.

"Check." The light blinked off. Peter saw it. He wondered if the APU had a leak somewhere.

"Flap lever up. Auto brake off."

"Check."

The thump of an air stair being shoved against the airplane was followed by the familiar sound of the main cabin door being released and swung back.

"Fasten seat belt sign off."

"Check."

It was five in the morning. Peter had an hour to meet his flight crew, pre-flight the airplane, compose and file a flight plan back to Frankfurt, and supervise the fuel load. The first passengers would begin to arrive at five-thirty, just as his first officer and engineer were going through their checklists.

Peter decided to climb down below the cockpit into the crawlspace that led to the instrument bay, ostensibly to inspect the blinking caution light, but really to steal fifteen minutes of solitude, to just close his eyes and think about the flight ahead. He was surprised to find that the auxiliary power unit caution light test functioned perfectly, meaning that its oil line really did have a slow leak.

No matter, he thought. *It's good for ten or twelve hours.* He decided it would hold until they got to Frankfurt. *I won't need it on the ground for more than an hour, not unless something else goes wrong.*

Something did.

ii.

What went wrong was Abu Nidal. Abu was not a happy man. A Palestinian, in 1948 Abu had lost his family farm to Israel, a country that didn't even exist in 1947 and, as far as he was concerned, still did not. He next lost his home, in Nablus, a few years later, again to the Israelis. He then went on to lose his job at Aramco in Saudi Arabia in 1966, an unfortunate experience made worse by the decision of the House of Saud to imprison him, then torture him, then expel him from the country.

Still, to say that Abu was not happy would be to suggest that he did not enjoy his pursuits, and that was not true. He took a great interest both in travel and in Olympic sports. In 1971, for example, he helped his friend

Abu Daoud design a successful training program for Palestinians. Daoud followed the program, successfully kidnapping Israel's Olympic athletes in Munich and killing eleven of them.

That piqued Abu's growing interest in aviation, a "developing sector." It began with a sightseeing tour for eleven tourists whom his employees had met at the Saudi embassy in Paris. Abu flew the tourists high above Kuwait, then over Riyadh, and then at thirty-five thousand feet above various uninhabitable desert areas, where he proceeded to broadcast that the tourists were to be thrown out of the airplane unless King Hussein of Jordan released Abu Nidal's old friend Abu Daoud from jail.

That tour was so successful that he and his friends relocated to Baghdad, where they formed the Abu Nidal Organization, or ANO, with branch offices in Syria and Libya. Abu went on to borrow, at gunpoint, his first 747 airliner, a KLM plane that he diverted to Malta. He also hijacked an EgyptAir plane and flew eighty-six new customers to Malta rather than back to Cairo, a flight tarnished by the deaths of sixty of the passengers.

His air tourism business became so successful that Abu attached it to El Al, using its ticket counters in Rome and Vienna to provide onsite training for his hand grenade employees, who proceeded to injure one hundred thirty-eight tourists, killing only nineteen, who otherwise would have made it home safely to Tel Aviv. Abu also cleverly once used a pregnant English girl, who unknowingly packed a bomb inside her luggage on an El Al flight to Tel Aviv, where she thought she was traveling to meet the family of her Palestinian boyfriend. British spies, being what they were, took her off the plane that day, disrupting Abu's intended light show over the English Channel.

Nevertheless, on the whole, Abu was in his peculiar way very knowledgeable about flying, and he did enjoy that. This made him quite happy to talk about travel with his friend and fellow tour guide, Zayd Safarini, about flights to Cyprus.

"Zayd," he said. "Would you like to fly to Cyprus?"

"Of course. Beautiful island. Warm seas, Mediterranean air."

"If you wear these uniforms you can fly for free." He gave Zayd four uniforms of the Pakistan Security Force, with 'Airport-Karachi' patches sewn onto the sleeves. "I have one for you and also for your coworkers, Wadoud, Jamal, and Mohammed."

"They would like to see Cyprus also. Larnaca is beautiful at this time of year."

Abu and Zayd laughed and slapped each other on the back.

"Enough," Zayd said. "You're killing me. Show me the maps."

Abu brought out the map of the Karachi airport.

"Here," he said, indicating, "is the service entrance. I have a very nice Toyota pickup painted in airport livery. It will meet you at the safe house. Drive it to the airport service entrance and then around here." He pointed to the east end of the passenger terminal. "There is the gate for service vehicles. When the refueling trucks leave the tarmac and pass out through the gate, just drive in going the other direction, and continue right up to the airplane boarding stairs."

They discussed the logistics of boarding the airliner, of moving the passengers from the front and rear of the plane for an impromptu group meeting in the middle. Abu explained that he had agreed with a Pakistani ("I hate Pakistanis, they always want more than the market price.") that, in exchange for the uniforms, Zayd and Wadoud and the travel agents would collect the passengers' passports so as to identify who was from India and America. "If needed to speed along the flight you should martyr one or two of them."

Abu then shared his last map with Zayd.

"Look at this. If your crew files an IFR flight plan to Kuwait, then on to Amman, the most direct route to Cyprus will take the plane right over Tel Aviv."

"I have never seen Tel Aviv," Zayd replied.

"You must see it. I suggest you drop in on the Israeli Defense Ministry," Abu told him. "It is right here." He pointed to the large building and marked its distance and direction from the Tel Aviv airport navigational aids. "And, this is important. You must be in the air by six-thirty at the latest, if you wish to visit Tel Aviv during business hours."

They discussed the possibilities of weather, climate, and which aircraft to hijack.

"Oh, I think there is only one choice," Abu said. "The Pan Am flight. It is scheduled to fly to Frankfurt. There will be a lot of passengers, and plenty of fuel to take you to Cyprus."

iii.

Peter had begun to climb out from the crawlspace beneath the cockpit when he heard thirty distinct pops coming from the area of the main cabin. His first concern was that a bank of electrical switches had sustained a serial bus failure and short-circuited one after the other. His second concern was that the voice over the cockpit public address system superseded his first concern. One of the flight attendants had had the presence of mind to grab a microphone and call the crew.

"CAPTAIN, GET OUT. THEY'RE SHOOTING GUNS IN THE CABIN. FOUR MEN CAME ON THE PLANE AND THEY'RE SHOOT...."

Peter knew very clearly what he was supposed to do and, if the engineer in the cockpit directly above him had not been standing on the hatch that led to his crawlspace, Peter would have done it. However, the engineer was busily locking the cockpit door while the first officer was jettisoning the crew escape window. Peter knew that he was stuck.

He waited only a few moments before trying again and, this time, the hatch was not blocked. He lifted it, peeked into the cockpit, and saw that the crew had made its escape. He began to lift himself out of the crawlspace to make good his own departure when the door to the cockpit was shoved open. It struck the lifted hatch cover and bounced back, during which time Peter dropped back into the crawlspace and closed the hatch above him. He heard the cockpit door open again, followed by the sound of footsteps above, then the growl of what was an undeniably angry hijacker. Five minutes passed before he heard Zayd speak into the pilot's microphone, very passable English with a Palestinian accent:

"Karachi? This is the ANO. Where is the pilot of the Pan Am airplane?" *Click.*

A few minutes went by before he repeated the question and, shortly, received the answer.

"This is Karachi airport ground control to the person speaking on the microphone of the Pan Am flight 73. Can you hear me?" *Click.*

"Where is the pilot?" *click*

"To the person speaking on the microphone of the Pan Am flight 73, it is my responsibility to tell you that there is no pilot on the airplane." *Click.* "I must say to you that the pilots have departed the airplane and have entered the terminal of Karachi International Airport. I also must add that clearance has not been issued for the Pan Am flight 73 to take off...."

"This is ANO. I am in command of the airplane and the passengers. At this moment we are collecting the passports of the persons in the airplane. You are instructed to send a crew of pilots to fly this airplane at once. If you do not, we will begin to shoot the passengers."

"Sir, to the person speaking on the microphone..."

"Do not answer me. Send a crew or we will begin to shoot the passengers."

"To the person on the microphone of Pan American Airways Flight 73, please listen. I must pass your message to the officials who can make such a decision. I am only the air traffic controller for the ground. I will instruct the proper authorities so that you may have their communications on the subject please. Do you understand what I am saying to you?" *Click.* "Do you understand?"

Peter heard the sound of footsteps on the hatch. The cockpit door opened, and the person on the microphone of Pan American Airways Flight 73 left the cockpit.

Peter's choice was no longer quite so clear. The crawlspace had an access panel that led to the instrument well. Behind the instrument well a pressure-sealed panel could be unscrewed to enter the top of the front landing gear service door. Peter could attempt to get into the cockpit and out the escape door as his crew had done. Peter could attempt to climb out of the plane through the landing gear. Or, Peter could remain where he was to see what might happen next. His Air Force training took over. He would evade, then escape.

Peter's Air Force training also included the use of a Smith and Wesson Model 15 revolver that had been issued to him in Ubon when he was assigned to his first combat crew. "Escape," he was taught. "If you can't, evade. If you can't do either, shoot the bastard closest to you."

With this comforting thought, and pistol in hand, Peter settled down in the crawlspace, where he waited for a long time before hearing the cockpit door open again.

Well, Mr. Hijacker, he thought. *If you open this hatch, you'll probably ask yourself, 'What have we here?' And you'll think 'I have a pilot.' You'll think wrong, because you should be thinking 'Why do I have a pilot who is pointing a gun right between my eyes?'*

He waited.

The hatch did not open. Instead, the footsteps continued to the pilot's seat, followed by the familiar click of the cockpit microphone.

"This is the Abu Nidal Organization. Karachi Airport, do you have the official who will send a pilot and crew to fly this airplane?" *Click.*

"He is here." *Click.* A different voice.

"This is Daroga. Who am I talking to?"

"I am Zayd Saffirini. I am in command of this airplane. I am in the cockpit and I do not see pilots walking to the airplane."

"Mr. Zayd? I am obligated to inform you of a very real problem. Pan American cannot order the pilots to come to the airplane and to fly it. We have asked for volunteer pilots. Will you be patient while we learn if there are pilots in Karachi who will volunteer to fly to Frankfurt for you?"

"Not Frankfurt. Cyprus."

"Cyprus? We do not have pilots for Cyprus. Cyprus is not an airport we know."

"You have fifteen minutes for the crew to come to the airplane." *Click* "Look out the window to the airplane. Tell me what you see." *Click.*

Daroga was in the air traffic control tower. He could see clearly, although the airplane was parked over a hundred yards away. He replied that he was looking at the airplane and was told to look at the front boarding door. Within a few moments Daroga saw a passenger—Indian, tall, skinny, young, dark, dark hair, very white eyes—appear in the open doorway. An indistinct figure loomed behind him.

"I see him," Daroga said from the tower. "His hands are in the air. He is kneeling down in front of the open door. Please, we are asking for pilot crews to volunteer...."

At that moment Peter accepted that escape would not be possible, not for him. He wondered who the bastard closest to him would be, because that was who he was going to shoot. He then remembered Shuja. Pleasant. Quiet. *Did Peter know Cyprus? Would a 747 land on its nice airport?* Shuja would be the bastard closest to him.

From the kneeling position, the skinny, young Indian with dark hair and very white eyes looked outside the airplane door and over the tarmac.

Daroga watched from the control tower when, after only a few seconds, there was a *pop* and the skinny, young Indian lurched forward, toppling out of the open door thirty feet down to the pavement. He bounced once as blood spurted out from what was left of his head, then lay dead and crumpled on the airport ramp. A man dressed as a security guard, holding a rifle, stood in the open doorway for a moment and gazed down at the body below him, then withdrew.

"Fifteen minutes."

Click.

Chapter Six

i.

Tog made the kind of mistake that any pilot could make, at least any pilot who hadn't been trained to fly the F-16. Every plane Tog had flown before he transitioned into the F-16 had design-intentional stability so that, even when he dropped the controls completely, at any speed or angle, the plane would try to correct itself and seek straight and level flight. The F-16, however, was designed with relaxed static stability. It would not correct itself, at least not in subsonic flight. It required absolute constant attention to avoid flying out of control, particularly when it rolled to the right, and entered a Mach .98 dive. He readied the weapons system almost thirty miles before the Osirik reactor would be in line-of-sight view.

Sweat began to form on Tog's brow as he tried to focus on the target lock while the TTT indicator ticked off the seconds to release. *Twenty-four seconds. Twenty-seconds. Lift Weapons-Arm switch cover, toggle switch to ARM, arm right rack, arm left rack, eighteen seconds.* The sweat boiled from his forehead and ran down the bridge of his nose.

Bambambam!

Focus, focus, focus!

"Bogey eleven o'clock nine miles closing at 1.8 Mach *EVADE!*"

Tog calmly moved the control stick, rolled right to force the MiG to overfly him, then rolled left to regain the target lock. The terrain raced past so rapidly that he made almost no attempt at feature recognition.

"SAM! SAM! SAM! EVADE!!!"

Bambambam!

And by the simple mistake of losing his focus, Tog had failed to see doors open on a desert bunker, to see the missile tips poke out above the sand. Dozens of intercepting defenses screamed upward to meet him and Tog exploded in a fireball of surface-to-air, Soviet-made missiles less than one second before weapons release.

Bambambam!

"Tog, are you in there? Coffee's on."

Tog sighed, looked at the fireballs and smoke rising from the Iraqi desert, then clicked Alt-F8 and hid the screen before reaching behind him to open his trailer door.

"You coming over for coffee? It's getting late, Tog." Lucille looked at him, completely unaware that she had saved Saddam Hussein's nascent nuclear reactor from destruction and thereby drawn the West into even greater danger of an atomic standoff over Kuwaiti oil and, ultimately, World War III. "Get off that damned computer and hurry up. Day's going to get away from you."

Tog grinned at his mother, turned back to the screen, and noted with relief that the computer monitor had replaced the desert southwest of Baghdad with the subdivision map of Burford Acres. Burford Acres might actually have been in Iraq, at least from a strictly aerial perspective. Both consisted of minimally productive dirt, mixed with clay, sand, and more dirt, and hundreds of years of dead roots from a tall grass prairie that had all but disappeared, in Burford Acres' case after the rush to plant wheat and the ensuing onslaught of the Dust Bowl. A lot of Burford Acres blew away each spring. A small amount of it simply broke off from time to time and fell into the encroaching edges of the Palo Duro Canyon.

"Look at this," Tog said to Lucille. He showed her the monitor, mentally proving to her that, no matter how early, he was being productive. "This is the outline of Bump Burford's land. Now watch." Tog pressed Shift-Alt-3, and a series of yellow lines crisscrossed the screen. He turned in triumph to show off his program.

Lucille wasn't impressed, indeed had no particular understanding of what Tog was trying to show her at all.

"And now, this." He pressed Shift-Alt-4 and a series of dotted red lines began to trot from the edge of the screen to the southeast corner of Bump's farm and then spread out in grid lines so that one solid red line transected the yellow ones, then branched off in smaller red lines. Each square in the grid had a red line that stubbed to an end. "That, Mother Dear, is mine!"

Lucille looked at his toy, rolled her eyes, and said, "That, Tog Dear, is keeping us from coffee. Come on." She grabbed him by the arm and pulled.

With a smile and feigned resistance, he rose from the built-in dinette by his trailer door, stood, and walked down the two metal steps that led to his parents' backyard. It was not a large trailer. *I'll come back after coffee and turn it off*, he thought. *I've got to get the file anyway.*

George and Lucille Grumman's backyard was barren, a seventy-five foot long plot on the edge of Bridle on which, more or less in this order: George had, during the first few years after the war, stacked lumber and shingles while he built their house on his days off from the bomb factory; Lucille had dug up and planted annual gardens, with the help of Ronald and Albert and, less often, of Tog, each of which had produced one harvest of tomatoes, corn, and okra before burning to shreds in the hot Panhandle summers; George had dug a tornado cellar whose doors looked remarkably similar to the Sam-7 bunkers that only moments before had saved Saddam Hussein's evil nuclear ambitions from Tog's F-16; Lucille had strung a three-wire clothesline; and the boys had erected blanket tents, wrecked their bicycles, and thrown passes before graduating from Bridle High School ('Broncos Forever'), marrying, going to work at the bomb factory themselves; and, in Tog's case, divorcing, losing his job at the bomb factory, spending his severance pay on a nineteen-foot Airstream Bambi, losing his trailer lot, and then relocating it and him to the rear of the backyard of the house in which he had grown up, his pride and need for occasional privacy in his thirties being too great for him to actually move back in with George and Lucille.

The Bambi was positioned to be perpendicular to George and Lucille's kitchen so that neither had a clear view through the windows of the other. This feature had sounded reasonable when Tog negotiated with George about where precisely to put the trailer but proved less advantageous than expected after Tog began to assemble computers on his dinette. The eerie green glow in the night worried Lucille that Tog would die from radiation poisoning and worried George that Tog would never re-enter the labor force.

"Hey, Dad. How's bombs?" Tog grinned at George who, in turn, elected to not throw a cup of coffee on Tog but instead make a 'kablooey' sound to confirm that the bombs he assembled were still bombs. "Anything exciting going on? A little SALT for your bacon?"

George did have to admit that jokes about the Strategic Arms Limitation Treaty were hard to come by and smiled back. He then made a show of salting his bacon and hummed the first few bars from the theme of *Star Wars*, a movie he had never seen and a missile defense plan he thought was crazy.

Lucille poured Tog a cup of coffee.

"All I can say is nothing's changed since you let the door hit you in the back. If anybody is dismantling bombs, it isn't us. Maybe it's Gorbachev. What are you up to today?" George asked.

George couldn't help himself. Tog was a complete fuckup who needed a good butt kicking and a job. Tog also was a complete fuckup who, every time George tried to have a decent talk with him, retaliated by not talking to either George or Lucille for weeks at a time, to Lucille's distress. They might see his trailer window glowing green in the night, or see Tog driving his battered pickup around Bridle with magnetic signs on the doors proclaiming his current enterprise, Tog's Car Wash, or Tog's Computers, or Tog's Fitness Training (We come to You). Eventually, Lucille would find him digging quarters out of seat cushions somewhere and take him to The Corral for a hamburger so that everyone in town would believe they were all one happy family; the next morning Tog would reappear in the kitchen for coffee. He was now on a forty-day streak.

"Great coffee, Ma." Tog sneaked a peek sideways to see if Lucille was making him breakfast. She was. "I'm going out to Bump's to stake out the cable lines and hot points for the terminal boxes and splitters. They're going to run electricity out there any day now." He looked up to see if George approved. George was non-committal. "It looks like they're going to wind up with about a hundred and fifteen of them when all's said and done."

"A hundred and fifteen lots?"

"Homes."

"On Bump Burford's wheat farm?" George was polite; incredulous, but polite. "There aren't a hundred and fifteen houses in Bridle." George wasn't sure of this but he was certain that with only seven hundred fifty people in town there couldn't have been many houses. "Who's going to buy those hundred and fifteen new houses? Three miles out in the country?"

Tog had been trained for this question. The seminar at Panhandle Investors had identified a growing need for homes. Mr. Robert Crawford of Crawford Strategies had already worked it out. "We don't call them houses.

We call them homes. They're what people dream about." The seminar was very thorough: Amarillo was in the middle of everything—crossroads north and south, crossroads east and west, the railroad. The airport was going to expand and the helicopter industry was going to put in a maintenance base. A new meat packing plant was set to open. Truck drivers needed a home. Railroad workers needed a home. Mechanics, both rail and rotor, needed a home. Tog knew the pitch perfectly. "Why live in Amarillo with all that bustle and the high price of lots and the school problem (*wink wink*) when for half the price you can live just thirty minutes from work in a community known for its great schools and churches? Who will buy all those houses?" The training had persuaded Tog, at least.

"You will, Dad. You will buy all those homes." Tog beamed. He was not arguing; he was quite pleased that he could be part of a dynamic and growing industry that would help hundreds of people all over the Panhandle realize their dreams. "You drive almost an hour to PanTex every day. Right? Right. Why don't you live next to PanTex?"

The question was so simple that it answered itself.

"Because I grew up here. Your mother grew up here."

"But there are a lot of people here and all over the Panhandle who don't work here. They work in PanTex or at the Celanese plant, but they barely make ends meet enough to pay for a house in Amarillo, if they can find one at all. Now they can do exactly what you do—live here and drive to Amarillo to work. It's cheaper, less stressful, better schools and churches. Crawford Strategies says that those one hundred fifteen houses will go in the first six months. In fact, Dad, why don't you buy one?"

The case for building a house at Burford Acres was solid, solid enough that Tog would be doing his parents a favor by getting them in on the ground floor and getting them out of the ramshackle wood frame house that George had hand-built over thirty years ago.

"Because our house is paid for. Who exactly do you think we need to build a new house for, anyway?" George didn't say it. Lucille would never say it. But Ronald had a house. Albert had a house. Everybody who worked for a living had a house. Tog did not have a house, not exactly, and George wasn't about to buy him one. Lucille defused the ticking bomb.

"That's really good, dear. Here, eat some breakfast before you go out to Bump's farm. What time are you supposed to be there?"

That was one of the great things about Tog's contract. He was his own boss. He could set his own schedule.

"I'm going to install a new cable over at the Millers, first thing. Terminal box is already there so I can run it from the corner over by the Catholic Church. Then I've got to figure out a route to run another one to the Brodickers and the Helmstones. Not sure how that's going to work, but I'll figure it out. After that I can go whenever I want. I just need to get the lots marked and flagged before they start laying the electrical."

"Can you help me with one little thing?" Lucille timed the eggs and the bacon precisely to serve with a personal helping of her needing one thing before Tog got away. "The Hastings house – they're selling it. I promised to help get it ready and there's this big old set of worn-out lawn tables and chairs in the back. Can you take them off to the dump for me?" She put Tog's eggs on a plate, shoveled the bacon onto the eggs, and laid them in front of Tog as if he were an honored guest. "There's so much rust they just started to fall apart. And look to see if there's anything down in the cellar that needs hauling off."

Tog knew the yard set. He and Frank had used it to climb Mount Everest and, earlier, to defend the Alamo. It had served, briefly, as a Panzer tank. He had hidden underneath it the night he and Frank had run away from home. Frank's cellar was their nuclear bomb bunker. It was hard to believe everything had rusted to despair but, on balance, it was hard to believe he hadn't set foot in Frank's backyard in about twenty years. It was only a couple of blocks away.

"I don't know, Ma. I've got my tools in the back of the truck, full of electronics. Cables and splitters. Terminal boxes ..."

Tog could feel George's eyes boring a hole in him. George had this power over him, this dark power, to make Tog feel like a thief. After Doc's funeral George had tried to make Tog feel like a jerk.

"*Who cares if I skipped the funeral?*"

"*Me. You should have gone. Frank was there, and Peter.*"

"*That's why I didn't go – Frank was there.*"

It wasn't fair, for sure not after he had tried to get George in on the ground floor. He could have gotten him a corner lot, too.

"Sure, Ma. When do you need it?" Tog already had heard through the grapevine that somebody wanted to buy Doc and Virginia's house. It had been empty for the last year or two after Doc quit the clinic and they moved off to Colorado. *And why would anybody buy that house when they could get one of the first new ones in Burford Acres? People are stupid,* he knew that much. "Best for me is after lunch. I can pick it up and take it out to the dump on the way to Bump's. Is that soon enough?"

"Maybe toward the end of the day. We're going over there to clean out all sorts of stuff, so if there's any more, you can take that too. Is that all right?" Lucille smiled and poured him a half-cup of coffee. George just looked away.

"Got to get with it. Thanks for breakfast. Get some sleep, Dad."

ii.

By noon, the Millers, the Brodickers, and the Helmstones had all been assured that with their new television cables they could watch the Dallas Cowboys on Sunday. "In fact, let me show you this." Tog had learned that he could buy more F-16s and Pac-Men and other graphic packages if, when installing cable, he waited until the men of Bridle were at work and the women of Bridle were stuck at home before he showed up to drill holes in their walls and snake coaxial wires into their living rooms. "I know that Joe Bob told me he wants to watch the Cowboys without all that antennae fuzz," Tog would say to Joe Bob's wife, "and you sure can do that, but watch this." Tog would then attach a decoder between the television and the cable slider to demonstrate a "barely more expensive" tier.

"This is the Seven Hundred Club." He would slide the channel selector to show Pat Robertson piously explaining God's plan to a confused but earnest teenage girl. "There are like five of these in the second tier. Don't get me wrong; basic cable gets you all the networks, the Cowboys, something called CNN. News from Chicago. There are twenty channels in basic. Cartoons. You get 'em all. But for just $3.99 more a month you get the Seven Hundred Club and about thirty more channels. At least five of them are the Bible." Maybe not five, exactly, but some.

Tog received forty dollars for each home installation plus one dollar a month from the $8.00 cable bill and one more dollar for the upgrades. Mrs. Miller and Mrs. Helmstone signed up on the spot. "Our little secret," they had said.

If there are a hundred homes in Bridle and I get a cable into every one of them I'll make, let me see, $40.00 times one hundred is four thousand dollars. Plus a dollar a month, forever. It's money on the ground.

"I've got computers, too," he always told them. "IBM is pretty good, everybody knows that, but this new one is what you need. It's called Dell. Do anything an IBM can do at a third of the price."

Very few people in Bridle bought a computer from Tog. The Helmstones, who were cheap at everything, refused not only the Dell but also the Seven Hundred Club.

I've already got sixty houses in Bridle. That's...

Tog was midway through a hamburger at The Corral when the math began to manifest itself. A hamburger at The Corral was eighty-five cents, a dollar ten with fries. A hamburger at McDonald's didn't cost as much but the gas it took to drive to Amarillo to get a McDonald's was a lot more. *Fuckin' Arabs. A tank of gas is over fifteen dollars.* Breakfast at home was free. Dinner was free when George was working the night shift; if George was home at night Tog ate in the Bambi. It was one thing to eat breakfast with him seven days a week, but one meal a day with George was all either of them could stand.

Tog had learned how to cook rice and slice tomatoes and heat up a can of beans and franks in the Airstream. Rice was sixty-five cents a bag for Uncle Ben's, tomatoes less than a dollar a cluster in season, beans and franks were three cans for two dollars at K-Mart. A tank of gas to drive to K-Mart was more than it cost to pay the extra price for frank and beans at Bridle Grocery. Okay, he would have over a hundred dollars a month once he had wired the whole town, and another hundred fifteen out of Burford Estates once he wired that. That was almost three hundred dollars. *Plus all the installs. I can make it. I can make it until something comes along.* Marshall Grey walked into The Corral, Marshall and his daughter. *Time to go.*

Tog had begun to fish the quarters out of his jeans to lay them on the table when Marshall spotted him. Marshall changed course to avoid Tog by walking around the other side of The Corral's tables to make it easier for both of them, but Marshall's daughter didn't know about the need for a course correction. She walked right up to him.

"You're Tog Grumman. Hi. I'm Elizabeth. I'm Marshall and Becky Grey's daughter. They went to school with you. I knew you would be in here because I saw your truck with the sign—Tog's Cable TV—and it was almost twelve-thirty, which meant you would be having lunch. I know who you are because I've seen your picture up there with Daddy ever since I was a little girl."

Tog tried hard to not look at her, but it was impossible. Elizabeth Grey was cute, seventeen or eighteen years old. He knew who she was, too.

She interrupted her outpouring long enough to point to photographs that hung on The Corral's wall above the sit-down counter. Thirty years of Bridle Broncos in thirty separate photographs of fierce teenage football demeanors looked down on The Corral's tables and chairs. In their uniforms the boys looked indistinguishable from one year to the next and, indeed, from the 1950s to the 1980s, a fact less remarkable since almost all of them were the fathers, brothers, and sons of each other.

"You were the running back on the team with Daddy." Marshall squirmed, unable to stop Elizabeth. "You were number 24. I can remember the number because the team averaged 24 points a game and gave up only two touchdowns all year. It was the best Bronco team in history, although the year before—"

"Yes ma'am, Elizabeth. Yes, I'm Tog. Nice to..."

"And your name is really George. George Grumman. But my mother told me that they started to call you Tog because your father is George, too, and so they called you The Other George, and then it was just Tog, T.O.G., which is an acronym, which is an abbreviation from the initial letters of a word. It's like a chemical symbol, like S, for sulphur, from the Latin *sulphurium*. Does your right hip hurt?"

Tog was startled. No one had mentioned his hip since the day he got Doc to write a letter to Pantex that said Tog could fulfill the duties of a job that required him to stand over a worktable for extended periods while using a variety of hand tools to assemble and disassemble sensitive and complex components of atomic bombs. That was ten years ago.

"It's your heel. The right heel is worn more than your left heel so you stand just a bit cocked to one side. And your jeans are worn on the right thigh like you put your hand there the way you did just now when you stood up, to stabilize yourself while your knee gets ready to walk. I'm going to run cross country in Austin next month." She paused for breath, an autonomic response to the inability of the human diaphragm to flatten further without the input of pressure on the walls of the airway in response to nerve impuls-es sent by phrenic and thoracic nerves, a process Elizabeth almost recited out loud before she stopped to catch her breath. She was instead interrupt-ed by Tog's own startled response.

"No, ma'am. It doesn't hurt. And yes, ma'am, I was on the foot-ball team with Marshall. It was a good team." Tog considered saying that Marshall was the best player on the team, not because it was true but be-cause Elizabeth Grey seemed like a nice kid, a bit too quick on her feet, all things considered, so he would be nice back to her. He decided instead, since Marshall had tried to duck him and was signaling to Elizabeth to stop being nice to him, to hell with Marshall Grey. Marshall hadn't been the best player on the team anyway; Tog was. "I read about you going to run. Good luck at State. "

He had read about it because there was a poster on the door of The Corral, as well as all the gas stations and the grocery store in Bridle, with the words "You're Number One!" and "Win State!" stenciled above and below Elizabeth Grey's picture. Everybody knew that Marshall and Becky's daugh-ter was the first Bridle girl to go to State in anything. She was pretty enough, too, not like Becky had been, more like a coltish kind of girl than anything. *She's not Becky, that's for sure. Still....*

"It's 3200 meters. That's two miles. That's not true. It's 1.98839 miles but most people call it two miles. 1600 meters is the metric mile. It's...."

Marshall had been as patient as he could be. On the one hand, his daughter knew more about biology, chemistry, even history, everything re-ally, than all but a fraction of the human race. Most of what she knew was unfocused and easily diverted from topic to topic because her seven-teen-year-old brain was almost four hundred times quicker than her mouth, which managed to catch up and say out loud only the most recent of the endless thoughts that raced through her mind, but not most of the bare-ly-earlier connector thoughts that had rolled through it between the last thing she said out loud and the next thing she would say. Marshall couldn't any more stop Elizabeth from being who she was than he could stop Tog from being who he was. On the other hand, she didn't need to be talking to Tog.

"Let's go, Elizabeth. Nice to see you, Tog," he lied.

"Bye," Elizabeth said. She was tempted to say that Tog's hamburger contained more carbohydrates than nutrients and might not satisfy his hunger level more than three to four hours, and that the French fries were both starches and fats, but the more insistent jerk on her arm from her father meant *Let's go, now!*, although she didn't see why. She smiled, then followed Marshall to the table. It didn't help Marshall's mood any when she chirped, "He doesn't look nearly as old as you, Daddy." She did not say, out loud, that she also thought that Tog looked like Tim Matheson, or maybe Judd Nelson, but with better hair.

She started to add that of the sixteen distinct personality groups, Tog was most associated with the 'mixed introverted' (solitary, a listener) and 'perceptual' (noncommittal, considering options) personalities. Before she could, though, and while she was considering whether she might have missed some traits because he hadn't talked much, the waitress asked her what she wanted for lunch, diverting her to describe the benefits of peanut butter and sweet potatoes to the diets of runners. It also occurred to Elizabeth that Tog was lonely, which was odd in Bridle, particularly for someone as old as her daddy but who looked a lot younger. She kept that thought to herself, too, and was actually somewhat furtive as she watched Tog leave The Corral.

iii.

Tog began to drive to Bump Burford's farm but stopped short, as he often did, at the high school football stadium. He had not gotten more than two blocks from The Corral when he realized that he hadn't installed a cable in the Grey house. It also occurred to him that hell would freeze over before Marshall or Becky Grey would ask him to put a cable in their house. He parked his pickup by the bleachers and climbed to the top row of seats.

From there, he could see the twenty-yard line where he had caught that kick-off from Plainfield and run it all the way back for a touchdown. He gazed toward midfield where a faded and bumpy strip of chalk marked the spot where he had crashed through the Sunset line and sprinted fifty yards for another touchdown. Tog could, and did, think about every place on the field where he had earned his scholarship. Then, inevitably, Tog stared at the raw and dirty 'S,' still visible almost twenty years later, where Frank had burned a mixture of diesel and chicken shit into the field. The

'S' was exactly on the spot where Frank had bent over to moon Peter, who was being treated like some kind of returning hero, all fancy in his Air Force Academy dress uniform, marching Rebecca Collins out to be crowned Homecoming queen.

Did he screw me good or what?

Tog was Homecoming King. Becky Collins (*Becky Fucking Grey!*) was Homecoming Queen. He had a right to walk her onto that field and put that crown on her head right there in front of everybody. Then he had the right to a date, one that he had planned for months, perhaps years. The king and queen always went to the dance after the game. Becky was supposed to meet Tog outside the gym and Frank was supposed to give her Tog's note to be sure she knew he'd be there. *We were gonna go off and do the twist and the hully gully. We were gonna slow dance. She was gonna fall into my arms. And then, after the dance....* Tog's imagination continued to be vivid, although limited.

Fate had intervened. Peter showed up at home from the Academy. The school broke tradition and asked him to escort Becky to the middle of the field. Frank mooned Peter at halftime, in front of the whole town, right when Peter and Becky marched past him to midfield for the crowning. Then Tog's jersey was torn in the second half. Coach made Frank take off his jersey and give it to Tog, a jersey Tog wore the rest of the year. Tog scored three touchdowns. Becky Collins stood outside the dressing room, waiting. Tog smiled at her. Becky smiled back. Then Becky looked right past Tog and smiled at Marshall (*Marshall Fucking Grey!*), who walked up. Becky took Marshall's arm, not Tog's. Becky went to the dance with Marshall, not Tog. Then Marshall had the gall to loan his pickup to Tog (*and that goddamned Frank!*) after the dance to ride around in because Becky had her mother's station wagon. Becky and Marshall went off parking. Tog (*and that goddamned Frank*) sat freezing in Marshall's pickup in front of The Corral until Becky brought Marshall back at two in the morning.

It wasn't Peter's fault, he thought. *Hell, he was special. But did I get screwed or what? God damn Frank to hell.*

Six hours later, Coach had rolled Frank out of bed to go clean Bump Burford's chicken houses. ("Okay, Hastings—if you want to act like a chicken shit, I'll teach you about chicken shit!") Tog did not know about the note, not yet, and went along to help. That was the beginning of the end.

Tog now looked past the field, beyond the visiting team's bleachers on the opposite side, across the autumn fields and prairies toward Bump Burford's farm just beyond the horizon, and decided it was time to quit thinking about Rebecca Collins and Marshall Grey and Frank Fucking Hastings. It was time to get on with life and go out to Bump's to survey the subdivision so that he could install cable television lines and terminal boxes to a new generation of homeowners. He walked down the bleachers and got into his pickup truck.

That Elizabeth! She is one cute kid, I'll say that. I hope she wins State.

He turned the pickup north on the farm road and left Bridle behind but couldn't get the thought of Becky Collins out of his mind. He imagined again the dance, after the dance, parking in Becky Collins' station wagon, and, as always when he drove past the old Collins farm, his thoughts became even more bitter.

That farm should have been mine.

He drove on and, a half-mile later, turned into Bump Burford's dilapidated barnyard. Bump was sitting on his kitchen porch, chewing on something. Tog knew he had to settle down to make any sense out of his business and tried hard to do so when Bump began to mosey toward Tog's pickup. However, one more thought crowded into Tog's already crowded brain, and it was a new one.

That Elizabeth—she should have been mine, too.

Chapter Seven

"Sonny, how are you? Bring your old man in for a haircut?"

Sandy Clayton was sitting in his barber's chair, reading the *Lubbock News*, when Hoyt and Sonny Carter walked in. Sandy folded the newspaper, laid it on the counter, and grinned at them both. Sonny stepped forward and reached out his hand to shake. Sandy grabbed it with his left hand and pumped it two or three times.

"No. Poppa doesn't get a haircut." Sonny struggled with the idea that Sandy might want to cut Hoyt's hair, there being none to cut. Sonny looked at Sandy, thought for a moment, then looked at Hoyt.

"Then it must be you," Sandy said. "Are you ready for a haircut?"

Sonny looked at Hoyt again, who smiled and nodded. Sonny said yes. Sonny remembered that Sandy was nice to him, but the barber might not be very smart if he thought Poppa needed a haircut. He did let Sandy point him to the chair, took a deep breath, and settled in. Hoyt told him that he would be all right.

"Can you hold this for a second while I put a clip on it?" Sandy reached over the young man's shoulder, lifted his hand up behind his neck, then threw the drape around him to put its corners right into Sonny's hand. Sonny saw in the mirror how it all fitted together, and smiled, then sat very still while Sandy clipped the drape and straightened it. "Perfect. Got it. Okay, Sonny, tell me how you want me to cut it."

Sandy waited a few moments, smiling, looking in the mirror at Sonny's face poking up above the barber's drape. Sonny smiled back and told him how he wanted it done.

"Cut?"

"Yes, sir. Cut. How'd that last haircut work out for you?" He smiled again, watching to see if Sonny would answer. Sonny's haircuts could be a bit of a challenge, mostly because of the electric clippers, but Sandy knew that if he hid them with a towel and went straight to the scissors, Sonny never said a word. He began by lifting the hair that had grown out over Sonny's ears, then his forehead, turning Sonny's head gently, in contemplation, as if he was weighing the consequences of a natural selection of the species, which in a sense he was. He decided to leave the neck alone for the present. "Let's start here first, okay?"

Sonny didn't answer, just took another breath, a nervous sigh more than anything. Sandy used a fine comb, lifting the hair, drawing it back, then putting the comb away and clipping no more than a half-inch swath of Sonny's thick hair at a time. Sandy could feel the man tense up in the chair, but he didn't move a muscle.

"Okay, Sonny, I've got one for you. There's this man sitting in a pub. Do you know what a pub is? It's like a bar, only it's in England, and he's sitting there having a beer and another man walks up behind him and says to the barkeeper, 'It is a pint o' Guinness Oi'll be havin', if you please.' Are you with me?"

Sonny nodded and grinned.

"So, the man watches while the barkeep pours a glass of Guinness, twirls a little shamrock into the foam on the head, and the Irishman takes the glass and goes over to the window and sits down. Then the man sees there's another fellow sitting there and this other fellow says to the Irishman, 'Aye, and it is a pint o' Guinness you're drinkin', lad. What a coincidence, because it is a glass of Guinness Oi'm having meself. Cheers!', and he drank it right up."

Sandy had practiced sounding Irish, mincing his words with clipped consonants, drawing out last syllables, wrecking the letters 'i' and 'y.' Sonny's eyes moved slowly back and forth, watching, as the scissors trimmed a bit from the side of his head, a bit from the top. The hairs fell quietly to the drape. He held his breath.

"And so, this second Irishman goes up to the bar and he orders a Guinness and then he sits down and starts to drink it and the first Irishman says to him 'Are ye from the auld country then?' And the other one answers, 'Aye, from Dublin, born and bred these thirty-five years.' 'No!' the other one answers. 'Oi'm a Dublin man meself! Cheers!' and they drink the glasses of beer and the first one says he'll stand the next round and—"

"Does he know Momma?"

"Know your mother?" Sandy lifted the scissors away from Sonny's head, a maneuver he had learned over the years whenever Sonny became restless. "It's just a story." He probably should have come up with a story about cows, or cotton. "You like my stories, remember?"

"It's a story. What's his name?" Sonny asked, then was fearful that he had stopped the story. He liked Sandy's stories, although he couldn't remember any of them.

"Who? The man in the pub? Uh, he's Lord Somebody. It's an English pub."

"Lord Somebody. Jesus is Lord," Sonny offered, helpfully. He relaxed again, comfortable that the man whose name he also couldn't quite remember who put scissors up to his head was telling him about somebody in Jesus is Lord's family, *probably Jesus' brother*, and the drinking men. It was a good story.

"So, he goes up to the bar and gets two more glasses of Guinness and they start to drink them and one of them says, 'If it is from Dublin you're coming, then tell me this—did ye go to school there?' and the other one says, 'Did Oi go to school there ye're asking me? That Oi did, at none other than St. Patrick's Cathedral School, none finer in the land.' And the other one gets real quiet, see, and then says, 'Jesus, Mary, and Joseph, a St. Patty's man Oi am meself.' 'No!' 'True it is.' And he says he'll stand the next round."

"Jesus is Lord," Sonny answers. Jesus is Lord's mother and father might be in the story too. It was a very good story.

"And so, the man listens while these two Irishmen talk about everything both of them knew back in Dublin: the same school, the same church, the same grocery store and, just as the pub's about to close, the barkeep says, 'Last call.' The two guys have one last Guinness and one of them says, 'And me mither, God rest her soul, workin' each mornin' from five o'clock to scrub the little house wher' we lived on O'Connell Street, keepin' it clean for the nine o' us and ....' And the other one stops him and says, 'O'Connell Street? It's a miracle. Oi grew up on O'Connell Street meself! Imagine the two o' us, all the way from Dublin, meetin' up here like this!' So, they finish their Guinnesses and stand up, they put their arms around each other, and walk out at closing time. Hold steady, Sonny. Just one moment. There.

Good. So, Lord Somebody finishes his drink and says to the bartender, 'That is a miracle!' And the bartender says 'What?' and Lord Somebody says, 'What are the odds of two Irish men meeting here in the bar like that, all those things they had in common back in Ireland?' So, you know what the bartender says?"

Sandy looked into the mirror to watch Sonny's eyes. It was a test. Sonny was thinking, thinking. Sonny didn't know.

"He says, 'That's no miracle... they're just the Murphy brothers in havin' a few pints on a Saturday night.'"

Sandy burst into laughter.

Sonny, who knew that Sandy was happy now, laughed too.

Hoyt looked at them over the top of the newspaper, wondering which of them was the bigger idiot, and smiled so that Sonny could see that Hoyt liked the story too. He really did like the story, much better than the one Sandy had told last time, about Kunta Kinte being taken up to the top deck to row because the captain wanted to go water skiing. Hoyt's favorite was the one about the Russian cosmonaut who said he only had one question before blast-off: "Mission Kontrol! How ve beat American capitalist pigs to land rocket on sun?" "Mission Kontrol to Yuri! Relax. Ve go at night."

Hoyt turned back to the newspaper. The government had decided that the Challenger space shuttle had blown up because some rocket scientist had made a miscalculation on the margin of error, leading to a mechanical failure that seemed to Hoyt to be so stupid that it had to be wrong.

"Jesus is Lord. Momma talks to Jesus."

"How is Momma?" Sandy asked. "I haven't seen your momma in a while. Hoyt, Shirley doing okay?"

The rain continued, more in fits and starts than as a downpour, but enough to keep them out of the fields. Hoyt needed to get back in and finish stripping the cotton before boll rot set in. Sonny needed to ride with Hoyt on the stripper because he liked feeling that he worked just like Hoyt. Shirley needed both of them out of the house because it was what women needed.

"She's fine, Sandy."

"Over at the bank?"

"She was still at home when we came into town," Hoyt said. She had been home when they left but he knew that sooner or later she would find a reason to run into town, check on Butch, then do whatever bankers did with their loan papers or books or deposits. The bank was Shirley's business. "I told her I was coming in and she said, 'You tell Sandy he owes me a peach pie.' Why on earth do you owe her a peach pie?"

"You tell her I'm working on it. She picked Clements. I picked Hance." Clements had won the Republican primary. Hance had finished third. Hoyt didn't care either way. "Tell her I said we're going double for nothing in November. Texas will never elect another Republican. Tell her I said that."

Hoyt admired the efficient manner in which Sandy trimmed Sonny's hair, the top, the left side. He was already spinning Sonny around in the chair so that he would not face the mirror while Sandy used the scissors on the back of his head, a known trouble spot.

"Where do you come up with all those jokes?"

"VFW. Hey, you want to go to the parade?"

"What parade?"

"Veterans Day. Remember when we were kids, used to pay a nickel for a poppy? Or a penny, I don't remember. Back then it was Armistice Day." Hoyt didn't seem to remember, so Sandy continued. "Anyway, the VFW post is going to be in it. You need to come on in with us."

Hoyt smiled, which meant that Hoyt would not march in the Armistice Day parade, not with the VFW. He wondered how on earth Sandy could afford the dues and the beer or even the gas to drive over to Lubbock for the meetings. He wondered if Sandy had anything in the house to eat.

Sandy took out his comb and began to sift through Sonny's hair, brushing the clippings as he went. He found a wedge that was out of synch with the rest, combed it, then picked up the scissors and trimmed a few strokes from behind Sonny's ear. Nothing happened. He made a few more passes with the brush, then removed the drape.

"All done. Sonny, I hope your father doesn't take you over to the square. Girls over there get one look at you with this haircut and I won't be responsible for what happens. You're through." He waited while Sonny scratched the itchy hairs from his neck and tugged at his collar, then studied all the hair that had appeared on the floor. "Still rainin', Hoyt.'" He looked out the window. The rain had increased, if anything, flicking dense drops against his barber pole. Pickups driving along the street had their wipers at full speed. "You going to get all your cotton in?"

"We'll be all right, Sandy. It's out of my hands. Hey, thanks. See you in a week or two." Hoyt walked over to the chair and reached for Sonny's hand. Sonny took Hoyt's. "Go? Are you ready to go?" Sonny stood up and waited. "What do you say, Sonny?"

"Thank you." Sonny looked at Sandy and wanted him to know how much he liked hearing about Jesus is Lord's brothers. "Good story."

"Glad you liked it, Sonny. See you in a week or two."

""Bye, Sandy. Good story." He shook Sandy's hand. "Kunta Kinte, Sandy. Jesus is Lord."

Hoyt's pickup was parked almost in front of the barbershop, no more than twenty or thirty steps from the door. He waited in the rain while Sonny studied the twirling red and blue of Sandy's barber pole, but the rain was coming down hard enough to get them both soaked if they stood around, so he tugged at his son's hand.

"Pickup, Sonny. We're getting wet. Let's get in the pickup." He led Sonny to the truck, opened the door, and started the engine, then made a decision. "Sonny? Sit here. Don't get out. I've got to run back in there because I forgot something. Will you sit here?" He waited for Sonny to process the question. "Just wait for me. I'll be right back." He patted the seat, waited for Sonny to nod, and then switched off the engine.

"Drive, Dad?"

"No, not this time. Soon." Hoyt felt the rain soak through the back of his shirt as he stood in the open door long enough to make sure that Sonny wasn't going to slide under the steering wheel and try to drive away. "One minute. Wait right there. Okay?" Sonny nodded. Hoyt trotted through the rain and back into the barbershop.

"Sorry, Sandy," he said. "Forgot to pay for the haircut."

Sandy waved him off. It wasn't important. He was glad to do it. He could catch him next time. Sonny had done pretty well this time. Forget it.

"Here you go." Hoyt handed Sandy six dollars, two bills folded together.

"Appreciate it, Hoyt."

He knew that Hoyt wanted to ask him but didn't know how to bring it up. Sandy made it as easy for Hoyt as he could. "Do you remember Will Hastings?" Sandy acted as if he was tidying the floor, folding the drape for the next customer. Hoyt's face reflected in his mirror, and he was sure that it was a sad face. "He died. In Colorado." He paused to see Hoyt's reaction. "I heard about it over at the VA in Lubbock. The VA docs were talking about how this Dr. Hastings they used to know died. I asked and they showed me the announcement."

Hoyt knew about Will's death, but not from the VA. He knew that Will had passed away because his wife had told him that Will had passed away, a fact he was reasonably sure that Shirley had learned from Sandy Clayton. They hadn't argued about it, nor even much talked about it. He expected Shirley to come up with some reason to run up to Amarillo for a bank meeting or whatnot, and he wondered what would happen between them if she did sneak away to go to the funeral. He wondered what he would say himself if she came right out and told him that she thought they should go. It had been well over thirty years since they had talked about Will or Virginia, but sometimes Will's ghost still walked around in his wife's head. Hoyt knew that much.

Shirley had not said she wanted to go, or that she had to run off to Amarillo on some new bank business. The day of Will's funeral came and went; Shirley stayed home. Neither of them mentioned Will, or Virginia, or the day that they had run Virginia and her baby out of Tierra. Things had been said then, hard things: "Virginia lied to us," and "Arnie says Will's coming back here with a war baby." Things had seemed so important then. She had read Will's telegram to Virginia before Virginia read it; Arnie let everyone in Tierra read the telegrams that came in before he delivered them.

Hoyt could remember it like it had happened just that morning, him carrying boxes out of Virginia's house and putting them in her car, then standing on the front porch next to Shirley, watching Virginia drive away with Peter in her lap. That had been the first time that Hoyt worried that he had married a woman who liked to meddle in other people's business. They ran Virginia out of Tierra before Will even made it home. It was so long ago.

"Sorry to hear he died, Sandy. Got to run before Sonny drives off in the truck. See ya." The more Hoyt thought about Will's funeral the less he wanted to hear about it.

Sandy watched Hoyt jog back through the rain, an old man's way of jogging, across the sidewalk to his pickup. Hoyt climbed in and backed out of the space. The wipers came on and Sonny's beaming face appeared in the windshield, happy as a ten-year-old in a thirty-five-year-old body. Sandy would have cut Sonny's hair for nothing, would have walked all the way out

JACK WOODVILLE LONDON

to the Carter farm to cut it for nothing, and knew that would never happen because Hoyt would never let him.

Sandy peeled the five-dollar bill away from the one- dollar bill, which, as he suspected, was a one hundred-dollar bill, enough to pay his electricity and water and have some left over for some groceries. He had the idea, for just a moment, to go to Nona's Café for supper. Butch wouldn't be there but Tommy probably would. That could be a problem because if Tommy saw that he had a hundred dollars he would start in on Sandy about them driving over to the liquor store. The idea passed and Sandy decided instead to just go back home, to microwave one of the TV dinners he had got at the K-Mart. They weren't very good but they were good enough, at least the Hungry Man meals. If he could stretch them out to the weekend maybe he could go to Nona's then. In the meantime, he would make do with what he had.

Hoyt and Sonny drove over to the bank. Shirley's car was there. Sonny wanted to go in and tell her about the story.

"Jesus is Lord, Poppa. And his brothers." He smiled and carried on. "Let's tell Momma."

"Yes, sir, Sonny. Jesus is Lord. But Momma..." and Hoyt changed his mind. "Momma's working. She's reading loan papers, and bank ledgers, and deposit slips." He said it with the singsong voice that he used to use when Sonny was three or four, or twelve, and he would tell him that Goldilocks found the first bowl of porridge was too hot, and the second bowl was too cold. "Not yet, Sonny. Not just right now."

Sonny nodded. Momma would be busy right now. She always was. Sonny remembered that.

They drove to the hardware store, looked at a half dozen different wrenches they didn't need that could be used to adjust the cotton stripper brush settings that didn't need adjusting, and bought a box of brushes, "just in case." They drove to town at the post office, where Hoyt let Sonny use the key to open the box.

Hoyt was not an atheist, neither was he a religious man, but he did sometimes wonder. He had decided, when he was hiding in the jungle from the Japanese, that there was no god. Later, he decided there was, that there probably was a Grand Plan, as Shirley put it. The Grand Plan had given him the wife he had wanted and, after Butch had run the new Studebaker

86

underneath a truck and killed Shirley's parents, It had given her the bank she wanted. It also had built Shirley a new plantation house on his family's old cotton farm and It had let Shirley mortgage enough irrigation pumps and pipes and John Deere cotton strippers that Hoyt could farm it without his brother or his parents. But It also had given him Sonny, who he loved more than he had imagined would be possible. On the other hand, no Grand Plan in Its right mind would have given Sonny a little less of a brain than he needed. No Grand Plan would give Hoyt Carter a box full of mail.

In the mail there was a federal farm tax credit form to complete. There was a solicitation for funds to support Jerry Falwell's trip to Bethlehem. There was a brochure for Golden Home Care Center, a cemetery assessment, and a letter to Shirley Carter and Hoyt Carter from Peter Hastings. The sun came out as well, but only sparingly.

Hoyt appreciated the sun because he appreciated cotton, the fine white bolls, the hardy stems, the clean fibers that became bales and clothes and everything people needed. He did not appreciate dealing with all the crop reports and taxes and whatnot that had begun to cover him up with paper as soon as they had started in with all that irrigation crap. He did not appreciate Jerry Falwell wanting everyone else to pay for his trip to Bethlehem, which seemed to defeat the purpose of pilgrimages anyway. He had no opinion about Golden Home except that it was too late for them to do anything for his own parents, who could have used some gold and a home in their later years after it had become apparent to Shirley that the McMansion she had needed in order to live properly on their farm had turned out to be not quite large enough for Hoyt's parents to live there properly too. He knew of, so was not surprised by, the cemetery assessment because Hoyt was on the cemetery board. Sonny liked the cemetery, helping straighten up the plastic flowers, holding the garden hose, raking the spaces between the graves. He threw the letter from Peter Hastings in the post office trash bin.

Hoyt's uncertainty tilted back in favor of theism for a few moments when he told Sonny, again, that maybe now he could drive the truck, and saw the look of joy on his son's face. *It takes so little to make Sonny happy,* he thought. It took very little to make anyone happy, when you thought about it. Hoyt had been happy with the old house, with his brother and sister and parents all living on the small farm, before all the pumps and pipes and cotton strippers and before Shirley told him that the bank was loaning them the money to build a two-story colonial with a porch and columns out front. Sonny was happy almost all the time. *And look at Sandy, for crying out loud. If anyone has a right to be angry it's Sandy, who gets by on a disability check and a few dollars giving haircuts, yet Sandy's happy all the time, never a complaint or a bad word for anyone.*

Hoyt's theology then tilted back slightly toward atheism, uncertain how there could be a Grand Plan that would dement someone like Sonny and wreak havoc on Sandy while, at the same time, reward someone as undeserving as Hoyt.

"Sonny? Want to drive?" Sonny's face lit up. Hoyt put the rest of his mail away, then helped Sonny get under the wheel. "First, back up. Just let the clutch out, slowly, slowly." He watched as Sonny backed the pickup into the street and stopped. "Put it in first." That was trickier, involving clutches and gearshifts and the crashing of transmission gears, but Sonny got the pickup into first and it began to lurch forward.

By a short series of commands, "Turn here, turn right there, no *right*, the other right, good, slow down," Hoyt directed his son for a few blocks, then paused the driving lesson. "Stop right here."

Poppy Sullivan's old house was a disgrace. The roof sagged, which meant that the foundation was broken. It probably hadn't been painted since Virginia and the baby, Peter, had lived there, and that was just after the war. They had lived there until the day Will Hastings had come back from the war for good and brought a damned baby back with him. *I never figured Will for that*, Hoyt thought. *Virginia must have been a saint, taking him back with some other woman's baby.* But, back then, Hoyt had told himself that it was like Will was spitting in Virginia's face. *Spitting in Tierra's face, too, planning to bring his war brat back here, after this town sent him to medical school and all that.*

The front door sagged on its hinges and the windows seemed never to have been washed. Hoyt knew that the old rusty plumbing froze and burst in the winter and leaked in the summer. The stucco plaster was cracked from the corner of the front porch to the roof. The wooden floors had to be close to collapsing. *The house should be torn down.* He wondered how on earth Sandy was able to live in there.

"Good job, Sonny. Here's what we're going to do next. Let's go home. Can you drive us home?"

Sonny could indeed.

Hoyt said not a word while Sonny pushed in the clutch, put the transmission into first gear again, and let the clutch out without stalling the engine. Sonny crept up to the corner, turned the steering wheel, and inched along each block until he arrived at the courthouse square. He drove past the courthouse at three miles per hour, drove past the granite memorial put up to honor:

Johnny Bradley and Bart Sullivan

and All Who Did Their Duty, 1941-1945

and turned south toward the highway. Nona's Café was surrounded by pickup trucks, farmers come to town to drink coffee and complain until the rain quit and the fields dried out. Sonny looked toward the café but Hoyt shook his head, no.

What do I know about Will Hastings, really? Hoyt thought. He told Sonny to stop at the highway and told him to wait for the cars to pass. *We all did crazy things in the war, things no one ever talked about.*

The question always hung over Hoyt: *Would Shirley have married me if I'd told her everything I did those three years hiding in the jungle?* None of the men in the war talked about what they had seen, what they had done. The one time Shirley did ask him where he had been in the army he tried to tell her about the Philippines; she misunderstood and thought he had been in the Holy Land, with the Philistines. *That,* he remembered, *was the night we took Virginia over to the hospital in Clovis, when Peter was born. Maybe there is a Grand Plan, just one with a Sonofabitch at the controls.*

Hoyt had seen that kind of thing before. He wondered whether he should have opened the letter and decided, again, that it was best thrown away. Right or wrong, he had put Will and Virginia and that baby of theirs in his rearview mirror a long time ago. One thing Hoyt Carter believed was that the past was in the past. He looked ahead.

"Okay, Sonny. Now, drive us across the highway. Good, turn there, good, and then steer onto that dirt road. Let's go home."

Sonny crashed the gears again, and they lurched onward. Sonny smiled again, and Hoyt remembered that it took so little to make Hoyt happy as well.

Chapter Eight

i.

Burford Acres consisted of a worn-out wheat field and a dilapidated farm where, on the roof of the chicken coops, there were painted the faded words 'Burford Egg Company.' Bump Burford had lived there all his life, apparently without the benefit of fresh paint or new shingles. His wooden farmhouse hid behind a couple of bois d'arc trees that, unfortunately, had been planted to block the morning sun rather than the evening sun. The barn risked imminent collapse, a feature that had compelled Bump to move his tractor and plows out of doors to rust, which they had done steadily over the last few years. None of it was any more charming than the last time Tog had spent any extended time there, a fact that he and Bump Burford both remembered.

"You were two of the laziest kids I ever saw," Bump began. "Took you three days to clean out my chicken houses."

"It took us three hours. That included taking your old John Deere tractor and spreading the chicken shit over your wheat field back there."

"You wore tennis shoes, you dumb nuts. You should have worn rubber boots. Got chicken shit all over you. What the hell were you two in trouble for, anyway?"

"*We* weren't in trouble. *Frank* was in trouble."

"That's right," Bump replied. "He did something at the Homecoming game, don't remember what."

Tog was surprised that Bump remembered them at all, and more surprised when Bump remembered that Frank Hastings mooned Peter Hastings at the Homecoming game. *Frank was a jerk*, Tog thought, *but at least he had the courage to bend over and show Peter his butt, right there in front of everybody. Maybe*

90

it had been the school's fault, breaking tradition, honoring an ex-player as the escort for the Homecoming queen, and Peter Hastings was an ex, that's for sure. They had marched out there, she in her gown, Peter in his dress uniform, and the crowd had cheered with all its might while the couple walked between the rows of lined-up football players, at which time Frank turned around and bent over. *Christ, Becky Collins was gorgeous in that gown.*

"I wasn't in trouble," Tog snapped. "I just came out here to help Frank."

"Why the hell would you want to help anybody clean chicken shit out of an egg house? That's stupid." Bump seemed to remember the whole thing better than Tog did. Why, indeed, had he helped Frank Hastings clean Bump's chicken coops? He couldn't remember, not exactly. That was a long time ago. "And what are you doing out here today?"

"The new house lots. Television cable's all lined up. That's where I come in. I'm the cable engineer." The idea that his labor could be called engineering had come to Tog as in a vision. "I figured it was a good time to put down some markers. I can start laying ground cable and putting up terminal boxes as soon as the electric is ready. Let me show you this."

Tog picked a folder off the seat of his pickup, took out the color plat that he had printed from the computer screen, a streaked and fuzzy testament to his need for more income than a dollar per cable customer per month. *Color printers don't grow on trees.*

"Here's your plots, see?" Tog showed the plat to Bump, who turned the page around three or four times, trying to figure out why there was a straight line along the right hand side, which was the paved road to Bridle, and a crooked line on the left hand side, which was the edge of the Palo Duro Canyon. "So, they've drawn these yellow lines to mark off the lots. The survey will put them down right on the money. Has the electric company been out here?" There was a noticeable absence of anything electric, on the ground or otherwise.

"Not as I can say."

Bump did allow as how three or four fellers had come out a couple of times with some tripods and some wig-wag paddles and wasted his time for a couple of hours.

"Said they was surveyin'. Ain't seen 'em since."

Worse, there were no survey stakes. The electrical company wouldn't mark off rights of way until the survey stakes were in place, much less begin to trench for power lines or pour concrete pads for the transformers. Burford Acres was still nothing but a dirt farm as far as the naked eye could see.

"Okay, not a problem." Tog's breathing was beginning to suffer some autonomic responses of its own. "Tell you what. I'll go ahead and put down some preliminary markers to site the terminal boxes anyway." That would let him estimate the amount he would collect for the whole project, a sum he was certain would dwarf any amount of money he had ever earned in his life. "The lots start from the corner of your barnyard, right? That's the northeast corner, that corner fence of your farm yard." Bump allowed as how it was. "And the subdivision goes all the way down to the marker by the Collins place, right?" Bump didn't know anything about any marker down by the Collins place. "Okay, this shows the subdivision is about a half-mile square. So, a half-mile toward the Collins place there should be a marker. That'll be the corner of Burford Acres. Right?" Tog was becoming aware that, as stupid as Bump Burford had been in 1965 when he was egg king of the county, he was twice as stupid twenty years later.

"It ain't the Collins place. They moved to town."

"Yes, I know. They built a house in town and moved into Bridle. But it's still their farm." It was coming back to him why he had been dumb enough to go help Frank scoop shit out of a chicken house when it was just Frank who got in trouble. Becky Collins had lived on the farm next to Bump's farm. Tog had found every excuse to happen by her farm, which was not easy since it was three miles from town. He had come out to Bump's with Frank just on the off chance that Becky....

"The Collinses don't live in town either. They're dead."

"Yes, I know. But.... Never mind. Wait here."

Tog left Bump and Bump's wheat field anarchy standing in the barnyard. He drove his pickup to the corner post, turned it around, and noted the odometer. He proceeded slowly along the paved road toward the Collins place and, at a half mile, pulled the truck over to the right of way and got out. The ditch was filled with tumbleweeds and soft dirt but, with a bit of scrambling, he found the barbed-wire fence that separated Bump's inert wheat field from the right of way. It took him another twenty minutes to find an ancient iron pin that had been hammered into the ground and left to serve as a survey point.

Now, twenty years later, he was back at Bump's with a different problem: Tog didn't know how to divide the field into one hundred fifteen squares on the ground. *I need my computer*, he thought. *That and a mile of electric cord. Somebody needs to come up with a little battery-powered computer. Nothing much, wouldn't have to be fast or anything, just something with a floppy disk to run some programs.* He daydreamed briefly about inventing one, then gave it up. *It'll never happen.*

He walked the fence line until he found an abandoned tow sack, which he tied to the barbed-wire fence to mark the location. He went back to the iron pin in the ground and scuffed the dirt away from it to make it easier to find the next time he came out. Bump was waiting for him in the farmyard.

"I been thinkin.' You're George's boy aren't you?" Tog agreed that he was. "You got the football scholarship over to Tech, but then you got in some trouble too, didn't you? Seems like there was something."

"I didn't get in any trouble. I broke my leg." His leg felt more broken now than it had in years, no thanks to stumbling around in sandy ditches and kicking iron survey pins. "That's what knocked me out of my scholarship."

"No, I'm pretty sure you got in some trouble. Something to do with that explosion over at the football field, that was it."

"That wasn't me," Tog insisted. Bump was turning out to be a lot like George, poking at him when all he was doing was trying to make an honest living. "It was Frank Hastings and, to be honest with you, it wasn't that much of an explosion." To be honest with him, Tog would have to add that Frank had figured out that mixing a great and messy quantity of Bump Burford's chicken shit would produce a small quantity of methane which, when mixed with a gallon or so of diesel fuel and a cherry bomb, would explode and scorch a substantial mark on whatever was beneath it, in that case the Bridle Bronco football field. To be really honest with him, Tog would also have to say that he had bet Frank that he couldn't do it, thus assuring that Frank would try.

"God, that was funny. Burned a big old 'S' in the grass. Hell, burned it right into the ground. You can still see it in the dirt, where you blew it up. They must have dug it up and tried to fix it a hundred times. Numbskulls ought to figure that all they're doing when they dig it up is make it stand out. Someday they'll dig up the whole football field just to get rid of that mark. You got any idea where you're gonna put your cable things?"

Tog didn't, not without enough arithmetic skill to divide a field that was one-half mile long on one side and bordered by a canyon on the other side into one hundred fifteen equal lots, not to mention measuring all the interior roads and alleys that would be put in.

"Tell you what I'll do, Bump. I'll set some markers where I think we ought to put the terminal boxes. It'll be rough until we get the streets marked and they put the electrical trenches in but I need to get an idea how much cable to run. Okay?" Tog needed to estimate how much he was going to make out of Burford Acres so that he could ask for a higher credit limit on his Visa and MasterCard. His computers were getting bigger and the Bambi was getting smaller. Bump said it was fine with him and wandered off to get himself some iced tea. Tog wandered off to get some red flags and a roll of measuring tape.

ii.

George Grumman received very few letters. Once or twice a year he got a form letter from the VFW, reminding him that he was eligible. He also received newsletters from the American Association of Retired Persons, the re-elect Senator Graham Committee, and SnowBirds of America, a group of Iowa farmers who lived in travel trailers in the Rio Grande Valley every year so that they could eat free grapefruit right from the trees and watch mildly pornographic Hollywood movies on outdoor screens at a motorhome park set up especially for them on the main road to South Padre Island. George carefully tore each one to shreds and, occasionally, considered filing a change of address form with the post office so they would stop bothering him.

George also had a few post cards. One had a picture of the Arkansas River near Buena Vista, Colorado, a view of steep-walled mountains, rushing river water, and a man clad head to toe in green waders and a rubber jacket hauling in an enormous fish on a doubled fly rod. Doc Hastings had sent it to him thirty years ago, and one year later he and Virginia had prevailed on George and Lucille to drive up to the mountains with them to stay in a cabin and breathe in the mountain air. George kept the card in a metal ammunition box, along with one from Ronald and his wife, sent from Corpus Christi on their honeymoon; another from Albert and wife from Six Flags over Texas ("Better than Disneyland," a sentiment George thought too frivolous for discussion, particularly since no Grumman had ever gone to Disneyland); and a few from here and there that had come in from friends at PanTex who had gone on vacations.

The mail that arrived that he considered important was kept on his dressing table. It was there that he first looked before asking Lucille what the hell she had done with the letter.

"What letter?" she had replied, an aggravating response that made George growl before he believed that she really didn't know. "I haven't touched your stuff. Everything's right where you left it."

His Old Spice, the comb, the Zippo lighter, and his key ring with the car key, the house key, the cellar padlock key, and his P-38 can opener were exactly where they were supposed to be. In fact, the water bill, the telephone bill, the electric bill, and the gas bill were exactly where he had left them as well. Frank's letter was missing.

"Are you talking about the bill from the highway patrol?" she yelled in from the kitchen. "I put it on the dresser, with the bills. Why'd you get a bill from the highway patrol, anyway?" *George is getting a little hard on the hearing side*, she thought. She waited for him to answer, then decided to yell louder. "What'd the highway patrol want with you?"

"What letter from the highway patrol?" he roared back. George had pulled the dresser away from the wall to check behind it. The dresser was heavier than it used to be and the carpet hadn't been touched in years. All he found when he got on his knees was a couple of nickels and pennies and the remnants of a Bic pen. He considered leaving the dresser pulled out, then stood up and began the process of shoving it back into place, endangering the Old Spice and causing his Zippo to careen off Lucille's Avon bottle and knock her hair brush to the floor. He was worse off than when he started. He stomped in to the kitchen to get to the bottom of it.

"The letter from Frank," he told her. Lucille was rinsing dishes and refilling the Mr. Coffee for his afternoon coffee. "I left it on the dresser. And what letter from the highway patrol?"

"What letter from Frank who?" she answered.

It was then that George realized he hadn't told her about the letter.

"And the highway patrol says you owe them a fine for not having a driver's license. When did they stop you? And why don't you have a license?"

95

George was indeed slipping. He couldn't remember if he intentionally hadn't told Lucille about the letter because he didn't want her to know about it, or if he might have put it somewhere else where she wouldn't find it before he decided what to do about it. *Where else would I have put it?* It was like the time he lost the flashlight and looked everywhere. Two days later he found it, still lit, inside the cabinet under the sink where he had used it to look at the leaking pipe.

"Highway patrol first. Here's my license." He took out his billfold, fished out his driver's license and showed it to Lucille. "It's got two more years to run. And they never stopped me. I don't owe them a dime." The highway patrol was getting out of hand, in George's view. Before they moved some snot-nosed kid to be the law in Bridle there had been no highway patrol. If a high school kid was speeding, his dad took the keys away. If a grownup was speeding, he'd hear about it at The Corral. And if someone even dared to break the law, the town men would settle it, quietly. Now everybody in town got a ticket for something, crooked license plates, mud on the parking lights, parking too close to the next car, anything to make the fines in town equal the salary of the snot-nosed patrolman who collected them. "Did it just show up in the mail?" he asked. It did.

"Well, I never saw it. I'll just go over to the little twerp's house and straighten that out in a jiffy." George took the coffee cup and put it on the table, then waited for Lucille to hand him the spoon. He stirred it and blew on it until it was cool, then added a spoonful of sugar and tasted it, adjusting and stirring until it was just right. "And Frank's letter? Nothing much." Lucille put the dishcloth down and poured her own cup, then sat next to him. "He wrote to say he appreciated us coming to the funeral. That's all."

Lucille had been within arm's length of George and within ear's length of both Peter and Frank at the funeral. She knew that if Frank Hastings had written a letter to her husband, it wasn't to say he was glad they came to the funeral.

"Oh," she answered. "That letter." She pulled a foot ladder out from under the table, opened the pantry door, and used the ladder to climb up to the ceiling slats above the top shelf. George watched from his chair as she removed a few slats from the ceiling and reached inside. "This letter," she finished, putting the slats back in place and climbing down from the ladder. "The one where he says he appreciated us coming to the funeral? Is this the letter you're talking about?" She handed it to him and put the ladder away. "If you want Tog to read your mail you should leave it where he can find it. The dresser is about as good a place as anywhere else. And I didn't read it. My name wasn't on it." She had the moral high ground on that score; she may have kept Tog from prying, but she was innocent of prying herself.

"Okay, you want to know what's in it? Here's what's in it." He took Frank's letter out and read to her:

> Dear Mr. Grumman: I know you were Dad's best friend. I need you to tell me something. Peter and I had a pretty ugly argument at Dad's funeral. He blew up, mostly in my opinion because of the picture of Mom and Dad on the front porch when they lived in Tierra, but I'm not sure why he thinks it upset her because that picture seemed to be the only thing she recognized. I'm writing because I'm pretty sure you heard him. To be blunt, he said I was not their son, that I had been brought to the USA as a war orphan and basically they raised me like a charity case or something. He used to call me names like that when we were kids but I thought it was just him picking on me, older brother/younger brother stuff. Can you tell me anything about that story? Thank you very much,
>
> Frank Hastings

"So there, it's out," George grumbled. "Peter spilled the beans and Frank wants to know the story. That's what the fight was about at the funeral." He drank a few sips of coffee and put the cup down.

The kitchen was as small as when George and the boys had built the house. He had never been a carpenter, but he had been the kind of man who did whatever he set out to do until he got it right. They had talked about adding a room or two, knocking out some walls, but George had built their home right the first time and he never really intended to change it. The kitchen was just large enough for the gas stove and the old Sears refrigerator, a sink, and counter top. They had a round dining table so that all five of them could sit together, but the room was so small that the back of George's chair at the table stuck out into the hallway that led to the two bedrooms and the front room. From where he sat he now could look out over the sink and see Tog's Bambi in his backyard and, beyond, a dry arroyo lake between their house and the high school.

"Okay, what are you going to say? Do you think he has a right to know anything?" Lucille wanted to know. George did not, but Lucille was hardly surprised by that. "I didn't think so. That's the last thing we need around here."

Lucille was tempted to write him back on her own and tell Frank she always had thought he was a little bastard. The two sides of her brain were in constant battle. One side was as much in love with Tog as when he was a baby. He had been cute, then nice looking, then handsome, and even today his best means of survival was his easy charm and disarming good looks. She went to movies to see Paul Newman or John Wayne and gazed at them without the least idea what the story was about, just to see what Tog might have become if Frank hadn't wrecked Tog's life.

That was the other side of her brain, the side that remembered Tog running away from home with Frank when they were ten or twelve years old and remembered Tog waiting for her at the justice of the peace office because someone saw him and Frank peeing off the roof of the grain elevator onto the cars passing below. In her mind's eye she saw every grimace of Tog's face when he and Frank were caught setting fire to a wooden outhouse on Halloween, and his grim determination when he told her he was going to go out to Bump Burford's to help Frank shovel out the chicken houses because the coach was making Frank pay for his ugliness at that Homecoming game. She loved that Tog was loyal to such a headache of a boy—right up until the day she found Tog in his room, gulping and almost unable to breathe, because Texas Tech had offered Tog's football scholarship to Frank.

"What?" she had shrieked. "Frank didn't play ten minutes the whole year. You were the star. You scored all those touchdowns and...." she had said.

Tog had just lain on his bed, gulping back his grief. After Coach gave Frank's football jersey to Tog at that same damned Homecoming game, the sports page had a picture of Tog scoring his fourth touchdown of the

98

night in Frank's jersey. The college scouts saw it and thought it had been the younger brother of the legendary Peter Hastings. They continued the mistake by watching Frank's number outrun, out block, out receive, and outscore every player in Bridle history. Texas Tech promptly offered a scholarship to Frank's number. True, it was straightened out, but it was the coach who got in touch with the college and told them what had happened. Lucille might even have let that go, but then Frank broke Tog's leg on that damned sheet of ice that Frank made with water draining out of Marshall Grey's pickup over on Main Street. Tog lost his scholarship to a broken leg.

Lucille had always thought Frank was a little bastard, and she still did. If it hadn't been for her husband, she would have picked up the phone right then and called Frank a bastard to his face, or at least to his ear. The only thing she cared about in life more than Tog was her husband, and the idea of making that telephone call lasted less than a second.

"I've got to tell him something," George said at last. For a few minutes he blew on his coffee, drank some, and blew again, thinking. For his part, he was ready to tell Frank the whole story. "Look, they're never coming back here. Doc's dead. Virginia's gone in her head."

"You don't know that," Lucille countered. "People wake up from those things all the time. For all you know, she knows everything that's going on, just can't say anything. Lost her voice or something." Lucille tried to prove her point with an example but couldn't remember any, trying to recall episodes of Virginia's absent-mindedness, of times when she and Virginia would drive off to go shopping in Amarillo or make a bunch of peanut butter Rice Krispies for the school and Virginia would forget to show up. Nothing exactly right came to mind. "She dresses like she always did, nice dresses and hose and all that, carries a purse. You saw her at the funeral; she looked normal as anybody. It's just like she doesn't know how to recognize you. But for all we know, she's in there in her head listening to every word." Lucille didn't believe that, but she wasn't sure. People did wake up from comas now and then, and they showed it on television. She didn't want Virginia to wake up and go on television and tell the story.

In the end, they decided to write Frank and tell him how sorry they were about Doc. They wished they had visited more after the funeral. George then told Frank what he had asked rather than what he wanted to know:

I don't know anything about you being a war orphan and never heard that story. I saw Peter acting up there between the funeral cars and thought it was pretty ugly but I didn't want to make a bigger fuss about it in front of everyone and it all seemed settled down there at the grave service and the church after. I saw the picture and it was the first time I saw them together with him in uniform. It was like something about the picture did set your mother off and maybe if you look at it you will figure out what it was. That should settle Peter down. I'm sorry.

George Grumman

He said, "There," and sealed up the envelope to take to the post office. "There. If he's got half a brain he can figure it out on his own."

"'There' my foot," Lucille replied. "You've said too much already."

iii.

For two hours Tog cursed the surveyors, the engineers, the electric company, and even Crawford Strategies, none of whom seemed to be in any hurry to start carving up Bump's farm and selling it to the truckers and meat packers who needed nice new homes without the cost and inconvenience of Amarillo. He pounded the last of twelve red flags into the dirt in roughly equal spacing somewhere along Bump's fence line and drove away. Bump was a good old coot but he had a knack of making Tog remember things he didn't want to think about.

By the time he reached the road that turned in to the old Collins place, his discontent extended to Becky herself. *What kind of sorry coincidence is it to run into Marshall and their daughter at The Corral? What were the* odds of Bump Burford reminding him of that whole sorry Homecoming weekend where everything started to fall apart? Now Becky Collins (*Becky Fucking Grey!*) was stuck inside his head and he couldn't get her out.

He thought about driving into the Collins farm, just to look around. He had been back there once, a couple of years ago. The old Collins house had been torn down but the elm trees that grew all around the farmyard were still there. He had climbed up in those trees a couple of times when he was a boy, just to see if he could spot Becky walking around. When Frank and he ran away from home, they made it as far as those trees before declaring them to be Sherwood Forest and falling asleep on the ground beneath them. Now there was nothing left but a set of Chrysler pump motors on giant irrigation heads, right where Becky's house had been.

Bump was right; it wasn't the Collins place anymore, just some kind of robot factory farm. It was the Grey farm; Becky had inherited it and Marshall had modernized it. In fact, now that Tog thought about it, that was probably why Bump was cutting his farm up into house lots – there was no way to afford robot irrigation to keep up his wheat farm, and the Lord knew that the big dollar boys in Amarillo had run Bump out of the egg business. Bump needed the money.

To hell with the Collins farm, and Becky too.

He shifted the pickup into third gear and stepped on the gas.

The closer he got to Bridle, the madder he got. There had been the Helmstones, too cheap to upgrade their cable. There had been Marshall Grey, gloating about his wife choosing him over Tog. There had been Bump, picking on him about Frank and the criminal destruction of Tog's football career. There had been Burford Acres itself, behind schedule and with not a thing in sight that looked like anyone but Tog was trying to turn it into the verdant community that Crawford Strategies had promised. And, as if his whole biography of insults wasn't already being put on instant replay to Tog's tiny attention span, he remembered that Lucille had asked him to go clean up the trash in the backyard of the old Hastings house because they were going to sell it. They were going to get rich selling off a house that hadn't been lived in for a couple of years and expected Tog to help them by being their junk boy. He had already been the junk boy for the Hastings family, *especially for that sorry Frank.*

Enough was enough, or, as Tog thought about it, *fuck that! Nobody named Hastings has ever done a damned thing for me except wreck my life. Fuck 'em.*

101

They can clean up their own trash.

He parked in the alley so that Lucille wouldn't see the pickup and slipped through the door of his Bambi. He pre-flighted his F-16 and loaded the bomb rack.

The Iraqi desert began to slide beneath his wings and Tog began to prepare for the missiles that would come after him as he neared the nuclear reactor.

Very clever, Saddam, hiding your missiles in a hole in the ground. They won't save you, though, because your bunkers look like, look like... and then Tog's memory dealt him one final blow for the day.

Saddam's bunkers looked just like the nuclear bomb shelter of his youth, the old storm cellar in the Hastings' backyard. It had been the scene of Frank's worst spanking, of good old Hercules' death, and of Frank's and Tog's decision to run away from home.

Chapter Nine

i.

The Tierra county clerk's office was manned by an efficient staff of high school graduates who had gone to bureaucrat school where they learned how to diligently file deeds and judgments, to record lawsuits and voter registrations, and to send out notices of taxes due, commissioners' hearings, elections, and such sundry public business. They were so good at their job that no one in the county had the least concern about their governmental affairs. The elected clerk, Mrs. Goforth, believed their job was to help the public. It was, therefore, with a sense of having failed in her mission that she wrote back to Mr. Hastings:

> Dear Sir: I have looked all through the vital statistics records of the county and regret to say that I cannot find any record of your family. We keep the marriage, birth, and death records all the way back to 1906 and there aren't any Hastingses in those records.
>
> I'm sorry that we couldn't be more help.
>
> Very truly,
> Brenda Goforth, County Clerk

Mrs. Goforth gave the letter to Betty Sue Noble with instructions to put it in an envelope to Mr. Hastings' address and send it out with the afternoon mail. Betty Sue prepared to do so and, in the process, read the letter. Betty Sue admired Mrs. Goforth and held no ill will over her having married into the county rather than being a local girl. It was only natural that she tell her employer that, while the letter was technically correct, there was one record over at the high school.

"We were cleaning all the senior pictures in the hallway for Help the School Day and I did 1935 to 1945. I'm pretty sure there was a boy named Woodrow Wilson Hastings who graduated from high school one of those years."

Mrs. Goforth told her to hold on to the letter and, if Betty Sue wanted to see if she could find out anything, that would be nice of her to do. Betty Sue said she would go over to the high school.

The school superintendent told her that she couldn't actually see the records, "...because of privacy and all that..." but it wasn't that hard for him to go all the way back to the files of 1937 and read out to her that Woodrow Wilson Hastings had been a pretty good student, had played football, had graduated, and that his transcript of grades had been sent to Texas School of Mines in El Paso and, later on, to the Texas Medical School in Galveston. He hadn't been heard from since.

ii.

It had been the custom of the First Bank of Tierra to stay open late on Thursdays, an unspoken declaration that the bank provided just as much service as the big banks over in Lubbock that advertised drive-in lanes and high interest rates and, of course, later hours on Thursdays. As a consequence, Shirley didn't cook dinner on Thursdays. She ordinarily bought a basket of fried chicken and French fried potatoes, with biscuits and gravy, and brought them to the farm for supper. However, because of the rain, she knew that Hoyt and Sonny would not be in the cotton fields so she called them to ask if they would like to come in to Nona's Café to have supper in town. Fifteen minutes later Hoyt and Sonny were drinking coffee and, in Sonny's case, a Coca Cola in the bottle, waiting for Shirley, when Betty Sue Noble came in.

"Mr. Carter?"

Hoyt looked up to see the young woman from the clerk's office. She was sitting at the next table and clearly trying to get his attention. Hoyt did a mental inventory to see if he had forgotten anything, his property taxes, or school taxes, or had ducked his jury notice. County clerks usually meant they wanted something, but he couldn't think what.

"Mr. Carter? I saw your picture today. Funny running into you like that. You know, small world?"

She was pleasant and had nice manners and Hoyt couldn't imagine where she had seen his picture.

"I was over at the high school and I went to look at your class picture on the wall there in the school hall. Yours and Mrs. Carter's, too. Of course, she was Shirley Fleming then, but it was so fun to see you and her."

It was in Hoyt's nature to be kind to people. Very few people said things or did things just to be ugly and, he knew, if you were pleasant to them, they would appreciate it. He was pleasant to Betty Sue.

"You must not have enough work to do over at the courthouse. My looks might have changed a little in fifty years. If you can look at that old senior class picture and recognize me, well, we need you to find some things to keep you busy." Hoyt smiled and turned back to see if Sonny was doing all right with the Coca Cola bottle. He was. Betty Sue did not have enough work to do.

"That's funny. It was work, sort of, that I was doing over there at the high school. I was trying to find out something about a family named Hastings and there was a boy in your class named Woodrow Hastings." She smiled and paused and waited for Hoyt to say something. He did not. "His picture was in your class."

It was also in Hoyt's nature to tell people what they asked, not what they wanted to know. She had not asked Hoyt anything, not yet.

"We had this letter from a man named Hastings and he thought maybe he was born here. That's what I was working on," she went on. "We don't have any records about any Hastingses at all at the clerk's office, not any birth records or deeds or marriages or anything. That's how come I went up to the high school." She smiled at Hoyt to show him that she was not only a reasonable clerk, but clever, too, the kind of civil servant any high school graduate would like to become.

Hoyt was already aware that there were no records of Woodrow Wilson Hastings' birth or marriage or anything else, at least not in Tierra. It wasn't anything he had thought about in a long time. He smiled back at her.

"He seemed like a nice man. I hate to tell him we just don't have any records. Did you know the Hastings family?"

105

Sonny had finished his Coca Cola and now was using the bottle as a spyglass, an idea he had gotten from watching *Captain Hook* or *Treasure Island*. He had the lip of the bottle pressed to his eye, trying to look out at the pirate world of Nona's dining room through the thick glass bottom. Hoyt wiped a dribble of Coca Cola off Sonny's cheek. The letter to the clerk was, he suspected, the same letter Peter had sent to Shirley. To Hoyt and Shirley.

"I didn't," he answered. "His parents weren't from here, so I don't know anything about them. Woodrow did go to school with us, but then we all graduated." Hoyt and Johnny Bradley had joined the army. Will had gotten into college, somehow. He wanted to tell the truth. He also wanted Miss Nobles to leave Nona's before Shirley arrived. "And then, after the war, he never moved back here. I don't know anything about the man who wrote you. What was his name?"

"Peter Hastings."

"No, sorry. I don't know the man." He was relieved that Betty Sue wasn't smart enough to ask if he had ever known a *boy* named Peter Hastings, a question that would have made Hoyt struggle a bit more. He wanted to add, *He must not have been born here,* or *Virginia Sullivan left town with Woodrow Wilson Hastings after the war,* but he didn't. He knew that the more he said, the more there was to know, and sooner or later someone would come around asking for the rest of it. "That was a long time ago."

He made a slightly bigger show of wiping Coca Cola off Sonny's collar, and putting the bottle away, and saying ARRRGGHHH like a pirate, so that she would know he had to go. Hoyt put two dollars on the table and told Betty Sue goodbye. He and Sonny left Nona's as quickly as he could.

Shirley drove up just as Sonny and Hoyt were driving away, an event that led to a flashing of headlights and a honking of horns.

"Hey," she yelled. "Hoyt?"

He stopped.

"Where you going? Let's eat."

Hoyt took a deep breath and considered the situation, then acted on the facts as they were.

"Sorry, we need to get it to go. Did you call it in?"

She had.

"Sonny got a little messy with a Coke while we were waiting." He waited for her reaction. "I'll run back in and see if it's ready." He waited for

Shirley to micromanage that plan as well and was relieved that she did not. "Just head on home and we'll be right there. Sonny? Sit tight. I'll be right back."

Shirley put her Cadillac in gear and drove away.

Hoyt looked at Sonny. Sonny looked at Hoyt.

"Okay?"

"ARRRGGGHHH," Sonny said. "ARRRGGGHHH."

iii.

Betty Sue Noble told Mrs. Goforth the next morning that she hadn't found out anything at the high school except that the man named Woodrow Hastings had graduated, just like the class portrait said, and then hadn't come back to Tierra after the war.

"How do you know that?" Mrs. Goforth asked.

"I saw Hoyt Carter at Nona's and he told me. He went to high school with him. They were friends."

Mrs. Goforth told Betty Sue to go ahead and mail the letter, but could she have it for just a moment? Betty Sue found it and brought it back. Mrs. Goforth added a handwritten note at the bottom. "We did find a man named Woodrow Hastings who graduated from high school here. He had a friend named Hoyt Carter. His wife runs the bank in Tierra. They went to high school with him."

Mrs. Goforth wasn't as careful with words as Hoyt so it never occurred to her that she was being anything but friendly when she added, "You should get in touch with them. They'd be glad to help you if they can."

She signed the postscript. Betty Sue took the letter along with the rest of the clerk's mail to the post office, where she had to wait a moment while Sandy Clayton collected his mail. She dropped the clerk's letters into the slot and then held the door for Mr. Clayton as they walked back onto the street. He asked her how she was and she said fine and then said she liked her job so much.

"Because you meet so many nice people and help them. Just today I was helping this man look for his family." She paused to think about it a moment, and continued, "I think it was before your time, though, Mr.

Clayton. It was a man named Hastings and he wanted to know if he was born here, that sort of thing. We couldn't find any records, though. It's a good job."

Betty Sue's reaction to Sandy wasn't recorded, but she must have had some kind of reaction because the next morning she asked Mrs. Goforth if she could look at a copy of Mr. Hastings' letter to get his address because she thought she might send that man another answer.

"You aren't going to believe this," she added. "I was at the post office and the barber was there. Well, we were chatting and he said, 'Woodrow Hastings? He lived here. Then he became a doctor and just died a couple of weeks ago. Tell him to ask me anything about them; I know all about it."

Mrs. Goforth was pleased, very pleased.

"Betty Sue, it's our job to help people. I think you just helped that man. I sure hope it turns out he finds what he's looking for." She smiled and patted Betty Sue on the shoulder. Then, because it was the clerk's office, she returned to her business, keeping the records of Tierra's affairs.

Chapter Ten

i.

When Frank was nine years old he watched Peter shoot a BB gun at birds on a highline wire and wondered, *Why don't they just fly away?* and then, *Why doesn't the electricity shock them?*

Frank wondered a lot of things. He wondered why Hercules liked to play fetch with him but not with Peter. He wondered why he had a used bike but Tog had a new one. He wondered why there were different churches for just one Bible, and why Tog seemed reasonably happy about not going to any of them. He wondered why he was invisible whenever Peter was present (Sunday school class, junior high band, school cafeteria and assemblies, Saturday night at the movie theater, any time they went to The Corral), and why he had a learning disability (*I'm retarded...*), a concern raised by the requirement of Bridle High School that all students had to take trigonometry and chemistry, neither of which he intended to use in his grown-up life.

He also wondered why he took little interest in the very things that Peter was so good at, such as football, basketball, track, girls, and Mother's 1962 Chevrolet. He wondered why he wasn't kicked off the football team after mooning Peter at the Homecoming game, suspecting (rightly) that the coach knew that Tog depended on Frank to help him pass English and history during the football season. He next wondered why he was disinvited from the school sports banquet after the season was over, suspecting (rightly) that it had to do with mooning Peter at the Homecoming game.

Frank once wondered, on a very cold and cloudless night one week after the sports banquet, why water does not freeze inside a town's water tower, but when that same water is filled into the bed of Marshall's pickup and then laid down in sheets on Main Street by driving the pickup back and forth as the water seeps out from the tailgate, it freezes on pavement like ice on a skating rink.

He also wondered why a couple of gallons of very wet chicken manure added to a gallon of gasoline didn't burn well but when fifteen pounds of dried manure, plus a box of saltpeter from the school cafeteria pantry, were added to gasoline, the mixture would scorch grass, chalk yard lines, dirt, subsoil, and everything beneath it in the shape of the letter 'S,' and continue to burn for quite a long time while the coach and superintendent slid around on the ice on Main Street before getting to the school football field to see what that odd glow was, visible in the night sky.

The following Sunday, while squeezed onto a pew between Virginia and Will, listening to a sermon on the fires of Hell, Frank wondered why no one preached the chapter in Luke where Jesus told the multitudes that he had come to bring fire to the earth and wished it already were kindled or, about the Prince of Peace telling the Twelve Apostles in the book of Matthew that he came not to bring peace but a sword. That Jesus sounded like someone interesting.

In his last few months at home, before graduation, Frank wondered whether Tog would ever come back to him. In his first few months at college he wondered why he had to take math and science, which he intended to never use in his grown-up life.

As a sophomore, he wondered why *they* seemed to be having so much trouble beating Vietnam and, later, after graduation, why *they* assigned to his birthday the very first number drawn in the draft lottery, the only lottery that Frank ever won. He soon wondered why he was sent to infantry training and then why he was so bad at it. He wondered if he would live to drive the used Volkswagen that Will had given him for college graduation and, when he did, whether going to graduate school and writing for a newspaper in Austin would give him the skill he needed to write about what he really saw in Vietnam. Frank soon came to wonder also why no one had told him sooner about live music, the Soap Creek Saloon, Willie Nelson's Fourth of July picnics, or longneck beers.

Frank's curiosity was not purely inward looking. He asked why, whenever anyone believed that if something could be separate but equal, they always wanted it to be separate. He asked his editor why a highway divided East Austin from rich Austin and why Mexican laborers were paid less to roof houses and pour cement than scruffy white guys who didn't work as hard or do as good a job; his editor said they were good questions. He asked why farmers who depended on government subsidy checks always voted for the candidate who would cut the farm budget, and why anyone thought that it was Ronald Reagan rather than Ayatollah Khomeini and the Fedayeen who really had defeated Jimmy Carter in the 1980 election. Pat C. Oh said they were rhetorical questions. He genuinely wanted to know why President Reagan thought that death squads for democracy were more likely to work in El Salvador than they had in Vietnam and why a coup in once-British Grenada was an American problem; no one wanted to talk about those questions.

Some of these wonders became files of clippings for stories that were never written. When Frank pitched them, Mr. Burnam said that Frank needed to focus on city council meetings and school board hearings.

Frank was not aware of everything, not even everything that mattered. He was unaware of interest rates, unaware that plastic is not biodegradable, and unaware that security investment regulations usually were enacted after some investment firm had figured out a new way to cheat its investors.

He was completely unaware that, during a graduate seminar on "Reporting Foreign Political Events," in which he asked why Margaret Thatcher thought that putting huge swaths of coal workers and shipbuilders out of work would make England a better place for them to live on unemployment benefits, a young woman was passing by the open doorway. He didn't know for a long time that she heard him question whether the rousing use of a crushing military action against a third-world banana republic would restore dignity to unemployed coal miners in Yorkshire and, hearing no answer to his question, that she stood in the doorway long enough to figure out which one of the people in the room had asked the very point she had read in a three-week-old copy of the *Manchester Guardian*, which she had stumbled across in the graduate school library reading room. Of course, she was unaware that he had noticed her reading the *Guardian* and had wanted to find out for himself what interested a person who looked like her.

In short, like younger brothers everywhere, Frank grew up largely invisible but observant, standing out from the crowd more often by doing something that upset someone's expectations rather by doing something that met them.

Frank Hastings had no clear understanding that the purpose of his life was to be the person who asked *why* as a means to making the world a more open place, if not a better one. Indeed, the only two people who clearly knew that were Eleanor, who for several weeks after hearing his voice in the seminar room had followed Frank at a discrete distance until he finally discovered her, and his father, Will, who now was dead.

The one question Frank didn't know how to ask was, "Why did Dad die?"

They were driving home from Will's funeral; he was telling Eleanor about Hercules' cross.

"Dad helped me. It was about the only thing I ever built."

"Rather a good job I'd say," she answered.

"It was the day after I ran away to California," Frank continued. "We were probably ten or eleven. Dad found us under some trees the next morning and brought us home. Mother grounded me. 'To your room.' 'How long?' 'A month. I don't know. All summer.' She put a wedge in my bedroom window so I couldn't get out again. Dad came in that evening and sat down on the bed. He never did ask what happened. He just asked me if I thought I shouldn't build a cross for Hercules' grave. He tiptoed me out the back door and we found a couple of boards in the garage. He let me saw them and nail them together to make a cross and put on a coat of white paint. He came up with some black paint the next day and I wrote 'Hercules' on the cross and put it up on his grave. I think he loved Hercules as much as I did."

"What kind of dog was he?"

"I don't know. Dog. Mostly brown, but with kind of some white on his chest and one of his legs, and big floppy ears. He slobbered on me when I fed him."

The funeral had drained both of them. She reached across the space between the seats and took Frank's right hand, forcing him to steer with his left.

Frank still was in awe of the general serenity of the vast plains. Lands larger than some states, little had changed from when Comanche Indians were driven out of the canyons barely a hundred years before. The colors of late summer turned from golden to white. Tall stands of maize gave way to cotton ready to be harvested.

For Eleanor, it was a land of wonder, the prairies and barren fields separated by occasional lines of trees planted to hold the soil during the Dust Bowl, vast plains separated by ancient canyons and wet weather gullies that crossed the road. There was a mosaic of almost identical towns ("Villages," she insisted), each with its courthouse, a brick-paved main street with overhanging storefront awnings, a Dairy Queen, a high school with a football field, and many, many churches. She let her mind wander until they passed a roadside rest area, nothing much more than a cement picnic table and an awning for shade.

"Yes," she said.

'Yes' made him smile. It wasn't a great smile, certainly not a grin, but there was at least a gentle lifting of the mouth that replaced the sadness that had cloaked his face since the moment she had handed him the telephone three days before.

"I will." She smiled her own gentle smile and finished her thought. "This is exactly where you asked me to marry you," she continued, her free hand drawing in the bleak landscape that stretched as far as the eye could see. "I waited all my life, I believe every girl does, for the bended knee, the silk box withdrawn from the tuxedo, the plea in the garden of roses. You, however, chose to propose to me on a concrete table overlooking a gully on a farm road a hundred miles from nowhere. I'll not forget that."

"That isn't quite true, not exactly," Frank answered. "That concrete table overlooking a gully on a farm road a hundred miles from nowhere is where you said 'yes.' The bent knee and entreaty of a life of devotion took place in the stacks of the graduate library. You were reading Chaucer."

"You were reading *The Pentagon Papers*. You were trying to impress me. And I did not accept your proposal in the stacks because at that time I had not actually met you."

Frank had been holding *The Pentagon Papers* because he was afraid that if she saw him reading *Catch 22* she would not have spoken to him.

"And I was not 'reading' Chaucer. I was preparing for class. At that particular time some of us were required to earn our corn."

Frank had found the girl who had been following him around the campus; Eleanor was sitting at a table in the graduate library, reading from a single volume. There was an orderly stack of crisp notes handwritten on lined sheets of paper. She did not type. She did not stack up three or four books as a kind of intellectual barricade to intruders. She did not nap or leave for coffee.

He had tried to not stare but found himself swimming in the color of her thick black hair and velvet skin, shades lighter than half of his platoon yet shades darker than the other half. At that moment he didn't care whether she was mocha or green or orange, and when he heard her voice he wanted to hear it again. He asked her a question.

"Am I from Boston? No indeed, and why would you ask if I'm from Boston?" she had answered.

He had said to her, "Hello, I'm uh, uh, uh, are you from Boston?"

"I've never been to Boston," she continued. She pronounced them 'neva' and 'bean' and, from Eleanor's lips, the word 'Boston' might have been the name of an exotic and secluded isle for lovers. "And why are you holding The Pentagon Papers upside down?" she had asked him.

He wanted to hide his face.

She did not let him kiss her for another two weeks. Six more months passed before he asked would she please come with him to the little town where he had grown up because he thought maybe she might want to meet his parents.

"I would not agree until your parents approved. No respectable girl would have done. What if your mother had said I should be packed off back to Croydon?"

"This is my mother," Frank had introduced her, fearful in anticipation of Virginia's almost certain disapproval.

"Ma'am," Eleanor had replied, and she shook Virginia's hand. Within a half hour Virginia had made it very plain that if Frank even hinted of sending Eleanor back to Croydon he'd be sorry.

Will had been late returning from a house call out at the Burford farm where he had been checking up on an old coot who smoked for his heart condition. When he saw his son and his son's girl standing in his kitchen, he looked at Eleanor, then at Frank, then back at Eleanor, and said "Oh, my."

"He then told me that perhaps if it wasn't too much trouble I might help you with your English. As for Virginia, of course she liked me—I didn't experiment with napalm in her potting shed. And you still didn't know how to properly propose to me," she laughed.

"It was the next day, we were driving back, we found the roadside stop, and I did what Dad said I should do. I proposed."

"You sat me on the cement bench and asked me if I would help you with your English until death do us part. Luckily for you, I interpreted that as a proposal of marriage, so I properly told you yes." Eleanor also properly said, "Whither thou goest, I shall go. Your people shall be my people and your home shall be my home. As long as we both shall live. Those are my terms. Take them or leave them."

"I take them."

Will had been his best man. Virginia had held Eleanor's bouquet. The roadside stop disappeared as they crossed a bridge over the Prairie Dog Town Fork of the Red River.

"Why is it called a river if there is no water in it? And what exactly is a prairie dog, and do they live in towns? And if they do, where is the town?"

"It's one o'clock," Frank said. "We've driven about seventy five miles from Bridle..."

"I'm not hungry." It had nothing to do with the fried chicken, which Eleanor found amusing, or the iced tea, which she believed but did not say out loud was uncivilized; she was almost as sad as Frank. It was as simple as that.

"... and I've never been to Tierra."

"Tierra?"

"Tierra. I've never been. I don't know anything about the town where Dad was raised. I know that he and Mother grew up there, well, Mother actually. Dad was raised by a family whose name I can't remember because they never talked about it. Mother's parents died before I was born. She had a brother but she never talked about him either."

"Kunta Kinte," she replied. "*Roots.*"

"Something like that, yes. At least you've got Croydon. They moved to Bridle and never went back, no Homecomings, no Christmas cards from people they went to school with, nothing. I'd at least like to see where Dad went to school, where he and Mother grew up. Family cemetery, that sort of thing."

Frank's internal editor was no better and no worse than most, improving on the good memories and obscuring the bad ones. He remembered when Will had put his hand on Frank's shoulder and told him that he shouldn't try to *not* get shot in Vietnam. "Don't stick your head up or anything like that, but then don't go around hiding, either, waiting to get shot, or you will get shot. You'll be all right." He remembered college graduation; Virginia had given him a piece of Samsonite luggage and Will had given him the used Volkswagen, which had lived inside the garage in Bridle while Frank was in the army. Will driving him to Lubbock for college, Will pouring down him a half-quart of bicarbonate of soda after Frank got drunk at his high school graduation. Will saying, "I thought you'd like a dog. His name is Hercules." Will drying Frank with a towel after he fell into the stream on a camping trip. Will driving out to the Collins farm to bring him and Tog home the morning after they had run away. Will saying it was time. Frank asking why it had to be a closed casket. It didn't seem to be too much to just want to walk where Will had walked.

"Is it far?"

"About a hundred miles. We could be there by three-thirty or so."

"Is it on the way home?"

"Not exactly. Actually, it's kind of in the opposite direction."

They drove on for a few more miles, uncertain whether to turn west or east, Tierra or home.

"You're not a bastard, you know," she said to break the silence. "I heard Peter. It was quite ugly."

"You heard, huh?"

"I did. I believe you should not give it another moment's thought."

Frank told her that he hadn't given it much thought. Peter had called him a bastard most of their lives; he had called Peter a momma's boy and a butt-kissser. Peter had also called him 'Darkie' because he was the only one in the family with black hair rather than fair, and 'Shorty' because he was, well, short. These were only vaguely in Frank's thoughts; he had just thought he should see the place where Dad had been a boy.

Just going to Tierra would be like taking the battle to the opponent, he thought. *I'm not the bastard in this fight. I'm not the one who dropped Mother off in a nursing home. I'm the one who wanted to see where our parents grew up.*

Frank didn't actually say it, but Eleanor had understood it from the second they crossed the bridge of the Prairie Dog Town Fork and the idea of driving on to Tierra had surfaced.

"I knew he was mad at me when we were in Colorado, but I didn't care. I was mad at him. Putting them in a nursing home was not the right

116

thing to do. Another winter in Del Sur wouldn't have hurt anything, and Dad knew better than anyone how to take care of Mother." Frank wasn't sure of that; Will hadn't survived even two weeks in Loving Arms, so whether he would have got through another winter in the mountains was far from clear, even to Eleanor. But that wasn't the point.

"The point is that, right up to the very second that I looked Dad in the eye and promised we'd come back up for Thanksgiving, he was as sharp as the day he was born. I had the right to say that Dad had the right not to want to live in a nursing home."

Eleanor knew he was right. She also knew that Will had indeed passed away, that Virginia was in a nursing home a couple of miles from Peter's new house, and that Peter was over a thousand miles away.

"I think you should let it go, dear," she answered. "What is there to fight about? He called you some ugly names. You did not call him ugly names back or demand pistols at dawn. You held your temper. We're a thousand miles apart. And they don't have anything we want."

That was true, except for Tiffany and Jeff. Eleanor did not want Tiffany or Jeff either, not them precisely, but she did want something like them, but of her own. It was the only subject she was reluctant to talk with Frank about.

"Let it go. Go back to work. Report on the Bluff Springs case. Write *An Khe*. You will promptly forget Captain Peter Hastings and his name calling."

Eleanor knew also, but did not say, that she didn't feel well, not ill exactly, but not right either. Such cramps were unusual, and the timing was not when it should have been.

"Let's go home, dear. We don't have to prove anything to anyone." She squeezed his hand and Frank agreed to put Tierra off for another day. The conversation about foundlings, however, was not quite over.

"Listen, I've got an idea," Frank continued. He explained the idea to her.

Eleanor thought it was a very bad idea and told him so.

"No, I won't call him names or pick a fight or anything. I'll just say, 'Read my birth certificate,' and that'll be the end of the bastard stuff."

Eleanor said again, "No, dear. Let it go. These things always turn out badly."

Frank didn't mention it again on the very long drive back home but, unfortunately, he also did not let it go.

ii.

On Monday, after Eleanor left for the campus, Frank went to their safe deposit box and withdrew his passport, whose details were very clear but did not, precisely, describe the circumstances of his birth. The box also held the mortgage to their tiny house in The Sisters, a lapsed life insurance policy, Frank's honorable discharge, and his military identification card. These provided even less information about who he was but said a great deal about what he owed, being, in order, $37,500 at 12.71% to City Federal Credit Savings and Loan; a statement for $23.32 per month plus a reinstatement fee of $233.20 for ten months of unpaid life insurance premiums and a $100.00 lapse penalty; and his life, for getting out of Vietnam alive. The military identification card said only, 'Franklin Delano Hastings' and 'Grade Sp4.' Eleanor's passport and her green card were bound together by a rubber band. Frank's passport and birth certificate were on the bottom. He took them with him and left the rest in the box.

He arrived before nine in the morning at the newspaper office, where he made a photocopy of his birth certificate and dropped it into an envelope, along with a letter to Peter:

> Dear Peter,
> Here's my birth certificate. Look for yourself—no bastards. No French whores. It's time to stop calling me a bastard.
> — Frank

He wrote a second letter to the army personnel office to request a copy of Will's service file, then dropped both letters in the outgoing mail cart and went to work. By late afternoon he had caught up on the pretrial proceedings concerning the socalled Bluff Springs rapist. By dinnertime, he had forgotten about Peter's accusation, exactly as Eleanor predicted he would.

He was not prepared for the rest of Eleanor's prediction to come true— that such things always turn out badly. When Peter's reply arrived a few days later, he expected a brief note of apology. That had been the pattern, more or less, when they were boys, and he was proud of his adult solution to the childish problem. He opened the envelope and, to his surprise, found his birth certificate inside. So was Peter's answer:

> Frank: I shouldn't have called you a bastard. I should have said 'dumb bastard.' Didn't you ever wonder why your birth certificate was smudged? Think about it.
> You are not my brother. You are not part of my family.
> Never contact any of us again, me, Mother, any of us.
> Peter

It wasn't much of a smudge, to be sure. Frank had to peer very closely indeed to see the ghost of a shadow around the word *Bridle*. The letter *d* originally had been different. The *l* and *e* may have been added. It was possible that the whole word had been changed.

Typos, he thought. *If it doesn't bother the Department of Vital Statistics, it doesn't bother me.*

It did bother him.

It was the address and date of birth that bothered him most, more even than the smudge. The address had not been changed at all but was entirely blank. He had never paid the least attention to it. He paid attention now because, like the town where he was not born and the blank address for the place where his birth had not happened, one indisputable bit of fakery stood out: *1948* really said *194B*, and the *B* looked like it had once been a 6. Will had signed it as the attending doctor of a birth 'not in a hospital.'

Why didn't I notice these before?

Frank still was sitting in the shadows when Eleanor came home from classes. She dropped her books and satchel on the sofa and was startled when they landed on him.

"What is it, dear? Are you ill?"

He looked a bit pale, even considering the time of day and the absence of light. When she switched on a lamp it was obvious that he had lost his color. Even his voice was off, a shallow voice that tried to be lighthearted, but wasn't.

"I'm all right," he said. "Just thinking about my story," a reasonably equivocal answer that was calculated to make her think he was talking about *An Khe* or the Bluff Springs rapist. He made room for her on the sofa and asked how class had gone. They turned on the lights and made dinner and did dishes and went to bed. He assured her again that he was all right and even marked up a few pages of *An Khe* before turning out the light. He believed that she was satisfied with his explanation until the dead middle of the night, when he realized that she was as awake as he was.

"Talk to me," she whispered. "We're in this together. I know what it's like to lose someone." She moved closer and comforted him, just as she had done every night since Will had died. "For better or for worse. Those are still my terms."

"All right," he answered. "I think this is part of the worse. It's not just Dad. It's Peter. The fight at the church." He paused to see if she needed more details; she did not. "I think Peter is right."

They turned on the light and read the letter together. She looked at the smudges and alterations in the most vital of her husband's statistics and saw for herself the cover-ups and changes.

"I think I'm not who I thought I was. Who they said I was."

Frank told her that he hadn't been able to stop thinking about times when he was a boy and Will and Virginia had stopped talking when he came in the room. "Don't ask," they had said. "Nobody," was who they had been talking about.

"Now I know who they were talking about. They were talking about me. I was the nobody."

Eleanor told him that it would be all right, and in her mind that was true, even if her husband turned out not exactly to be Franklin Delano Hastings. "You are who you are," she assured him, "and my terms haven't changed. Whither thou goest, I go. Your home shall be my home. As long as we both shall live."

She intentionally omitted *your people shall be my people*, just for the time being. *We can sack the lot of them if need be.* She knew something of sackings and funerals, which reminded her of something she almost had forgotten, that a funeral is the worst place to learn family secrets.

Chapter Eleven

i.

As the news stories of August faded, the news stories of September unfolded. Suspicion mounted that the *Challenger* space shuttle had blown up because of something called 'O' rings. Compact discs appeared in stores and Sony Discman players appeared in time to play them. Doctors figured out that they were spreading AIDS through blood transfusions, and stopped. The trial of the Bluff Springs rapist commenced. Burman expected *The Gazette* to cover them all. Frank expected Burman to cover *An Khe*.

"Let me read you what I finished last night," he said. "It's a chapter called '*Night Mission*,' where Hood's new major makes him torch a village. Listen to this."

Burman raised his hands to stop Frank but was too late. Frank read:

```
Night Mission
```

Would Two Fuck go up in flames? The village was invisible in the dark but, Hood knew, the dozen or so huts were there in a circle just on the other side of the rice paddy. Major Liddy, in his second week in country, believed in the good-gook/dead-gook version of the war and said he was going to teach every village a lesson.

"So this place is named Thuy Phuoc but they call it Two Fuck. And Major Liddy found out that this village was siphoning off gas from the pipeline so he wanted to run some jet fuel through it so it would burn their huts down when they put it in their cook stoves and Hood's trying to stop him and ... what?"

"It's a quarter to nine, Frank. You should have been in court half an hour ago," Burman answered.

"I'm on it," Frank went on. "But, read the chapter today, okay? Ignore the typos. Tell me what you think." Frank handed the *Night Mission* manuscript to his editor. "Just if you've got time. Listen: one more sentence, okay?"

```
...at that moment, Tuy Phuoc hamlet exploded
in flames, the smell of JP-4 jet fuel fouling
the air.
    "That'll teach 'em," Liddy said.
```

"Leave it. I'll read it," Burman lied. Burman found it painful enough just to read what the *Gazette* paid Frank to write without wasting his life reading another chapter of *Ditch Close to An Khe* or *Leaky Pipes of An Khe* or whatever Frank called his dull novel at the moment. "Go!"

"I'm headed to the courthouse now. Day Two of the trial."

"I'll read it when I can. Say hi to Judge Leatherman for me. See you after court."

Frank thought "*Night Mission*" was a good chapter, a really good chapter. He was confident that no one would think it was just a thinly disguised memoir with names changed to turn it into a novel. The storyline was really coming along, to the point where Hood had begun to question the war. Frank left the typewritten pages on Burman's desk and drove to court.

Judge Leatherman's courtroom was on the third floor. Frank slipped into a wooden bench and took out his notepad just seconds before the trial resumed.

"Call your next witness." The judge leered at the assistant DA, a woman doing a woman's job. The prosecutor called Phyllis Vines, who stated her name and occupation for the jury.

"Tell us, Miss Vines, where were you the evening of June 7."

Miss Vines was at home, in her apartment. Her apartment had a front door and a back door. The back door led to a patio. The patio had a wooden gate. It was why she had chosen the apartment, so that she could live right on the Bluff Creek greenbelt.

"I like to jog and walk my dog. I've been jogging on the greenbelt ever since I moved here."

"What happened the evening of June 7?"

"I went out to the greenbelt. I was training for a race so I ran a little longer than usual, an extra mile or so. About the time I turned around to run back home I saw someone else on the trail. He wasn't anyone I recognized. He wasn't wearing jogging clothes."

"Hey, Nitro, what are you doing here?" Frank looked up to see Pat C. Oh, a television reporter, slide in beside him. Pat whispered like an anchorman so that only half the jury heard him instead of the testimony. "New beat?"

"I'm doing double duty," Frank whispered back, more quietly. "The Bluff Springs trial and a fluff piece about Judge Leatherman's retirement." He noticed that the judge was paying more attention to the prosecutor than to Miss Vines. Some of the jurors were staring at the defendant. The defendant seemed to be the only one in the courtroom who was listening to the witness. "I've been sentenced to journalist rehab after my teacher story. I stepped on some toes over at the school district."

"What teacher story?"

Frank had asked a school board member why no one talked about the effects of busing students, and a news story grew out of the conversation. It might have been a good news story if Frank had studied math.

"I reported that more white kids are failing after they started busing them over to the black schools and, surprise, a lot more black kids are failing after being bused over to the white schools. You didn't read it?"

Pat had not.

"School board's up in arms. Burman said the paper gets a hundred calls a day from parents demanding we go after the teachers and fifty calls a day from the school board demanding they go after me. " Frank neglected to mention that he had made a slight mix-up in the pass-fail statistics and the teachers had threatened a defamation suit. "So *The Gazette's* putting me out of harm's way—the jury'll say either that Artemis Washington is the Bluff Springs rapist or that he isn't and no matter what I write, the paper won't have to issue any retractions."

"Hard to screw that up, true. Listen to what she's saying." Pat nodded at the victim, who was answering another question.

"I looked up and he was right inside my kitchen. I didn't hear the gate open or the back door. I was turning around to get something out of my refrigerator and suddenly I felt a hand around my throat." Miss Vines was beginning to shake. "He was choking me." Judge Leatherman nodded at his bailiff, who poured a glass of water for the witness. "Then his other hand clamped over my mouth so I couldn't scream."

The prosecutor paused long enough for the jury to absorb the shocking image of unwanted, black hands around their own throats and clamped over their mouths, then asked Miss Vines to tell the jury what happened next.

"He pushed me back through my apartment, looking around like he was trying to see if anyone else was there. He was very strong and I couldn't stop him. Then he shoved me onto my bed and, and, and..." and she burst into tears.

"Do you need to take a break?" the prosecutor asked.

Miss Vines had been prepared for the rigors of a fair trial. She knew that in order to properly inflame the jury she was supposed to say she didn't want a break and push bravely on.

"Then he ripped my shorts off, my underwear, and held me down. He raped me." A giant sob gulped out of Miss Vines' mouth. She lowered her head and looked away. The jury began to froth and twitch.

"I hate to ask you these questions but, as the prosecutor, there are some technical things that the law requires. When you say rape, do you mean he sexually penetrated you?" She did. "Did he insert his penis into your vagina?" He did. "Did you consent to his inserting his penis into your vagina?" Miss Vines had not. "And is the man who did this to you – do you see him in the courtroom today?" Miss Vines did see him.

The defendant's lawyer objected. Leatherman overruled him.

She pointed to Artemis Washington, a black man dressed, improbably, in a business suit, white shirt, necktie, and a leg chain that was padlocked to a deputy sheriff, the jury's view of that device being blocked by a box of files and papers that Judge Leatherman had ordered to be placed under the defendant's table. The defendant, despite the mirage of dressing for court as a young businessman about town, glowered at her and bristled in his chair. His lawyer patted him on the arm and whispered to him to be patient.

"Let the record show that she has identified the defendant, Artemis Washington." The prosecutor spoke triumphantly to the jury. The jury nodded in agreement, twelve as one.

"Old Artemis is in deep shit, Frank."

Frank agreed. It didn't sound like they had named the wrong man.

"I pass the witness, Your Honor." The prosecutor held her head high and crossed her arms. Judge Leatherman leered at her again, then scowled at the court-appointed defense lawyer.

Artemis was in deep trouble indeed. His lawyer had told the jury that it was a case of mistaken identity, but his now-frightened defense counsel didn't know where to begin to prove it. He timidly asked Miss Vines what time of day it was when the attack occurred. It was six in the afternoon, and her apartment was well lit. He asked her if she had ever seen the defendant before that day, which she had not. He then asked if she had ever seen him since that day, a not-terribly bright question since Miss Vines had attended every pre-trial hearing of the last six months and had seen Artemis in court dressed in his jail clothes, now in a cheap business suit and, at his first arraignment, wearing a tight white tee shirt with the slogan 'I like it white and tight.' Artemis' lawyer didn't think to ask Miss Vines if she had heard Artemis' voice or compared it to the rapist's voice. Leatherman called a recess and the jury disappeared.

Frank tried to catch the judge, but a lawyer sneaked in from a side door and caught Leatherman first, a moderately bold move given that the judge was going straight for the prosecutor.

"Mr. Dean," the judge acknowledged. "What can I do for you?"

"I just need five minutes, Your Honor. " Mr. Dean looked to Frank like a poster for blue-suit, red-necktie blond lawyers. "A default judgment, if you have time."

The judge had the time. One of the jurors, a bit nauseated by the testimony, had asked for an extended recess to compose himself. The judge sent the clerk to get the folder from the central court office. She came back with a stack of twenty or thirty folders.

"I'm not sure I've got the right one, Your Honor," she said. "They're all City Federal Savings and Loan against somebody." She handed them to Mr. Dean, who rummaged through them, then gave one to Judge Leatherman, who began to act as if he had discovered the Ten Commandments.

"I call for trial Case Number 1986-255-L, City Federal Savings and Loan versus I-35 Condominiums, Phase II. Plaintiff is ready. Is the defendant ready? The defendant does not answer. I therefore review the file. I find that the defendant has executed a loan and received the funds; that the loan is past due; that the plaintiff has made a demand for payment, and the defendant has not paid. I find that the defendant has been duly served and more than thirty days have passed, yet there is no paper answer in the file. The clerk affirms that as of today, none has been filed. I therefore enter default judgment in the amount of $4,287,000 in favor of the plaintiff, together with attorney fees."

It was a great performance. Leatherman signed the judgment that Mr. Dean handed to him, gave the documents to the clerk, and walked out of the courtroom. Frank had never before seen ownership of four million dollars change hands in less than a minute.

Dean disappeared and, to Frank's dismay, so did Judge Leatherman. Frank chased him down to his office and asked the clerk if he could have five minutes to interview the judge for a feature article before he resumed the inexorable crimination of Artemis Washington. She said no, to come back later, then piled the court files on her desk to make clear that she wanted to leave herself. Frank was not going to give up so easily.

"Can I just you ask a dumb question?" She said she was used to it. "How can someone default on over four million dollars? What happened to the money?"

She shrugged and showed him the stack of files, then told him she had to leave for her break. Her getaway would have been complete if the phone hadn't rung, but it did, and she transferred the call to the judge's private line. Frank gambled on catching the judge walking out of his office after the call, and sure enough, Judge Leatherman came out.

"Who are you?" he asked. He didn't wait for a name. "You the reporter that Marty Burman sent over? I've watched you scribbling away there in the courtroom. Can't talk about the trial, unethical, that sort of thing. Marty said he wanted a feature. I don't do that sort of thing either. Public doesn't want to read about judges. I said to Marty okay, just this once, since I'm retiring. Guess you knew that." For someone who didn't do that sort of thing Judge Leatherman seemed to know what Frank should write about him. It would be an easy interview.

"I promise not to ask you about the trial. The paper wants to get your thoughts on the law, career highlights, what you'll do when you retire. But first, can I ask a question about that savings and loan case you just heard did this morning? Four million and something dollars? Off the record."

"The I-35 Condominiums. Yes. What about it?"

Frank asked him the same questions he had asked the clerk, how someone could default over four million dollars, and what happened to the money.

"Do you own a house?" Frank did; he had just looked at his loan statement a few weeks before. "I'll bet you that if you go to the bank today and open up a certificate of deposit they'll pay you a higher rate on the CD than you're paying them for your mortgage. It's something called ERTA and deregulation. Congress let savings and loans start acting like banks and suddenly, all the S&Ls started selling their mortgages to investment houses and investing in things they couldn't do before, like new subdivisions and construction projects, just crazy stuff for them, and a lot of it goes to people who spin it to somebody else until finally, the money goes to somebody who has no intention of paying off the loans. That's why we've got all these new houses all over town. In a couple of years, we'll have a bunch of new empty houses and there'll be lines down the block in front of the savings and loans with people who want to get their money out before they crash. And they will crash. It's nuts."

Frank had never had it explained that way before and didn't hear most of it. The idea that he could make more money on interest from a savings account than he and Eleanor were paying for their mortgage made his gears turn to see if they could do something, maybe borrow against their home loan, to make money. He had to pinch himself to restart the interview.

"Okay, wow. Here we go. First, Mr. Burman told me you had been a lawyer since before I was born and a judge since before he was an editor." Frank put on his eager-to-please face and, sure enough, the judge who didn't do interviews opened his office and let Frank in.

Leatherman's office was not what Frank expected. Judges were supposed to be revered figures perched on majestic chairs behind enormous desks in wood-paneled offices, walls lined with law books and diplomas. Judge Leatherman's office was a dingy room with sheetrock walls and linoleum on the floor. His desk looked like it was bought at an auction of used public school furniture, large enough to contain a jumble of papers that

Leatherman swept to one side as he sat in a cheap chair that might have been borrowed from a courtroom. The sole concession to progress was a chunky white computer console with a chunky white monitor on top, electric wires dangling free of the power outlet.

"Fire away," Leatherman said. "You got a tape recorder? If you do, give it to me. I don't do tape recorders." He gazed across at Frank, who was shaking his head no, he didn't have a tape recorder, and was fishing out a pencil and spiral tablet. Leatherman didn't wait for a question. "Okay, here goes. You want to know what's changed since I've been a lawyer? Everything. Drugs. Credit cards. Free agents in baseball. Sunday closing laws. Integration. Television. Ambulance chasers. Everybody wants to be rich and no one wants to wait until they earned it."

Frank wondered what the question was that Leatherman had answered. It didn't matter; Leatherman was talking faster than Frank could write. He stopped and listened.

"What's worse—easy credit or drugs? I don't know. When I first got on the bench you came into court charged with marijuana and you were going to prison. If you got caught with heroin you could kiss your family goodbye. Now, and don't write this down, this Washington kid. I don't know if he's guilty or innocent"—a contention that would have been more believable if Leatherman hadn't rolled his eyes—"but I'll bet you a T-bone steak he was hopped up on drugs. They're everywhere."

"So, can I say that in your career you've seen changes in society with more drugs being used?" Leatherman nodded, told him he could say it but not if he said it was a quote. "Why do you think that is, Judge?"

"Kennedy, pure and simple. Johnson and Kennedy. When I started out as a lawyer it was right after the war. Everybody was on the same team. We were the most powerful country on earth. Everybody had a job, everybody knew their place, and then—don't quote me on this—then we start seeing people want to change things. Blacks. Women. Farm workers. Everybody. Hell, I read the other day some article about white teachers flunking black kids and black teachers flunking white kids, you know what I'm talking about? That wouldn't happen, didn't happen before Kennedy, because Negroes went to their own schools and the good ones got into college, you know? Then these two came along with their civil rights and their voting rights and their great society and you know what happened?"

Frank didn't know what had happened, much less what Leatherman thought happened. He shook his head and prepared to write some more.

"They're the ones got us into Vietnam, that's what happened. Got us in and didn't get us out. Next thing we know, we've got a whole country full of kids taking drugs. Half of them growing marijuana in their dorm rooms, the other half of them smoking marijuana in the army. Were you in the army?"

Frank nodded that, yes, he had been in the army.

"You know what I'm talking about, then. I look up in court one day and some kid is up there charged with using drugs and the next thing I know his parents are up there pleading not to send him to prison because he was in Vietnam and then some guy shows up from the veteran's outfit and says not to send the kid to prison because he served our country but when he came back from Vietnam he was hooked on drugs and he needs rehab, not prison. I had to pinch myself to believe I had heard it right. Then there's another one, and then some more, and the more I dug into it, the more it looked like every soldier in Vietnam was on drugs the whole time he was over there. You were in the army. You know what I'm talking about."

Frank wondered if he was going to have to plead the Fifth Amendment, or lie, or just not answer, but Leatherman went off in a different direction.

"You think I'm going to say we should have bombed those fuckers out of existence and won the war, don't you? I have no idea what we should have done. I wasn't in charge. But I'll tell you what Kennedy and Johnson should have done. They should have pumped all that war money into fixing up schools instead, and sending kids to college. Remember the Space Race, beat the Russians to the moon and all that? Know any astronauts who went to prison for doing drugs? Hell no. They went to college, flew jets, competed, went to the moon. It was the kids from the crap high schools, segregated schools, they just dropped out, they couldn't get jobs, got tired of all those people in the South pushing them around, and when the army drafted them, they blew up. I was in the army and I'll tell you what, everybody was on the same team then. If we'd kept that up after the war, we wouldn't be having this interview because people wouldn't be getting in trouble and all the drugs and credit cards and color televisions for no money down and crap like that. They'd work all day and go home tired and be with their families."

"You were in Vietnam, Judge?" Frank knew it was a stupid question but couldn't stop himself before he asked. "Or did you mean Korea?"

"Hell no, kid. World War II. I was in the *real* army. We didn't smoke marijuana and we didn't screw around. We killed more Germans in France in six months than all the Vietcong or whoever we killed in six years. Were you in Vietnam?" Frank nodded that he was. "Can't imagine fighting a war by running out of the fort every day, killing some people, then going back into the fort at night to smoke marijuana. Crazy."

"What'd you do in the army, Judge?"

"MPs. My unit did everything from cover the combat landings in France to scout and patrol missions. All that crap about MPs running around arresting soldiers for getting drunk on leave is Hollywood. We spent months in a place called Cherbourg where we were digging out the Germans and the French sympathizers who had wrecked the docks and the port. We had to cover the engineers who were fixing it up, plus we had a slew of POWs in holding pens that we had to ship back to England. Then somebody discovered I'd been to law school so they started adding court martials to my job."

"You were an army judge? What was that like?"

"Not a judge, just a lawyer. I didn't think much about it at the time but after the war I realized that it was like being on Planet Nuts. Here we were with hundreds of thousands of soldiers fighting Germans on every street and building and in the hedgerows and whatnot, I mean full-scale artillery going off and planes dropping bombs and point-blank rifle duels, and then somebody'd come get me and the next day I'd be in a court martial trial over a GI who'd done something stupid, like steal a bottle of wine. Most of them stole something or went AWOL or got drunk. There was this one case where someone was charged with breaking through a window to get into a bar to steal some wine or something, and when I got there to investigate you couldn't even find the bar. The whole town had been turned to rubble because we had bombed it and called in artillery on it. How do you charge a man who's been in combat with breaking and entering a bar that we had already destroyed?"

Leatherman turned around to a bookshelf that was on the wall beside his desk. He picked one picture from the shelf. The black-and-white picture showed a tank rumbling through the streets of a town that must once have been a picturesque village but now was clearly the mortal victim of combat, every building and chimney crumbling and blasted to bits, nothing but piles of rocks and craters and pock-marked walls. He handed it to Frank.

"Here, look for yourself."

Frank studied it. Saint Lô looked to Frank like the radio station inside his unit headquarters back in Qui Nhon, a block building that the Viet Cong obliterated during the Tet offensive with thousands of bullet and grenade strikes that had knocked out every door and window and blown the roof and porch to bits. That was just one building; the rubble in Judge Leatherman's picture of France extended to every building and street in town.

"So then one day they stuck me with prosecuting some poor black guy who had just been with his unit eleven days. He got drunk with some buddies, then took off in the dark to get some more wine somewhere and wound up trying to bust into a farmhouse. He tried to shoot the lock off, and the bullet killed a farmer inside. Then the dumb bastard went inside and let the man bleed to death while he busted the place up looking for something to drink. It was crazy. There I was, a great lawyer with a stacked jury full of angry white combat officers who had fought on their bellies for four months of sheer hell. They weren't very sympathetic to a black truck driver who went AWOL and killed a civilian eleven days after he got to France. Patton said we had to prove to the French that we weren't like the Germans. I watched them hang that poor kid in the town square."

Leatherman paused to see if Frank was taking it in. Frank felt like a little boy, listening to Will read stories. He hadn't written a word in ten minutes.

"So, I look up one day thirty years later, I'm on the bench and I'm listening to lawyers tell me the reason I shouldn't send some kid to prison is because he was in the army. 'Yes, Your Honor, he was in combat, it was traumatic to him so his brain got relief by getting under the influence and so he got hooked on getting high, he's got PTSD, so it's not his fault.' And I'm thinking that is the very same reason we hung that black kid in France. Yes sir, I've seen a change in the law."

"Wow," Frank said. *Wow*, he thought. "So, I'm not going to ask you about the Bluff Springs rapist, but in general how does that make you feel when you have to sentence somebody? You've seen it from both sides. Do you believe in the death penalty?"

"I don't know. It's the law. It's what people want. We've never sent an innocent man to death row, black or white, I guarantee you. Science brought us that far, anyway."

"Retirement, Judge. Why are you retiring?"

"I want to spend time with my family." Frank listened to the answer and wondered what the judge's family thought about him leering at the prosecuting attorney's bosom. "I want to take my grandkids fishing, go see the Grand Canyon. Maybe write a book."

"What will you do about being a judge? Run for the Supreme Court, maybe?"

"Got to wrap this up. Back to court. Say hi to Marty for me. Do not print anything that I said wasn't for print." Leatherman grinned to make clear that he was just being a sport.

ii.

The trial lurched onward. A policeman testified about capturing the Bluff Springs rapist.

"One last question, Officer. When you arrested Mr. Washington, where was he?"

Officer Foster didn't hesitate.

"There's a creek that runs behind an apartment house over near the university. A line of cedar trees hides it from the apartments, about twenty or thirty yards in the back. Dispatch took a prowler call and when we got there we walked around the apartment house. Some of the students who lived there were huddled around a barbeque grill. They weren't the ones who made the prowler call. Then I saw something over in the tree line and when I went down to check, that gentleman was hiding in the creek." Artemis was that gentleman.

Washington's defense lawyer was prepared this time.

"Officer Foster? How far away from the Bluff Springs Apartments did you arrest Mr. Washington?" No answer. "Five miles? Six miles?"

"Maybe, I didn't measure it."

"And there was no running trail there at the creek where you arrested Mr. Washington, was there?" No answer. "No place where people go for a jog out behind the apartments."

"Not as I could see, Counselor."

"This was almost a half year after Miss Vines was assaulted in her home, right?"

"That's about right."

"And Mr. Washington was wearing a jacket over his tee shirt, right?"

"Yes."

"So you didn't read what was on the shirt, did you?"

"That's right."

"So there was absolutely nothing to connect Mr. Washington in that creek to Miss Vines' events that took place five miles away and six months before, was there?"

Frank hunched over his notes. For some reason, he began to think how easy it was to misread the facts. *How often do we walk around believing someone is somebody else? All the time. Maybe even that poor slob Artemis Washington isn't who they say he is, just a case of mistaken identity. Another case of mistaken identity.* The police officer answered the question.

"No, nothing except Mr. Washington," the officer testified. "I wouldn't have made the connection myself but he heard me coming through the trees and told me to be quiet. He said that he was trying to get a good look at some girl who lived there in those apartments."

No further questions.

iii.

"How was court?" Burman was in a good mood. "Heard from Judge Leatherman. He enjoyed the interview. Glad to hear it. Told him we'd work up the story and put it in a Sunday edition."

"How was court? I can tell you this: Artemis Washington is going down. They caught him sneaking around at night trying to window peep in some woman's apartment. I'll have about a thousand words for you in an hour or so."

Burman heard enthusiasm in Frank's voice and was pleased. Frank had been sliding downhill ever since his father had passed away, which Burman understood, but he didn't know how to help Frank get his grief under control. He would have suggested a vacation or even a leave of absence, but Frank had already used up his time with a trip to the Bahamas right before Dr. Hastings died. It was a mess. He was pleased to hear Frank sound like he wanted to write the news again, even if it was just a criminal trial.

"Did you get a chance to finish 'Night Mission?'" Frank looked at Burman; Burman looked confused. "The new chapter? *Ambush at An Khe?* Sorry I keep changing the title. Maybe I should just call it *An Khe.*" He had already decided to change it again; *Ambush at An Khe* wasn't quite right either. *Maybe Burman can help with the title, too,* he thought. "What do you think? Did you like how the ladies in the village turn out to be the unit's 'sexually agreeable laundry ladies?'"

"*Night Mission*" lay crumpled on Burman's desktop, stained by a coffee cup ring.

"Ah, no, sorry, I did not. But I can't wait. It'll be good. A couple of things and then you get to work on your thousand words. First, no to you fixing the school story, the white teachers and the black kids and vice versa. Your mistakes are just too hard to explain. It's a tar baby and fixing it might just make it worse. Sorry."

Frank was disappointed but not bitter; he knew that he might not have been the best choice to write a story on racism. He told Burnam not to worry, that he had an idea for a new story, about the local savings and loans getting in over their heads on real estate deals.

Burnam looked up from the desk and looked carefully at Frank, making sure Frank would look carefully back at him.

"And that's the other thing, Frank. No go." He paused when he saw Frank's puzzled look, but he had no choice. "Judge Leatherman also said to tell you: 'Do not write a story about those savings and loan suits over the condominiums. Not one word. Period.'"

Chapter Twelve

Eleanor was awake again, this time around two in the morning. When she opened her eyes she realized that, yes, she had been dreaming in Chaucerian rhyming couplets (*"...I would tell a legend and a life both of a carpenter and of his wife..."*), but that had been in early sleep.

The more vivid dream of recent sleep was of her and Virginia in the kitchen in Bridle, making goodbyes. She could hear Will talking to Frank in the next room. "Ask her to help you with your English," he had said.

"I write for a newspaper, Dad," Frank had answered.

"All the more reason," Will pointed out. "In fact, why don't you ask her to help you with your English for a long, long, time. Like, forever." She had promised Will that she would.

But in her dream, instead of helping Frank she had let Will down. Will was gone, now, and Virginia was gone too, in her way. Eleanor woke up and felt for her husband. He was still there.

Frank was asleep, breathing, tossing, turning, but asleep. She slipped out of bed and tiptoed into the tiny living room.

The facts are pretty clear, she thought. *Peter was born in Tierra while Will was in the army. Peter is doted on as the golden boy. Will comes home. They move away from Tierra. Frank is born in Bridle. Peter is no longer the only child, the idol of everyone's attention. Peter is too small to see exactly where the next baby came from and thinks Will brought him home, rather like from a cabbage patch, and Peter is no longer the center of attention. Peter believes that Will brought him back from France, something that requires a 'French whore', proved by the fact he and Frank looks different and acts differently. Peter accepts that fiction is fact. Frank believes that Peter is always right and Frank is always wrong. Frank therefore believes he's a foundling.*

The difficulty wasn't in understanding it; older children have told younger children that they're foundlings since the beginning of time. *The difficulty is in knowing how to correct it,* she thought.

Her promise to Will came to mind at the same moment that she saw on the lamp table the battered pages of *An Khe*. It wasn't as if Frank had not asked her to read it or, at the least, to listen as he read a line here, a sentence there, and concur that it was 'really, really good.' *I read a hundred bad papers a week at school. Why haven't I read this?* She took the typewritten sheets in her hand, opened to a place at random, and began:

```
                AMBUSH AT AN KHE


                Chapter Five


        The Hamlet Night Mission


Would Two Fuck go up in flames? That was the
question Hood asked himself over and over.

Specialist Fourth Class Hood was sure the wom-
en would hear them. The village was invisible
in the dark but, he knew, the dozen or so huts
were there in a circle just on the other side
of the rice paddy.
```

Eleanor read that 'Hood' had been ordered by Major Liddy to help burn a village in retaliation for their taking a bit of cook stove gas from the army's pipes.

```
"Sir," he yelled. "Come on, Sir. We've got to
get out of here." It wasn't hard to see Liddy
in the dark because, at that moment, Tuy Phuoc
hamlet exploded in flames, the smell of JP-4
jet fuel fouling the air.

The men formed a perimeter around the jeep
and stayed put just long enough to watch what
until an hour ago had been a hamlet of sexual-
ly agreeable laundresses convert itself into
```

another village of rice farmers who were now
sympathetic to the Viet Cong.

"Hey, Hood?" Liddy asked as they climbed into
the jeep. "Who do you think you are? For a
spec 4 you're way too squeamish about torching
a gook village."

"Me, Sir? Me? I'm nobody." Hood answered.

"I've got it," Liddy smirked. "I know who you
are. You're 'Nitro.' Ha ha ha. That's it.
We're gonna call you 'Nitro.'"

'Nitro?' Hood thought. *Not bad. But I still
want to frag the ~~little bastard~~ prick.*

Eleanor was fascinated. She knew only tiny bits of Frank's time in
Vietnam. That he was writing a thinly veiled novel of himself was immediately apparent, as much from his Robin Hood hero as from naming him
'Nitro.' She looked in the dictionary for 'frag' and found nothing, then
turned to the chapter named *The Hairpin*.

Vietnam Diary of Sergeant Robert Hood:

August 11: Seven days to R&R in Bangkok with
~~my brother~~ Locksley. Major Liddy told me to
file an after-action report for burning down
Two Fuck.

Major Liddy flipped Hood's diary back across
the desk. Hood caught it and put it in his
fatigue jacket. Hood wondered how much of his
personal diary Liddy had read.

Eleanor quietly padded into the kitchen and put on a kettle for tea. For the next half-hour she read 'Nitro's' diary, in which Hood and his team, Dale, Little, and Tucker, were variously sent to repair more pipeline leaks, lost track of a land mine, found the land mine, and wondered whether they should frag Major Liddy, which Eleanor now suspected meant shooting him. Unfortunately for Hood, Major Liddy had found the diary and punished him by sending him to 'The Hairpin.' Eventually the band of merry men was taken by helicopter to a bend in a road near An Khe to repair a pipeline that the Vietcong had blown up.

The rifle squad stood guard over Hood while he probed the jagged metal to see how much damage the mortar strike had done to the fuel pipeline. He peeled away the punctures and patched up the hole until a real engineer unit could come ~~fix it~~ repair it.

Hood was certain that there were VC somewhere ahead, concealed behind the sharp bend in the road, waiting to ambush them. He felt it in his bones. After repairing the mortar strike they were supposed to patrol on foot to the next section, less than a kilometer away.

"Your mission, Nitro, is 'depart helicopter, kill enemy, fix pipe, walk back' ha ha ha," Major Liddy had ordered. "Kill ~~and capture~~ Charlie in the act of sabotage. And look out for booby traps ha ha ha." Hood radioed the helicopter to pick them up.

"Slick? This is Oilcan Harry. Landing zone clear. Come get us." Fuck walking another kilometer.

SNAP went a branch. His repair team hit the
ground, elbows down, weapons up.

"Just a branch. Be careful, you hear?" he
hissed at the men.

It might not be a branch.

"SLICK - Oilcan Harry. Correction. Do not repeat DO NOT LAND YET. LZ MAY BE HOT! Out."
Hood released the microphone switch and waited
for Slick to confirm.

Eleanor made a second pot of tea. The writing was terrible, she knew,
but she couldn't help reading more. Some of it was confusing, such as the
first chapter, where Hood was called a specialist 4 but in the next chapter he
was Sergeant Hood. *I'll ask someone if those are the same rank.* It was Darjeeling,
the tea, and Eleanor couldn't have gone back to sleep if she had wanted to.

Hood heard the *whop whop whop* of helicopter rotor
blades flying just above the ground level, out
of sight behind the ridge. Hood radioed again.

"SLICK - this is Oilcan Harry. Do not land.
Repeat, do not..."

The last thing Hood saw was the helicopter.
The door gunner faced the road, the crew chief
shouted, the pilots maneuvered toward the
landing zone, and all of them gaped when someone fired a B-40 bazooka, its fiery trail headed
straight to the helicopter. A burst of white
fire flashed as the grenade hit the helicopter
fuel tank...

The diary ended the next day. Eleanor poured the last of her tea and read.

August 12:

Only one survivor on chopper. Battalion clerk brought me a message from my sorry fucking ~~brother~~ friend Locksley: 'Sorry Brother, can't go to Bangkok with you. Secret mission. R and R canceled.'

It was five in the morning now, but Eleanor had no wish to sleep. She turned to the last chapter.

Chapter Seven

~~Brothers~~

Moment Quite at Bar Cielo

The helicopter landed at Tan Son Nhut and Lieutenant Hood walked to the transit area. He gave his R & R orders to a clerk who told him that there was a plane headed for Bangkok in an hour and directed him to a provisional travel office where he was given clean khakis and a pair of lace-up shoes.

"What's it like in Bangkok?" he asked. His squad had told him that the REMFs in Tan Son Nhut were crooks but they knew everything. "Hey LT," Tucker had said, "if you want to be treated right, slip them a ten. They know all the bars and whorehouses. They'll steer you straight." The REMFs steered Hood to the Florida Hotel.

It was dark in Bangkok by the time Hood cleared the R & R processing center at the airport and converted his dollars. He hailed a pedicab and ten minutes later was looking up at a cinder block and neon wonderland.

"Weccome to da Florida Hotel Lieutenant." Hood thought the desk clerk sounded like Elmer Fudd. "We give you escort. Twenty-faw dolla. Room and escort, we give you twenty-faw dolla and room also twenty-faw dolla da dey. Army pay room. You pay escort. Fust tum Bangkok?"

"Escort?"

"You like? Vey pretty. All clean. Vey pretty." Three Eurasian girls drifted up to the desk. They looked like they were twelve years old. "Vey pretty, my dottas. You like which please?"

Hood picked the shortest one, who also might have been the oldest one, somewhere between twelve and, on closer inspection, thirty-five years old. She had thick dark hair and pouty lips.

"I Busabong. I go you room now we drink dance go PX longtime," she said.

Hood didn't understand exactly what she had said.

"Room, fo to leave you tings. Go drink dance. Dinna, otha tings. You like take me PX. Ready." She was already trying to feel Hood's pants pocket to see if she could locate the bulge of a billfold. He made a decision.

"Where is the bar?" She pointed upward. "I'll go to my room and meet you in the bar in ten minutes."

"What you room numba?" she asked. He made another decision.

"I don't have my key yet. Here's five dollars. Get a drink. Wait for me in the bar." He was about to make a third decision when she grabbed the five dollars and turned around.

"You no be long Lootint I know who you ah and fine you no come ten minute." She gave him a look that left no doubt she would indeed come find him, no matter where in Bangkok he might try to flee and hide. With that, she began to punch the elevator buttons. Hood watched the doors open, the nympho-sprite disappear, the doors close.

Hood would have left the hotel altogether but didn't know if he could find his way back to the army reception center at the airport to see if he could get them to find him someplace else. He gripped his bag and took the key, then headed for his room.

In the room there was a faded card that explained the virtues of Hotel Florida. Café Miami was a 'fine GI dining of fame international with steaks and drinks refreshing.' There was a picture of Busabong and a dozen other escorts sitting at a table spread with lumps of meat and pink drinks with bamboo umbrellas. Bar Continental had a floor show with, Hood suspected, a review featuring Busabong and her sisters stripping to some kind of electric sound and light show. Bar Cielo was a haven on the roof, to watch the stars and have 'moments quite with someone.' He was stuck.

Hood found the Bar Continental. Busabong, standing across the room near the bar with a dozen GIs and another dozen of Busabong's identical twins, had her head turned. She did not see him and seemed to have gotten over Hood's lack of enthusiasm. To be safe he found the elevator and made his way to the Bar Cielo.

The Bar Cielo was unlit, a cluster of moldy rattan tables and chairs jammed together onto an open-air rooftop. Hood took a moment to adjust his eyes to the twilight and considered, briefly, the dynamics that would have to fit perfectly for anyone to have a moment quite. A slight man wearing a slight shirt, white with short sleeves, appeared at his elbow.

"Beer, please."

"You no go like Thailand beer Sir. Me bring you whiskey vey fine whiskey."

"Beer, please. I don't like whiskey." The white shirt grunted and disappeared back into the shadows of the Bar Cielo.

Liddy hadn't taken too kindly to finding out that the spigot at Tuy Phuoc had been a long-standing deal with the local girls. Hood tried to remember the exact words that Liddy had said to him when he got back from the Hairpin. The gist of it was that Liddy was sending Hood away on R & R and when he got back Liddy was going to ship him out to some other unit with more helicopters, more pump stations, and the words 'An Khe.'

The white shirt glided back up to Hood's elbow. A warm glass of fulvous whiskey appeared on his table.

He was right, Hood thought. *I no go like Thailand beer.*

Someone else walked into the bar.

The man looked familiar, even in the dark twilight. He made his way over to a table beside the open-sided wall where his table had a decent view of the Bangkok bustle and lights. From that table, Hood could tell, it would be easy to watch airplanes taking off and landing at the airport a couple of miles away.

Hood took a sip of the wretched whiskey and started to call the crooked waiter back, but stopped. The new customer had turned a certain way and his silhouette stood out clearly against the backdrop of city lights. That was why it was so easy for Hood to see that the man who had walked into the bar and sat down near the open-sided wall was ~~Peter~~ Locksley.

That lying son of a bitch, Hood thought.

Hood waited for five minutes, maybe ten, but no one moved. He thought of accosting him, maybe verbally, maybe pounding him to a pulp for lying about being sent off on a secret mission, then remembered what his father had said once: 'Don't try beatings to see if morale improves.'

He left two dolla on the table and disappeared from the Bar Cielo, then sneaked back to his room and packed his suitcase.

It was six in the morning when Eleanor sneaked back into their bed. She lay for a long time with her arms around Frank, sensing that she had learned something she wasn't supposed to know, something about laundresses and napalm and wanting to shoot superior officers. Something about how hard it would be for her to help undo Frank's fear that he was nobody.

Chapter Thirteen

i.

Frank stuffed the typed pages of the manuscript back into a worn briefcase and took out his notepad just as Judge Leatherman told the bailiff to bring the jury in.

"Call your next witness," Leatherman instructed the prosecutor.

"The State calls Detective Rigere."

Detective Rigere was an excellent policeman. He had spent three years as a patrol officer before his talent for ferreting out obscure clues was brought to the attention of the chief. The happiest day of Rigere's life was when the department issued a check to him for a clothing allowance, a policy designed to make the plain clothes officers equal to the uniform officers when it came to the matter of clothing benefits. Rigere took the $350.00 and bought a new Smith and Wesson .357 Police Special, a Bushnell pistol scope and a couple of boxes of hollow point bullets. He spent the rest on three or four suits, one of which he now wore on the witness stand.

"When were you assigned to the Bluff Springs rape case, Detective?"

"In February, a year ago. I took a statement from the victim, then went over to her apartment on the Bluff Springs greenbelt."

"Did you observe anything at her apartment that moved your investigation forward?" The prosecutor loved working with Rigere because he knew better than she did what ordinary, frightened, white jurors would believe to be proof that a black man or, in a pinch, one from Mexico, had done everything the police accused him of, and probably more. Rigere was a storyteller.

"A pan of spaghetti on the stove. A jar of spaghetti sauce on the counter. A lamp knocked over in the living room. A hole in the sheet rock where a door had been shoved open and the doorknob was punched into the wall. The doorstop of that door was bent double. The bed in that room all messed up, not just sheets and blankets and pillows pulled every which way but the leg at one corner of the bed broken off, like something heavy or forceful had pushed down on the bed...."

"Objection. Speculation."

"Sustained as to the comment about what broke the leg on the bed."

"Blood on the sheets. I took some pictures. Some shorts, like running shorts. Some underwear, torn at the waistband. I had the forensic lab technician take charge of them and the sheets. Some things on the floor that looked like they had been knocked off a table or something..."

"Same objection."

"Sustained," Judge Leatherman ruled. He could not imagine the jury being too stupid to speculate on the same facts and reach the same conclusion, but *a rule is a rule.*

"There were five items on the floor. They were not stacked in an orderly fashion. There was a book. There was a magazine. The book was face down, pages open, and the front and back were bent. The magazine was wadded up. The alarm clock was on the floor seven inches from the edge of the magazine. A sheet of notebook paper with a written list that said 'Saturday, six miles, Sunday, ten miles, Monday, three miles, Tuesday, five miles' was on top of the alarm clock. A lamp with a broken shade and a broken bulb was on the floor immediately beside the bed. I don't know what caused any of those things to be in the location or condition in which I found them."

Of course he knew. The jury knew. Everybody knew. Artemis Washington had knocked them over while he was raping Phyllis Vines on her bed. How dare Washington's lawyer object to Detective Rigere. Frank wrote down every word, then made his own observations of the jurors' faces. As far as the jury was concerned, the case was over.

"Did these facts lead you to take any particular steps in your investigation, Detective?" The prosecutor could have been filing her nails at the table. The jury was riveted to every word Rigere had to say and every picture he showed them.

"Yes, ma'am, they did. I turned over the biological items, that would be the sheets and the clothes, to the laboratory. I am not a laboratory scientist, ma'am. I believe the department blood technician would be the best person to ask whether the blood on the sheets matched Miss Vines' blood, or the blood on her panties matched Mr. Washington's blood, or the semen matched his semen." Of course they matched. The jurors didn't need a witness to tell them that. "What I did was to compare the crime scene to other investigations to see if there was a pattern that might lead us to a suspect."

"What does that mean?"

"Similarities. It could be anything, like similar descriptions, clothes, that sort of thing."

"Did that lead you anywhere?"

"It did. I found that there were seven pending investigations in which a white woman who was in or lived on Bluff Springs was raped by a black man. In each case the black man choked the woman with one hand, put his hand over the woman's mouth with his other hand, and threw her on the ground or on her bed and pulled her clothes off, then raped her. Two of these cases happened outdoors, right on the Bluff Springs trail. Five of these cases happened where someone came in the backdoor of the apartment of the women, all of whom lived on Bluff Springs."

Detective Rigere spoke for almost two hours, comparing photographs of Miss Vines' sheets to the sheets of other Bluff Springs rape victims, of her panties to the panties of the others, of her wrecked bedroom to those of the other five. There was no doubt that she had been raped by someone who had figured out that hiding in the woods along the Bluff Springs jogging trail was a good way to catch scantily dressed white women alone.

"Pass the witness."

"Cross examination, Mr. Cheatham?" asked Judge Leatherman.

"Just this one question, Your Honor. Did you find any physical evidence at any time in Mr. Washington's home that came from any of those poor women's homes along Bluff Springs, Detective?" The defense lawyer waited, and asked the same question in a different way. "Did you find any of the women's underclothes, or sheets, or some book or purse or anything that belonged to any of those victims, in Mr. Washington's home?"

"No, sir."

"So you found no tangible evidence to connect Mr. Washington to any of those crimes, in particular to the rape of Miss Vines?" The lawyer had said one question but had asked two, and they were different.

"Oh, yes, of course we did." Rigere adopted the blank patronizing look that trained police witnesses have used for years to clobber lawyers. "We found the blood...."

"That we understand from the RH tests could be Mr. Washington's blood type, but also could be shared by as many as one out of every thirty black men here in this city. True?"

Defense lawyers should never get cocky.

"True, Counselor. But you didn't let me finish my answer. You asked me if I found any tangible evidence to connect Mr. Washington to any of these crimes. As I said, we found the blood, the pattern of the cases, *and one other thing.*"

The defense lawyer knew he had done something stupid. He only had to wait to find out what it was.

"What was tangible," Detective Rigere said, "was that once we arrested Mr. Washington and put him in jail, the crimes stopped."

"Objection."

"Denied, Counselor. You asked the question."

"Before we arrested Mr. Washington the rapes and crimes against women along Bluff Springs happened every three or four weeks. He's been in jail awaiting trial for over seven months and there hasn't been one more incident on Bluff Springs since then. No rapes. No burglaries. No assaults down in the creek bed or on the trail. In short, when we stopped Mr. Washington, we stopped crime on Bluff Springs."

No more questions.

"Prosecution Rests, Your Honor."

"Defense Rests."

The assistant district attorney had an easy argument. "She was raped. She pointed to Artemis Washington and told you, the jury, 'that is the man who raped me.' And when Artemis Washington was arrested, crime in Bluff Springs stopped."

Washington's lawyer had less to work with. While he said, "There is not a single piece of physical evidence, no blood, no clothing, no hair or fingernail or other scientific evidence to connect Mr. Washington to a crime that took place five miles and six months away from his arrest," the jury spent the time looking at the white t-shirt which he had worn, which made no bones about his preferences for tight and white women.

149

The only barrier to convicting Artemis Washington right then and there was that it was five in the afternoon. The jury retired to elect a foreman, then told the bailiff, "We'll come back and convict him tomorrow morning."

ii.

The index to *The Gazette's* morgue files was hopelessly out of date. The files themselves were stored by year, not by subject, making the search something like looking for a needle in a needle stack. Frank began with the date that Miss Vines had been raped and worked his way forward, looking for clippings under her name and under the name of Artemis Washington. As he suspected, there were none. What he found, instead, was a headline that ran across the first page of the local news section of the paper: **Bluff Springs Rapist Strikes Again.** The story was reported by Steve Gates, who had quit *The Gazette* a month ago to become a publicist for Dell Computers. There was an undeniable plea in Gates' story, the tale of an un-named victim who had been dragged off the Bluff Springs trail and raped behind some trees not fifty feet from where others were jogging and riding their bicycles. A second story, a week later, **Police Warn Women in Bluff Springs**, provided some detail about a young white woman who was attacked near the parking lot a quarter mile from Miss Vines' apartment. She gave a description of her rapist as a young black male, very strong. A third story, **Epidemic of Violent Crimes in Bluff Springs**, reported that the victim—who, according to *Gazette* policy to not identify rape victims, remained unnamed—told police that "I suddenly I felt a hand around my throat. He was choking me. Then his other hand clamped over my mouth so I couldn't scream."

Christ, Frank thought. *That's exactly what Miss Vines said in court.* He checked the date of the story; it was two months before Miss Vines was attacked. *Something's not right.* He looked at the first story again. *Why does the headline say 'strikes again' if it was the first one? And why isn't there a description in the others? I mean, don't they want to tell people who to look out for?* Not until he read the last story, **Another Rape at Bluff Springs**, did he realize what was missing. "Police artists are composing a sketch of the man based on the victims' descriptions."

iii.

The jury went right back to the jury room at 8:30; Frank arrived in the courtroom at 8:45. Artemis Washington, chained to a deputy, arrived at 9:00; his lawyer arrived at 9:05 and was told the jury was already deliberating. "Call me at the office when they come back. I'm just across the street. I can be here in three minutes." The bailiff told the lawyer that he would call him the minute anything happened. The deputy told Artemis to stand up; they marched to a holding room adjacent to the courtroom and left the door cracked open. Frank went to the door.

"Psst," he hissed.

Artemis looked up, then peered through the cracked-open doorway and saw Frank standing beside the doorframe, out of the deputy's line of sight. Frank arched his eyebrows and pointed to a sheet of paper rolled up in his hand. Artemis responded with his own arched eyebrows. Frank unrolled the paper and showed it to him.

Gates' personal file of news stories was not in the stack that Burman had given Frank, nor was it in the morgue. Instead, it was in the *Gazette*'s personnel office, apparently left as an artifact of Gates' employment when he turned in his building pass and severance documents the day he went to work for Dell. It contained a copy of the stories that Frank had read in the morgue files and a smattering of pages from the police file that Detective Rigere seemed to have shared with Gates. There was the arrest report, some of Rigere's statements written for the grand jury, and a police composite sketch of the man victims had told police had raped them. The police sketch had never seen the light of day, not as a news item and not as an exhibit in the trial.

The sketch looked nothing like Artemis Washington. Frank showed it through the door to Washington. Washington's face clouded and he clenched his jaws.

"Who is this?" Frank mouthed.

Artemis shook his head.

"Police sketch of rapist." Frank mouthed again.

Artemis frowned again, and shook his head violently.

"Your lawyer," Frank mouthed. He pointed at Artemis, at the sketch, and shrugged to try to communicate that he wanted to know if Artemis' defense lawyer had seen it.

You are not who they say you are, Frank thought. *Artemis Washington, you are a free man.*

In the thirty seconds before the deputy came out of the anteroom Frank was proud of himself. He had pursued a story. He had believed that something was wrong and proved that the man they were looking for was not the person Miss Vines had pointed to in court. He had the proof. *I've done a good thing for this man, finally.*

"Officer!" Washington said to the deputy. Frank waited for the wheels to begin to turn. The wheels did not turn. "That newspaperman is outside the door..." Washington said, "...trying to sneak around and interview me without my lawyer. He's bothering me."

The deputy did come out and told Frank to get the hell away from there. "You know the rules. Get out."

iv.

Frank was sitting in the hallway, contemplating that no good deed goes unpunished, when the clerk said that Judge Leatherman would like to talk with him, and led him to the judge's office.

From ace detective to contempt of court. One more thing I'm not any good at.

"Mr. Hastings, come in. Nothing to do about waiting for the verdict except wait for the verdict. Still can't talk about the case, but I did want to mention something I thought about after you and I met the other day."

Frank let his breath out.

Leatherman had told him what not to write instead of what he could write, so piecing together his retirement story had been harder than he had expected. The judge's computer was still on the desk, apparently never used. The desk was still cluttered with papers that seemed to have not been touched since Frank had been in the office a few days before, nor for months before that. However, the cabinets were empty and the mementos and diplomas—the certificates of proof of how well Judge Leatherman had done at college and in the eyes of the local YMCA, the local Chamber of Commerce, the local business and church communities—all were missing. His pictures had been taken down. A dozen boxes bulged with Leatherman's personal books and memories, waiting to be carted away. Frank wondered what Leatherman wanted to mention.

"I had this case in the army, when I was in France, where this corporal murdered this major. The major had stirred up a firefight in this old chateau, probably stupid of him, and the Germans shelled the dickens out of his unit, killed or wounded nearly everybody, then drove away. This corporal traps that major up in this old farmhouse and shoots him, then runs away. He shows up a few days later in a POW cage and so we try him for murder. You would call it fragging. Isn't that what you said in Vietnam, 'fragging an officer?'"

"We always heard about it. I don't know that it every really happened." Frank could have said that he didn't know if it ever actually succeeded, but everyone he knew in Vietnam had agreed to never mention it again. "But yeah, we heard about fragging."

"Anyway, this medico shows up and says the guy we're trying is the wrong guy, it isn't the corporal who was in his unit. And you know what? He says the way he knows it is because this guy on trial, this corporal, had some kids. But this doc says the actual person we were charging didn't have any— get this—any balls. No balls, no kids. He had done short arm inspections on this guy we had on trial and, guess what? The guy had no balls. Commander said 'Stop the trial' and sent the guy right back into combat. Wonder why I'm telling you this?"

Frank did. It was kind of like tales they used to tell around the bar in the PX, stories he heard in the army, more like a joke, but this one didn't have a clear punch line.

"Justice," Leatherman went on. "I don't know if this guy really killed this major or not, or if we really had the wrong guy. I thought the medico was a liar but I couldn't figure out how. I mean, the man we were going to shoot had no balls, just like he said. But the CO didn't really care. He said only God knows if we had the right guy or not, so let God sort it out. If the guy needed shooting, God would let the Germans shoot him, something like that. He sent that soldier right into the middle of the Battle of the Bulge. I never heard another word about him. We do the best we can; sometimes we just don't really know if we have the right guy. Do any of us really know who anybody else is, really?"

The clerk knocked on his door.

There was a verdict.

Chapter Fourteen

i.

September began nicely enough. Late summer rains brought the flowers back out. Tiffany and Jeff started back to school. Mitsubishi announced that it would sell a home television with a forty-inch screen. But then Candace made a simple mistake, the kind that people make when, after dinner with parents, a penance of spinach salad with bacon and apple canceled out by a slice of apple pie, they come home, send the babysitter home, then walk past the blinking lights of kitchen clocks, by the stereo system ready lights, by answering machine lights, by electric toothbrush standby lights, and by hallway night lights; they push the 'play/record' button on an otherwise silent video recorder; they take off all their clothes except undies and a t-shirt, they go to bed, and they go into a deep sleep, during which they are annoyed but not awakened by the sound of knocking on a door that they mistake for the sound that Crockett and Tubbs make right before they burst through some drug dealer's South Beach condo to make a spectacular and sometimes noisy arrest. Deep in stage four sleep, made deeper by the cheap red wine she had added to the slurry rolling around in her stomach, Candace made that kind of mistake.

Bambambam.

She pulled the pillow over her head and went back to sleep.

Bam. Bam. Bam.

Miami Vice, she thought. Candace opened one eye, then a second eye, and shook her head just enough to collect her senses. *Crockett is killing Tubbs. Or is it Tubbs killing Crockett? Maybe some drug lord's killing them both. I hate Miami Vice.*

Peter loved *Miami Vice*.

She squinted across the dark bedroom where the video recorder winked at her, '3:43,' blink, blink, '3:43,' blink, blink, '3:43.' A red light scolded her for not turning it off, 'Recording Complete,' blink, 'Recording Complete.'

Crockett and Tubbs must have killed each other and finished up for the day, she thought. She couldn't remember, at 3:43 in the morning, whether she was supposed to turn the recorder off or turn the television off or just leave them. In fact, the only instruction she could remember was to set the television to channel 3 and, at 10:00 p.m. on Tuesday nights, push 'play/ record.' "It's all set up," Peter had said. "Just push 'Play, Record,' and go to sleep. It'll do everything else."

Bam! Bam! Bam!

She decided that she would do everything else herself. She scrambled across the floor, pulled the dresser away from the wall, stuck her hand into a nest of electric wires, and jerked them out of the wall socket. The Trinitron ready light blinked out. The 'Recording Complete' light blinked out. At 3:44 the green clock lights shrank, blinked once in protest, and dissolved into the magic hole where LED lights swirl to their unpowered graves. Back to bed.

"Damn!" she hissed, cursing the darkness and its stubbing of toes on pedestals of beds, feeling her way, climbing back in and covering herself.

Something hummed. *The heater.* A low hum came through the bedroom window, a thrum of motor sounds that could only be the heat pump, outside, kicking in for no reason. *Why is the heater turning on?* It was not cold. It would not be cold for a month, two months. *This new house has so many bugs. When Peter comes home he is definitely going to work on these bugs.* Thrumm. Or was it a car?

Bam! Bam! Bam! "Candace? Are you in there?"

It wasn't Crockett, or Tubbs. She woke up.

Candace put a housecoat over her tee shirt and stumbled into the hallway, past the children's doors, past the breakfast nook, into the living room. *Turn on a light. Turn on a light. No, don't turn on a light. Look out the peephole.*

Two men stood on the other side of the peephole. She rubbed her eye against the door, trying to get a better look, never seeing completely who they were.

Way down inside her a valve opened, a *cush* of adrenaline slipped through the valve and into an artery, bathed itself briefly, and began to send hints to Candace's brain. *Something's gone wrong. Dad suffered a heart attack.*

Mom's had a stroke. An eighteen-wheeler crashed into them on the interstate. The men were burglars, burglars in uniforms. They were not police, not ambulance. They were... *Oh, my God, no. No.*

She fumbled with the deadbolt and chain, jerked too soon, remembered the porch light, switched it on, pushed open the door, and looked at them.

"Candace?" one of them said. "Candace? Have you heard anything?"

And then she recognized them, one of them, anyway. They were from Pan Am. Rocky was from Pan Am.

"Rocky?" She looked at him. Rocky nodded his head. "Rocky?" she screamed. He shook his head. "Rocky? Is he....?" And she began to feel herself losing complete control. Eyes clouded. Voice cracked. Knees buckled. The porch hit her in the face. Rocky caught her.

"No. He isn't. Candace, we've got to hurry. Get some clothes on. We've got to get you to the airport. Hurry." He helped her to her feet, helped prop open the door. "We don't know anything. It's not a crash, nothing like that. Get some clothes on."

Rocky and the other man walked her into the living room, found the light switch, found the kitchen.

"He's all right. Drink some water." *Peter might actually be all right,* he thought, except that Rocky didn't really know anything other than it was urgent and to go find Candace and bring her back to the Pan Am operations office in Denver. Someone had called someone who had called a highway patrolman to pick Rocky up and race to Colorado Springs in the middle of the night. A police car had met them at the exit ramp and led them to Candace's home. "We've got to get you up to Denver. Do you understand? We need to go to Denver, Candace. I'll be with you. Don't worry, there's nothing to worry about," he said. "Just get your things."

She pulled on a pair of blue jeans, some running shoes, and tucked her tee shirt in, then realized that he had said, 'your things.'

"What things?" she called through the bedroom door. She didn't want it to be a *things* kind of emergency. "What do you mean get my things?"

Rocky didn't know, but the patrolman did.

"She needs whatever women need to spend a couple of nights. Meds. Woman things. Some clothes."

Rocky tapped on her door, repeated what the patrolman had suggested.

"Clothes?"

"We may have to go somewhere else too. I don't know. Just get whatever you need for overnight, you know, if you take anything, pills, toothbrush, hairbrush. I don't know."

She knew. Pilot wives lived in two worlds, they all did. In one world they were all alone, and they puttered around the house and drank coffee and mowed the lawn and read cheap novels. In the other one they kept a bag ready to be taken off to Sioux City or Dallas or some mountainside in the middle of nowhere to grieve in front of television cameras. She didn't actually have such a bag but she knew what went in it. A black dress. Pantyhose. Shoes, no heels. A scarf. Undies. Sunglasses. Toothbrush. Toothpaste. Advil. Credit cards. Purse.

"The kids?"

The kids. She had to call her mother. *The kids.*

Candace was never to have any memory of calling her mother in the middle of the night, nor of how her mother got to her house. She did remember opening the children's doors and watching them, asleep, and of leaving with Rocky and the highway patrolman. Beyond that, Candace would never remember the details of the knock on her door.

The patrol car turned north on the interstate. It would be five in the morning when they got to Stapleton Airport. She waited for a siren, a hundred-mile-an-hour race with lights flashing, swerves in and out of traffic. A few lights of the city blinked and the spires of the academy chapel loomed in the darkness, disappeared, then nothing but night blackened by the forest and the towering Front Range.

"What happened, Rocky? You've got to tell me."

"We don't know anything, Candace. Operations in New York called. The station chief told me to find you and get you to the airport. That's all I know."

She knew Rocky would say this. 'Operations' was not a name. 'Station chief' was not a name. When a plane crashed suddenly no one had a name. No one knew anything, some voice with no name would appear and tell wives and widows to go here, go there, be quiet, be patient, that they were doing everything they could, that someone would be along in a little while to bring things up to date. She pulled her sweater around her and began to twirl her scarf and stare out the window.

"Where, then? At least tell me that." She tried to calculate from memory. It was pitch black in Colorado so it was around ten in the morning in London, maybe noon. "In London? Did he crash in London, Rocky?" *Or in the ocean,* she thought. *They'll never find him.* "Tell me that much, at least. Don't make me just sit here."

She had known Rocky almost as long as she had known Peter. Now, he and the patrolman were like Peter's stupid video recorder, blinking at her, whirring, hiding Crockett and Tubbs and their stupid Ferrari that Peter thought was gorgeous. When she should have been watching CNN she had been trying to put the Trinitron on channel 3 and press 'record' and read *Secrets* and just go to sleep. No one would tell her anything.

Where did it happen? He was flying London – JFK – home. He would be home tonight, except now he won't. She began to shake so badly that Rocky heard her chattering teeth from the front seat and tried to reach past the patrol car's prisoner screen to comfort her in the backseat. No one said another word until they arrived at the airport.

Denver Stapleton Airport was waking up as Rocky led her around behind the Pan Am ticket counters and into the local operations office. The din in the room was unnerving, people rushing back and forth, talking loudly, shouting out numbers and weights and complaints of excess passengers and fuel balances, faulty landing gear lights, a flat tire on a catering truck. One crew was calling in a flight plan to JFK, another was debating what constituted reasonable service for passengers "...*just in coach, just to Chicago.*" Somewhere, a dot wheel printer chirped and an un-bodied voice told no one in particular that Denver Stapleton winds were "variable, five degrees at ten knots, visibility fifteen miles, skies broken seven thousand...." She wanted to scream.

Plate glass windows looked out over the ramp where baggage handlers were backing a loading cart to the open well of an airplane and where Candace looked up to see a gaunt woman, a homeless woman maybe, with hair flying and ratty blue jeans and running shoes, looking back at her. Someone else saw the same woman reflected in the glass and figured it out, and the room stopped. She could hear necks turn, feet press against the floor and freeze, arms poised in midair with sheets of paper flopping about. They gaped at her, then quickly looked away.

"Will someone now tell me what is going on? Rocky, you got me here. I'm here. Now, I want to know: where is my husband? What is going on?"

Rocky shook his head.

"Ma'am, I'm the station manager. Let's go inside my office." A man appeared at her elbow, his Pan Am uniform stained and mushed from sweat and cigarettes. "I'm Jim Burton. We met at Christmas. Or Thanksgiving. Anyway, come in and sit down." He opened the door to a glass-wall office and led her in. "Rocky, come in or not. Would you like him here?"

He asked Candace, she nodded, and Rocky came in and closed the door.

"First, I'm very sorry to have come gotten you in the middle of the night. Second, we don't know what's going on. We've got people on the ground in Karachi with an open line to Systems Operations in New York. They're telling us whatever they learn as fast as they learn it."

It took Candace a few seconds to filter what he had said. *You don't know what's going on? You've got an open line? Karachi?*

"Karachi? What's Karachi?" She looked at Rocky. She looked at Jim Burton. Karachi was not good, whatever it was.

"We had a flight takeover at the airport in Karachi. On the ground, actually. It never got off the ground. Some people we think are, well, no question about it, they're terrorists. They hijacked the plane."

"Why are you telling me this? Peter's not in Karachi. He was going to London. Is that some airport in Iceland or somewhere? He's coming from London to home." *If I just will him to be somewhere else it doesn't matter if someone hijacked a plane.*

"It's not London. Karachi is in Pakistan. Peter deadheaded to Karachi and was going to fly the turnaround back to Frankfurt. Didn't he...?" *Christ,* Rocky realized, *He didn't even tell her he was flying into a hellhole. How am I supposed to tell bad news to a woman who didn't even watch the news, then tell her it isn't really all that bad?* His shirt gushed from a new round of sweat.

"What's happened to Peter?" *You know. I can tell when you're lying and you know what happened.* Candace's adrenaline splashed around, raced to her Alpha-1 neurotransmitters, told Candace to raise her voice, tremble, demand something, to act right now! "I have a right to know. Just tell me." She shouldn't have shouted at him.

"We don't know." Burton did know that if she had been watching television at two in the morning she would have seen what he and nearly everyone else in Pan Am ops had seen. Whoever had taken over the airplane had dragged a passenger whom, as the BBC reported, "We believe to be an

American of Indian descent, whose name is being withheld until authorities can verify..." to the main door and forced him onto his knees. There was a pop, a jerk of the head, a bullet hole spouting blood, and then the world watched as the American of Indian descent plunged twenty feet and thumped down onto the pavement, followed by the televised image of a very serious man waving a gun while standing in the airplane's doorway, then slamming it. Someone else could tell her that.

"We thought you should be here until we do know what's happened. Let me be as honest as I can, ma'am ... we don't have any report at all that Captain Hastings has been hurt in any way. But we don't have any report of anything about anyone specifically who was on the plane. It's surrounded by army or police or whoever they have in Pakistan. The plane isn't going anywhere. It ran out of power somewhere in the night and is just sitting there."

Except it's sitting there with Peter on it.

She closed her eyes and tried to remember what Peter had said to her when he left. He had a flight bag. He had a hanging bag with a spare uniform. He had put them in his Corvette and grinned like a boy with a new rocket. Why did she remember crap like *Miami Vice* and Danielle Steel novels and not remember what Peter said to her before he backed out of the driveway and zoomed off in that stupid Corvette?

"Drink this. Sit up." She had slumped toward the floor, then jerked awake in time to keep herself from banging her head on Jim Burton's desk. "Don't faint on us. Want me to call a doctor?" He opened the door to yell into the operations room and scare the wits out of everyone; she stopped him.

"I'm okay, no doctor. Just let me sit here." She did sit, and remembered.

Peter had backed into the street, stopped, and revved up the motor like a teenager. 'See you Thursday,' he said. *That's what he said, 'See you Thursday.'* His soft blond hair had drooped across his forehead and he had grinned. She was supposed to have gone with him to get his hair cut but they had run out of time. He would get in trouble if the line supervisor at JFK saw him with his shaggy hair, and he had flipped it with his hand and grinned at her and yelled something and driven off and she had turned away like she always did because he was always coming back, and she had forgotten everything he had said. *And he had said something before that.* She couldn't remember. *I'm a horrible wife.*

She watched CNN at six in the morning.

"The aircraft remains on the tarmac some sixteen hours after armed gunmen pushed their way onto the jumbo jet shortly before it was scheduled to take off. A source has reported that it is believed they dressed as security guards and walked into the aircraft through the main cabin door before drawing their weapons and ordering the passengers to..."

A white 747 with the Pan Am logo sat on a tarmac pavement that appeared to be in the middle of a desert. Isolated carts and buggies stood at a great distance. A man in a blue costume with a stiff collar was filmed at a desk inside the airport, telephone in hand, waving off reporters and cameras.

"...seen escaping through the crew emergency door above the cockpit. It is apparently that act of escape that led to a burst of gunfire inside the cabin, but without a flight crew, the airplane will not be going anywhere. This is...."

At seven o'clock both Rocky and Jim Burton came for her.

"Mrs. Hastings, we just spoke with the security command office in New York operations. The crew got out of the plane...."

She brightened visibly and began to stand up to hug them.

"...but Captain Hastings wasn't with them. He's still on the plane."

Someone knocked on the door. Burton looked up. His deputy manager came into the office.

"Jim? I think you should see this." He pointed to the portable television that was perched on the counter outside his office. The 747 was visible on the screen. They all rushed out to gather around it. As they watched, two evacuation slides erupted from the aircraft's passenger doors and stretched to the ground. A talking head on CNN reported:

"The auxiliary power unit of the airplane died after sixteen hours and the aircraft lighting went out. Someone inside the airplane opened the doors and the emergency slides were activated, at which time gunfire and explosives could be heard inside."

Every employee in the operations office stopped work and ran to crowd around the television. The screen was filled with the scene of passengers spilling down one of the slides, pushing, shoving, falling, tens of them, dozens of them.

Peter Hastings was not among them.

ii.

Eleanor's slender arms reached forward, one after the other, and stroked downward into the water, her hands forming paddles as they dug below the surface, pulled her across the water, and cycled behind her. Her legs had become quite firm and powerful, her feet strong and fluid. They gave Eleanor the freedom to swim, back and forth, to enter into a diving flip turn at the end of the neighborhood swimming pool, and to kick away and swim another length. They also gave her freedom of silence, of motion and purpose, each of which enabled her to spend an hour in thought as her body worked itself out quite independently of her mind. Swimming was Eleanor's quiet temple. She turned, kicked, and thought about what she had done.

She did not like to lie to Frank. *Technically*, she thought, *I am not lying.* Technically, however, she had withheld something. It had been a misunderstanding, a silly one, and she had not mentioned it to Frank because it was embarrassing. She had allowed herself to be drawn into a discussion (stroke, stroke, stroke... *Admit it—it was an argument!* ... stroke, stroke, stroke) with a student about the literary merit of Chaucer versus the literary merit of Becket. It began with Chaucer's Proem to *Troilus and Criseyde.* Some of the students thought that Proem was a printing error; most of the others had not noticed it at all. One, however, was dismissive. The girl (*She was trying to show off in class...* stroke, stroke, stroke) had said that Chaucer, even if revised into modern English, "offers little or nothing in the way of insight or contemplative literature. You just need to read anything written by Becket, anything, to open up the mind to literary experiment and the human condition." (*Stupid cow.* Stroke, stroke, turn.) "Have you read anything by Becket, Miss Herald?" (*Bitch.*)

Eleanor had struggled to remember. There had been some letters she had read at university, chiefly to do with bishops failing to timely excommunicate miscreants and some edicts regarding legal process.

"Very little," she had admitted. "I found it tedious and, frankly, presumptuous." Her student had beamed the smile of righteousness.

It had not been until Eleanor got home that it registered on her that the stupid cow had meant Beckett, two 't's', as in Samuel, Nobel laureate, not Becket, one 't', as in Thomas, murdered archbishop. Without thinking, Eleanor had removed from the bookshelf *The Complete Works of Beckett*, two 't's', that Frank had brought home from Colorado on the last day he had spent with Will who, Frank said, had handed them over with his fishing gear while Peter was moving Will and Virginia out of their cabin and into a nursing home.

Eleanor had removed the plastic wrapping from the volumes. She began to read Beckett, two t's.

Her first impression was that still she was correct, that apart from not understanding at all what it was that Beckett, two 't's', was writing about, Beckett also was tedious and presumptuous. Her second impression was that the title plate in the first volume of *The Complete Works of Beckett* only listed four volumes, yet there were five books. Her third impression was that the fifth book was not a book at all.

The fifth volume was only a binding that looked exactly like the first four books. Inside, however, instead of pages, there was a hollowed shell that contained a half-dozen pencil drawings. Eleanor had never seen them before, nor had she been able to stop looking at them despite the strong warning light coming from her internal alarm. Not only were the drawings remarkably clear and detailed, Eleanor had known as she looked at them why Frank's father had hidden them inside a book that no one would read and secured them with plastic wrapping. The only thing worse than the fact that she was looking at something that she was not meant to see was that she had hidden from Frank that she had seen it.

That the drawings were Will's secret memoirs was beyond dispute. The first sketch was of Virginia, only a very young Virginia. Her beautiful high cheekbones and strong forehead, the thick hair tumbling about her shoulders, her wide, open lips and slightly downturned eyes facing the artist at a provocative angle, were shocking. Eleanor's late father-in-law had in some manner captured a ripeness in Virginia's soul that was erotic and, Eleanor had no doubt, if the drawing had shown more than Virginia's head and neck and shoulders, it would have shown a girl who was not only nude, but quite naked. This art was more than Will's imagination, she knew. There was a story behind it, she knew that too. Eleanor couldn't stop looking at it and imagining, for the first time, how her parents-in-law had lived before life overtook them. Stroke, stroke, kick, turn.

The next drawings were memoirs of a very different kind. In one there was a view across a meadow to an open-sided shed that appeared to be erected on the banks of a stream. Flowers and willow tails grew at the stream's edge and trees lined the far bank. A small, empty rowboat was floating, tethered by a rope to the shed. In the distance, behind the trees, there were the remnants of a gothic building, high walls with arched windows. If Will had rendered it in paint, or even ink, it could have been mistaken for a photograph taken through a strongly filtered lens.

Another drawing was made from across a different riverbank. It showed a hillside in a city that was reduced to rubble. On the left of the drawing were the damaged bell towers of a cathedral and, filling the edges and centers, row upon row of demolished stone buildings and narrow, rubble-filled streets. High on the slope of the hill there was a stone building, wide, grim, two rows of windows and a steep slate roof. A line of very small and indistinct figures formed a procession of people who seemed to be trudging up the hillside to the front porch where a few others, perhaps nuns or nurses and some men, gazed at them.

A fourth drawing seemed out of place, a view of a cluster of small, rectangular wooden buildings that might have been farm coops or the houses of a group of efficient, boring, and very poor people who all used the same whitewash paint. In front of a wooden path was a sign that on careful reading could be made out as *Hôpital Irlandais*. There was no doubt that the scene was something from Will's time in France, a subject about which he had never spoken.

Another drawing in the book showed the town square of a small village, a stone church on one side, a row of shops or houses leading away down the other side and into the town. Yet another sketch depicted rows of trees, perhaps an orchard, growing down a hillside in an orderly pattern that ended at a walled farm. Inside the walls, the roof of a sturdy stone farmhouse rose at one end of the farmyard, the caved-in roof of an old half-timbered barn at the other. There was a gate leading to the orchard but something, a cannon perhaps, had demolished the stone wall around it.

Eleanor had forgotten completely about Becket, one 't.' She tidied up the drawings and the books and prepared herself to make a full confession when Frank came home, then spend the evening with him looking at the drawings and making up educated guesses about where Will had been and what he had seen when he drew them. It was possible that Frank might see in the sketch of Virginia exactly what Eleanor had seen (stroke, stroke, stroke, 'The ick factor,' stroke, stroke) but he also might see it in a completely different light. It didn't matter, she thought, because Will had given them to Frank and it was for Frank to discover and see in them whatever he would see. That was her conclusion until she turned over the last drawing.

There gazed out at her a face she had never seen before. Round, simple, a young woman who, for her rough scarf and locks of hair spilling from it to cover her forehead, might well have been a farm girl, or a peasant. She was not beautiful, certainly not in the way that Virginia was beautiful. She might have been pretty, but only in a clean and simple way. Her eyes, clear, accepting, were set gently into her face, her nose small, turned up very slightly. Her mouth, however, was somewhat elegant, the slightest shape of a 'w', and wide, a fine lower lip hooded by the upper lip and a slight, contented smile. A rough sweater cloaked her shoulders and some of her open throat and neck. It was the drawing of a kind, simple woman.

Eleanor had never before seen art like this, art that captured the soul of someone who was so clearly and unconditionally in love.

Eleanor looked up from the pool and saw that the morning sun had somehow managed to climb higher above the sycamores along the creek bed. She had been in the pool at least an hour longer than she had intended, and swam to the ladder. Her towel lay on the cement bench at the edge of the pool, a sturdy old seat built for a sturdy old pool at the bottom of a hidden park at the end of The Sisters. She and Frank had wondered often how their neighborhood had been called The Sisters. Most likely, the actual sisters had been heirs to a rich family who a hundred years before had lived in the mansion at the top of the bluff that overlooked the creek and the park. The Sisters, down below, consisted of a dozen or so tiny wood frame homes, shotgun homes that were one room wide and several rooms deep, all with gabled roofs and small porches where every neighbor sat in the summer evenings to visit in the breeze of the sycamores until the sun dropped behind the bluff.

She wrapped her towel around her bare legs and tight swimsuit and stepped into her sandals to walk the worn path back to their tidy little cottage.

I must tell him, she decided. *I ought to have done last night.*

She would have told him if he had not been so upset. The jury had indeed convicted Artemis Washington of raping the woman, as Frank had told her the day before was almost certain to happen. "Why are you upset?" she had asked, partly forgetting the drawings and partly thankful for the diversion.

"They have the wrong man," Frank had said. "It really is a case of mistaken identity." She had never seen him so upset.

Now, she stepped onto their porch and opened the door, girding herself to tell her husband that she had gone behind his back and, worse, not told him what she had found.

"I'm home," she called out. Frank didn't answer. "Frank?" She walked through their small front living room, into the bedroom, and looked at the alarm clock. It was past nine. She had lost track of time. Frank already had gone to work.

Indeed, she thought, *I must get to work myself, else I'll be late for my ten o'clock class.* She toweled her hair, stripped off her swimming suit, and started the shower to heat the water. She stepped back into the bedroom and began to look in their small closet for the day's clothes when the telephone rang. *No time for a phone call.* She shook out her hair to keep it dry in the shower and opened the curtain to step in.

The phone rang again, and again. It rang fourteen times.

"Hello?" she answered.

"Hello, Eleanor?" Eleanor recognized the voice, a woman's, but could not place it. "Eleanor, this is Wanda Barnet." *Who is Wanda Barnet?* "I'm Candace's mother. Peter's mother-in-law. In Colorado Springs. Listen, something terrible has happened."

iii.

Saddam's anti-aircraft bunkers looked even more like the Hastings' storm cellar than Tog had remembered. Lucille had thrown a fit when Tog hadn't come to clear out the backyard.

"I was over there all day cleaning. All I asked you to do was spend ten minutes over there picking up some junk to haul off. I scrubbed the floors. I washed the windows. I vacuumed the curtains and polished up the cabinets.

And I asked you to come by for ten minutes."

At eight in the morning Tog parked his pickup in the driveway of the Hastings' wooden garage and walked into the backyard. The clothesline sagged badly between two cast iron posts that once not only had held laundry, but also had been the center support for the Indian teepees of his and Frank's scalping days, the goal posts of his and Peter's football practice days, the booby traps of all their GI Joe days, and the UHF antennae of countless nights spent in space travel. The picnic table, a former Panzer tank and Mount Everest, had fallen on hard times and was collapsing under its own rusted weight. Indeed, the only two things in the backyard that looked exactly the same were the clean, painted white wooden cross where he and Frank had buried Hercules and the nuclear bomb shelter/storm cellar. He hurried to get the chore over with.

The rusted tables and chairs took Tog only a few minutes to drag across the yard and lever into the pickup. *Can't believe I spent half a night hiding under these damned things, waiting for that little bastard to crawl out of his window.* The picnic table had been midway between the door of the cellar and Frank's bedroom window. Tog could no longer remember why Frank had said he was running away from home but he clearly remembered shivering while he waited for Frank in that October night. *Something to do with Peter's airplanes, or maybe it was the dog. Something.* Tog had waited until Lucille was asleep and George was off in the middle of a nightshift at the bomb factory, then stuffed some clothes into a pillowcase and walked right out the kitchen door. He had expected Doc or Virginia to catch him in their backyard but they never came outside and, around eleven, their lights went out. Tog had waited another hour and was about to take his bag of runaway clothes and go back home when he heard a 'screeee' and saw the sash of Frank's bedroom window rise up from the windowsill. A few moments later, Frank's pillowcase came flying out the window, followed in short order by Frank's hands, head, shoulders, arms, and the rest of him.

"Let's get out of here," Tog had said.

"Just a minute," Frank had whispered back. "Wait here." Frank had tiptoed across the backyard to the bomb shelter and tried to open the steel door that led down into it. "Hssss – come here," he hissed. Tog had gone over to him and Frank had told him to help try to tug open the stuck door. "I'm going down. Be right back." Frank never made it. The two of them tried a dozen different ways to get the door open but the padlock was too secure, the hinges too tight, the handle too weak. In the end they walked away, their vagabond bags slung over their shoulders.

They made it as far as the Collins farm, where they slept hidden in the bushes at the foot of the elm trees that grew up around Becky's house. Mr. Collins was up doing farm chores the next morning before they woke up; they stayed hidden half the day before sneaking away to the road, where someone from Bridle saw them walking and called Will. Will and George drove out and picked them up, and their escape from Bridle was ended. Becky had never come out of the farmhouse. Tog was pretty sure that it had been when he was twelve years old. He pulled on the handle of the storm cellar door and, despite some rusty resistance, managed to pull it open.

There wasn't much junk left inside. Wooden shelves that once had held jars of canned vegetables and peaches were sagging with age and inattention, filled now only with dust. There was a rusted washing machine and, under a tarp, a contraption that looked like a huge typewriter, with wheels and pulleys and a large flat plate at the top. Tog wasn't sure what to do with it because it was far too big for him to muscle up the steps. There was Peter's old bicycle, a worn-out floor lamp, and a wooden Zenith radio. He wrestled them one by one up the steps and into the bed of his pickup, then returned to see what else was down in the cellar to haul away. There was an assortment of worn-out vacuum cleaners, brooms, paint cans, and garden tools, which he carried away one load at a time. By midmorning, the cellar was reasonably empty, apart from the linotype machine.

Tog was beginning to think he liked poking around in other people's things. *I'll wrestle this around a bit and maybe take it apart*, he thought. It was covered in oil and dust but might be worth something at an antique store or maybe he could take it apart and sell the metal for junk. *Whatever that is*, he thought, *there's money in it*. It was when Tog tried to remove the keyboard from the chassis of the linotype machine that the letters fell out.

What's this?

The letters were bundled together by several loops of thick string. Tog's first thought was that they were exactly the kind of junk that people start to throw away and then forget. His second thought was that the letters had been stuck up inside the bottom of a keyboard of an old newspaper type-setting machine of some kind, hardly the place that someone would put letters to be thrown away. His third thought was to look at them.

All but one or two were addressed to Virginia Sullivan. Most of them had to do with places whose names didn't make sense.

> *9 July Ste Marie du Vire France: Please ignore my last letter....*
>
> *11 June Portsmouth: Back in England. ...*
>
> *May 15, 1944: Dear Virginia: I finished field hospital medical officer school...*
>
> *June 1, 1944: Dear Virginia: A last letter. Well, I hope not. ...*
>
> *20 June Isigny France: I told the army to put Peter's things in a box and ship it to me in Tierra in care of you. I don't have anywhere else to send things. If I make it back I'll come to Tierra for it. Thank you – Will.*

So, Tog thought. Old Doc wrote Virginia from the war. Big deal. Wonder who that Peter was?

But the letters were boring and Tog's hands were getting cracked from the dry dust. He started to put them away but, like the curious cat, he couldn't stop.

> *14 June, Portsmouth, England. Virginia. Peter is dead. A major in the 8th AF confirmed it to me as Peter's next of kin. He crashed somewhere around Carentan. I don't know more than that....*

Tog read the letter twice. Whoever Peter was, he bought the farm. *And, better still, it looks like good old gorgeous Virginia didn't write back to good old Doc for months and good old Doc wasn't waiting any more.*

The last piece was a telegram, this time to Virginia Hastings. Tog read it, then read it again, and the thick gears of his dull mind ground away, as fast as they ever had done. Tog had struck gold.

"TOG! Are you down there?" Lucille's voice echoed down the stairs. He turned around in the dim light of the cellar to see her stepping slowly through the open doorway and down onto the wooden steps. "TOG! Get up here. Hurry!"

Tog hadn't planned to discover anybody's letters, so he hadn't planned on what to do if he got caught with them. "Wait Ma! I'll be right there." Flustered, he stuffed them back into the linotype machine and hoped they wouldn't fall on the floor. "I'm coming up. What is it?"

He stepped through the dust of the cellar, around the empty shelves and onto the rickety stairs, and climbed up into the bright sunlight. Lucille was standing in the yard a few steps away and, despite the heat of a late summer day, she seemed to be trembling.

"Ma? Are you okay?" He lowered the cellar door behind him and rushed over. She was doubling over, her arms crossed, and rocking back and forth on her feet. When he lifted her face, tears were running down it and her hair was flying loose. "What is it?"

"Tog, hold on." She collected her breath and gasped so badly that Tog thought she was dying. He took Lucille by her upper arms and held her up to look at him, and the sight of him helped. When she composed herself, she looked him in the eyes and said it the way she had heard it on the television.

"The Arabs have hijacked a plane over there in the desert somewhere, and started shooting people. Listen to me, Tog." He held her, and listened. "The airplane... it's Peter's. Peter Hastings. I just seen him on TV."

She stopped to catch her breath again, then finished what was on her mind. "It's bad, Tog. Real bad."

iv.

"Momma says Christ looks just like his Father," Sonny said. He was walking with Hoyt across the floor of the big barn. "We might be going to go see him."

The big barn was one of Sonny's favorite places. Hoyt took Sonny to the barn nearly every day and Sonny helped him work on the big machines. The cotton stripper was parked near the front of the barn, close to the tool bench where Hoyt had put the roller brushes and the wrenches. This morning he had asked Sonny to help change them out so they could get back in the fields as soon as the ground and the cotton dried out from the rains.

What Hoyt had said was, "Sonny, hand me the brush. The brush." Sonny had carried the lint brush to his father and handed it to him. Then he had said, "Okay, Sonny, hand me the wrench. It's the heavy steel bar with the round socket on the end," and Sonny had gotten the right tool the first time. It was important, Hoyt knew, to say exactly what he meant to Sonny because there were in Sonny's sunlit mind neither shadows nor clouds of nuance.

The barn was Poppa's work and Sonny liked it. Sonny was fascinated by the cotton stripper and the tractor, but he also liked the little things, the coils of rubber hoses, the drum of grease and the grease gun, the case of motor oil and the boxes of filters at the workbench. In fact, Poppa's barn was nothing like Momma's bank, which was mostly just papers and typewriters and money and there wasn't any work for Sonny to do. But Momma had said that they were going to see Jesus and his family, and he wanted to tell Poppa.

"That's good, Sonny. So, what do you think about going to see Jesus?" Hoyt had no illusions about Momma wanting all of them to see Jesus. Shirley said so often enough and loudly enough that Hoyt suspected that she was trying to make sure she was heard Upstairs. "Do you think we will?"

"Yes. Jesus is Lord, Poppa. And Momma says that Christ looks just like his father."

Hoyt did not challenge the idea. On the one hand, he was not prepared to say that Jesus was not Lord. Hoyt himself had been saved, although not by baptism but by the *Narwhal*. The submarine had delivered two tons of rifles, ammunition, and mortar rounds to the Philippine Scout resistance on Mindanao, then taken Hoyt off the island and removed him to Australia. Hoyt was in no position to say whether Jesus looked like God or looked like the commander of the *Narwhal* or, for that matter, looked like Dandy Don Meredith or Howard Cosell. On the other hand, Hoyt was not prepared to say that Jesus was mythology just because Hoyt hadn't seen Shirley rescued from much of anything, not personally. He certainly was not willing to tell Sonny that Jesus was not Lord or that no one really knew what Christ looked like. For all he knew, Sonny might have a direct link to Jesus. He hoped so. Still, he was curious.

"So, what does Jesus look like, Sonny?"

"He's blond and has a nice face. Momma showed me his picture on the television."

Sonny had believed that Jesus looked like a man in a pink dress with a blue robe draped over his arm, sitting at a big white table where twelve other men who had girl's hair and colored robes were arguing about something. Now he was relieved to find out that Jesus looked a lot like that other man on television, the one who lived on a sailboat in Miami and wore white suits and had a black friend and drove his Ferrari around very fast so that he could arrest angry people.

The Jesus that Shirley had seen on television wore a blue uniform instead of a white suit, but Jesus' clothes didn't trouble Sonny. He had seen Hoyt change clothes, sometimes into a suit when they went to Jesus is Lord's house on Sundays, and lots of times into coveralls, and he had seen a picture of Hoyt wearing an army uniform. Jesus is Lord could wear a blue uniform if he wanted to.

"Momma looked at his picture on television and said, 'Jesus Christ, he looks just like his father.'"

Sonny was content. He looked at the socket wrenches and at the oil filter strap wrench. There were a half-dozen rubber belts, fan belts for the pickup, different fan belts for the John Deere tractor, yet other drive belts for the stripper spring idler pivots, and he took each out of its cardboard sleeve, studied it, put it back. Hoyt kept one eye on the brush rolls and bats he was adjusting and another on his son.

"And we're going to go see him if there's a funeral. Jesus's father was a doctor and they had his funeral two months ago, but we didn't go." Sonny was studying the switch that turned the work light on and off above Hoyt's work table. "Momma says you were his best friend a long time ago."

Hoyt put the wrenches down and crawled out from the tight workspace. Sonny was holding his hand under the glow of the work light, letting it get hot, then taking his hand away before it was burned. Hoyt put his arm around Sonny.

"I don't exactly understand what you're saying, Sonny. "

"Momma says you were his best friend. She said it was a long time ago. God is older than everybody." He put his hand back under the lamp. "And Momma says it looks like we might be going to Jesus is Lord's funeral. If they shoot him."

Hoyt had to think about what Sonny was doing as well as what he was saying.

""It's not always easy to see how things work, Sonny. If you hold your hand up close to the light it just gets warm, but if you touch it, it burns you." Sonny touched it and Hoyt watched him wince with the burn from the metal. He held his son's hand and waited for him to quit blowing on his finger. "Sometimes things seem obvious but then when you touch them they're kind of tricky. Understand?" When Sonny looked up at him and nodded, he went on. "Let's walk up to the house. I need to talk to Momma."

The white mansion that Shirley had built on Hoyt's farm was a hundred yards or so across the farmyard from the barn. There was a white picket fence around the house and, in the front, an expanse of struggling lawn that separated the columns and overhanging front porch from the drive. In Shirley's mind it looked like Tara.

Hoyt never used the front door. He led Sonny around to the side gate and up the back stoop into the kitchen. Shirley was sitting at the kitchen table with her back to the door. She didn't turn around when she heard her husband and her son scuff their way into the house and walk into the kitchen. Hoyt could see from the back of her head that she was facing downward, her neck bent, her hands drooped in her lap. Something was wrong.

"What's going on, Shirley?" He waited for her to turn around or say something, but when she didn't, he pulled a chair up beside her and sat. He took her hand. "Sonny tells me that...."

"It's Virginia's boy, Hoyt. It's Peter. It's on the television."

Hoyt never completed Shirley's sentences or, as a rule, even asked her what she was talking about. People tend to not only say what they mean, he believed, but they tend to take a while getting around to it. Shirley always said what she meant and, in Hoyt's experience, if he asked her what she meant, she would say he wasn't listening and say the same thing again and then add two or three things more so that by the time she quit talking she no longer meant what she said the first time. He waited.

"They can't find him, Hoyt. It was on the television, some terrorists or Arabs or somebody pulled a gun on his airplane. They shot one of the passengers right there on television." She had to stop to gather her thoughts.

"So, they got all the pilots off, but not Peter."

Hoyt looked at the television set that Shirley had insisted on buying for the kitchen counter, a portable to watch while she was cooking or doing the dishes or, more often, drinking coffee after Hoyt went out to the barn. He turned the channels and saw David Hartman and Joan Lunden talking about Martina Navratilova. He switched channels and found Jane Pauley and Bryant Gumbel talking about Jerry Falwell. He decided to ask.

"What happened, Shirley?" He wanted to ask her why she told Sonny there would be a funeral but, again, he let her come to the problem in her own time.

"It was on television. It said that some Arabs hijacked a plane in the Middle East somewhere, a Pan American plane, and that the pilot was Peter Hastings. They showed his picture on television and it was surely Virginia's boy. Then they said that the Arabs were shooting people on the plane. They can't find Peter."

Hoyt had not seen Will since they graduated from high school. Hoyt and Johnny Bradley had signed up for the army right after graduation but Will, somehow, had come up with the money to go to college. When Hoyt came home on leave Will was away in the army in France. When Will came home on leave, Hoyt was back on active duty. Then, on the very day they dropped the bomb on Japan, the army called Will back. For all but a few days, Virginia had been alone from the day that Peter was born. Shirley had convinced herself that she had raised Will's baby, at least until Virginia took him and left town when Peter was about two years old.

Jane Pauley interrupted the news of Jerry Falwell's ordeals to announce that there was a bulletin. The screen switched to a live image of a 747 airplane sitting on a remote airfield in what looked like the desert.

"Gunshots have been heard inside the cabin of the jumbo jet," Jane Pauley said, "and a team of commandos is storming the plane."

At that moment, one of the 747's passenger doors popped open and a giant rubber evacuation slide spilled out of the plane and down to the pavement. Frantic passengers crowded to get out the doorway and onto the slide.

"Stay on this channel. Live coverage will continue," Jane concluded. Shriveled raisins with white gloves and tennis shoes began to dance and sing that they had heard about something on a grapevine. Hoyt turned the television off.

"It was Peter, and you told Sonny that he looked just like his father," Hoyt asked. "Is that it?"

Shirley nodded, yes, and began to shake a little bit. At length she said what was really on her mind. Her mind was filled with the memory of standing next to Hoyt on the porch of the house where Sandy now lived but, until then, had been Virginia's house. Shirley's father had stood on the ground next to the porch. Hoyt had stood next to the door, and Shirley next to Hoyt. Virginia had walked out the door with Peter and marched straight to Poppy Sullivan's old Ford. She and Peter had looked to neither the right nor the left nor in the mirrors and, when she started the engine and drove away, Virginia hadn't looked back. Shirley knew what she had done, she and her father and, in her mind, she and Hoyt. *Now, thanks to us, Will's dead and Peter might be.* She said what was really on her mind.

"Yes, Hoyt. Yes. I told Sonny that Peter looks like his father." She paused and took a deep breath, and confessed for both of them. "And, you know that this is our fault."

v.

There really wasn't much for Frank to do but wait. The prosecutor had called one witness in the sentencing portion of Artemis Washington's trial, a jailer who said that while Artemis had not actually attacked anyone in the jail during the months before his case to come to court, he had scowled at everyone and the jail staff was afraid of him. Artemis had taken the witness stand and said just one thing: "I didn't do this." He had scowled at Frank from the chair.

The prosecutor had told the jury to give Artemis a life sentence. The jury was now deliberating what punishment to assess to the now-convicted Bluff Springs rapist or, as Pat C. Oh had put it in the courthouse coffee shop, "whether a life sentence was long enough."

With nothing to do but wait, Frank took out the chapter that he had worked on the night before and began to proofread it.

"Mr. Hastings? Why so serious?"

Frank looked up to see Judge Leatherman in front of him. Leatherman

175

seemed to be in a festive, even friendly frame of mind, the probable consequence of an unfettered flirtation with the assistant district attorney now that
the Washington case was in the hands of the jury. The prosecutor, for her
part, seemed no less amiable for having been flirted with. Washington himself had been taken back to the holding cell to wait for the jury to decide his
sentence. His attorney was nowhere in sight.

Does he know that they're going to send the wrong guy to prison? he wondered.

Burnam had said to forget it, stuff like that happens all the time. *Does
it?* A more worrisome question was whether the prosecutor knew it. *Or Judge
Leatherman?*

"Good morning, Your Honor," he answered. He put away the typed
manuscript and stood up to say hello. "Everyone seems like they're in a
good mood. How long do you think the jury'll be out?" Leatherman didn't
know. "And, is this it? Is this your last trial?" That would explain the good
mood and, with no voters, no lawyers, no courts of appeals looking over his
shoulder, it would also explain why Leatherman was willing to be so open in
his frankly salacious coquetry with the assistant prosecutor. *She's quite good
looking,* Frank conceded, *but still.*

"Finito. Adios. Goodbye. Once this case is over, I'm through. Got your
story written?"

Frank did, mostly. It had taken less than an hour to finish the thousand words about Judge Leatherman's career, titled "A Life of Service,
then...?" It was a good piece, a history of Leatherman's view of the changes
he had seen in court cases and in society, but Frank had not mentioned
Leatherman's army career.

"Yes, but it's never finished until the paper runs it. You know what I
never asked you?" Leatherman didn't. "I didn't ask about your family."

"Nothing to write about. Don't have one. " The answer was snapped
out so quickly that Frank knew he had touched an exposed nerve.

"My mistake, Your Honor. I'm sorry."

"Forget it. Lost my wife, kids moved away. I'm just like any other old cowboy, spent too long out on the range and never very good at the bunkhouse
part of it. Hey, you know what a real Texan is, don't you?" Leatherman's
eyes weren't precisely a twinkle, more of a leer. Frank did not. "None of that
sheep stuff. No sir, maybe back on the range, lot of sheep out in San Angelo.
But a real Texan's a man who's screwed Scarlett O'Hara, Rosie from the

Cantina, and the Yellow Rose of Texas, a real triple hitter. Ha ha ha."

Ha ha ha? Do I laugh? Do one better? He tried to remember any sheep jokes, pig jokes, cowboy jokes. The main door to the courtroom opened behind him. *So this Australian guy, sheep herder, was engaged to this girl but he kept putting the wedding off and...* He realized that Leatherman now was leering over Frank's shoulder at whoever had walked in.

"Like that one. That's one good-looking girl. You a real Texan, Hastings?" He gouged Frank in the ribs and leered again. Frank turned to look.

"I guess not, Your Honor. She's definitely not a yellow rose."

She was willowy, and very pretty. Her thick dark hair, however, was naturally straight, and her skin was a shade that was neither light black nor dark white, an opalescent luster that defied category.

"How do you know?"

"Well," Frank replied, "mostly because she's my wife."

Eleanor paid no attention to Judge Leatherman or, for that matter, to anyone or anything in the courtroom. She saw Frank and walked straight up to him.

She should be in class....

For his part, Frank started to introduce her to someone he now would have preferred to not know himself, but there would be no escaping. He then realized that Eleanor had come to the courtroom to find him, but not to learn the fate of Artemis Washington.

Eleanor was taking very deep breaths. Her eyes seemed to have lost their light and her mouth seemed afraid to speak. Frank ignored the judge and the prosecutor and met Eleanor halfway to the courtroom door.

"Are you all right?" he tried to ask. She clearly was not. She took his hand and studied his face.

"Frank? Sit down. Something's happened."

vi.

Candace asked Rocky and the station manager if they would tell her anything more. The grim station manager admitted only to what Candace was going to learn from watching television anyway.

"Somebody named the Abu Nidal Organization is demanding a crew to fly to Cypress. Apparently the Pakistanis in charge of the whole thing tried to play him for time. They strung him along for about ten hours until the airplane's auxiliary power unit shut down and the lights inside the plane failed. Then the hijackers opened fire inside the cabin. We think they've shot some passengers and flight attendants. There's no reason to think Peter is one of them."

He didn't know how many were dead or injured but he did know that someone inside the 747 had had the presence of mind to blow the emergency evacuation slides. Hundreds of passengers had tried to jump off the plane and run to safety.

"Look, we've got a room for you at the crew hotel, somewhere to rest and get away from this crowd. I know it's hard but... go get some sleep. Call anybody you want to, check on the kids. Get something to eat. It looks like it's going to be a long day. We'll come get you the moment we know anything."

Candace wouldn't have needed a doctor at all, nor even a sedative, if Rocky had escorted her out through the ticketing area the way he had escorted her into Stapleton Airport. Unfortunately, they walked out through the concourse where hundreds of passengers were jammed into the Front Range Coffee Shop, all of them watching CNN on satellite television.

"In a dramatic development today in that Pan Am standoff, Pakistani security stormed the plane when gunfire erupted inside the cabin..."

Candace turned, looked, and saw grainy footage of the bleak desert landscape, of the 747's rubber evacuation slides erupting from each boarding door, and a scrum of humanity pushing and sliding and jumping out of the airplane to get free of whatever unseen thing was inside. Police officers, armed with automatic rifles, pistols, and batons, frantically climbed up the air stairs and disappeared into the plane. CNN continued,

"... one of the terrorists chased the passengers all the way to the ground when...."

She watched a figure climb out from inside the airplane's front landing gear door, crouch low, and jog underneath the plane to the underside of the passenger emergency slide. Peter, still wearing his navy blue captain's uniform, sprinted back to the main landing gear and stepped out in full view from behind the slide. He walked quietly up behind the swarthy, frantic, Pakistani man who was waving his pistol at the fleeing passengers at the foot of the slide.

Peter raised a pistol from his side and shot Shuja in the back of the head.

The terrorist jerked, slumped, and fell face forward in a pool of his own blood. Frantic passengers screamed and raced away as best they could.

Candace watched as Peter stepped over the man's body, lifted his pistol, and fired a second shot into Shuja's head. She watched the body twitch, twitch, stop. Then someone ran up behind Peter and raised a hand with a gun in it.

Peter jerked forward, his eyes bulging, blood spurting from under his captain's cap. His pistol flew from his hand and, as Candace fainted, Peter crumpled to the ground.

Chapter Fifteen

Family and Friends Remember Hero

Third in an Exclusive Series by *Gazette* Reporter
Martin Burman

AUSTIN, TX—The Gazette, in an exclusive report in Friday's edition, detailed how terrorists from the Abu Nidal group of extremists stormed Pan Am flight 73 as it waited to take off from Karachi, Pakistan, for Frankfurt, Germany, with the loss of at least twenty lives and over one hundred injured passengers. Yesterday, *The Gazette* reported that the hijacking was thwarted by the bravery of the Pan Am crew, including pilot Peter Hastings.

Today, we regret to report that Peter Hastings was killed as he tried to protect a group of passengers who were escaping from the jumbo jet when gunfire erupted. At press time his widow could not be reached for comment. This exclusive report by the *Gazette* draws on memories and information from his family and friends.

The Pan Am Airways pilot who, two days ago, saved unknown numbers of lives by shooting an Abu Nidal terrorist who had hijacked his plane in Karachi, Pakistan, was a long way from home. Peter Hastings was born during World War II in the cotton farming town of Tierra, Texas, while his father was in the army in France. His mother, remembered as the daughter of a revered local newspaperman, worked in the local war ration office. Family friend Shirley Carter remembers the day she and her husband, Hoyt Carter, raced to get Peter's mother to the hospital, an early sign that Hastings would live life at high speed. "I was there when he was born and it was a close call. I thought she was going to have that baby in the truck. His daddy was five thousand miles away fighting in France and my own husband had just come home from the war. We loved that baby like it was ours. Everybody did. We still do."

The family moved after the war to the sleepy town of Bridle in the far north of the Texas Panhandle, where Hastings grew up as the son of the local country doctor. He spent countless hours lavishing his attention on an addition to the family, baby Frank, and Hercules, the family dog. His love of flying was apparent from an early age when he learned not only how hard it was to build model airplanes but also how easily they broke when he made a mistake, many of them having to be assembled over and over as Hastings learned by trial and error. He first flew in the backyard, where he practiced the art of takeoff and landings and taught Frank how to fly off the backyard picnic table, and by dropping bombs on the family storm cellar, which they called their "nuclear bomb bunker."

Boyhood friend George Grumman, Jr. remembered Peter Hastings as a superb high school athlete. After years of playing touch and tackle in the backyard, Hastings went on to excel in football and basketball and to run track, setting records for the local high school. He even won fame riding bareback at the summer rodeo at archrival Sundown. He was the first student from Bridle to win a place in any military academy. "I remember that Peter came back from the academy for Homecoming my senior year too. The school superintendent changed our tradition just for him and Peter escorted the Homecoming Queen to the center of the field during the game. People still remember that night." Grumman revered him so much that he wore Hastings' jersey as a senior and it brought him luck

– Grumman was the first Bridle athlete to win a major college football scholarship.

Hastings also turned heads at the Air Force Academy. Academy officials remember him as the only cadet in academy history to so successfully complete the boot camp escape and evasion course that he was never caught by his drill instructors. Friends also remember when Hastings became famous for rescuing Billy XV, the Naval Academy mascot, who broke free of his pen before the first-ever Air Force–Navy football game, and returning him to a grateful throng of midshipmen.

Hastings went on to a distinguished career in the Air Force where he reached the rank of major during the Vietnam War. A C-130 pilot, his missions and exploits during that conflict were so secret that they have not been disclosed to this day, according to a family spokesman. After he left the Air Force he flew for Braniff Airways and, more recently, for Pan Am.

Hastings is survived by his wife, Candace Hastings, and children Tiffany and Jeff of Colorado Springs, Colorado, and by his mother, Virginia Hastings. He will be sorely missed by family, friends, and colleagues.

Arrangements have not been announced.

Chapter Sixteen

i.

Bridle took Homecoming very seriously. The familiar navy blue and white horseshoe of the Bridle Broncos appeared on the windows of the gasoline stations and at The Corral, the bank, and the dry cleaners. Drivers peered out windshields darkened by shoe polish horseshoes and commands to "Beat Sundown."

By all appearances, the current and former students of Bridle High School were festive. Those who had played and graduated and moved away returned in large numbers. Those who had played and stayed welcomed them back. At The Corral, at the barbeque and the parade, wherever two or more of them were gathered, they replayed past glory and cheered for the team. It appeared to be a happy time.

Appearances were deceiving.

"They ain't a damned thing I can do about it, Tog," Bump said. "Money's gone."

Tog stood in front of Bump's farmhouse and asked one more time, when would construction begin? When would the dreams of new homes, close to work, in a community of good schools and churches start to come true?

They would not.

Somewhere between the electrical utility trenches and the cable distributor pads, the lot surveys and street surveys and set-asides for septic fields, Burford Acres had passed away. A small road grader had carved some temporary paths across Bump's emaciated wheat field. Little orange flags sprouted at regular intervals to mark out for the home-seeking workers of the beef packing plant and the helicopter factory, the railroad workers and the bomb assemblers, the plots that would have been theirs. Then, everything stopped. The unfortunate fact was that the bank that had promised millions of construction loan dollars to Panhandle Investors and Crawford Strategies had itself gone broke.

"Feds took the bank over, Tog. Don't you read the newspapers?"

Tog did not. He leaned against the window of his pickup truck to keep from falling, watching Bump's bald head and the ragged bois d'arc trees weave and dip before his eyes, mirages of failure that Tog knew well. If his chest hadn't hurt so badly, Tog would have believed that he had died and gone to Hell. He took a deep breath, then asked Bump if he could borrow a couple of gallons of gasoline from Bump's tank to get back to town. The only thing worse that Tog could imagine was being forced to attend the other event on the Homecoming calendar, the one not written on the official schedule.

Peter's memorial service was arranged to take place at the church in Bridle at two in the afternoon, to be followed by an open house at the old Hastings home at three. All were invited. All were expected.

"I don't care if Satan himself shows up, Tog," George had said. "You're going. At noon you're going to sit up there on the parade float with the rest of your class and ride up and down Main Street and you're going to be nice to everybody. Then, when the parade's over, you're going over to Doc and Virginia's house to help your mother."

"They're selling it," Tog interjected. It was a mistake.

"It's not sold yet and you're going to shut up and help your mother get it ready for the open house. Then at a quarter to two you're going to be sitting in a pew at the church and you're going to keep your mouth shut and shake hands with everybody and that includes Frank, and you're going to listen to them talk about Peter and then, when it's over, you're going back to the Hastings' house and eat cookies and drink tea and listen to whoever is there tell stories about Peter Hastings and probably about Doc too and maybe even Frank and Virginia and you're going to keep your bumblebee in your butt and your mouth shut and help clean up when it's over. Got it?"

Tog's mouth was shut but George could read his face as easily as if it was open. Tog's face said, 'And if I don't?' George answered that as well.

"And if you don't, you can be the first tenant of Burford Acres because you aren't sponging off me and your mother for another ten seconds. I'm unhooking Bambi from my electric line and my telephone line and taking off the gas and water hoses and I'm dragging it out to Bump's farm. Got it?"

Thus, although George didn't know that Burford Acres had ceased to be a budding paradise to which he could exile Tog, George did have the minor satisfaction of seeing Tog accept defeat. For that reason, and no other, at a quarter to two, Tog was forced to scoot over in the church to make room for a fat woman, a balding farmer, a slender man with only one arm and a tall young man dressed in a polyester suit.

"Jesus is Lord, Momma." Sonny's face beamed with joy and he trembled with pleasure, gripping Shirley's hand first, then Hoyt's. "Did you know Jesus Christ?" he turned and asked Tog, who was shifting over on the pew to make room. "Momma says that he looks just like his father. Poppa was his best friend. There is a lot of water under the bridge."

Tog turned to his left to find that the tall young man not only was talking to him but also touching his leg and pointing to the front of the church where a large easel displayed a collage of pictures of the late Peter Hastings. Tog's newfound companion appeared to be a couple of years younger than himself, tall and slender, and with gently flowing blond hair, a sort of defective Viking prince whose breathless enthusiasm made Tog think that Sonny might be the introverted tenor of a barbershop quartet who had suddenly discovered hootenanny music, or an insurance salesman.

"Did I know Jesus? I don't getcha," Tog answered, pushing Sonny's hand off his leg. He concluded that Sonny was the youth director of an out-of-town Protestant church. "Jesus? You come all the way from Colorado?"

"Don't mind him," Shirley interjected. "Sonny's special. He thinks that Peter Hastings looks like Jesus Christ. I'm Shirley Carter. We live in Tierra. You probably knew that because they wrote a big newspaper story about me when Peter was killed. This is my husband, Hoyt, and our friend, Sandy Clayton. He's the barber. It's a real nice town." Hoyt and Sandy nodded hello to Tog.

Tog made a mental note of Sandy's empty coat sleeve and wondered how he could cut anybody's hair with just one arm.

"Nice to meet ya."

"Sonny's just a little confused, sir." Shirley nodded at the pictures of Peter. "He saw that picture of Peter Hastings in the newspaper and thought it was a picture of our Lord and Savior. He loves everybody. What's your name?"

Tog told them his name, then looked around the church to see if it could be any worse. It could.

Most of the boys who had played football with Peter Hastings had come as a group to the memorial service. Tog saw them take seats together nearer the front of the church and he now understood what had been meant when someone on the parade float had asked whether he was going to wear his football letter jacket to the church with them. Even worse, Marshall and Becky sat beside them. Their daughter Elizabeth was there as well, dressed in her blue-and-white Bronco cheerleader sweater and skirt. A defilade of old school teachers crowded in behind. Mr. Grumley, who had been their superintendent, sat next to Mr. Lancaster, their old football coach. It was, Tog realized, the first time he had noticed them together since the night that his leg was broken on the ice on Main Street. They turned to gaze around the church and saw him, nodding in recognition. Tog nodded back. He should have been with them, the old team back together, but now there was no place for him. He stayed where he was.

The next rows were filled with the current football team, followed by the cheerleaders, the pep squad, and the town officials of Bridle. These consisted of Mr. Altgelt, the mayor, Miss Blanchard, who kept books at city hall, and Mr. Hunt, a general factotum who emptied Bridle's trash barrels, sprayed DD-T on the streets in the summer, and mowed the weeds around the water tower. The remainder of those who crowded into the church were the ordinary people of Bridle, friends of Doc and Virginia, retired school teachers, the men who had run the booster club for the last thirty years, and church ladies. Most of them gazed at Peter's pictures and nodded and whispered about him.

That could have been me, Tog thought. *I could have gone off to Tech and made the pros and Bridle would have retired my number and then they would have held a big funeral for me when I got killed, but hell no. I'm just the one who got screwed because the younger brother of the man this retard thinks looked just like Jesus Christ caused me to get my leg broken on that fucking ice so he wouldn't get caught firebombing the football field.* Tog looked around the church to see if the man who had wrecked his life had entered the building.

A thought nagged in the back of Tog's mind, that being honored by a state funeral meant he would have to be dead. *Better him than me,* he thought. That led to a different thought—Peter Hastings again was upstaging him with the Homecoming queen, *except this time it's not Becky. It's Elizabeth, Becky's daughter.*

"I'm sorry, ma'am. I didn't catch all that," Tog replied. He wondered how long the fat lady had been talking and what she was talking about.

"Well, Virginia and I were best friends. And my husband here, well, he and Will—you probably knew him as Dr. Hastings—they were best friends, too. The four of us were just like the Musketeers. And then the war came and scattered us across the world like so many flowers in the wind." Tog watched Shirley lift her eyes to Heaven to emphasize the dark days of World War II when "...we all did our share to save mankind. I don't see Virginia. She's the reason I came ... to support her. Virginia always did run late."

"I don't know, ma'am. Mrs. Hastings, well, she's not doing too well." Lucille had told Tog she would be surprised if Virginia came at all. "I'm not real sure she's gonna make it this time, not with her mind like it is and all."

"What do you mean, her mind like it is and all?" Shirley asked. "Hoyt, did you hear that? Virginia's not doing well with her mind and all. What's wrong with her mind?" Hoyt looked away.

"Well, you know, she's kind of old." Tog realized from the look on Shirley's face that a woman her age didn't want to be called old. He plowed on. "Like, she doesn't remember anything. You talk to her and she can't remember your name five seconds later. You'd see her all dressed up and all and you'd think she was the most normal woman you ever saw. But then there at the end, when you'd talk to her, she got so she didn't even answer you, just kind of looked off, you know?"

The minister came in, followed by Candace and the children, and a man wearing a Pan American Airways dress uniform. Frank and Eleanor entered last, and Tog saw that the gossip was true.

He did marry a nigger! Tog had a hazy and unkind notion of octoroons and mixed bloods but nothing in his experience included women of the raj.

The congregation rose, just as it had done for Will's funeral, this time to honor Peter. Peter's body, however, was not there to be honored, the diplomatic wheels of Pakistan being at a standstill.

"We're here today to honor our friend Peter Hastings. Peter was the husband of Candace and the father of Tiffany and Jeff. He was the son of Virginia Hastings, and, of course, our beloved Doctor Will Hastings. Turn to number 322."

Number 322 was *The Battle Hymn of the Republic*. The football players and bankers, the coaches, farmers, teachers, pilots, and ordinary cheerleaders sang, "Glory, glory hallelujah..." joining their voices to proclaim that Peter Hastings had, "...with a fiery gospel, writ in burnished rows of steel, as a man born of woman, crushed the serpent with his heel." Even the worst of voices sang praise for the dead man who had put Bridle on the map.

"Be seated. That was beautiful. I believe Peter would have loved hearing you sing," Reverend Antsley continued. He took a deep breath. "When I learned about Peter's heroic last hours and moments, and when Candace called to ask me if I would conduct this memorial service, I thought of all the memories of Peter and realized that this young man was destined to die for us." The collage of pictures of Peter, the pilot, the running back, the bridegroom, the cadet, the hero of the Vietnam War, beamed down on them all. "I am going to call on several of you to share with us the story of Peter Hastings, beginning with the woman who was witness to his birth."

Tog was startled to see the reverend point to him. Instead, it was the fat lady next to the retard who stood up and made her way to the front of the church.

"Hello, most of you probably know from the newspaper that I'm Shirley Carter from Tierra," she said to them, without the least self-consciousness. "I was a witness to the birth of the baby Peter. His mother was such a frail little thing that when she came to me and said, 'Shirley, I need you, I think this baby's coming,' I thought, Well my goodness this baby's already a month late, and no wonder. I turned to my husband, Hoyt, who wasn't my husband then, but he had wanted to marry me for years and years, and later on I did let him, and I said 'Hoyt, we've got to...'"

Shirley told of the birth of the baby Peter as she remembered it. Some of it was true.

"Well, we had lost our doctor to the war, and Dr. Hastings, that was Peter's father, he was off in the war too, so I had Hoyt drive us all the way to Clovis for Virginia to have that baby. It was the war."

Clovis? Tog thought.

Clovis? Frank thought.

"...and that little hospital, we sat for hours and no one would tell us anything, and we could hear the screams back there. Now I knew what it was like, being a woman, but Hoyt you could see he had never heard screams like that, and I had to tell him she'll be all right, it's normal and sure enough..."

Shirley spoke for thirty minutes.

"... and that was the miracle of Peter's birth. Well, I practically raised him until they moved off up here. We taught him to walk and to talk and to feed himself and his numbers and letters. That's how we taught babies back then, so it broke our hearts when Virginia and Will, who you call Dr. Hastings, moved off after the war. So when those Arabs killed him it was like they killed our own little boy." She smiled at the grateful throng and took her seat without the least notice that Hoyt, wide-eyed, appeared to believe she had lost her mind.

"Well, that was, that was... especially important." Reverend Antsley, worried that half the congregation was ready to flee, hurried the service along.

Lucille Grumman told them about Peter as a very small child being chased by a bull. The shop teacher was astounded at Peter's carpentry when, at age 12, "...he showed me this whole fleet of model airplanes, every one of them perfect." They laughed when the sheriff said that as boys he and Peter had "...poured a radiator bag full of water into an old bottle of MD 20/20, and got a bunch of freshmen boys drunk on 'Chateau Eau.'"

There was a last speaker.

"My name is Robert Hammond," said the man in the Pan Am uniform, "but Peter called me Rocky, and it stuck. We were roommates at the Academy. I've heard about the big Homecoming here in Bridle where Peter wore his Academy uniform, and it's fitting that we're here on that same weekend. But, you know Peter, and so you know there's more to it than that. The Naval Academy came to Colorado Springs that weekend for a football game and brought their mascot, a goat. How do I say this?" Rocky paused and thought, then plowed ahead.

"In plain English, Peter kidnapped their goat. Everybody knew he did it but nobody could catch him. He swiped the goat right out from under the noses of a couple of Navy cadets. The next day there was a bigwig lunch with the admiral in charge of the Naval Academy and the general in charge of the Air Force Academy and they were furious about the goat disappearing and, well, it took them a while to figure out that what they were eating was—the goat. Candace cooked it and fed it to them right before the game. When those big shots figured out that they had just eaten the Navy's mascot they wanted blood."

Every single person in Bridle believed unblinkingly that Peter Hastings could steal the Navy's goat and feed it to them without getting caught.

"Now, you're not going to believe this next part. Peter brought that goat back to life, as sure as I'm standing here. I don't know how he did it. In the middle of their rampage, the admirals and generals walked up to the chapel. The goat they had just eaten was there, on a leash, eating the lawn. No one knows how Peter did it, but he did, and the dean hustled him out of town fast to keep the Navy cadets from killing him."

Rocky was infectious. Every person in the church knew full well that Peter Hastings had done everything Rocky said he had done. There was more.

"After that, I would have followed Peter Hastings any place on earth. I followed him to active duty. I followed him to Vietnam. When we got home, I followed him to the Academy chapel where he and Candace got married. I followed him to Pan Am. I wasn't as good a pilot as Peter so eventually I wound up in the office while he wound up flying 747s. I watched Candace become the wife and mother she is. I watched his kids grow up. I watched Peter take care of his own mother, Virginia, and just recently he moved her to a nursing home to be close to where they live."

Rocky began to cry.

"I think Peter Hastings could have walked on water. I am proud to come to this town where he grew up and say these few words about him. You knew him as a boy, a brother, a football player, a great kid and son. I knew him as a prankster, a pilot, a loving son and husband and father. If I have any honor in my life, it is that I knew Peter Hastings by the most important title of all, though, and that was—friend. And, if I had been half the friend I thought I was, I would have been there when Peter Hastings tried all by himself to save a plane full of passengers from a dozen armed terrorists. His sacrifice was great. I have no doubt that you're up there now, watching over us. God bless you, Peter."

Even Sonny began to cry.

ii.

George removed the For Sale sign from the Hastings house and put it in the garage before people arrived for the visitation. Lucille had cleaned the empty house, leaving only marks on the linoleum where there had been a stove and refrigerator, imprints in carpets of a long-removed bookcase, a sofa, two chairs, corners of beds, a tear in the wallpaper near the boys' bedrooms. She wondered if maybe Virginia would come back home to live now, and wondered who would take care of her. *She'd be closer to Will, here,* Lucille thought, then decided to put off thinking about it for the time being.

People filled the little home and searched for something in common to talk about, the way people do at weddings and funerals. It was a relief after the church service.

"Those pictures up at the church, of Peter. My, oh my. Especially that wedding picture, them walking out of church under those swords and all. What a shame."

"The pilot picture."

"The one where he was quarterback."

"He was even better lookin' grown up than when he was a kid, even playin' football."

"Nobody played ball like Peter Hastings, that's for sure."

"And that story about the goat!"

"Did you know he flew a gunship in Vietnam?"

"It was a Puff. Puff the Magic Dragon."

"AC 130.

"A 707?"

"A 747?"

"He could fly anything. Pan Am says that boy knew more about airplanes than the Wright brothers. What a shame."

"It's not a shame. It's a crime. See his kids? They look just like him. At least he had kids. *They* had kids."

"His poor wife. The Arabs don't care anything about the families. They just kill people."

"They're crazy."

"Poor Virginia."

"Maybe it's best she, you know, kind of lost her mind."

"Well, she's still got the other one. Thank goodness for that."

"Not that she knows it."

"I'll tell you one damn thing. We ought to...."

Once the Arab question was settled, and the family pitied, they were free to talk about themselves.

"Not much. Haven't seen you in a long time. You doin' okay?"

"Yeah. Been pretty dry. Maize barely topping out."

"Cotton. Fields are wet."

"Cable TV. It's like being an engineer."

"Oh, yes. Clovis, it's true. We didn't have a hospital, so I up and drove her there myself and waited right by her side until he was born. Well, Hoyt drove. He was a beautiful baby. I run the bank there in Tierra."

Candace retreated to a cot that Lucille had put in the bedroom and cried herself to sleep. Jeff and Tiffany hid in the backyard. Sonny looked at the walls and windows and tried to work out where that long table had been, the one with Christ and the twelve men dressed like girls. Shirley told him and Hoyt to go stand in the corner of the living room.

"And don't drink anything, you hear? You've got to drive us home. I saw that Budweiser in the kitchen."

Becky introduced Elizabeth to the retired coach and the retired high school superintendent who had driven almost a hundred miles for the service.

"Yes, sir, I did win State. I'd never been to Austin before. Austin's different from the Panhandle. Did you know that the geological structure of the Central Texas hills has a fault line where the limestone gives way to rich alluvial farmland? Here I just run on flat ground but there where we ran the cross country meet there were hills and I had to adjust my breathing to six more respirations per minute and I shortened my stride by about four percent and it worked, which surprised me because I expected it to slow me down, but it made it easier to maneuver within a crowded pack. That newspaper story about Captain Hastings that said Mr. Grumman wore his jersey was mistaken because Captain Hastings wore number eleven in high school and Mr. Grumman wore number twenty-four, but you knew that because you were the coach then. They gave me number twenty-four to run in and I think I ran harder at State because I was wearing it. My favorite subject is chemistry. I want to be a doctor. Yes, I won."

The men had never seen anyone like Elizabeth. During the drive home they would wonder aloud if she was really Marshall and Becky's girl. She was.

Sandy made friends.

"I took care of Peter when he was a baby and I was about twelve. I was in love with his mother and she was twice as old as I was. She took in laundry, even helped in the cotton fields. Soon as I graduated I joined the army. Wanted to fly. We all wanted to be pilots. I feel really bad that I didn't see her before she, you know."

"Open that for you?" Marshall opened a Budweiser and handed it to Sandy. "What about Frank? Did you take care of him too?"

"No, today's the first time I saw him. Virginia, Mrs. Hastings, she just had the one, Peter. Someone told me they adopted the other one. I guess that's Frank. Oh, this? Vietnam. Had a helicopter shot out from under me. It could have been worse."

Marshall had heard before that Frank was adopted, but couldn't remember where. Becky told him she didn't believe it and to hush until they got home.

Eleanor led Sonny into the backyard where they found Tiffany and Jeff, who asked her why she was black. "I'm not black, the way Americans think of it. I'm partially Indian, from my mother's family."

"You're not an Indian. Indians are red."

"I'm not an American Indian. I'm an Asian Indian, sort of. I've never been to India, but that is where my father met my mother."

"My father said Uncle Frank broke all of his model airplanes." Jeff crossed his arms to clarify that he held Eleanor responsible for her husband. He wanted to be mad at someone and was prepared to attack Eleanor, even though she was quite pleasant and he liked the way her words sounded, like she was talking on television and didn't say the letter 'r,' not quite. Her skin wasn't quite black, but it wasn't red either, like an Indian should be, but he liked looking at it. Nevertheless, he hoped that she would argue with him so that he could yell. "My father made a model of every airplane that ever flew and painted them perfect and now they're all destroyed and I never got to see them. I hate Uncle Frank."

Tiffany said, "We're not supposed to ask Eleanor about being black and you don't know anything about the airplanes because it happened when Daddy and Uncle Frank were boys."

It was then that Eleanor learned why the memorial service was in Bridle rather than in Colorado Springs. By bits and pieces they told her everything.

Tiffany was not mad at Uncle Frank. She was mad at her mother, who had left her with her other grandmother and gone away in the night, then had come home later and sat on Tiffany's new bed and told her that her father had been murdered. Nothing since then had gone right and none of it seemed to have anything to do with Uncle Frank. If anything, Tiffany didn't care about model airplanes; she had decided to hate all airplanes because her father was flying one when he got killed.

"You don't know if it's true that Uncle Frank broke all of Daddy's model airplanes and, besides, that was a long time ago." Tiffany also kicked Jeff in the shins in hopes that he would shut up about Eleanor's skin.

"Oh, no, Tiffany," Eleanor answered. "I do believe it's true. Uncle Frank told me that he did break apart your father's model aeroplanes. I told him that it was a wicked thing to do."

"Then why did you marry him?"

"Because I only knew him when he was grown up. People usually become very different than when they were little boys. And because when he brought me here to meet your granny and your gramps he brought me to this very place and told me about Hercules. Your Uncle Frank loved him very much." Eleanor considered telling them that Hercules was the only thing that Will had given just to Frank as a boy, but did not. "That is why he always took care of Hercules' grave."

"I hate this yard. I don't want to live here," Jeff volunteered. "There's nothing to do." To prove his point he walked over to the cross above Hercules' grave and kicked at it, then wandered to the cellar door and sat down. He ignored Sonny, who tried to straighten the cross, and also ignored Tiffany's finger-to-lips admonition to keep hush. "Mom says now that Dad is dead we may have to move here. I hate here."

Tiffany then remembered what else they weren't supposed to say to Aunt Eleanor.

"To live here?" Eleanor asked.

"Mother says our new house costs too much because Daddy is dead and the bank is going to take it away from us. I want to move back to our old house but she said they already sold it. Mother says it would be nice here because we'll know everyone but I don't want to know anyone else. You didn't grow up here. You don't live here."

Jeff wondered aloud whether Eleanor had grown up in a teepee, or had seen cowboys, but Eleanor only smiled at him and shook her head 'no,' while thinking about what Tiffany said. Eleanor knew not to pry. Instead, she told the children what they wanted to know.

"My mother's family was Asian Indians, not red Indians. But I grew up in England. It's very small and rains a lot and you don't know everyone, even when you think that you do. When I was out of university I had the chance to come to the States to go to school, so here I came. Your grandparents were already living here when your uncle Frank brought me here to meet them. I like it very much."

"My father said you worship cows." For Jeff, where there were Indians there were cowboys and where there were cowboys there were cows, which caused the cowboys and Indians to fight.

"On the contrary, I do not worship cows. I did have a rather nasty accident with a cow when I was in university. There was a bomb, really, a very old bomb, from a war a long time ago, that was hidden under the earth, and it just blew up. It did kill a cow and nearly killed me. So, I suppose I am a little afraid of cows and very afraid of bombs that surface after a long time and blow one up. Are you afraid of cows?"

Tiffany said no, that she was only afraid of losing her home.

"Momma will give you money."

They looked at Sonny. He was straightening the cross and trying to spell out 'H E R C'... when he heard the word 'bank.'

"Momma has a bank and she gives people money for their houses. She has a lot of it, and she's a cheerful giver." Sonny smiled because that's what you do when you want people to know you're telling the truth, and also because Sonny now could help Momma in her work too. "Was H E R C U L E S in Jesus is Lord's family?" He liked being at Jesus is Lord's house. It didn't look like the house with the big table and the twelve men dressed like girls, but it was a nice house, and Sonny liked that they kept a cross right there in the backyard. He also liked when people were happy, and the two children and the woman with the skin that wasn't white but wasn't black had been serious before, but now they were smiling, and that was the kind of thing people do at Jesus is Lord's house.

There was no furniture in Jesus is Lord's kitchen, no range or refrigerator, apart from two galvanized tubs of beer and Dr. Peppers and a large picnic table that Lucille had borrowed from the church to set out chips and snacks. A coffee urn and some paper cups hovered at the end. Hoyt felt like an intruder, a sneak who waited until Will was dead and now was trying to reconstruct his life by looking at an empty kitchen with a couple of dozen strangers wandering through Will's barren house.

"You're from Tierra, aren't you?" George intruded. Hoyt said that he was. "Didn't see you at Doc's funeral. Wasn't sure." George waited a few moments to see if Hoyt had anything to say, and continued. "Is that your wife, the lady who said ya'll grew up with Doc and Virginia?"

Hoyt realized that this man wasn't talking to him to pass the time of day; he had gotten to the point and it seemed like he had something on his mind.

"We were running buddies in high school," Hoyt answered. "I went off to the army and he went off to college. We kind of lost touch after that." Hoyt wondered why he lied to this man in Will Hastings' kitchen, not lying exactly, but putting out false signals. "They moved off up here after the war and I stayed home to farm. How about you?"

"Doc and Virginia showed up here one day," George answered. "Just young and dumb and broke like the rest of us, and needed a town that needed a doctor. The town loved them, both of them. Fit right in. Built this house. Well, we all built it, what I mean is, after a couple of years it was time for them to build a house, so we all pitched in. They could have built a mansion, you know, but they weren't showy people, just wanted something that was nice and simple and a good place to raise the boys. I drive by here every day and see this house and think about playing bridge right here in the kitchen, Doc smiling and Virginia tossing that red hair around and the boys playing football in the backyard. Good people, you know. Doc never talked about Tierra after the war." George looked up to see if Hoyt caught the distinction.

Hoyt did. He had the distinct sense that George Grumman already knew everything there was to know about Hoyt and Shirley. He also had the sense that George Grumman knew what had happened before Bridle, in Tierra, when Will had come home for good. Hoyt hadn't said a half-dozen words to this man and he felt his face changing color.

"So, that's your wife, isn't it? That one," and George pointed to Shirley, who was standing in the living room and dominating a conversation with

196

Becky Grey and Lucille. "Didn't know you raised Peter as a baby. You and your wife."

"She might of stretched that a little," Hoyt said. "I was home on leave when Peter was born and went back to duty after that. When I got discharged we got married, Shirley and me, and lived out on the farm. See that man with one arm? That's Sandy Carter. If anyone in Tierra raised Peter it was him. He followed Virginia around like a puppy and worshipped the baby. " Hoyt felt the urge to tell George the whole story about Virginia leaving town but couldn't imagine why. He didn't know the man; if Will and Virginia had already told the Grummans what had happened in Tierra, there was no need to tell them again, and if they didn't know, he couldn't see any point in hashing it out now, not with Will dead and Virginia's mind gone. *Let sleeping dogs lie.* "You said Doc never talked about Tierra after the war. Did you know him before then?"

George's mind left Hoyt, left Will's kitchen. In the brief moment that he looked away he remembered a skinny, sandy-haired army doctor doing short-arm inspections on a hundred GIs at midnight. He saw Will listening as Major Halliburton accused him of lying about something, about girls, about leave, about stealing rubbers, something. He was right back there, the night that Halliburton showed up at the Windmill Club in Piccadilly, drunk and mean, when all Will had wanted was to wait for his brother Peter to show up. Will scuttling through machine gun fire in hedgerows to care for some poor wounded guy. Will and Reverend Antsley's brother driving a jeep with Major Howie's body strapped to the hood into the rubble of St. Lô. Will pining away for a letter from Tierra. Will giving up on Virginia and falling for a simple farm girl. Will shot in the back in the courtyard of the chateau, gasping to stay alive. George Grumman would have done anything for Will Hastings, and did.

"Yeah. We were in the army together, for a while. In France," George answered. "Until he got wounded. I knew he was from Tierra." George stopped before mentioning the months that he had watched as Will waited to hear from Virginia. He had decided a long time ago that if Will could forgive her and marry her after what she did then George's place was to be Will's friend, not Virginia's enemy. His dying didn't change that. "He may have looked like a boy then, but I watched Doc crawl through hell to save a lot of shot-up kids. He had more guts than any GI I ever knew. And never said a word about it. Like I said, I'm surprised I didn't see you and your wife at the funeral. If you were running buddies. This is my boy, Tog."

Tog had been caught in the dual act of trying to avoid Frank and trying to get a Budweiser. He recognized the man talking to his father to be the father of the retard who sat next to him at the church; he seemed pretty quiet. Frank came up.

"And Peter's brother, Frank? You know him? How are you, Frank? Sorry about Peter. You doin' okay?" George waited for Frank to nod yes and shake hands. "That was real nice, what you wrote about him in the paper, Frank. Real nice. You and Tog go out back and catch up." It wasn't a suggestion; it was an order. "I'll talk to you in a while."

George waited until the two were beyond hearing, then resumed his attack on Hoyt. "To tell you the truth, I didn't see that Peter was raised all that great. He was a bit of a momma's boy. Virginia took on over him, new clothes, new footballs, new this and that, but when it came to Frank, he picked on that kid every day of their lives. Never saw two boys fight like those two."

Hoyt felt his face turning red and turned to look out through the kitchen screen door. In the backyard he saw Peter's two children and his own boy, Sonny, sitting in their best clothes on the ground. They were in a circle, calm, listening intently to a story being told by that dark, slender woman he had noticed, and it finally registered on him that she was married to Frank. Hoyt watched her look up at Frank and smile, not a romantic smile, but an assuring one, a smile that said she was fine and that Frank could go about talking with all the people in the house who thought that Peter was a wonderful brother and that he need not worry because she was there to catch him if he fell. Hoyt watched Frank draw a deep breath and smile back, and disappear around the wooden car garage with Tog.

Hoyt closed the door and turned to look for Shirley, only to see George Grumman walking around with a plastic bag, picking up empty cups and paper saucers and napkins in the living room. Shirley dropped some of her mess into the bag without looking at George and without interrupting herself as she explained to a half-dozen strangers, "... I love how it feels to help so many people with our little bank. I was raised to help people..." and Hoyt was ashamed of himself.

He had made a devil's bargain when he married Shirley, and the devil had won. Virginia had done nothing to him. Will had done nothing to him. The only thing the devil let Hoyt keep was Sonny, but the rest of it, his farm, his family, the little moral compass that had kept him on the right path, they were long gone. He knew that they had to leave.

iii.

"Hey, Tog," Frank said. "You're lookin' good." He leaned against the garage wall and gazed over the fence in the general direction of the school. A bass drum could be heard, thumping in rhythm to the blare of a badly tuned trumpet and some squeaky clarinets, booming across the blocks from the high school where the Bronco band was tuning up for the game.

He tried to not stare at Tog but the change was unnerving. Instead of the slightly loopy buddy who for seventeen years seemed to never change his tee shirt or blue jeans, Tog the grownup looked like a movie actor. He was dressed in a pair of denim slacks and a jacket, boots and a Stetson. His long hair drooped and curled over his ears and forehead and down his collar, framing a fine, handsome face. Frank figured that if Tog had ever had the brains to leave Bridle he could have married into a string of car dealerships, that or become a male stripper. "Lookin' good."

"Hey, Frank. You look all city slicker yourself." Tog actually thought that Frank looked like a cheap Sears Roebuck window mannequin, and gloated. He had imagined that Frank had gotten fit and masculine and was pleased indeed to see that the boy he had followed around like a dog had grown up to look like a clerk at the K-Mart in Amarillo. "You don't make it back here much, Frank. Nothing here, eh? Not for you. Guess you made it out of the war okay, huh?" Frank did not appear to limp or to be missing any arms or legs. Tog stared, looking at Frank for telltale marks of needles or a draining sinus like the head cases Tog had worked with at the bomb factory who had been in Vietnam and come home with a drug habit. Frank didn't even have that to show for it. "Married now, I see." Tog jerked his head in the direction of the backyard, where Eleanor was trying to keep Peter's children and Sonny entertained. He wanted Frank to know that he was on to him. "Big-shot writer for the newspaper." He did everything but bare his teeth, and Frank accepted that he had been asked to go outside for a fight. Frank didn't want to fight.

"What's on your mind, Tog? You seem to know all about me. Your dad said we had to catch up. What about you?" Frank had heard that Tog had married and divorced. "I haven't heard from you since, whenever."

'Whenever' was the night of their high school graduation. "What are you doing now?" It was awkward.

The bass drum boomed again. They looked down the driveway to the street to avoid looking at each other and saw Elizabeth and Becky Grey walk out of the house and across the yard. Elizabeth turned to wave goodbye and they got into Becky's car and drove away. It was time for Elizabeth to dress for Homecoming, to put on her ball gown and tiara and collect her bouquet.

Maybe it would be better, Frank thought, *living here in the Shire. Everyone a Bronco, loyal and true. No wars or stock markets or Bluff Springs rapists, just lucky blue-and-white horseshoes, forever.*

"I'm not doing a fucking thing, Frank. Not a fucking thing. You remember all that shit you got us into at Homecoming? Coach sent us out to Bump Burford's to clean out his chicken houses? Well, turns out Bump's a good old boy and he and I got to be pretty good buddies out of it. We were going to make a land deal out of his farm, but it went to shit. So I'm not doing anything. You remember that Homecoming don't you?"

Frank didn't say anything; the words coming out of Tog's mouth seemed to come from somewhere else, not from the good-looking stranger standing three feet away. He wondered if Tog was on drugs, or if he should be on drugs.

"You see that girl just walked across the yard there? That's Becky's daughter, Frank. Becky's daughter. Now do you remember Homecoming?"

"You lost me there, Tog. Are you talking about when Peter came back from the Academy? Sure. But I'm the one who got sent out to Bump's to shovel out his chicken houses, not you. And what does that have to do with Marshall and Becky's daughter?"

Frank had no idea, nor any way to guess, that Tog had planned his speech for twenty years. Tog had driven his pickup back and forth to K-Mart and dreamed of telling Frank about his painful hip, his scholarship, and especially about Rebecca Collins Grey. He had awakened in the Bambi and rushed to write down certain words that had come to him in his sleep, the perfect and accurate recital of a history that would make Frank grovel in shame at the things he had done to wreck Tog's life. He had stood on the bomb factory assembly line, before he was fired, and daydreamed of exactly what he would say to Frank for his perfidy. Tog had pushed yards, miles, of coaxial cable through sheetrock and had assaulted Saddam Hussein's bunkers and dropped hundreds of pounds of high explosive on Frank Hastings' home, wife, and car, all while practicing the last words Frank would ever hear.

Unfortunately, at the moment that Peter's death and George's order to talk to Frank had delivered to Tog the supreme opportunity to tell Frank off, Tog forgot what he had planned to say. He said only, "That girl should 'a been mine. You fucked me."

"What?"

"You fucked me, Frank. That Homecoming. You fucked up my whole life." There was nothing in what Tog had planned to say that would have made any more sense, so the accusation that he did make was as good as any.

Frank stared at him the same way he had stared at copy editors, drill sergeants, economics professors, and parking meter maids, each of whom spoke English but in the style of untutored nut jobs rather than as rational human beings. Frank then made the same mistake with Tog that he had made with them: he asked for an explanation.

"Explain?" Tog snarled. "Explain? I busted my hip on that goddamned ice on Main Street that you made to cover up your firebomb over at the football field. Didja forget that, huh? Didja forget that?"

Frank had forgotten it. It had been a boy's prank, and he and Marshall had moved on. *Marshall.*

"I made? I wasn't even there. It was you and Marshall, Tog. You used Marshall's old pickup. You filled the bed with water and drove back and forth on Main Street and let the water seep out the tailgate and freeze on the pavement. Marshall said when you heard the fireworks go off at the football field you jumped out of the truck and fell flat on the very sheet of ice you had just laid down." Tog made the ice so the men in town would slide around on it instead of chasing after Frank at the football field; Tog should have known not to step onto ice he had just made on the street.

It sounded rational to Frank. "And what's that got to do with Becky's daughter?" And, he wondered, *why are you so mad at me over it?*

"Your goddamned ice rink broke my hip and there went my scholarship, that's what."

Frank concluded, correctly, that Tog was so angry that he couldn't make sense. It was time to say goodbye. He concluded incorrectly, however, that Tog was ready to let him go.

"You ain't going nowhere, not until I'm through with my say. You think I didn't read that chickenshit you wrote about me in the newspaper last week, that crap about me wearing the great Peter Hastings' football number? That was your number. When my jersey got tore up you gave me your number, and you knew damned good and well from Day One the only way you could get any attention was for me to run your number into the record books and people would think I was you. When I did, Tech gave you the scholarship, not me."

"Tog, I'm going to go now. I'm sorry things didn't go the way you wanted. Take care." Frank tried to walk around him but Tog shifted and moved to block his way like a street thug. "What do you want, Tog?"

"I want my fucking life back, asshole."

"I didn't take your life, Tog. The only reason I played football that one year was to be on the team with you. Did you forget that I spent every day after practice and every road trip on the bus helping you do your homework so you wouldn't flunk off the team? And when Tech wrote the scholarship letter, it was obvious they were giving it to number twenty-four, not to me. I took it to Coach Lancaster to fix before you ever heard about it, and he fixed it. I ate crow for you, Tog, ate crow to the football coach who basically had kicked me off the team after Homecoming, and I did it so that you would get your scholarship, not me. Remember that? The only reason I set off that chicken-shit bomb on the football field was because you dared me to, after Lancaster told me he wouldn't let me go to the football banquet. 'You're not a real Bronco,' he said. And you got your scholarship."

Tog had forgotten all of that. Frank was turning out to be an even bigger jerk than Tog had planned, not even man enough to admit that it was his fault for Tog's life being such a wreck.

"And what about all the things we planned, Tog, you and me? We didn't leave town after graduation, Tog, because you didn't show up to go with me. We didn't go to college together because you didn't want to if you couldn't play football. We didn't join the army together, either, and when I got drafted, you didn't show up to go with me."

There could be a million reasons why Tog had not shown up. Frank had figured out long before then, long before graduation even, that his blood brother Tog, the one he had loved from the day he first laid eyes on him, had dropped him. By then he had not expected Tog to show up, certainly not for the army.

"I even wrote you letters, from Vietnam. I never heard back from you. Christ, you didn't even show up for my dad's funeral."

If Frank had stepped around Tog then, nothing more would have happened. Tog would have watched Frank walk into the backyard, say goodbye to Tiffany and Jeff, and shake Sonny's hand. Frank would have gone inside with Eleanor, said goodbye to whoever was still in the house, then gotten in the car and driven away. He knew, in his mind, that Tog had not agreed with him and certainly had not forgiven him, but Frank had done no more than list some facts that Tog had forgotten. He also knew that Tog was too addled to suddenly rethink the course of his last twenty years in the driveway of the Hastings house at a memorial gathering for the missing one, Peter. Unfortunately, Frank didn't step around Tog and walk away, because the last time Frank had come to Bridle he had walked away after being accused by someone else, Peter, of wrecking someone's life, Virginia's. Frank wasn't going to do that again.

"And you still haven't told me what any of that has to do with Becky's daughter."

Frank knew before he was through saying it that he should have stopped when he was ahead. Tog's face lost its color. His Stetson slipped on his head and his knees sagged. He leaned against the wall of the garage to keep from falling over. There was not any possible way that Frank Hastings had anything to do with Becky's daughter, except that there was.

"It was then, man. It was then. Becky was all I ever wanted. She was why I played ball. I was going to be a pro, and she was going to be proud of me, man. She was the reason I went out to Bump's with you after the Homecoming game, just so I could ride by her farm on the way out there and back. It was her place we ran away from home to that night after you busted all of Peter's airplanes; we walked out to her farm and went to sleep in the trees outside her house. And all I ever asked from you was one thing, to tell Becky to meet me after the Homecoming game and go to the dance. One thing, and you let me down."

Frank couldn't know it, but Tog still had the note he had given to Frank for delivery: 'Becky, meet me outside the gym after the game and we'll go to the dance. — Tog,' and that Frank had given back, undelivered, a week later.

"She liked you, man. Marshall didn't care about her, not then, and if you had asked her she would have said yes. But you didn't even give her the note, so off she goes with Marshall. Well, the rest, as they say, is history. One fucking thing in my entire life, and you stab me in the back."

For no particular reason, Frank remembered sitting in the dark on a rice paddy, watching two or three women in a village prepare to light their cook stoves with the most volatile and combustible liquid in southeast Asia, helpless to stop them from unknowingly making a bonfire of their homes and helpless to stop the colossally stupid major sitting next to him from turning a village full of hardworking peasants into a VC outpost of anti-American hatred. It was folly, and it was beyond his control.

Of course I didn't give her your note or try to get Becky to go to the dance with you—she was already married.

"I'm sorry, Tog. You didn't know, did you?" *Was Tog the only human being in Bridle who had not known that Marshall and Becky had eloped before their senior year?*

"Know what?"

Frank explained.

Not only did everyone else in Bridle know about their elopement, everyone knew to never mention it. Marshall would not have been allowed to play football. Becky would not have become Homecoming Queen. They might have had to withdraw from school. It was a different time, then, different rules. Parents, coaches, teachers, everyone knew that it was more important to leave them alone than to rock the boat. They were good Broncos, all of them, and the Broncos had to win, the team had to have its queen.

New facts rarely change settled history. The events of the past are interpreted by their outcomes, and only the facts that support the popular memory of the event are relevant to it. When new facts are uncovered they don't change history, only serve to reinterpret it. Tog's new fact, that Becky was already married, didn't change Tog's settled history, the one in which his life had unraveled because Frank had failed him. Indeed, it clarified his history.

"You son of a bitch."

"What?"

"You son of a bitch. You knew Becky Collins had already eloped and you didn't say a word. Hell no, you leave me in the dark like a piece of coal and I spend my whole life believing Becky would have loved me if she had just had the chance. If I'd 'a knew I could have moved on, but hell no! You let me sit around pining for that woman when I could 'a done better. College. The pros. Who the hell knows? Thanks for letting everyone in town think I'm a worthless has-been."

It did not affect Tog's history that he was just as worthless after Becky and Marshall formally married a year later as he had been before. "I'd have done anything for you, Frank. Run away from home. Gone off to LA. Hell, I'd of gone to Nam with you. But you fucked me. I'm glad I see the light now, you sorry son of a bitch. You never did anything with your life. Not a damned thing. You're nothing."

Frank had no doubts now; it was time to go. He moved to step around Tog and succeeded. He could feel the heat of Tog's hatred glowing on his neck as he walked into the backyard and found Eleanor. He took her hand, tried to hug Tiffany and Jeff, and shook Sonny's hand. As he stepped into the house he saw out of the corner of his eye that Tog had followed him into the backyard and now was shooing the kids away from the cellar door. Frank heard the heavy door squeak open and flop back against the berm, and saw Tog's Stetson disappear down the steps.

"Goodbye, Mrs. Carter, sir. Goodbye, Mr. Grumman, Mrs. Grumman. I think we need to go." Frank whispered in George's ear that he had upset Tog, and apologized. "Bye, Marshall. It's been good seeing you, even under the circumstances. Take care of yourself."

He also said goodbye to Sandy Clayton. For the briefest moment he felt as if he had seen Sandy somewhere before, but couldn't think where. Sandy put down his Budweiser and shook Frank's left hand with his own.

He left to go to his parents' bedroom, where Candace had taken refuge, and knocked on the door.

"Candace, it's Frank. I've come to say goodbye." He waited and, shortly, the door creaked open. Candace looked as if she had been run over by a truck. "Is there anything I can do for you?" He wondered why people said that, suggesting to the bereaved that they could do something vital, such as bring back the dead. Eleanor was the only person he had ever known who always made sense, and he hoped that she had found a way to comfort Candace. He wanted to tell her that he was sorry that he and Peter had argued, that if he had another chance he would not have upset Peter or Mother, but he didn't.

Candace said no, there was nothing he could do, and hugged them both and thanked them for coming. She wiped her eyes on her sleeve.

Tog was back in the living room when Frank and Eleanor made their way to the front door. He had a bundle in his hand, a bundle of letters, tied with string.

"These are for you, Frank." He handed the bundle to Frank and stepped back. "Found 'em when I was helping Mom clean out your cellar."

The letters were in faded envelopes, addressed to

> Virginia Sullivan
> P.O. General Delivery
> Tierra, Texas

Some were addressed to Virginia Hastings instead of Virginia Sullivan. At least one was a telegram. They all had an army post office address; the last few had the word 'France' scrawled below Captain Will Hastings' name. It took Frank only a few moments to realize that Tog had handed to him a bundle of his parents' war letters.

"Found these, Frank, thought you ought to have them," Tog said, and smiled his best smile. *Fuck you, Frank Whatever-Your-Real-Name-Is.* "Something to read in the car."

Frank and Eleanor were standing in the doorway when Rocky appeared and asked for Candace. Frank realized that Rocky was a better brother to Peter than he had ever been, that as Peter died he probably would have thought about Rocky a hundred times before he thought once about Frank. They shook his hand as well, and told Rocky that Candace was in the back of the house, resting.

They were thirty miles from Bridle when Eleanor began to read the letters. They were fifty miles from Bridle when she read the telegram, the one that Will had sent to tell Virginia:

> The baby and I made it out of France, now in New York, leave for Tierra, arrive Sunday on the 3:15 train. Now Peter will have a playmate.
>
> Love, Will and Francois

Eleanor expected Frank to slam on the brakes or skid off the road, and braced herself. In fact, now that it was out, Frank was almost relieved. No more wondering about rumors, about smudges on birth certificates and birth dates that seemed wrong, of doubts and whispers. He drove for another hundred miles, wondering what to do next.

Eleanor understood but, for the first time in her life, had no very clear way to sort out what should happen next. It didn't matter to her where Frank had come from nor, she was sure, would it matter to him once he found out. But, she also was sure, he had as much right to know who he was as Eldred Potts might have had the right to know more about who she was, had Bossy and the Luftwaffe not intervened. She had no intention of letting them or anyone else interrupt what she had to say to Frank. *And*, she remembered, *there is Beckett. Two 't's.*

"Dear," she began. "I don't think it will be that difficult." He stared straight ahead, over the steering wheel and over the two-lane highway. "To find out. Do you remember the books that your father left to you? It seems that one of them was not actually a book."

Thus, in the hours-long drive home, Eleanor soothed Frank. She comforted him and let him talk in circles about things suddenly being clear, of dark eyes and blond hair and stocky bodies and hugs not given equally. In the end, she listened as he rambled about what he should do. She listened to his plan, one that even if it succeeded would not likely tell her husband who he was, and she knew that she would be alone for a while. They did not turn on the radio, and did not hear the last news of the hijacking.

iv.

The Carter car rolled toward its destination without clear channel radio. Hoyt drove in complete silence, although Shirley did not.

"Did you meet that young man?" She described Tog with reasonable clarity, a good-looking man in a cowboy hat. "He's in development himself. He's going to put a hundred fifteen or so houses up on the outskirts of town. It's less than an hour to the major jobs in Amarillo. You know, the railroads, the airport, the nuclear bomb factory. He just needs a little financing."

Hoyt listened to her and understood that his wife was about to use the Bank of Tierra to carpet the outskirts of another farm town with cheap, poorly built houses. The Suburban ticked off the miles as it crawled down and up the road through Palo Duro Canyon, then south past endless cotton fields and windmills. *I'm almost seventy. It's time for me to stop sleeping with a woman who's sleeping with the ghost of Will Hastings.*

Hoyt let the miles tick away, contemplating whether he would tell Shirley to get off his farm or, instead, he would just build a house for himself and Sonny on the other side of the barn. He tried to remember the intricacies of what loans and deeds she had got him to sign, and when, that had resulted in his family home being torn down and Shirley's mansion built, in wells drilled and fields irrigated where once he and his father and his brother and his sister had scraped out a bale of cotton in a year, and lived together.

It doesn't matter, he decided. *She already took my dignity. She can have the farm, too, as long as she leaves Sonny and me alone.* He would go into Lubbock the next day to find a lawyer. He did worry about Sandy, quiet in the backseat.

"I think he was there," Sandy said. There was a note of wonderment in his voice but, even so, Hoyt asked 'who,' and Sandy said it again. "I think that other son was there. Frank."

"Sure he was, Sandy. He was the one with the black woman, not black, you know, foreign, whatever." He thought about describing Frank in more detail but Sandy continued.

"Not at the house, Hoyt, but *there*. I think he was in Vietnam." Sandy tumbled over the memory of losing his arm in a fireball at the edge of a twisting mountain pass. "I think he's the one who pulled me out of the helicopter."

In Bridle, George, cleaning the house after the visitation, asked Tog what he had given to Frank in the living room. Without much difficulty, he got it out of his drunk and angry boy that he had found the fountain of Frank Hastings' youth in the form of Virginia's war letters, and the telegram.

George listened until Tog told him everything, then went home and immediately began to unhook the Airstream Bambi from his water, electrical, and sewer line. He was dragging it off his lot and out into the street when Lucille found him.

"What are you doing?" Lucille shrieked at him. She wrung her hands and even pounded her bony little fists on George's back, but he had hitched the Airstream to his pickup and was preparing to tow it to Bump Burford's farm in the middle of the night. "He's got no place else to go!"

"I don't care if he goes to Timbuktu or Shanghai. Or if Bambi and the computer king become the first happy residents of Burford Acre's hundred and fifteen deluxe mansions close to Amarillo and work and play. Do you understand what he did?" George explained it to her, to be clear, and that was all that George said.

They had talked about it before, dozens of times, hundreds, but only once in the last year and that was after Will's funeral. She knew that it could be bad, but pleaded anyway.

"It doesn't matter, George, not anymore," she argued. "Will's dead. Virginia's demented as a bedbug. No one's left. Who cares?"

George cared, even if Lucille no longer did. Thus, when Tog arrived after the Homecoming game he discovered that he had become a man without a trailer lot. Tog was not homeless but he was without a place to park his nineteen-foot-long aluminum demesne. No amount of hammering on the kitchen door succeeded in getting George or Lucille to open it.

A special edition of *The Bridle Bronco* was pasted up with the photographs from the memorial service. Tog Grumman was quoted to say that he fully believed that Peter Hastings was immortal. Peter's graduation photograph was re-framed and put above the football photographs at The Corral. Main Street was renamed Hastings Avenue.

Chapter Seventeen

i.

For several days Frank considered not going to France to look for his mother. Eleanor was wise enough to only think, not say, *Every time I suggest that you let it go, you don't, and it gets worse.*

Frank was smart enough to remember her advice and at least thought through the possibilities: *I don't find her, then what? I find her, then what? She's a lovely victim of the war who has wasted her life away wishing she had not let me go. She's a retired hooker who thought she had got rid of me. She died and everyone forgot about her.*

And he had unfinished business. He left Artemis Washington's file with the court clerk and walked across the street to his lawyer's office.

"Mr. Cheatham will see you now."

Cheatham's office was even grubbier than Judge Leatherman's. A garish wooden desk separated Cheatham in his overstuffed swivel chair from two armless, wooden side chairs that might have been rescued from a defunct insurance office. Stacks of unfiled sheets of paper that looked like rumpled copies of the sheets of paper Frank had just seen in Washington's courthouse file were piled at random on the desk. Cheatham himself rose and shook Frank's hand and asked what kind of trouble he was in.

"Trouble?"

"Okay, first rule. Everything you say to me is confidential. I won't repeat it to anyone unless in my opinion it helps your case. DWI?" Cheatham noticed that Frank was rotating his wedding ring with the fingers of his right hand. "Divorce. I'm real sorry. I can see it hurts. Let me get out a divorce questionnaire for you." He reached into a desk drawer and withdrew a form for Frank to fill out.

"No, I'm not in any trouble. I came to ask you about Artemis Washington. I covered the trial for *The Gazette*."

This put a different spin on things for Mr. Cheatham. Even when you lose a case, just getting your name in the papers is good advertising.

"We're going to appeal. There are very good grounds. No evidence connected Artemis to the scene, no scientific evidence. And all that blather about 'the rapes stopped.' That's not evidence. The real rapist might have died for all we know. You can quote me on it."

"I'm not doing a story on the appeal," Frank replied. "In fact, I'm going to quit the paper."

"So, then, what can I do for you, Mr. Hastings?" The lawyer took out a notepad to jot down whatever Hastings would say. Maybe Hastings was one of those do-gooders who wanted to do justice, or maybe he was applying for a job.

"Tell me why."

"Why what?"

Frank handed him the composite drawing that the police had made of the Bluff Springs rapist. The lawyer handed it back and looked at Frank with a cool, level gaze.

"Why you didn't tell the jury that this is the man they're supposed to be looking for?"

Cheatham's eyes narrowed; Hastings was the worst kind of do-gooder seeking justice, the kind who blames the lawyer.

"Washington told me that you showed up outside the courtroom and tried to talk to him. Bailiff ran you off. Any other lawyer would have reported you for that, Hastings. Leatherman would have tossed you in the clink for contempt of court. Then you wouldn't be quitting the paper; you'd be the news. 'Reporter breaches confidentiality, causes mistrial.' They'd talk about you right up until the day you go on unemployment. Me, I figured no harm no foul." He sat back in his big chair and crossed his hands to show how fair a man he was. "I let you off that time."

"That doesn't tell me why you didn't show this to the jury." Frank put the drawing back in his folder and looked up. The lawyer was having none of it.

"You're a smart man, Hastings. You figure it out. Time's up."

The interview was over.

ii.

Burman stopped editing *The Gazette* long enough to listen to Frank resign his job.

"Martin, I'm leaving the paper. I've got to do this."

Burman told Frank that he wouldn't authorize another vacation. "Christ, Frank, you took off to the Bahamas back in July, then to Colorado when your parents moved, then to.... Well, you know. I can't do it. Now, if you want to go up to Colorado and write stories about Peter I'll wangle something. But no, I'm not giving you a month off."

"No, thanks. I'm really leaving."

"Why, for crying out loud?"

"It's a long story. It turns out that, well, it's a long story. It's not easy being the little brother of a man people worship, somebody who had a miraculous birth and then dies so that others may live. It's even harder *not* being the little brother." He had never talked with anyone except Eleanor about being a foundling. "I'm going to look for my mother."

In the end, Burnam gave him a month's leave without pay. Frank was leaving Burman's office when he brought up the one thing that couldn't be left alone while he was gone.

"Artemis Washington. You've got to get someone on that before they ship him off to prison and Leatherman retires. He's innocent."

"It's yesterday's news, Frank. It's over. Forget it."

On the last day before he went to France, Frank drove to the address that was listed in the court record on Washington's application for a bail bond. To his surprise, it was not a housing project or tenement. A woman answered the door.

"Who are you?" she asked. She was used to white men coming around, most of them Mormons or police officers. "I got things doing. Come back later." She moved to close the door, but Frank asked her to wait a moment.

"It's about Artemis Washington," he said. When she raised her eyebrows, he continued. "I'm looking for this man," he said. "Do you know him?" He showed her the composite drawing of the Bluff Springs rapist.

"Sir, I don't know who you are or what you want, but you get off my porch, you hear? Get! Right now!" She slammed the door.

Frank heard noise inside the house. It wasn't clear whether the woman was talking to someone, or using the telephone, or just screaming, but his welcome was worn out, that was clear. He knew then that he would not learn why Artemis Washington was going to prison.

iii.

Eleanor agreed that she would keep a bag packed herself, just in case.

"I'll call you every Friday from somewhere, I promise."

"It's seven hours difference. I'll wait by the phone from the minute I get home until you call."

"And I'll write you every day. I'll send you a fax number from the hotel when I get set up."

"Are you sure you want to do this?" She wanted to give him one more chance to back out.

"No, I don't want to do this. It's just that not doing it seems worse. How else am I going to find out?"

"You have the drawings?" she asked for the eleventh time.

He opened his backpack to show her that Will's drawings still were where she had put them, along with the copy of Will's army personnel file and his passport and plane ticket.

They kissed, and then it was time. She felt the pain and hoped again that it was nothing. *Stress, probably, a little irregularity, that's all.* It was just a thing, a little mass, nothing more. That and some bleeding. It probably was nothing. Eleanor also told herself again that there wasn't any reason to worry him about it, not yet. *He'll find what he's looking for, and maybe even why. Then he'll come home. He is who he is, but he must learn that for himself.*

She watched him go into the airplane, watched the plane push away from the gate, watched it taxi and take off. She found the car and drove back to The Sisters, hoping that her snug little house with her cozy sofa and the little bed they shared and the kitchen so small that they bumped each other while they cooked would not seem like an empty mansion while she waited home alone.

"The Bar Cielo," she said aloud, and no one answered. It was the first time they had been apart since they married. "With moments quite."

Children of a Good War
Part Two

Chapter Eighteen

By late October, the days had less than nine hours of daylight. Sunset fell before six in the evening, causing long shadows to drape the garden table in semi-darkness well before the staff came around with the six p.m. medications. This had an effect on the poker game in that all bets were made in pills that the women took directly from the paper cups that the dispensary used to provide their medicines before dinner. It was much easier in the daylight for friends to sit at the table at the far end of the garden and nip a couple of capsules from their pill cups and recycle them through endless rounds of blackjack and five card stud. The effect of autumn, combined with the shortened time before darkness arrived, both lunar and absolute, was to drive their game indoors where the nurses and volunteers hovered over them like turkeys, watching every movement and quacking whenever any of them dropped a Catapres, or even so much as a Fibrelax, into their laps.

"Oh, dear, Coco," one of the volunteers clucked at Madame Dubois, "you've dropped a pill. Must not skip your medicine." The nosy pest smiled and plucked a furosemide from Coco's skirt. "Why don't you take it now so you don't forget?"

"I'll wait until we're through with the game, *cherie*. It makes me, you know." Diuril pills made Coco leak from time to time. Coco waited until the volunteer patronized her with a warning that she would come check after the game, then tossed a pill on the table next to the stack of cards that hid Madame Lavois' warfarin and Madame Dupré's Calderol. "You don't have to wait for the leaves to drop to tell the seasons. The little do-gooders show up like clockwork every October. Are you in or out?" She held her cards close to her chest.

"In," said Madame Lefèvre. "Top this." She spread her cards on the table, a deuce, a four, a nine, a ten, and a queen.

"No, not yet! You're supposed to bet first. Then, after you put your bet on the table, you say 'See you,' or 'Raise you,' and put another bet on the table." Coco was already exasperated at having to hide her pills from the medication volunteer; explaining the rules again to Madame Lefèvre was one more straw on her back.

"Can I say 'hit me?'" Madame Lefèvre asked. "I like saying hit me."

"Not in this game. That's in five card draw. Or blackjack. Take your cards back. I didn't look."

"Me either," said Madame Lavois. She quickly rummaged in her pockets to look for some Reglan to raise the ante. "Do you have any Darvocets? Those would make a nice bet."

Madame Dupré kicked Madame Lavois under the table and leaned over to whisper, "Leave her alone. She's doing the best she can."

They disagreed whether to let Madame Lefèvre take her cards back. Madame Dupré argued that she should be allowed to draw five new cards since everyone had seen that Madame Lefèvre had a rotten hand. It was put to a vote; the motion was denied three to one, Madame Lefèvre voting against herself because she liked Coco more than she liked Madame Dupré.

"Does it smell in here? This parlor always smells bad. Or maybe it just carries the smells. That's another reason to be outside. It doesn't matter who does what, you never smell it when you're outside. I call you all. Show 'em."

They played until the gelatin bell sounded. The volunteer came back to announce that Jell-O was being served in the dining room.

"I like Jell-O, dear. What kinds are there tonight? I hope there's red. I really like red Jell-O."

"I think there's red," the volunteer answered. "Would you like me to go and see? Or do you want to come with me? Here, let me help you stand up. My goodness, how long have you four been playing cards? I arrived at three o'clock. I think you were already playing then. I hope you're not cheating," she added with a smile.

"Since my husband died."

"I beg your pardon?"

"Since my husband died. You asked how long we'd been playing cards, I said since my husband died." Madame Dupré smiled up at the girl, a skinny sixteen-year-old dressed in a long skirt and buttoned shirt that was covered by a loose bib embroidered with the name of the nursing home, *Maison Feuilles d'Automne*, Autum Leaves Retirement Home. "That was in 1948."

"You've been playing this game since 1948?" She was astonished. "My parents weren't even born in 1948. You've been playing cards since before my parents were born?" The volunteer held Madame Lefèvre's arm to keep her from wandering away. "That's... thirty-eight years."

"She's telling tales, *cherie*. She moved here, when?" Madame Lavois looked at Madame Dupré, who sniffed the air and looked away. "You moved here when Dr. Genet died. When did that old coot die?"

"I don't remember."

"Yes you do. He had his last heart attack about the time that they put the new electric lines through Sainte Marie. When was that?"

"I don't remember." She did remember; she had lived in Autumn Leaves since 1966.

"I came here in 1972," Coco added. "You were here then. Playing cards, too. Both of you."

"Imagine," the volunteer chirped, "all those years and not going anywhere. I guess you do go out when your family comes. That must be nice."

Coco and Madame Lavois both tried to tell her to hush but the girl missed the signal and kept talking.

"I saw your son here last Saturday. I guess it was your son. He was all dressed up. Where does he live?"

"He wasn't my son. Why don't you take Madame Lefèvre for some red Jell-O before it's all gone?"

"Oh, they've got plenty of Jell-O. I'm always amazed at how much Jell-O you ladies eat. You must really like it. I don't like it so much myself. My family isn't big for eating sweets, not even chocolate. Have you all taken your medicines?"

"Yes."

"Yes."

Madame Lefèvre didn't remember taking her medicine, or betting it or even losing it to Coco, but she agreed and said yes as well.

"Are you sure you don't want some Jell-O? I'll bring it to you if you want. I'm going home in about fifteen minutes, but I don't have any plans tonight so I can bring it to you."

"No thanks, *cherie*, just take Madame Lefèvre for hers. That's a good girl." Madame Lavois waited until the volunteer had walked Madame Lefèvre out of the parlor and toward the grim little dining hall before continuing. She turned to Madame Dupré. "I'm sorry. She didn't mean anything by it. She's just a girl."

"I don't want any Jell-O. I want a cigar."

"Do you think the doors are locked yet?" Coco was pretty sure that the doors were not locked, at least not the doors that opened to the courtyard. "Besides, it's dark now. If we smoke, they'll see the cigar end glow in the dark." She had added the 'we' in a clever attempt to see if Madame Dupré had cigars for all.

"What are they going to do? Throw us out? You go have some Jell-O. I'm going outside." Madame Dupré glanced around the parlor to see if any of the staff was watching them. "The coast is clear. I'm breaking out of here." She pulled her sweater over her collar and buttoned it, then gathered her purse and stood up.

"Let's just watch some television. It will be cold outside now." Madame Lavois was still somewhat new to television, and liked it.

"Cold? You call this cold? When I was a girl we were in the orchards until we froze. And the cows. Every morning we had to be out of bed at four, freezing or blazing hot. We milked the cows, then led them out to the pasture, then roosted the chickens and the doves. There was this one cow..."

"Now see what you've done? You've got her going on about the cows and the chickens. 'There was this one cow that gave five litres of milk a day. I had to milk her every day for sixteen years. That's how I got such big....'"

"Stop it," Madame Dupré snapped. "It's true. All of it. Then I married Dupré and it started all over, only we had a bigger orchard. And the monks. The monks chimed out services from matins before dawn until nocturns after midnight. The bells rang a hundred yards from my bed. You could hear the monks chanting right across our pasture." She paused, remembering the early days of her marriage, more or less as they had been. "Then the girls came along and I had to teach them how to work. They learned real work because I taught them, none of this do-gooder meddling in nursing homes. I had them in the barn before the sun came up, while they were still in diapers. I'm going outside."

They let her go on talking. Madame Dupré told the same stories over and over; they all did. Madame Lavois had married too soon and spent her life washing and cooking for a lusty carpenter who died of liver disease when she was sixty. Coco had lived in Saint-Lô every day of her life. She felt some obligation to tell stories about indoor plumbing and visiting the museum, all to refine Madame Dupré and Madame Lavois, who for years had lived across the river from each other in the country. Coco had been delighted to learn that Madame Dupré's daughters had gone to school in Saint-Lô but dismayed to learn what had happened to them in the war. She tried to turn the subject.

"We didn't have cows in the city, dear. My father sometimes brought out the cart and we rode to Pont-Hébert to see the sheep. They looked to my romantic mind like clouds in the fields. I have always had a romantic mind. In fact, I was something of a poet. Sister Agnes told me I should apply myself. I wrote a poem before my *bac*, *On A Summer Evening*. It was about two lovers whose families hated each other."

"Yes, you've told us. None of the words rhymed and the lovers died. Are we going out to smoke or not?"

"I just have one cigar. Do you have your own cigars?"

"I have some chocolate. I'll give you a nibble if you want to share the cigar."

"Dr. Genet told me that I should have some chocolate every day." Madame Dupré disappeared for a moment, thinking back on the day when Dr. Genet had told her exactly that. 'Eat some more chocolate,' he had said, 'and smoke a cigar too. Best way I can think of to kill yourself. Do it every day.'

That would have been on her birthday, in 1964 or 1965, she thought. Madame Dupré always went to the cemetery on the anniversary of her death. Until he died, too, Dr. Genet always walked across the street to the churchyard to sit with her; then they would walk back to his clinic and sit quietly in his reception room, eating chocolate and smoking a cigar. "And take a little brandy. Every day. Before bed."

"Brandy, hah!" Madame Lavois chimed in. "Calvados more likely. *Fermier*." Madame Lavois had a healthy taste for farm-made brandy, having lived most of her life within two hundred yards of the Sainte Marie du Vire Calvados cooperative barn. On the other hand, drinking farm-made

Calvados was one of the most peasant-like things that Coco could contemplate.

"We had real brandy," Coco asserted. "And not just Calvados. Until my father died we had very fine brandy. And port, too. Did you girls ever drink port?" She liked to put on airs for the farm girls. Madame Dupré once confided to Coco that she even had made her own cheese, but that had been before the war, and Coco had mentally forgiven her for that hardship. "People gave Father all sorts of fine things. Brandy, AOC. Real Camembert." Coco looked up to see if Madame Dupré and Madame Dubois were listening. "And after the war, well, more than ever. People loved my father. He was the sub-prefect, you know."

"We know. Damn, you've talked so long we've missed the boat. Here they come."

Mademoiselle Garnier approached, a patronizing smile on her face. The rumor was that the only reason Mademoiselle Garnier was employed at *Feuilles d'Automne* was because when she ran the dog pound the dogs had refused their last meals.

"Dinner, ladies. Come along, time for dinner." Mademoiselle Garnier hovered over their card table, her little eyes darting back and forth for signs of contraband. "You've already missed the gelatin. Come along. Why are you wearing a sweater, *Puce*? Are you cold? Let me pick up your cards; you go ahead."

The three women hurriedly snatched the cards and their bets off the table and scooped them into their pockets.

"Hurry. You don't want to be last at the table, ladies, not tonight." Mademoiselle Garnier glared at them with what she thought would be interpreted as a kindly authoritative face, and walked on to the next table.

"Ah, dinner; duck with cherry sauce. And scalloped potatoes." They all laughed.

"I don't think so. It's Saturday. Saturday is steak *au poivre*, with fried potatoes." More laughter.

None of them had enough teeth to chew duck or steak, nor had *Feuilles d'Automne* attempted to cook or serve either since Christmas the year before. It was commonly agreed among the residents that the ducks sacrificed for that holiday meal had been raised in a stone quarry.

"Chanterelles. Onions, and braised chicken."

They laughed again and agreed that chanterelles, onions, and braised chicken would be lovely, a last meal fit for a duchess. They stood, patted their pockets to hide the Darvocets and cigars, and followed Mademoiselle Garnier in the direction of the dining room. The odor of salted cabbage baked into softened white bread crusts hit them before they left the parlor, and each of them wondered whether they would survive the autumn.

Chapter Nineteen

"I call to order this Cabinet Meeting of the Democratic Parliamentary Federal Islamic Republic of Pakistan. The ministers will please identify yourselves for the tape recording."

The ministers knew that the tape recorder would preserve the meeting for review. They also knew that it was bugged, since Abdur Rahman was not present in the meeting.

"Foreign Affairs, please. I am Khan."

"Law, please. I am Pirzada." Pirzada paused after announcing himself, wondering if Foreign Affairs, Khan, would make a play to take over the meeting.

"Interior, please. I am Khan." Khan, Interior, had already informed Khan, Foreign Affairs, that this was entirely an internal affair. Law would have his day, of course, but Law would not conduct this train. "Praise be to Allah."

Seven voices chanted as one.

"*Allahu Akbar.*"

"Defense, please. I am Khan."

Please to be quiet, Khan, Defense, for Allah's sake, the others thought, collectively summarized as, *This is not a war. The hijackers did not attack Pakistan. They attacked India, or Israel. Maybe America.*

"Media, please. I am Salik."

Salik was generally considered to be nothing but a button pusher whose sole function was to push the broadcast button when the president or one of the ministers gave him a script to broadcast.

"Internal Security. I am Khan."

"Intelligence, please. I am Farman Ali. Let us begin."

All of them, particularly Ali, Intelligence, assumed that Rahman, ISI, was listening on the bugged taped recorder. It might have been Abdur Rahman's secretary. It might have been his brother or his aide or just the man who cleaned his boots. It might have been Abdur Rahman himself, hence the suspicion that even if the cabinet meeting was ordered by the prime minister it was really Abdur Rahman's show.

"Agenda Item Number One: the hijackers."

Internal Security. Khan spoke up.

"I am pleased to report that we have captured each of them, praise be to Allah. General Tariq Mehmood directed the commandos at Jinnah Airport, but at our cost of two martyrs inside the 747. He captured two of the terrorists inside the airplane and two who attempted to flee in the crowd. Zayd Safarini was arrested at the hospital. Wadoud al-Turki, an Iraqi, was seized while trying to flee the country."

Iraqi dog, one of the ministers thought.

Iraqi warrior for peace, another believed.

"Of the two captured inside the airplane, one is Muhammed Abdullah ar Rahayyal, a Palestinian."

The bug heard a sigh of resignation come from an unknown minister. *A Palestinian attacking an American airplane and killing Indian Hindus is not automatically a bad thing,* the bug thought, *but he should not have killed our Pakistani commandos. The Palestinians never know when to stop.*

"Are you sure ar Rahayyal was a terrorist?"

"Who asked that?" No one answered.

"Yes. A passenger pointed to him hiding in a passenger seat, sitting on a Kalashnikov with only two bullets still in the magazine. He is a terrorist. I am certain of it." Internal Security paused. "Jamaal Rahim, a Palestinian. Muhammed Ahmed al-Munawar, another Palestinian. All of the men are in custody, God be praised."

"Where? Where are the hijackers?"

There was a silence around the table. In the end, a voice announced quietly, "I have them." The ministers were silent. The man who had them was Ali, Intelligence. "Continue."

"May I speak?" said Law. "We have prepared the most thorough and complete report of the activities of the hijackers. We shall charge them with murder, conspiracy to murder, and *mot sharia.*"

"No, my brother Law," said Foreign Affairs. "Such charges are not sufficient." He waited for their attention. "The Americans are angry. Very angry. May I—"

"Please stop, my brother Foreign Affairs. America is not an agenda item."

"Forgive me, please," said Foreign Affairs. "I believe America is related to Item One, the hijacking."

The thought balloons around the table would have surprised no one.

America transships arms across Pakistan to Afghanistan to fight the Russians.

America is the enemy of our ally's enemy so America is our ally.

But America is infidels and Jews. It is the ally of Israel.

The ally of my enemy is my enemy.

Why are we helping the Americans fight the Russians?

"Please, sirs. We must be decisive and immediate," Khan, Foreign Affairs, continued. "It is not just rifles for our Afghan martyrs. There is the matter of...."

Foreign aid. All of them considered it; none said it. *American money.* Realizing, or at least suspecting, that they were being listened to, Law and Justice broke the silence with a statement of principle for the record.

"I will not pervert the course of justice to please American money," Law announced.

No one bothered to answer Law since he already had surrendered custody of the hijackers to Ali, Intelligence. The course of justice would be perverted until Intelligence told Law to tell Media to announce the date of the trial and, it was hoped, before they told him to announce the verdicts and the hangings.

"I am Khan, Defense. It is the policy of Pakistan to cooperate with the American defense of our Afghan allies."

No one really cared what Khan, Defense had to say. The hijacking was not an invasion.

"What do the Americans want, please, Foreign Affairs?"

"They want us to deliver the terrorists to them."

The recording was quiet for a very long time. The collective thought balloons of the ministers reflected the sting of such an insult.

The attack on the airplane was most unfortunate, yes, but nothing personal. The Palestinians do that sort of thing in Libya, in Rome, in Malta. This one just happened to have taken place in Karachi.

The thought balloons also reflected individual concerns.

The real enemy is Israel. The enemy of our enemy is our friend. Palestine is our friend.

But if I mess this up Rahman might hang me. It is nothing personal.

"Hand the hijackers over to them? No. We will not do it." Internal Security went to a great deal of trouble to capture Israel's enemies and hand them over to Law. "We are not dogs. America is not our master. I vote No."

"I say to you, brothers, do not be hasty in your judgment. The Americans want the hijackers? Fine. I say give them to the Americans," said Foreign Affairs. "Abu Nidal blew up our airport"–an exaggeration– "and he will lob bombs into the trial of his martyrs. Let him lob them in the courts in Washington, not here." To his surprise, Khan, Defense, seconded Foreign Affairs.

"No," said Law. "The world looks to Pakistan for a model of proper law and justice." It would have been hard to find anyone in the world, at least in the non-Islam world, who looked to Pakistan for law and justice, but the world would be watching the trial of the hijackers. "Pakistan will not tremble at the threat of a bomb in the courtroom. We must put them on trial." *A show trial*, he meant, *to improve the image of Pakistan*, no bad thing at the moment.

"No," said Media. No one really counted Media's vote; Media would broadcast what they told him to broadcast.

Intelligence had the deciding vote.

"I have not concluded my investigation," Intelligence announced. "The men will not be given to America. They will remain in..." Everyone listened to hear exactly where Ali had hidden them, and everyone was disappointed. "...my custody. I will find the coconspirators who gave them the uniforms and an airport truck, passage through the airport gates, and the murderer of our fellow martyrs. I will not vote on the American question until my investigation is complete. Until then, I will keep them," Ali finished.

"In Central Jail?"

Ali, Intelligence, ignored the question.

"Is there anything else?"

Most were relieved. The tape recording would reflect a lively discussion of all points to do with the investigation and the disposition. They hadn't been cornered into making a decision. Ali, Intelligence, had taken charge of the direction the matter would go, as they knew he would. Indeed, if Salik, Media, had not been contacted by the United States Information Service desk at the consulate in Karachi, the meeting would have been over.

"Yes, please," Salik said to them all. "Agenda Item Two." He paused. He was proud to have an agenda item for his brothers. "Or is it Three? The American consulate has requested the last body."

"Please, Brother Media," said Foreign Affairs. "Have you been given some new authority to discuss affairs of state with the American consul?"

The others were quiet, relieved that Foreign Affairs had put Media in his place.

"The last body?" Khan, Interior, asked. "What last body?"

Salik, Media continued to volunteer.

"Yes, please. The American survivors were put on a hospital flight to Germany on September 15. All the dead were transported to their countries of origin, also on September 15. The only one still in Pakistan is the body of the American who shot Shuja on the tarmac. It was taken to Jinnah Hospital with the other victims and the martyrs."

No one knew quite what to say. Media continued.

"Let me read from the communique:"

The United States officially requests that the body of Peter Hastings, American national, who died in the attempt to seize Pan American flight 73 at Jinnah International Airport, Karachi, September 5, 1986, be provided to representatives of the consulate for transport to the United States and next of kin in accordance with the Vienna Convention on Consular Affairs and the SEAC Endorsement of the Strasbourg Treaty on the Transport of the Bodies of Deceased Nationals, 1973.

"The consul also has delivered to me the certificate of transport for our signature. He also personally gave me a letter from the man's wife, in an American state named Colorado. So, we should accommodate that." Salik paused. No one breathed. "Internal Affairs should repatriate the body."

"I don't have it."

No one had considered that Internal Affairs might have lost the body.

Maybe Internal Affairs had buried it. It was nothing personal. It could be dug up.

At some length, Ali, Intelligence, told them.

"I have it."

No one had anticipated that.

"Yes, sir," Media chirped. "Shall we direct the consulate to you? To collect the body?"

"No," said a voice from inside the tape recorder on the conference table.

A chill suddenly reached through hundreds of miles of listening devices and bugs and telephone lines and tape recorders and gripped Salik, Media, who had not appreciated until that second just how badly he had mistaken his position in speaking with the American consulate. Visions raced through his mind: loss of his house, and his automobile; his children removed from school; his wife followed through the streets, like a prostitute; assignment to a 500-watt radio studio in Hyderabad. Abdur Rahman had spoken. Salik prepared to quietly withdraw the question and pray he would not be arrested after the meeting. Ali saved him.

"No, Brother Salik, Media," said Ali, Intelligence. "Advise your American friends that we are continuing the investigation. There are, how shall I put this? Forensic questions."

Forensic questions?

"Yes, sir."

"But say nothing else, Brother Media. This is a matter of state security."

"Yes, sir."

"I will say no more." Ali closed the subject. Everyone, even Ali, Intelligence, breathed outward through their nostrils.

"We are not prepared to make a resolution of these matters today just to please the Americans. There will be a thorough investigation, as I have said."

"Yes, sir. Thorough. And if they ask?"

"Tell them in good time," Ali answered. "We do not humiliate ourselves and bend to the ground and touch our chins to deliver the Abu Nidal terrorists to America to beg for foreign aid. But tell them only that the decision will be communicated to them. In good time. Let us adjourn."

And that good time, Media, will be never. They will get the body of Peter

Hastings when I am through with it, his clothes torn by the wind and scattered to the vast wasteland, its eyes bulging, tongue blackened, when the last ounce of putrid flesh is stripped by the vilest crows and his coffin eaten into dust by termites and scorpions surrounded by thorns and weeds and rotting in the hardest stone ground. That is when they may transport the body of Peter Hastings.

"Praise be to Allah."

"*Allahu Akbar.*"

Chapter Twenty

i.

Officer Prudhomme walked out of the mayor's office, then down the cobblestone street past the pharmacy and the hair salon. The Renault, parked facing the wrong direction, was just beyond the bakery and only twenty or thirty feet from Dr. Genet's long-vacant house on the corner. Prudhomme walked across the square, past the fountain and onto the rutted path that led to the river-

The apple barn, a quarter mile from the town square, faced the meadow that stood between the river and Sainte Marie du Vire. Pup tents, pop tents, and random sleeping bags and cots dotted the meadow. Prudhomme was tempted to nose around to look for drugs but the mayor, Emil, had told him to fetch Jeremy and bring him right back. Making a mental note of what would be adequate cause for a future search, he walked past the campground and through the open doors of the old apple barn.

The village had converted the old Calvados apple barn into a summer youth hostel with camping in the meadow. Jeremy ran the hostel during his summer break from school and slept in a rough room inside the barn that served as the office. Prudhomme glanced around inside the barn as well, just in case any campers were smoking marijuana or, better still, going naked to the showers; saw nothing and no one, and so proceeded directly to Jeremy's room. Music, wretched and metallic, like locomotives going off the rails, blared through the closed door.

BAM! BAM! BAM!

Prudhomme giggled and banged on the bedroom door again.

BAM! BAM! BAM! He knocked a second time, then threw open the door.

A partially dismantled TRS-80 computer lay in piles around the floor, circuit boards here, a keyboard there, a clutter of cables and expansion slots alongside. In the middle of them there sat a twenty-year-old boy, his round clean face almost hidden by wire-rim glasses. He was quietly studying two thick black wires and apparently oblivious to the Wrang Buggas blaring from a boom box three feet away.

"Âllo? *What?*" Jeremy looked up to see the village policeman filling his doorway. "Oh, it's you. *Bonjour.* What?"

Jeremy was accustomed to Prudhomme's abrupt arrivals in the mornings. Convinced that the campers created a free-love drug zone every night, one in which all the evidence seemed to disappear by the time the sun came up, the policeman had made the campground something of a crusade.

"I have come for you in the name of the law!" Prudhomme stood to attention and tried to seem authoritative. "And turn that noise off."

"I'm adding a videotext card to the TRS," Jeremy said, holding up a small circuit board, "and a modem. I think I can interface it to the Minitel. Do you see?" He was a quiet boy, and polite. He looked somewhat hopefully at Prudhomme, who did not seem to grasp it. "I need to attach these three..."

"Turn it off," the policeman insisted. "The music. It's public disorder. And dress immediately. I am taking you in." Prudhomme knew that he wasn't taking Jeremy in but he thought he should let Jeremy know that he was in charge. "You have five minutes."

"For?" Jeremy pushed a button on the boom box. The Wrang Buggas shrieked and died as the cassette tape crunched to a halt.

"I am under the instructions of the mayor to bring you in. That is all I may say. Dress yourself." He stepped backward through the door and closed it approximately halfway, watching to make sure Jeremy quit tinkering with the computer.

"Inspector?" Jeremy called through the doorway. "Do you know where the kitchen is? Would you fix me a coffee please, while I put my clothes on?" Five minutes wasn't enough to screw the 40-pin connectors into the computer chassis and test the circuitry. "Plug the kettle in please, red switch. There is coffee in the blue jar next to the hot plate. I'll be right there." He found a crumpled shirt, pulled it on, and buttoned it, then turned back to the computers. "And please prepare one for yourself. Do you know what Uncle wants?" Jeremy feared that one of the campers had broken something in town or pestered the priest's duck, and that his uncle Emil, the mayor, wanted to tell Jeremy that it was his responsibility to keep the campers in line.

"No time for coffee," barked Prudhomme. "Let's go!"

Jeremy tied his shoes, pulled a jacket over his shirt, then led Prudhomme away from the barn. The morning had turned grey; light rain fell on them as they walked up the lane to the village.

"I have arrested a master criminal, a burglar. Doesn't speak a word of French," Prudhomme resumed. "He wants you to translate," The policeman led the way back up to Sainte Marie, where an elderly priest glared at them from the top step of the ancient church, his knobby hands gripping a walking stick. "Morning, Father," Prudhomme continued. Father Jean swiveled his head, scowling, to watch Jeremy and the policeman walk by. They turned in front of the church and walked to the first street alongside it, then up the cobbled pavement toward the city hall. "He might even have been planning a murder. It's very serious."

Jeremy noticed the Renault parked the wrong way on the street and suspected that Prudhomme's imagination outpaced his investigation; he would not have left a murderer sitting in the mayor's office with his uncle. They made their way along the street to the red, white, and blue flags over the entrance to the two-room city hall.

"Good morning, Uncle," Jeremy said to Emil. "It's about to rain outside." Jeremy pulled off his anorak and draped it over a wooden chair in front of the mayor's desk. "Who's in trouble? I'm trying to put my computer together, if it can wait. I haven't even had my coffee yet. Who's in trouble?"

Emil Lavois looked at Jeremy from across the cluttered span of a desk that was considerably older than he was. Emil had been chosen as mayor precisely because he had lived in Sainte Marie all his life and because he respectfully tried to help whomever in the village came in to apply for a marriage license or to register one of Sainte Marie's rare deaths or even rarer births. There was neither a window nor a countertop to separate Emil from anyone who walked in the door. Every time Prudhomme proposed installing something to make the mayor's office look more like a government office, by which Prudhomme meant a police booking desk, Emil said he would take it up with the council. Every time the council met, Emil's agenda consisted of keeping the gas, sewer, and water lines intact and the market stalls rented and the school in repair. His most difficult task was to keep Prudhomme from arresting every person in Sainte Marie for petty complaints, a service that Prudhomme believed was his duty but that Emil believed would change Sainte Marie into another zone of officious intolerance. The hostel, the campers, boom boxes that played the Wrang Buggas were battle lines that often divided them.

"*Bonjour*, Nephew. Sorry, no coffee," Emil answered. He nodded toward a pile of debris on the desk and continued. "But I do need a translator."

Jeremy tried to make himself look as if he was starving, but he did like his uncle and his summer job at the hostel and would do a lot of favors to keep them both. "Translate what?"

"Not just what but also who. Come with me." Emil picked up the pile of clutter from his desk and led them into the village's council chambers.

Frank's eyes darted around with the urgency of someone who might be in a great deal of trouble. He sat in a wooden chair at the council meeting table, barefoot, shivering in a stone room that was even colder than the street. Prudhomme walked over to take a position between him and the door, in case Frank wanted to make a run for it.

"Translate him," Emil said. "I want to find out what he's up to."

"So none of the campers are in trouble?" Jeremy looked at the man in the chair, the table, the silly policeman, and inwardly wished that everyone had just waited an hour.

"No. Your campers tend to be gap year half-wits, but at the moment, law-abiding half-wits. I'm not so sure about this one." He pointed to Frank. "I can't tell if he's a law-abiding half-wit or a criminal half-wit. He is an American, if that helps. He doesn't speak a word of French. Prudhomme thinks he was trying to kill his mother but I'm not so sure. So, help me to find out what he's up to," Emil asked. "Who he is. Why he was trying to get into Dr. Genet's empty house. What this man is doing in Saint Marie at all. Everything."

"Who is Dr. Genet?" Jeremy, a student, lived with his parents in St. Lô. His summer job in the village wasn't enough to make him one of them, not quite. "Where does he live?"

"Dr. Genet was the doctor here when I was a boy. He died a long time ago. His house is the empty one on the corner, just before the square. Prudhomme found him there,"—nodding at Frank.

The mayor dropped Frank's clutter onto the council table. There was a backpack, the ignition key to a rented Renault 5, a pair of Nike running shoes from which the laces had been removed, a man's belt, a pocket edition of a Larousse English-French dictionary (subtitled 'With 300 Useful Traveler's Phrases,') a Casio wristwatch, a wedding ring, a billfold that contained several one-hundred U.S. dollar bills and almost one thousand French francs and a Visa credit card, a wallet-sized photograph of Eleanor, a Texas driver's license, two sketches, one of which even Prudhomme conceded was a very old drawing of the center of Sainte Marie du Vire, and a handwritten note.

"So, Jeremy, just start by asking him who he is and what he's doing in Sainte Marie. And ask him about this." Emil held up the note that Frank had written. "Find out for me what he's up to," Emil asked.

"Oh, Uncle, I don't know if my English is good enough." Jeremy drew a deep breath.

"Do your best."

"Hello," he began. "They want me to ask you some questions. The policeman thinks you're a man of crimes but my uncle wants to know why you are in Sainte Marie." Jeremy's English was a shy blend of classes at the *lycee* and two summers of learning slang from campers. He didn't think that Frank looked much like a criminal. "I begin with who are you?"

"I'm Frank Hastings. I came here to look for my mother."

Emil said something to Jeremy, who continued.

"The policeman has told that you were breaking the door of an empty house. That's what he told me to say from you first."

"To ask me. It looked like it was a doctor's office. I wasn't forcing the door. I was trying to see if anyone was there. I looked in the window, knocked on the door. I thought..."

"Why do you crime into a doctor's office? The policeman asks you are for taking drugs."

"If I'm taking drugs. No. And I did not crime the doctor's office. I was not breaking into it. My father was here in the war, in France. This town and the house, they look like where he was in the army. Look." Frank picked up one of the drawings and showed it to Jeremy. "He drew this. I saw the house and it looks like the drawing. I thought maybe whoever lives there could help me."

Will's drawing was so detailed that it could have been a black-and-white photograph. He had stood on the opposite side of Sainte Marie's square and sketched the church and steps, the fountain, and the corner. The only obvious change was a red traffic sign with a horizontal white bar that meant **Do not Enter**, something Frank should have learned by reading the margins of his Michelin map. The same house where Prudhomme had arrested him was there next to the corner. Sainte Marie had hardly changed at all.

"When did he draw this?"

"He wrote letters in July, 1944. I think that's when he drew the pictures."

Jeremy explained that to the men. Emil told him what to find out next.

"The mayor says that no one goes inside that house for some years. That's why he thinks maybe you were a crime."

"Thinks?"

"I don't think the mayor is so sure you are a crime. He says the policeman was being careful."

Officer Prudhomme had begun to back away from burglary as a reason his prisoner had been at Dr. Genet's long unoccupied clinic; his retreat had been occasioned by Emil pointing out the absence of anything resembling burglar tools, either on Frank's person or in the Renault. "Not even a tire tool, Prudhomme?" Emil had observed.

Prudhomme's second theory had been that Frank was casing the house, a crime that would have called for burglars to hide in waiting inside an obviously empty house on the town square two doors away from the town hall but in no proximity to any structure of value, such as a bank or jewelry store.

Emil said something to Jeremy. Jeremy repeated it:

"He says that's why he sends the policeman to bring me. He tells me to ask why you do it."

"I'm trying to find my mother. I think she may live here. It's that simple."

Frank pointed to the note. Emil handed it to Jeremy. It was handwritten, laboriously worked out with the Larousse: '*Vouler aider moi chasser pour ma mere?*'

"Is you chasing your mother?" Jeremy smiled, then underlined the word '*chasser*,' and handed it back to Frank. "You have written a message that you are chasing your mother, like with an *arc?*" Jeremy didn't remember the word for bow, so he drew his arm back as if shooting an arrow. "*Chasser* means to find deer and rabbits to eat them. And you give your message you are *chassent* your mother to the only man in Saint Marie who does arrest you."

Frank began to suspect that translating vernacular American English might not always give him the right phrase.

"Okay, I'm not *hunting* my mother. I am looking for her. I'm trying to find her."

"I think maybe you should write *chercher*, not *chasser*. "Jeremy turned to Emil, translated, and silently agreed with Emil that their subject was more foreign than criminal.

"Good work, Prudhomme," Emil announced. You've arrested a man who's searching for his mother." He turned to Frank. "Do you speak any French at all?" he asked in French.

Frank did understand that phrase; it had been the third or fourth repetitive exercise on the language cassettes he listened to in the rented Renault. He also understood that now was not the time to practice French phrases. He shook his head, no.

"*Monsieur le Maire*," Officer Prudhomme insisted, "the note admits that he is trying to kill his mother. He was going to break into the old clinic to hide the body." A new theory.

"Ah, of course, Prudhomme," Emil answered. "He wrote a note in terrible French just in case he found a place in Sainte Marie to hide his mother's body but didn't find anyone who speaks English. That's plausible." Emil had objected the first time the Prefect had assigned a policeman to Sainte Marie, for fear that he would turn out to be someone exactly like Prudhomme. "That's even more complicated than your burglar theory and your casing a hideout theory." He turned to Jeremy. "Tell him to explain exactly what he's doing here." Jeremy translated.

"Let me start over," Frank said. "I can see where a policeman might misunderstand, but I wasn't trying to get in the house. I was looking for my mother."

Jeremy translated; Prudhomme replied.

"You thought your mother was inside Dr. Genet's house, waiting since 1944?"

"Slow down and hear me out. My father just died. After he died we found some letters he wrote, and some drawings, from the war. My father was a doctor in the army. He was here in the war, somewhere here, I don't know exactly where. And I was born here."

Emil watched them, expecting Jeremy to break in and translate. Prudhomme drummed his fingers on the council table and played with Frank's shoelaces, for which Emil smacked him on the back of his hand.

"He sent the letters from Sainte Marie and Sainte-Lô. Then he sent a telegram that said he was bringing me home from France, a year after the war." He waited to see if Jeremy understood. "I only just learned any of this. He never told me anything about it, that I was born in France or that my mother in America wasn't my real mother. This is the first time in my life I knew that I had a mother in France. I just want to find her, that's all."

"Didn't you ask your mother? Your American mother?"

Frank had not, but that took more explaining before anyone understood.

"She never said a word. Now she has aphasia. It's like Alzheimers, and she lives in a nursing home. It's like her memory was erased, everything blank."

He paused.

"The only one who ever said a word about any of this was my brother. He called me a bastard from the time we could talk, but nobody ever takes it seriously when your brother calls you a bastard."

Jeremy looked shocked; he would have taken it seriously if his brother had called him a bastard.

"I didn't pay attention to him. Not much. But after my father died and we found his army letters, and a telegram that says he's bringing me home from France after the war, well..."

"So why do you try to go into a doctor's house? Now I don't think they believe you."

"I wasn't breaking in. I was just curious. I don't know, it was just one of those 'Oh, I wonder if Dad knew this Doctor Whoever in the war?' things. The house, the street, everything looks just like Dad's drawing."

It was difficult for Jeremy to understand Frank's story and even more difficult to explain it to Emil and Prudhomme. Prudhomme didn't believe a word Frank had said.

"I do have a picture of her in the car," Frank went on. "My mother. Well, it's another drawing, not a picture, but it's pretty good. It was my plan to go to the places where I knew Dad had been, like here, then see if anyone recognized her from the drawings. Will you ask the policeman if I can go get the drawings out of the car? And I've got all sorts of records. If I can get my things out of the car I can prove that's what I was doing. Okay?"

It was okay. Five minutes later Frank, the mayor, Prudhomme, and Jeremy were back in the council room, looking at the rest of Frank's papers.

"Okay, these are my father's army records."

There was a copy of the remnants of Will's military service personnel file, the only records the government sent to him. The first was part of a microfilmed army order assigning Captain Woodrow Wilson Hastings to the 261st Medical Company, 29th Infantry Division, June 9, 1944. The other page appeared to be a record that listed the officers assigned to the court martial of a corporal Curtiss who was charged with the murder of a major Halliburton, to be conducted at Fourth Infantry Division Headquarters at Cherbourg in October, 1944. Will was listed as a witness. It took a while for Jeremy to understand what the pages meant and explain them to the mayor.

"He wants to know what this is." 'This' was the brief reference to the court martial.

"I don't know, to be honest," Frank answered. "I've never heard of any of those people, or a court martial. I'm guessing my father was a medical witness of some kind."

"The mayor says to ask if you go to Cherbourg to search?"

"Not yet, but I expect to."

"And the other papers?"

"These are the letters," Frank said. He showed them two letters that Will had written that mentioned that he and his medic were in Sainte-Marie in July of 1944 and the telegram Will had sent when he and Francois got off the boat in New York in 1946. "I'm Francois. Frank. And this."

'This' was the drawing. Even Jeremy saw what Eleanor had seen. Will had captured Géraldine, twenty or twenty-one years old, gazing back at him with a kind, gentle, face. She was not beautiful, certainly not in the way that any of them thought of beauty, but she had a slight and peaceful smile. A rough sweater was draped over her shoulders and around her open throat and neck. Wisps of her hair escaped from the edges of her scarf as if she had just tied it on her head, something she would have done only as she was getting dressed. Her expression was remarkable, wide, open, and she undoubtedly was in love.

"What's your mother's name, sir?" Emil asked, quietly.

"I don't know."

Prudhomme nodded skeptically at Emil; Emil sent him a look that was more than a shrug.

"Her first name? Her family name? Anything?"

"I don't know. I didn't even know she existed until a couple of weeks ago."

"The mayor says, so you are walking around the village, staring at women and looking in windows, and you don't even have a name?"

"These are all I've got to find her with. I don't know what I don't know. I thought if I found where Dad was in the army, the town and the farm and the other places he drew, if I showed her picture to people, sooner or later someone would recognize her."

Jeremy translated. Emil answered him.

"I understand," Emil said. "But tell him he has to stop."

"Stop?"

Frank had spent twenty hours on airplanes and another ten getting to Saint-Lô, worrying every minute about everything that could go wrong. The village he was looking for might have been taken over by factories. The river with the little hut on the banks might be covered up by new tract houses. He had faced the possibility that the girl wasn't even French: 'Dad was in Belgium, too – what if she was from there?' He also had admitted that he might not find her at all, or that she might be dead. Then there was the worst possibility: *Maybe she just didn't want me.* He had thought of everything that could go wrong except being ordered to stop looking.

"He can't just tell me to stop."

"He can. He's the mayor. And it's because of the police. They're, I don't know how to explain this. They are arresting people everywhere. Do you see the newspapers?"

"Of course I read the papers. I write for a newspaper. That's what I do." *At least, that's what I used to do,* Frank thought. "Why the newspapers?"

"Sainte Marie is a village, maybe there is five hundred living here." Frank had no idea what Jeremy was explaining. "This police will arrest for everything. He even comes to the campers and searches them. But in every town every police in France searches for bombs." Frank looked blank. "You understand? Bombs? In Paris, in the metro, you know?"

Frank didn't know.

"There is bombs in Paris. Bombs in shops and embassies, even bombs to the police station. The Arabs, they is killing people in France so the police now they look at everybody. If you only walks slow by a window a police is watching you." Jeremy paused while Emil told him to add something. "If you has done this in a door or a window in Saint-Lô they put you in the jail. The gendarmes are looking very much at foreigners right now."

Emil didn't speak English but he did speak 'bomb.' He picked up one of Will's drawings, of a faded building on a hill, surrounded by rubble, people trudging up toward it.

"*Bombes,*" he said. "*Saint-Lô.*" He tapped the drawings and Frank understood what he already assumed, that some of the drawings had been sketched in Saint-Lô. "*La guerre. Bombes.*" Then he spoke to Jeremy for a few minutes.

"This is what he says to you. Stop doing like you are trying to crime a house. If you go walking and looking, you must tell the police before you commence, not after. "He paused. "And the mayor, he says good luck."

"Good luck?" Frank began to pick his drawings and letters from the table.

"Yes. He does never see anyone like her. He would know her if she was from Sainte Marie. Everyone knows everyone. But he says good luck and he will make copies of the picture and send them to other polices and mayors to ask if someone knows her. And then he says you are to go."

Frank stood up. Prudhomme put a hand on his shoulder. Frank sat back down.

"At least charge him with the parking violation," Prudhomme growled. He was not sure that Frank was telling the truth about anything and his pride was at stake. "He broke the law with his car."

The mayor couldn't disagree; the Renault was still parked facing the wrong way on a one-way street, fifty feet beyond a red and white Do Not Enter sign. *I suppose I need to fine him for that; otherwise he'll drive around charging through street signs and scaring the wits out of people.* He retrieved Frank's wallet, counted the money, took out ten francs, and told Jeremy to tell Frank he needed to learn how to drive.

"You may go."

Jeremy followed Frank out to the Renault, then waited while he unlocked the car and started it. Prudhomme stood in the portal of the *mairie* and glared while Frank inched the car backwards toward the town square, then parked and got back out of the car. Frank then walked back to the house where Prudhomme had arrested him a couple of hours earlier and signaled to Jeremy to come stand with him.

"Look at the window," Frank said.

Jeremy had walked by the vacant house dozens of times without so much as glancing at it. It was modest, paint faded, glass dirty, and with ancient electric wires dangling above the doorway from a rusted light. There were a dozen houses in the village just like it. He squinted to make out the faded lettering on the window.

Docteur P. Genet
Heures 9:00 – 10:00 14:00 – 20:00

"I was just trying to find some connection to my father," Frank repeated. "I thought maybe, who knows."

Jeremy nodded, then pulled the hood of his anorak over his head to ward off the rain.

"Thank you for, helping. Translating." He waited while Jeremy nodded a polite acknowledgement. He walked alongside the boy until they arrived at the car. "Can I drive you anywhere?" Jeremy shook his head, no, and turned to walk away.

Frank saw the apple barn down the lane. There were still several tents in the meadow. A river flowed along its edge, bordered by trees and shrubs. No one was about.

"Is that where you live? I can drive you there, if you like."

"No, is just a normal walk. Goodbye sir."

"You don't believe me, do you?" He wanted someone to believe him.

Jeremy didn't know what to say; he had no experience in such things. He considered telling Frank that he had an American computer, even asking if Frank would like to see it. He instead decided to say nothing and walk on; he didn't know Frank and would never see him again. And, he thought, if Frank's story was true, Frank would go back to America without finding his mother. If she had wanted her son to find her, she would have found a way in the last forty years.

ii.

Emil waited until Prudhomme wandered off on patrol, then went back to his office and found his rain jacket. He hung a *Back Soon* sign on the front door of the *mairie* and locked it. Small gusts of rain drifted down the sidewalk and guttered off the roofs of the buildings. It was a two-minute walk to the corner, where he stopped for less than a minute to study the door and windows of Doctor Genet's decaying house and clinic. There were no scratches on the lock, no prise marks on the doorframe or window. Emil was satisfied that the American had been telling the truth, that he was who he said he was.

He crossed the street to the porch in front of the church, then walked around it and entered the churchyard through a rusting iron gate that was slung into the wall. The squat stone church was much older than the town and the churchyard was even older than the church. Many of the tombstones had begun to collapse into the soft dirt of the graves so that some looked like broken piano keys, others like no more than rocks, eaten away by centuries of hard rain.

Emil had attended the burials of a few of the people in the graves, friends of his mother and father, widows from the two wars, schoolmates who had gone away to work and come home with cancers and failing hearts. He had been the registrant of some of the deaths, people who already were ancient when he was a child and one couple he had known since boyhood who had been killed in a car crash. He picked his way through the graves, reading some names for reference, stopping for a moment just to pay respects and to recall good memories at others. The rain continued to fall during the fifteen or twenty minutes it took him to find the grave.

The Dupré plots were nearer the back wall than to the entry. The family had always been frugal; their tombstones were not adorned with carved roses or elaborate angels, nothing more than their names and the dates of their deaths. Emil had no memory of any of the family apart from old Madame Dupré, who had been his mother's friend for the last twenty years or so. He didn't believe he had ever met Monsieur Dupré. He already had concluded that if his suspicions bore out, he would ask Father Jean for details; the old priest was cranky and self-important but he was a source of town history whenever Emil had a question. There were no footprints on the path to the Dupré graves and, indeed, the stubby growth of weeds and clover that had survived the summer suggested that no one had visited them in quite a long time.

He found her grave next to her father's and wrote down the date of her death on a notepad that he carried in his shirt pocket. The grave was not well tended and he took a moment, even in the rain, to pull a few strands of nettle and bindweed from the edges of her tombstone, then brushed the clumps of resulting mud away with his bare hands. It was the part of being mayor he didn't like, the uncertainty, the looking into places where people hadn't asked him to go, making news where there really wasn't any news. He wiped her stone clean of the mud and stems and stood up, then made his way back to the *mairie*. No one was waiting for him.

The commune's registry of deaths was kept in bound books that were maintained in the locking metal cabinet behind his desk, on the side nearer to the door that led to the council meeting room, along with the registry of births and the index of criminal charges in the mayor's jurisdiction. It took several minutes to find the 1940s.

There were very few deaths in 1938 or 1939 or even in 1940, but he detected a perceptible increase in 1942 and 1943. The year 1944 recorded almost as many as the other years combined, but 1945 had fewer entries. He found it.

She had died April 16, 1945. The cause of her death was complications from the delivery of a child. Her mass of Christian burial had been celebrated the following day and she was interred in the Sainte Marie cemetery next to her grandparents. Emil was sad to see that she was not a married girl; he had suspected that she was not. For that reason alone he made the decision to not see what Father Jean might remember, at least not yet.

Chapter Twenty-One

"Hsst. It's that Arab again."

Madame Dubois came out of the examining room and jerked her head around, winking and nodding at the other women who were waiting to be called in for their monthly consult. She bristled and tugged on the collars of her blouse to imply that no Algerian doctor had succeeded in poking around on her septuagenarian bosom, not even in the sanctity of the examining room. It didn't matter that Dr. Joseph, as they called him, had been the doctor for all the women of *Feuilles d'Automne* for over a year or that he had never inflicted the least indignity on any of them. "Keep your hands on your purses." Madame Lavois and Madame Lefèvre winked back, and Coco took her seat next to them.

The nurse called out, "Madame Dupré," who rose and went to face the Arab.

Dr. Yousef Ben Khedda began very simply: "I would like to talk with you about your laboratory results. Your blood count is a bit low and you may be anemic. Your electrolytes are on the high side, meaning that you're retaining fluid. Your glucose levels are high." He showed her a sheet of numbers and medical symbols, which she waved away. "Do you know what this means?"

"Does it mean I'm going to die?" she answered. There seemed an odd note to her voice. "How long have I got?"

"How long have you got? I don't know. Patients just like you live for years if they take care of themselves. We just need to…"

"No," she interrupted. "I mean, how long must I live, Dr. Joseph? When can I go? I'm ready." She smiled to be sure that he understood that it was nothing personal to him, that she wasn't seeking attention or complaining of pain, just ready to go.

"Go? You're not going anywhere. As for as how long you've got, you might have a little congestive heart condition, I'm not even sure of that, but we can manage it if you'll help." Dr. Ben Khedda liked Madame Dupré. Of all the ladies at *Feuilles d'Automne* she never complained, never asked for prescriptions, and never disagreed with him. "Where would you want to go, anyway?"

"I've lived long enough, Dr. Joseph." She liked him also, even though he was Algerian, and his real name was Yousef. "I'm ready. If you'd just move things along I'd be grateful." She crossed her hands and smiled. He was very kind to her, she knew.

"Or it could be that you haven't lived enough, and you've just been taking someone else's medicines." He sat back on his swivel stool and folded his hands. "I know all about your card games. Madame Lefèvre always asks me if I'd like to sit in." He tried to appear stern by squinting his eyes and crossing his arms, but he knew it didn't work. "Let me listen to your heart. Then we'll talk. Okay?"

She agreed. He took out a stethoscope and moved it around her chest and her back until he was satisfied that he had a good sense of her heart. He peered into her eyes and made her stick out her tongue and cough a few times. He took her pulse and poked at her feet and ankles.

"Okay, I'm ready. Let's talk. Tell me what's going on with you."

"Nothing's going on, nothing new. I'm just tired of this life and ready for the next one. I'm well past eighty, you know."

"That's not a reason to want to die. You're past eighty and could live to be a hundred. Your heart and your lungs sound like a woman half your age. If you'd stop smoking cigars I wouldn't even be able to get you to cough."

"If I had to stop smoking cigars I'd take one of Mademoiselle Garnier's butcher knives and kill myself."

"Yes, cigars. That and your chocolates. I know about that, too. Look, let's go over some things. Today, you have a few of the signs of congestive heart failure. A month ago, you had gastric distress. Before that it was jaundice. You have something every month, but it's never the same. Do you know what I think?"

"No. I feel fine. I just don't want a life of playing cards with women who play for a year or two and then die. Do you know what it's like to live in a place where everyone you know is about to die?"

246

"I'm Algerian, Madame. What do you think?"

"Sorry."

"Look, here's what I think. Number one. Your symptoms change every month because you're taking other people's pills. You never get enough to put you in full-blown organ failure, and the pills I prescribe for you aren't strong enough to make a mouse sick." He paused; she sighed. "Number two. If you don't stop giving your pills to Madame Lefèvre you are going to kill her. She needs the Darvocet and she does not need your sedatives; they just make her worse." He paused again. All the women denied trading their medicines for Madame Lefèvre's Darvocets, but her lab tests didn't lie. "Number three. You're not telling me everything. The only thing I can say for certain is that you're depressed. Why?"

He waited for her to answer. He could hear the rumbling in the waiting room. There were more patients waiting to see him. To compound the problem of spending more time with Madame Dupré, the nursing home driver always took the ladies out for ice cream on their way back to the nursing home. He decided that they could wait.

"Let's talk about Feuilles d'Automne. Are they mean to you, or don't take care of you?" Dr. Ben Khetta knew that women in nursing homes hated being there until they made friends, but Madame Dupré had lived at Autumn Leaves so long that she didn't risk dying from loneliness. "Is something going on there that you want to talk about?"

He studied her, flipped back and forth through her chart, looked again. She had lived there for almost twenty years. She came from a farm on the west side of the river, and was a widow. Her husband had a stroke after the war and had died almost forty years ago. She had no particular illnesses apart from colds now and then, and a bit of cholesterol from a lifetime of milking cows and making cheese and cream.

"There's a note from the nurse at Feuilles d'Automne. 'Son came for visit. Patient locked room and refused to come out for dinner.' Two days later, 'Decreased affect.' That means you weren't your normal self, not talking to people or acting sad, or preoccupied. Do you not get along with your son?"

"He's not my son," she answered. Her affect changed from sad to angry.

"So who is he? Is this what this is about?" He waited again. Something in the way she flashed her eyes, for just a moment, suggested that he had hit a nerve. "If someone's bothering you, or trying to..."

"He's the son of a distant cousin. His name is Jean-Claude."

"Is Jean-Claude upsetting you?"

"No," she lied.

"Then it's something else. Can I ask you some questions, just general questions?" She nodded and he proceeded. "Number One. Are you basically satisfied with your life?"

She laughed, the old laugh he had seen before, and he was encouraged. She was not satisfied with her life.

"Number two. Have you dropped many of your activities and interests? I think they mean in the last month or two."

She laughed again, and said that she had not.

"Number three. Let's skip number three. Number four. Do you often get bored?"

"Yes, of course I'm bored. What was number three? Why did we skip that one?"

"It asked if you felt like your life was empty. I don't think we need to..."

"Do I feel like my life is empty? What kind of dumb question is that? I'm a widow. My best friend has breast cancer and another friend is losing her mind. My daughter, my beautiful daughter, well, she died. My husband lived through the war and had a stroke. I live in a nursing home. I haven't been home in over a year. And..."

"You haven't been home in a year? Why not? Where's your home?"

"North of Pont-Hébert, a very old farm."

"Did you lose it when he died?"

"No, it's mine."

"Why haven't you been home, then? Have you rented it out, is that it? It's normal to feel sad when you look back and you feel like all the things you lived with all your life—"

"Because I'm afraid of the guillotine." She was very clear on the point.

That stopped Dr. Ben Khetta cold. Madame Dupré was unusually composed for a woman her age. Their doctor/patient visits had been reasonably pleasant and she knew exactly what smoking cigars and drinking Calvados meant for her health. He expected her to say that the tenants had not taken care of the farm, or had cheated her rents, or simply didn't want her to come bother them on her farm; it was a familiar story. The guillotine was different. No one had ever told him they chose to stay in the nursing home because they were afraid of the guillotine.

"I left Chateau Dupré because Dr. Genet and Father Jean told me that if I killed Jean-Claude they would cut my head off. Not them. The judge."

Dr. Ben Khetta let his breath out. He had been a doctor for fifteen years, most of them in Saint-Lô. He actually liked being employed by the *Départment* to care for elderly patients and understood that his primary job was to keep them from dying too soon, or in pain. Some of them, like Madame Lefèvre, would develop Alzheimer's disease and he would lose them. Others, like Madame Dubois, would succumb to cancer and he would lose them too. They often confided their fears to him. But never, not once, had one of his old ladies told him that she wanted to murder someone. These were the rare moments that broke up the monotony of Yousef Ben Khetta's life.

He raised a forefinger to Madame Dupré to indicate that she should keep her seat, then went out to the nurse's desk and canceled all his appointments. He told the nursing home driver to take the others for ice cream, now, and that he personally would see that Madame Dupré got back to *Feuilles d'Automne*. When the clucking and rearranging were done he returned.

"Are you willing to tell me about this? Why you want to murder Jean-Claude?"

"I would kill him before I would let him inherit Chateau Dupré. He destroyed my family. He tried to steal my farm when my husband had a stroke. If I could cut his head off, I would."

"And this is the man who came to see you two weeks ago?"

"Yes."

"Why did he come to see you?"

She waited for a very long time before replying, and then said only that she didn't understand the details, not very well.

"Maybe you can understand it better than I can. Maybe you can explain it to me. Would you like to read this?" She reached into her handbag and took out a large envelope, then handed it to the doctor. He took it and noticed immediately that it was from a notary lawyer in Saint-Lô, addressed to her. He inquired by his expression whether Madame Dupré really wanted him to read the contents, and she nodded.

Dear Madame Dupré:

I hope that this finds you in the best of health and that you are comfortable.

I have the honor to represent your heir, Jean-Claude Martel. Jean-Claude has engaged me to study the most efficient manner to avoid Chateau Dupré going into escheat. That means that through no oversight of your own, the government of France will take ownership of Chateau Dupré on your passing away if you do nothing. The facts are very straightforward. You have no direct heirs within the French civil code. Your husband passed away in 1948. Your daughter died in 1945. Your sister Julia died in 1960. There are no other heirs who may legally inherit.

Jean-Claude has managed Chateau Dupré for you since 1945. He is the son of your husband's distant cousin, Roland Martel. Thus, he is your heir. However, due to the remote degree of consanguinity it is likely that the government of France will try to seize Chateau Dupré in escheat.

I have a simple solution. By signing the enclosed *Compromis du Vente*, you may rest assured that Chateau Dupré will not go into escheat and that your heirs will not have to sell any of it to pay the expenses of preserving your fine estate for the future. Accordingly, I ask that you read these documents and, then, call my office to arrange a convenient time when I, acting as a *notaire*, may supervise the execution of them.

With my best regards
Adolphe Trichet, Notaire

Of course it was depressing; even a doctor could appreciate the need to prepare for the inevitable. He put the letter down.

"Let me see if I understand. This notary asks you to sign your estate over to Jean-Claude. That's what these documents would do, I presume." He waited to see if she agreed with his reading of the letter. "But you hold Jean-Claude responsible for all those things you said, harming your family when your husband had a stroke." She nodded again, vigorously. "However, according to the lawyer, if you don't do this, the government will take your farm."

"I would rather suffer the death penalty than let Jean-Claude own Chateau Dupré."

"And this is why you're depressed. Jean-Claude manages your farm and wants to inherit it. He came to see you at the nursing home to pressure you into signing the documents, which you refused to do. That's clear to me, now. But, what else is there?" He waited for her to answer. Dr. Ben Khetta also had learned that one of the features of helping elderly patients with depression was easing them through the process of making difficult decisions at the end of their lives. "You have to make a choice, as I see it. Do you see that? Once you make a choice, this will all be behind you. But I'm not the one to guide you through this. You should get a lawyer of your own, someone who knows about these things." He smiled. It was painful but straightforward, a temporary sadness.

"Oh, I've already made a choice," she replied.

"Good, then. I think you'll find that this will make things easier for you."

"Oh, I made my choice a long time ago. That's why I moved to *Feuilles d'Automne*. I just haven't told Jean-Claude. I left everything to my grandson."

This time Dr. Ben Khetta was startled. He had taken care of her for years and she had never mentioned a grandson. It was clear to her; it was another mystery to him.

"You have a grandson?"

"I do. At least I think I do. He'll inherit all of it. The chateau, the farm, the orchards, even the land where the monastery stands. Do you know the monastery, Dr. Joseph?" His startled look was misinterpreted as a shake of the head, and she pressed on. "It was beautiful before the war. The monks were a kind group, very devoted, very industrious. My daughter loved it especially. She found reasons to go there every day and by the time

251

she was in school she said she wanted to take religious orders. But then the Krauts came and took all the monks to Germany. It's been falling down ever since."

"I know you lost your daughter. It's in your history. Is this her son?"

"Yes. He was a tiny thing, no bigger than your thumb when Jean-Claude tried to kill him. He got in trouble for it, too, but he got off. That's why I hate him."

The clearer the facts became, the less Dr. Ben Khetta understood them.

"What do you mean, 'you think you do?' Do you have a grandson?"

"Oh, I haven't seen him since he was a baby. That's when he was taken away."

"Taken away? What do you mean? Who took him away?"

"Jean-Claude tried to kill him, so the soldiers took him away. My grandson. He was only a year old. They took him to America." She paused to let her thoughts catch up with her. It was pleasing, she found, to be able to confide in Dr. Joseph. She had told the girls about her grandson, Madame Dubois and Madame Lavois, and others before them. None of them believed her. 'When is he coming to see you?' they would ask, or, 'What's he say in his letters?' It eventually evolved into 'Where is he, this grandson of yours?' And, when she answered them that she didn't know, just 'America,' they all decided that she made the grandson up. "But I thought when he grew up he would come home."

Dr. Ben Khetta also was accustomed to elderly patients who had fantasies. The poorest ones all had rich relations who would come for them. The sickest ones always knew someone who had survived the same illness and lived another twenty years. The loneliest had sons and daughters who would come next visiting day. He was not a cruel doctor; he didn't ask Madame Dupré the questions that her friends and Mademoiselle Garnier and the volunteer girls always asked to put her in her place. He wished he hadn't asked the next question, but her story was so different from the run-of-the-mill abandonments that he plodded onward:

"And this cousin tried to kill him?"

"Jean-Claude. Yes. He left him in the river to drown."

"How did Jean-Claude get off with trying to kill him?"

"Oh, by the time it came to court he insisted that there was no baby. The prefect believed him and dropped the charges. By then the Irish had closed up the hospital and the Department couldn't find his birth certificate. The baby wasn't here anymore, so that was the end of it."

"Did the baby have a name?"

"Of course he did. Francois. He was a beautiful little thing."

"Okay, here's what I want to do. I want you to remember these three things. I'm going to ask you to repeat them in a minute after we talk about some other things. Okay?"

She had been through this before, and knew that the doctors thought she was demented. *I'll show him,* she thought. *I shouldn't have trusted him. I should never have let him see those papers. He's just an Arab.*

"Triangle. Plow. Weathervane. Can you remember those three things?"

She could. She also could tell him who was the president of France and the day of the week and she could count backward from one hundred three to eighty-four. She remembered that the couple in *A Man and A Woman* met when the man gave the woman a lift back to Paris after leaving her son at boarding school, in 1966, (*That would have been Francois' twenty-first birthday; I thought that would be when he came home, after he turned twenty-one,*) and that she had eaten a croissant with jam for breakfast four hours earlier (*The croissants there are awful; I think Mademoiselle Garnier puts bran in them,*) while listening to Madame Lavois natter on about her son Emil, whose ear infection Dr. Genet had cured with a wonder drug and who now was the mayor of Sainte Marie du Vire.

Five minutes later, however, she correctly repeated the words: "Triangle. Plow. Weathervane."

Dr. Ben Khetta was satisfied. *She's not demented,* he concluded. *She's just depressed. Sometimes depression makes them create fantasy lives.*

"Listen, Madame, I'm going to add some nortryptiline to your prescriptions, just a little dose. It'll keep you steady while I do some reading up about your symptoms. But promise me this—I want you to stop asking me to help end your life."

"Oh, don't ask me to promise that," she answered. "I've thought it all out. If Jean-Claude steals the chateau from my grandson, I don't want to live. But after forty years, I don't think I'm going to ever see him again, not in this life. Why would you want me to keep on living like this? I'm ready for it to be over."

"Well, because there's hope." He didn't really believe there was much hope, but that didn't entitle him to tell a patient to give up hope. "No one has written to say he's dead, have they?" Even Dr. Ben Khetta was confirming her fantasy now, and he felt uncomfortable about patronizing her. "So, let's try the nortryptiline and let me see you in a week. Okay?"

She agreed; another week wouldn't matter in the grand scheme of things.

"And don't give them to anyone, especially Madame Lefèvre. Agreed?" She agreed. "It's noon. I'm going to drive you back to *Feuilles d'Automne* myself. I fancy some ice cream. Would you like some ice cream? Shall we?"

Madame Dupré was full of eighty years of milk, cheese, cream, and now, from the nursing home, ice cream, and said so: "If you don't mind, I'd rather have a crepe, a real one. Not one of those bran ones."

"Agreed."

"And maybe a little brandy, if you don't mind."

Thus it was that, when Dr. Yousef Ben Khetta delivered her to *Feuilles d'Automne* more than an hour later than her friends, Madame Dupré was resigned to at least another week of the diminishing sunlight, falling leaves, and rigged poker games of the depressing life. She was not resigned, however, to putting up with Mademoiselle Garnier's unwelcome comment that a visitor was waiting for her.

"No. I don't want to see him. Tell him to go away. He's not my son." She pulled her jacket tightly around her shoulders and made to go along the residents' hallway to find the girls. Mademoiselle Garnier blocked her way.

"It's someone else, Madame Lavois' son. He's in the visitors' parlor."

"Is she all right?" Ill-formed notions of tumors and failed organs crossed her mind. "Is she still here? I didn't see an ambulance. What..."

"She's fine. He seems very intent on talking with you and, what could I say? He drove all the way over from Sainte Marie."

The visitors' parlor was not Autumn Leaves' best feature, furnished with fake leather cushions on the imitation Empire furniture to guard against catheter leaks. Emil sat stiffly with his mother and, seeing Madame Dupré enter, trailed by Mademoiselle Garnier, stood and gave his best now-the-mayor-who-has-known-you-since-I-was-a-boy smile. It took only a few moments to greet, cheek-kiss, and assure everyone that no one was worse or dying.

"But I do have something I need to ask you about. It may be nothing, so I don't want to give you a shock or anything."

"Me? What?"

Emil wasn't sure where to start. He decided to begin with Prudhomme.

"We arrested a man who seemed like he was trying to break into Dr. Genet's vacant house." He described the discovery of a Renault parked the wrong way on the one-way street, a figure on the stoop in front of Dr. Genet's house. "He was peering in through the windows, then he tried to open the door, so Prudhomme arrested him."

Madame Dupré seemed unsure what it had to do with her.

"I haven't been to Saint Marie in years. Well, not years. I go every April, but just for a couple of hours, to the cemetery."

Emil took a deep breath.

"That's what I've come to see you about." "When we talked to him at the *mairie*, he showed us this drawing."

Chapter Twenty-Two

Four thousand, seven hundred and eighty-seven miles west of Saint-Lô, a specialist fourth class sat on a plastic chair in the clerk's office of the deputy adjutant of the Fourth Infantry Division headquarters command in Fort Carson, Colorado. He plucked from the wire in-tray two separate sheets of paper.

On one sheet there was the duty roster of the day. It assigned one clerk of the adjutant's office to assist the duty lieutenant as base charge of quarters for twenty-four hours, beginning that evening.

The other sheet of paper consisted of a personal letter from a retired judge who described himself as "...an old warhorse of the Fourth Infantry Division," who wanted a personal favor. He attached Form SF 180, requesting records that, if they existed at all, hadn't been opened in over forty years. The clerk, being a specialist, suspected that such boxes were most likely in the archives of the Fourth Infantry Division gathering thick coats of dust in a warehouse in the back reaches of Fort Carson. The clerk compared the implications of the two sheets of paper in the in-tray.

Inspection by the CO. Class B uniform. Shoes polished, can of Brasso. Drive lieutenant around in jeep for twenty-four hours....

Or.

Hole up in warehouse and smoke a few joints.

He thumbed through the post adjutant services directory. Archives were divided into two categories: 'Permanent,' and 'Division Museum.' 'Archives, Permanent,' were stored in Building 662, on the other side of the abandoned airfield and some four plus miles from the deputy adjutant's office. He resumed daydreaming.

Found location of warehouse: one hour. It had only taken ten minutes, but no self-respecting military clerk does anything in ten minutes. *Find building supervisor: one hour. Check out key. One hour. Go to warehouse.* This was actually a matter of driving four miles but, since the warehouse was all but off-post, he allowed himself a half-day. *Open warehouse; wander up and down looking for records from World War Two. Half-day. Find record. Or not find record. Either way is okay. Another half-day. Lock up warehouse. Return to deputy adjutant general.*

It was no contest. The duty sergeant nodded and went back to what he was doing. The specialist then returned to his apartment in search of a decent package of rolling papers and enough marijuana to keep him numb for twenty-four hours. By midafternoon, he had gotten the key, found the warehouse, opened the door, and found an exhaust ventilator fan switch and turned it on.

Twenty hours later, he got up from the lawn chair where he had been having a toke and listening to his Walkman play an endless reel of Mike and the Mechanics. He stretched, rolled his eyes in the dim warehouse light, walked twenty feet to get the kinks out of his knees, and tripped on a tube roll of the division's maps from 1944, causing him to fall in front of six boxes marked 'Normandy – ADJ – Misc.', which reminded him of his mission. Bored with Mike and the Mechanics, and entertaining the fuzzy notion that he might be rewarded in some indefinable way if he actually did find the records, he began to open the boxes.

In Box 7, 'MP, Normandy, Court Martials, 1944,' he dug out a file labeled 'Curtiss, Corporal, George, and began to read.

Judge Advocate's Summary Notes:*General Court Martial of Curtiss, George Corporal, 29ᵗʰ Infantry Division*

Date: *October 11, 1944*
Location:*Temporary Courtroom (School), 4ᵗʰ Infantry Division HHQ Command, Cherbourg*
JAG:*Leatherman, Major, 8ᵗʰ Inf. Reg. JAG Det.*
Charge: *Art. 92, murdered Major Halliburton while on TDY at Chateau Dupré;*
Art. 58, desertion;
Art. 75, endangered post.
Witnesses: *Capt. Deere, Inf., CO D. Co. 2d/ 116ᵗʰ 29ᵗʰ Infantry Division*

Pvt. Rogers, Inf., Fourth Platoon 2d/ 116th Infantry Division
Capt. Hastings, Med. Officer, 261st Field Hospital Infantry Division,
TDY Chateau Dupré

The specialist still had four hours to go on his duty day. He dragged his lawn chair over to the Normandy court martial boxes, lit another joint, and began to read.

Chapter Twenty-Three

i.

F rank felt like he was alone, but wasn't.

Telephone calls with Eleanor were expensive and hurried.

"He told me to stop looking, especially at people and places. He says it makes them think I'm with Khadafi or Arafat, like I'm looking for something to blow up."

"I've been to the doctor. I'm fine. I swam four thousand yards this weekend."

"Everyone has a dog. They even take them right into the restaurants and they sit on the floor and wait while you eat, like it's normal. Well, except at the farms. Those dogs bark and scare you to death."

"Judge Leatherman called for you. It was on the answering machine."

"And traffic circles everywhere. It's crazy."

"The right rear tire on the Volvo is losing air."

"I've been driving up and down back roads until I'm blue in the face, trying to find the farm in Dad's drawing. Mostly I just get lost."

"Don't stop looking; you'll know when you find it."

"I miss you."

"I miss you."

When the calls ended each of them lay down on their beds and worried that they were losing touch.

Emil's order to stop attempting burglary did challenge Frank's creative skills. He found a hotel in Saint-Lô. He walked around town looking for the places Will had sketched. He looked sideways at sixtyish women in shops and on sidewalks. He drew the attention of a beat cop.

"What are you looking at?" the gendarme demanded, in French.

"Do you know where this is?"

Frank showed him Will's drawing of the pitiful hospital clinging to the top of a hill in the bombed-out city, a line of wretched patients making their way up to the nuns waiting on front steps to care for them. The gendarme misunderstood and thought Frank was asking where to find the children's playground on top of the old city ramparts. Frank misunderstood the policeman's directions and walked several blocks the wrong way before walking up a back lane that led to the side entrance of what once had been a dungeon. He felt the policeman's eyes boring into his back the entire time.

On another walk, several days later, he stood in front of the abbey church of Saint-Croix and saw a plaque with the words '*Juillet 1944*' and '*Major Howie*.' A man who was walking his dog asked Frank if he was a tourist; Frank asked if he knew where to find the site of Will's drawing of the '*Hôpital Irlandais*'. The man, who turned out to be a dog trainer for the police, had never heard of the place.

Both officers made notes of their encounters and read them out at the next days' morning reports.

The hotel staff were, for the most part, from Paris; they knew even less about Saint-Lô's history and geography than Frank knew. They helped him find a Laundromat and a newsagent where he could buy day-old copies of the *Herald Tribune*. They also learned from the housekeeping staff that Frank had bought an electric kettle for instant coffee and canned soup, thereby avoiding spending for meals in the hotel restaurant.

Slowly, but surely, he carved out a routine that was more than tourist, less than resident. He watched the BBC in his room. He drank one cup of *café noir* and ate one croissant for breakfast each morning and wished he knew whether and how he was permitted to ask for seconds. He declared a mediocre bar two blocks away to be his local pub. He learned to listen for English in the background of the broadcast as it was being translated on French television news.

"The Soviet Union has expelled American diplomats over a row that...."

"In by-elections in Greece...."

"The American custom of Halloween is taking hold in Britain with...."

"Officials in Washington accuse Pakistan of falsifying a report concerning nuclear weapons..."

He took another sip of the coffee and turned to *Calvin and Hobbes* in the *Herald Tribune*. Calvin turned Mrs. Wormwood into a slobbering, tentacled monster. Hobbes helped Calvin blast off in the space rocket. The letter 'B.'

Of course, he thought. *Bridle begins with a 'b'; that much of my birth certificate isn't smudged.* He finished the croissant in two bites, the coffee in one gulp, and pulled on his jacket. The newsagent sold him Michelin map 52, 'Normandy.' By noon he had located the first 'B' town on the map, Baudre, not more than five miles away.

Baudre looked promising, apart from the fact that was never mentioned in any of Will's letters. It was near Saint-Lô. It was small. It was surrounded by farms. Half the buildings were more or less recent vintage, the other half rebuilt, evidence that Baudre had been steamrolled in the war. There was within a few hundred yards of the center of town a stream that might have been the site of the laundry wash house in Will's sketch. And there was a *mairie*. He went in.

He showed them Will's drawings; the clerk shrugged. He asked if he could look at the town's registry of birth certificates, last name uncertain. The clerk didn't understand what he wanted. He hand-wrote his request, using the Larousse for every word. The clerk said no.

He drove from Baudre to Beauvrigny. The mayor said no. He drove from Beauvrigny to Bavent. The mayor said no. He drove to towns and hamlets whose names began with a 'B' for almost a week, and found nothing.

And he wrote to Eleanor.

> I found ten more 'B' towns between Saint-Lô and Cherbourg - Bricquebec, Brix, Brillevast, and so on. Nothing. That part of Normandy is swamps and hedgerows and farms without walls and chateaus without orchards, no wash houses on the streams. I'm running out of ideas.
>
> Love, Frank

She replied:

It might go more easily if you had someone who knows the way of things where you are. Perhaps you should ask the translator?

Their letters weren't very satisfying. What was satisfying though, was the fax machine. Both of them looked for something that was out of the ordinary, a cheaper car rental agent, an annotated set of *Creysida and Troilus*, something special enough to justify the cost of sending and receiving a fax.

Dearest: Candace called to say that the government is having difficulties with Pakistan about returning Peter's body. She's very depressed and unsure how to make decisions, but is going forward with selling their new house. She says your mother seems (to Candace) to understand that something is happening, and is lonely. Please think about it, as I know you will.

Don't doubt yourself. I'm well; don't worry.

Love, Eleanor

Post Script: Mr. Burnham delivered this message from Judge Leatherman.

A separate page followed, written on Judge Leatherman's personal stationery.

Dear Mr. Hastings. I was sincerely sorry to learn that the Peter Hastings who was killed in the hijacking was your brother, and so close on the heels of your father passing away. Please accept my apologies and condolences.

Once I figured out who you are I started turning a few wheels, to see if I can help you. I think I may have something coming.

Sincerely,
Judge Leatherman

It wasn't the oddest sympathy note Frank had received, although it was the most obscure. He sent a fax in reply:

> Dear Eleanor: They make me show my passport everywhere. Someone blew up a synagogue a couple of days ago, police now on every corner and inside every public building.
>
> Maybe it wasn't a good idea to come. Things have ground to a halt. All the little towns are shut down for apple festivals, priests blessing the harvest, drunk-in-the-square celebrations. I'm going to the 1944 landing beaches to retrace exactly where Dad's unit landed and went. If no luck, I'm out of ideas.
>
> I'll call you tomorrow night.
>
> Love, Frank
>
> PS: What on earth was Judge Leatherman talking about?
> PSPS: You're well?
> PSPSPS: Do you really think Candace would move to Bridle?

She sent another fax back within the hour:

> Dearest, no quitting. But yes – I'll be waiting by the telephone.
>
> Love, Eleanor
>
> Post Script: Candace is overwhelmed. Peter took care of all the finances, now their bank account is overdrawn and Pan Am is not sending anything to help.

ii

Frank parked at the Omaha Beach monument and walked toward the shingle. The wind blew in from offshore under a flat midday sun. Several people walked across the parking lot, bundled against the wind, and he nodded as they passed.

He had expected something dramatic, rows of steel girders rusting in waves, a Sherman tank on a cement pedestal, anything, but once he stepped onto the sand itself, the beach was free of the tourist debris of war. Even the speaker's platform from the grand Fortieth D-Day celebration of two years before had been removed. There was something about that event that nudged at his memory but he couldn't recall what so he walked past the flags in front of the Omaha Beach monument and beach. A newly paved footpath had been installed, separating the sand and shingle from the hillocks of sand clumps and shrubs. He thought of Tog.

Tog had walked into the kitchen and found Frank so agitated that Peter was home from the Academy that he was trying to leave the house without a jacket.

"No you don't, you two," Virginia had intervened. "It's cold out there. And you've got to eat something before the game." She had made chicken soup, warm and thick with carrots and potatoes, and served it to them in big crockery bowls. When she turned her back, Tog handed him the note to give to Becky Grey. Frank had said he couldn't eat, but when Virginia asked why, he didn't say a word about Peter. The next morning he and Tog were spreading chicken shit over Bump's wheat field.

The wind went right down the neck of Frank's shirt, making him shiver, and he hurried along the empty stretch of sand.

Omaha Beach was quiet under a changing grey sky that hinted at rain. A stone pillbox up the hill sprouted out of the sand and shrubs. Frank looked out to sea and tried to envision what it must have been like to come there, under fire and with a huge mass of ships firing shells overhead at Germans high above who were firing back down at them. Every quarter-mile or so clefts in the hillside formed ravines which, Frank's slightly military mind told him, had to have been the routes the men had to fight up to get off the beach and into France.

Almost a mile east of the parking lot, midway between the summit and the path, a thick blockhouse emerged between the seawall and the hilltop. Concrete igloos hid at irregular intervals alongside the ravines. When Frank looked all the way up to the ridge, he realized that anyone who survived as far as the gun emplacements still had to get past them to attack the summit. He began to understand why Will never talked about it. He tried to imagine Will smoking a joint and getting drunk on Omaha Beach or in the hedgerows and apples barns around Saint Marie. *That's what we did in Vietnam— we would jeep out in the morning and patch holes in the pipes, walk back to the firebase in the afternoon, go to the PX and sit in the hooch and drank Budweiser and smoke dope and count the days we had left in country.*

Vietnam was worse than that, but worse in its own way.

Then they would call in a dust off and the helicopter would take the bodies away and drop them back inside the wire. At the end of the day, we would go look for the laundry ladies and fuck them for a little bit of cooking gas and maybe something from the PX and then the next day we went out and did it all over again. It was just the war, that's all. Everybody does things in war.

Will's drawing of Géraldine was embedded so deeply in Frank's mind that he knew he was trying to make excuses for his father.

Maybe that's all she was to Dad, his laundry lady. So, why the rest of it?

He had done the math a hundred times. Every time, he was an illegitimate child.

They conceived Peter in 1943 because he was born in September, 1944. I was born here in 1945 or maybe 1946 while Mother and Peter were back home. So, why would Dad do it?

Most of his life Frank had watched the way that Will loved Virginia. He had loved her with kindness. He had loved her with jokes shared between them. He had loved her with touches on the back of her hand and with joy in watching her while she cooked or cleaned or sat in the car or went to church or played bridge with George and Lucille. Will had loved Virginia more than any other man Frank had known in Bridle, more than any soldier he knew in the army or any newspaperman or lawyer or school teacher or judge he had ever known, better and kinder and more honestly than any of them had loved a wife or a girl.

So, why did he cheat on her? Why did he bring me home for her to raise? And why did she agree to keep me?

At least he understood why Peter was her favorite; Peter was hers. He hadn't written a word of *An Khe* since the day Peter was killed.

I was a shit about Peter. I don't care if Candace and the kids have the house in Bridle. I need to write her and make sure she knows that.

He took out a note pad and scribbled 'Write Candace,' then remembered: *But if she moves to Bridle, what about Mother?*

The wind and the chill and the intrusive thoughts were not helping. He continued along the beach to a point where the hill rose steeply to a summit high above the shore. A path wound back and forth up the hill and disappeared into the trees at the clifftop. It took fifteen minutes to reach the top. He stepped over the parapet and found himself facing almost ten thousand graves in perfect rows across a huge expanse of green lawn.

A dozen people wandered quietly among the crosses—a couple walking arm in arm in one part of the cemetery, a family with children in another part, others sat on the steps of the loggia. The only sound was the wind blowing through the leaves of the trees encircling the cemetery. Frank knew he had to sit down. He made his way to the reflecting pool and sagged to the pavement.

"Are you all right, sir?" someone asked. "Can I help you?" A kindly hand attached to a kind man stood over him. He was older than Frank, not as old as Will, about the same age as Emil, the mayor, but welcoming. "It can be overwhelming." He seemed to understand that Frank just needed to take in the endless rows of graves that stretched to the horizon.

"My father was here," was all that Frank could manage to say. "I just came up from the beach and over the wall and suddenly here I was, and it hit me." He paused to catch his breath. "I can't imagine how he did it."

"It's only a hundred feet or so high," the docent said, "but it seems a lot higher because of the slope. What's your father's name?" He was dressed in a blue blazer and slacks, a flag lapel pin in his jacket. Frank had avoided people dressed like that ever since he had gotten out of Vietnam alive.

"Hastings. Will Hastings. He was a doctor. 261ˢᵗ Field Hospital."

"Are you going to be all right?" Frank said he was. "Let me see what I can find out for you. I'll be back in a little while." He paused to be sure that Frank really was going to be all right. "It's fine to wander. I'll find you." Frank had no idea what he was talking about.

The cemetery was soothing, in a painful sort of way. A metal sculpture rose in front of the reflecting pool, modern art, almost shapeless, but still the image of a young warrior rising from the earth and pointing to the sky. Urns embossed with dying soldiers stood near the columns of the loggia. Seagulls drifted overhead, then turned to fly away.

He remembered the night they burned the village down, the major cackling at the sight of the women trying to put out the fires on their straw roofs. Two days before the fire the major had ordered Frank's team to see if there was a leak there, at Thuy Phuoc. A guy Frank knew, Pierce, a good guy from some town down by Houston, went up the highway with the other leak team to check on a mortar strike near pump station twelve. When Frank came back inside the wire he watched the corpsmen unload Pierce's body out of a helicopter. It could have been him or any of them; snipers shooting at the pipeline repair teams was a condition of the job.

He went over to Pierce's hooch to drink with his crew that night. They were already drunk and making plots how to frag the major. All of the white crosses and stars were identical, and he began to wander among them, reading the names and where they were from and when they had died.

Quiet cloaked the cemetery. Somewhere to the west a few visitors arrived, some left. Even the seagulls seemed to hold their cries. He read the names of some of the crosses:

'James Brooks, PFC, 115th Inf, June 8, 1944.' 'Daniel Banks, Lieutenant, 116th Inf., August 11, 1944.' Richard Colson of New York had died there, too, and Arvin Redebacker, some Whites, some Blacks, some Forrests and Rivers, side by side in endless graves. He stopped before one cross in particular, read the name, and felt ill, then made his way back to the cliff to stare down at the English Channel and wonder how anyone had the courage to get to where he stood.

"I didn't find your father."

"I beg your pardon."

The docent was back. He had come back to Frank, as he had said he would do.

"I didn't find your father. You said Will Hastings, didn't you? I looked for Will, for William, for Wilson, for any Hastings that might have had the name Will in it. I'm sorry, he's not here." He was embarrassed; families came thousands of miles to find their fathers. It was difficult to say to them, 'I can't find him.' "I'm sorry. We do have some three hundred Known but to God. Three hundred seven to be exact." He saw that Frank had a blank look on his face. "Tombs of The Unknowns."

There was an awkward silence. Each waited for the other to speak.

"I think I didn't understand you before, when you asked me who my father was. I just told you his name. He was here, but not buried here. He lived until just a couple of months ago. He's buried at home, in Texas. I didn't mean to send you off on a wild goose chase. I apologize."

"It's quite all right. I'm glad to look. That's why we're here, to help find family members and people you care about. I was happy to do the search, although I confess I was a little concerned when I found only one Hastings and it wasn't your father. I thought it might have been a nickname or something. I'm happy it wasn't him."

"Me too. Thank you very much." Frank thought the man's job was either very good or very bad, or both.

"And he was from Texas, too. A lot of men from Texas. It's such a shame."

"Who was from Texas?"

"The other Hastings. Like I said, I only found the one. Peter."

Peter Hastings. Frank took a deep breath and sat back down on the cliff's edge.

"Oh my, I didn't expect that. That's my brother's name. Peter Hastings. Or was." The docent waited patiently; there weren't many visitors in late October and his job was to be available. "He was a pilot for Pan Am. They killed him at the airport in Karachi." The docent sat down beside him. "You just caught me off guard. I'm fine."

"Of course. I'm supposed to help the visitors, not shock them. I shouldn't have said anything."

The docent had found three pages of men named Hastings in the Commission's directory, but only one buried in France from World War II. The delicate balance of saying too much or too little never involved volunteering other names when visitors came to find one specific person; he told himself that he should have known better. "I apologize to you, sir. And I'm very sorry to hear about your brother."

"Not at all. I appreciate you're trying to help. I'll be all right." Frank waited until the docent patted him on the shoulder and left to walk back toward the visitor center at the far end of the cemetery.

The beach stretched as far in either direction as Frank could see. There seemed to be no way for boats to float up to the beach under those guns and land enough troops and get them up the cliffs to win the summit, no matter how many men there were.

No wonder there's ten thousand graves.

Frank wondered how many of them were men whom Will had tried to keep alive. He was pretty sure he couldn't have done it himself; he had seen the Germans' cannon emplacements and enfilading machine gun pits.

The girl in Will's drawing began to seem even more remote. Every single soldier and airman and sailor in Vietnam had hunted down girls because they all wanted to get laid before they got killed. Village girls, bar girls, donut dollies, whores in Hong Kong and Bangkok and Sydney, they were more or less part of the hazard duty pay, a tacit agreement between command and soldier that nobody talked about whatever anyone did in Vietnam.

I have no doubt that the men who climbed up these cliffs and crawled through the hedgerows and got shot up by antiaircraft fire and Panzers and machine guns, all of them wanted to sleep with girls as much as we did, but nobody in Vietnam brought a bastard kid home in his barracks bag. Why did Dad bring me? Frank was missing something.

He had avoided thinking about Will's death, avoided it from the minute Candace called and avoided it right through the funeral and the fight with Peter and then avoided it again in Peter's memorial service and even after Tog handed him the package of letters, when it began to be clear what Will had done. After that the thought never entirely went away, but when he looked from the parapet of the cemetery and down to Omaha Beach he had to face it.

After living through all this, why would he jump off a highway bridge?

He wished he hadn't come. It was only midafternoon, but grey clouds had begun to build up into the flat northern sky and approaching darkness. It was time to leave.

Walking back to the Omaha Beach monument took even longer than walking to the American cemetery had taken. When he reached the beach, the wind changed; sand and salt and sea spray and light rain hit him in the face. It was almost four o'clock when he climbed back into the car and took out the map to ponder which roads to explore on the way back to Saint-Lô.

He made the decision.

None of them. It's over. I don't belong here. France belongs to Dad, not me. He twisted the ignition key and waited for the starter to whir and the engine to rumble, then put the car in reverse. *I don't speak French. I've driven all over Normandy for weeks and found nothing. They don't like me. Asking hotel clerks and the tourist information office to translate for me is stupid. I can't read a newspaper. I don't understand the television. I hate instant coffee in my hotel room and I'm getting fat from bread and cheese.* He clinched his fists and admitted to himself that he had failed.

And then...,

I don't care who my mother was. She was no one until a month ago, and she's no one, still.

And then...,

I'll tell Eleanor that I'm coming home.

He drove away from the Omaha Beach monument and up the narrow D road to the traffic circle but, instead of turning west toward the motor-way, he drove back to Colleville sur Mer. The parking lot was empty and, for a moment, he thought it had closed for the day. It had not. He left the Renault and made his way through the entrance, along one of the orderly sidewalks, and found the reception desk in the visitors' center.

"Hello," he said to the man on duty. "I was here an hour or so ago and, I apologize for this, but I got lost in my thoughts. I meant to ask something, if it isn't too late."

The docent on duty was as kind as the man who had spoken with Frank on the grounds.

"Not at all, I'm here at least another half-hour. What did you want to ask?"

"I read this name on one of the graves, Antsley. I'm pretty sure my father knew him, because there's a man in my hometown named Antsley. He's the minister. Do you have anything on him?"

"Let me look for you. Do you have a first name?"

"No, I didn't think to write it down. Just Antsley."

"Won't take a sec. Stand by."

The docent turned to a desk a few feet away and opened a binder filled with green and white-lined computer printout pages. He flipped through it, stopped at a page, and made some notes, then closed it.

"Here's what I've got, sir. "Micah Antsley, Corporal, 261ˢᵗ Field Hospital. From Iowa. August 12, 1944. He was awarded the Purple Heart and a Bronze Star, posthumously. He's in Plot K, Row 20, Grave 14. I'll be happy to go back with you, if you like."

"No, thanks. I can find it. I just want to write his family and say I've visited his grave and that I believe he's in a peaceful place, with his friends." Frank took a deep breath, and continued. "May I ask you for one more?"

"Of course."

"Is there a record of a soldier from Texas named Peter Hastings?"

Frank had only the foggiest idea of how many men had been in World War II, even less of the number from Texas, and had never met anyone named Hastings, not in the army or in school or in writing for *The Gazette*. Still, he calculated that the odds of there being someone from Texas who was buried in the American Military Cemetery at Colleville-Sur-Mer, who had his father's last name, his brother's first name, but wasn't related, were a zillion to one. "I think he's from my family."

"Standby." The docent returned within minutes. "Hastings, Peter, Lieutenant, 434ᵗʰ Troop Carrier Group, 101ˢᵗ Airborne, from Texas, died June 1944. The exact day isn't stated. Sometimes that happened. He's in Plot L, Row 2, Grave 2. Would you like me to escort you to the graves?"

"Yes, please."

iii.

Seeing Peter's grave reinforced Frank's decision to go home.

Dad loved whoever Peter Hastings was enough to name my brother after him. My half-brother. And there was a medic named Antsley that he cared enough about to bring one of his brothers to Bridle to be the preacher.

He decided to skip driving the back roads and took the fast motorway west across the river.

No more wrong turns in hamlets and roundabouts. No more getting lost in hedgerows. No dead ends in swamps.

Everything he had told them at Will's funeral had happened. They had left Peter and Candace and Virginia in the cabin in Del Sur to go fishing. They had driven the jeep high up on the mountain, just below the tree line, and Will had wandered away, fishing for hours. They had dug a

271

cooking pit, gutted the trout, grilled them, heated a can of pork and beans, and eaten like kings. They had packed up and gone home late and the house was almost completely emptied. Mother had been confused, of course, and Candace and the kids were very tired, but Peter was furious:

"You left everything for us to do, all the hard work, and then when you do show up you go off fishing with Dad, like you and he were old friends."

He had snapped back that it was Peter's idea to move Dad and Mother to a nursing home in Colorado Springs "to be close to you, as if you were ever home anyway. I took Dad fishing because it was what he wanted. It was helping, helping Dad, at least."

Will had been as happy that day as Frank had ever seen him. He smuggled the books and the other things out of the house and told Frank to hide them. "These are for you."

Then they had driven to Colorado Springs and unloaded his parents at Loving Arms. He had promised that he and Eleanor would come for Thanksgiving.

Loving Arms must have felt like death row. Mother couldn't talk. He was lonely, that's true. I should never have left him there.

And then...

The drawings were long forgotten, hadn't been touched for years. They were inside Beckett's books, yes, and Dad knew Beckett at the Irish hospital in Saint-Lô, yes, but he just wanted Eleanor to have them. Nice books, that's all. He didn't jump.

And finally...

She was just someone he met on a farm. He sketched her because she was pretty and he could get her to smile. If he had wanted me to find her, he would have told me. I'll tell Eleanor that I'm coming home as soon as I can book my return flight.

iv.

However, when he asked the hotel clerk to place the international call for him, the clerk said there was a message.

"Come please? I show you." He led Frank behind the reception counter to the hotel manager's office. "Is there." He made a courteous gesture toward a cheap gadget that looked like a homemade TRS-80 computer. Green lines of blinking cursor movements and text displayed in rows across a black screen. The clerk pecked a few keystrokes and the message appeared:

☐M. Hastings, 39 11 Hotel du Selles: Emil has a question. He wants to know if your father had any particular recs, like a sport or a pastime. Jeremy Tanner@ 39 11 Mairie SMDV☐

"What's this?" Frank asked.

"What is what?"

"This computer? Why type a telephone message onto a computer? Why didn't you just hand write it?"

"Is not from the telephone. Is here in case you reply, just to make the reply."

"I don't understand."

"When message comes on the Minitel you keep it here to reply."

"The Minitel?"

"Yes, don't you have it?" Frank had come from the Philistines.

"I've never heard of it. So, the message." He read it again. "Do we call them, or write them? What?"

"You type it. I send it to them. Here."

Frank sat at the keyboard, found the letters, and typed 'Fishing.' It appeared on the screen as

'☐fishing☐'.

The clerk tapped some keys and the Minitel sent Frank's message on its way.

It was almost seven in the evening, noon for Eleanor. He decided to wait long enough to clean up from the beach, to make up some instant soup, maybe splurge for a Calvados and settle his thoughts, and then call her when night rates applied. He hadn't reached his room before the clerk came to find him.

"Another message, Monsieur."

They walked back into the office. The clerk waived toward the glowing Minitel screen. Frank looked at the message.

273

☐M. Hastings, 39 11 Hotel du Selles: Emil says to wait for him tomorrow at your hotel.

Garth Tanner@ 39 11 Mairie SMDV☐

Chapter Twenty-Four

i.

E leanor found the fax in her faculty in-box:

Le Voix du Nord

Réunis Après Près de Quarante Ans

Madame Marie -France Dupré avait abandonné tout espoir de revoir un jour son petit-fils infantile, François, qui a été emmené aux Etats- Unis après la guerre quand la mère de François est mort. Cependant, après près de quarante ans, l'enfant , maintenant appelé Frank Hastings , retourné à la recherche de sa famille. Hier, dans un retrouvailles émouvantes à Maison Feuilles d'Automne, ils ont vu une autre fois ....

She took the fax to a friend in the Department of Romance Languages, who translated the newspaper story for her:

Madame Marie-France Dupré had given up all hope of ever again seeing her infant grandchild, Francois, who was taken to the United States after the Second World War when Francois mother died. However, after almost forty years, the child, now named Franklin Delano Hastings, returned in search of his family. Yesterday, in a tearful reunion at Autumn Leaves Nursing Home, they saw one another again.

"He was a very fragile baby," said Madame Dupré, "and barely survived his first year. My relative Dr. Genet, in Sainte Marie du

Vire, and the doctors at the Irish Hospital in Saint-Lô, took care of him." She cried when she told Mister Hastings, through an interpreter, that his mother had died in childbirth. Life was very, very hard in Saint-Lô and throughout Normandy after the war. The city was named 'Capitol of the Ruins' for the destruction caused by D-Day and the German defense of the city. Chateau Dupré was badly damaged in a battle in August, 1944, and the family was taken to Saint-Pellerin, near Carentan, and later to Brix, near Cherbourg, where Francois was born. Mr. Hastings took very hard the news that his mother had not survived his birth. She is buried in the family plot in the churchyard of Sainte Marie du Vire, across the river from Chateau Dupré.

Mr. Hastings only learned of his birth in France after the recent death of his father, an American army doctor in World War II who, said Madame Dupré, was loved by her daughter and by all of the family. Emil Lavois, the mayor of Sainte Marie, remembered when American medical troops put a field hospital there after D-Day.

Asked his plans, Mister Hastings seemed resolute: "Call my wife. Get to know my grandmother. Learn French." He said that he does not yet know much about his new family or about life in France, but when asked, he smiled and said, "I might even get a dog." Madame Dupré hugged him, and then asked reporters to let the family have some privacy and get to know one another.

The department secretary had placed Frank's message written on the cover sheet:

Dear Eleanor: I've found her! This was in the morning newspaper when I came down for coffee. The waiter said 'Bonjour' and pointed to the story, then brought me a second croissant. So much to talk about but, will you come? I'll call you this evening / noon your time.

Eleanor waited from noon until four o'clock but, when the phone didn't ring, she sent a reply by fax:

> Dearest: Very happy for you. I waited for your call. This is not the time for me to travel to France. Please call me.

ii.

Monsieur Trichet said good morning to Philippe, his clerk, and to Mademoiselle Prix, his personal secretary, went into his office, and closed his door.

For the next few hours his employees quietly busied themselves with drafting conveyances, balancing the accounts of widows and orphans, and recording entries in the firm's ledgers. But, by late morning, no sound having come from behind Trichet's closed door, straws were drawn to determine who would enter and endure the wrath of a lawyer struck down by apoplexy at the newspaper story of Madame Dupré's fortune-hunting American. Philippe knocked.

"Yes, come in."

Philippe looked cautiously through the doorway, only to see Monsieur Trichet very much alive and humming at his desk.

"Monsieur Trichet? Shall we... that is to say, have you...?" Monsieur Trichet held aloft a fountain pen, green ink dripping from the nib, poised to write agreeable entries of profits from shares he held in Banque Populaire du Nord. "May we bring you anything?"

"Not at all." He smiled and turned to look down at the ledger. "Is there something else?" He smiled and seemed pleasantly occupied with doing administrative chores at hourly rates. A newspaper rested on the corner of the desk.

"No, sir. We hadn't heard from you and thought, perhaps, did you need something?" Philippe glanced at the newspaper. Trichet saw it.

"No, no. Not a thing."

"You saw the story, sir?"

About the surprise grandchild? "Of course. A nice story, heartwarming. It's the best possible thing we could ask for."

"Sir?" Philippe did not see how their client, Monsieur Martel, could benefit from the existence of Madame Dupré's direct descendant.

"And very convenient—not more than a few weeks after we sent her the *compromis* to sign and presto! A lost heir appears? It's better than I could have imagined. This is wonderful."

"I'm sorry, sir. I don't follow."

"Before, if everything went exactly as Jean-Claude hoped for, she signs the *compromis*. We supervise the transfer of what's left of Chateau Dupré into becoming Chateau Martel, and collect a few thousand francs for our trouble. But now? She'd be crazy to sign. All goes to the surprise grandchild, every rock and tree and dilapidated chicken coop, all of it. "

"Of course. The *réserve légale*." Philippe's duties often included explaining to unhappy clients that the law preserved land to their heirs, no matter how badly they wanted to disinherit someone or sell the pile to buy a flat in Paris. "Jean-Claude Martel has lost it all. Very sad."

"So, what will Monsieur Martel do? He will fight, of course. He grew up believing he was going to inherit the place. He has believed for forty years that he's the only heir, no matter how remote. He will call out the American. He will sue, of course."

"Of course." Philippe knew Jean-Claude's history as well as he knew his own. Jean-Claude would stand up for himself; history was on his side! He also knew Jean-Claude was quite poor.

"But he has no money, not for such a fight." Monsieur Trichet smiled and rubbed his hands together.

"I don't see how we can help him if he has no money..." Philippe paused when Trichet held up a hand and smiled. Philippe suspected that there was a spider web; Monsieur Trichet always wove a spider web. It would be small, threads slinking outward from here and there, a few cross-threads looping across the long threads. But it was not clear, not to Philippe, what the thread would look like when Trichet finished spinning it.

He remembered the morning that Jean-Claude had engaged them to persuade Madame Dupré to sign her chateau over to him. He was a pathetic old man whose children had left him to live alone on the farm. He hated them for bringing him electric appliances he didn't know how to use instead of staying home with him to cook and take over the farm. "They want me to make coffee with an electric pot. That's not how you make coffee."

Jean-Claude had thought the electric coffee pot was stupid, an insult. He refused to even try it.

Philippe had expected Monsieur Trichet to send him away within minutes. Instead, Jean-Claude told Trichet a story of his being falsely accused of trying to steal the family farm and of trying to kill a baby that didn't exist. He had tried to redeem himself by helping the Duprés, his distant relatives, by restoring their orchards and meadows and rebuilding their dairy. The old man died, Jean-Claude stayed, and forty years had passed. No baby had ever materialized. Monsieur Trichet had agreed to persuade the old woman to convey the chateau to Jean-Claude. But now Madame Dupré had a real heir and, Philippe realized, there was *le bref*. A mess.

"And, alas," Trichet went on. "Jean-Claude will not give it up. He will say to the American 'Prove you are who you say you are. Where is your proof?' Of course, there will be no proof."

"Sir?"

"There is no birth certificate. There was no child." Trichet beamed and picked up the green fountain pen. "I expect Jean-Claude will propose signing over to me as much of Chateau Dupré as necessary to win his case, in lieu of fees and expenses. To fight for what is his."

Philippe saw it at last. The web would require a good deal of legal work, but it was being spun by a patient, thorough spider. When the prey was caught, Monsieur Trichet would own a chateau.

"What do we do now, sir?"

"Do? We do nothing. Did you not read the story?" Trichet smiled again, and took up his green pen. "We let the family have some privacy. We let them get to know one another."

iii.

Eleanor almost missed the telephone call. Frank's voice was strained through the line connections and cables of international telephony and, even though he sounded like Frank, he didn't.

"And I have so much to tell you. There's this incredible machine called a Minitel and Jeremy sent me a message at the hotel and it was on the Minitel and it asked me a question about Dad and when I answered it he replied that the mayor wanted to see me and when he came the next day he said to come with him and we left the hotel and..."

"Slow down. You're so excited I can only hear a third of what you're saying. You left the hotel."

"And went to a nursing home. We walked there, it was that close! We went in and...there she was! I knew who she was the moment she stood up. She's over eighty and I didn't know what to do or say but then she looked at me, rushed to the door and hugged me, and said ,"Francois!" And something in French. I have to learn French. Then Jeremy started trying to translate..."

"The boy from the hostel?"

"Yes. And she talked too fast so Jeremy only got part of it but all these other women came in and started talking and smiling and kissing me on the cheek. It's the first time anyone here even shook my hand, and now they kiss me on the cheek! Then *Grandmere* hugged me and laughed and hugged me some more. Did you read the story?"

She had.

"Then you know. My mother died when I was born. It was in a house about thirty or forty miles from here, and she didn't survive. And they told me her name."

"Yes, dear?"

"Claudine. Claudine Dupré. She was just a girl, really. Not even eighteen."

Eleanor let Frank breathe for a moment, then asked:

"Dear? Now what?"

"I don't know, exactly. I'll go back to *Feuilles d'Automne* tomorrow morning. It means Autumn Leaves. Then we're going to Sainte Marie du Vire. To the cemetery."

"Ah, of course. And then?" She wanted to ask him if that would satisfy him. She wanted to ask him when he was coming home. She instead asked him what to do about the slow leak on the Volvo tire and having the heater inspected before winter.

"Take the car to Floyd's Mobil station to check the tire. He'll put on a new one if you need it. And it's too soon to worry about keeping the house warm in the winter."

She wasn't so sure.

"Dear?" he finished. "I need to go. But do you know what? All this has been pretty easy. *Bon soir.*"

Chapter Twenty-Five

i.

"You sound like my doctor."

"You say that like it's a bad thing."

"He's a good enough doctor, for an Arab." Madame Dupré lit her cigar, sucked on it to get it fired up, and inhaled a huge volume of smoke, then blew it out. "But he's always trying to take things away from me. Don't you start, too."

"Like cigars," Frank said. The translator scrambled to keep up. "He doesn't sound like a bad doctor to me."

"And Calvados. He's griping about that too. I was drinking Calvados before I could milk a cow. Do you like Calvados? Very good for you." She tried to blow a smoke ring but was just showing off for her new grandson and the glob that came out her mouth evaporated in the cool garden of the nursing home. "I let him take away my chocolate, but never the cigars. What do doctors know anyway?"

Cigars and apple-based white lightning certainly didn't seem to have killed her. Frank decided that he would never attempt to wean her off anything.

"So, about my mother."

She had told him that Claudine was the dressy one, the pretty one. The Duprés had been beside themselves when the allies landed on the beaches and the Germans flooded Normandy with reinforcements.

"She was trapped in Saint-Lô. She was in her last year in school, staying with her Aunt Julia when the bombing started. The Americans dropped sheets of paper down on us that said they were going to bomb the city and everyone had to leave Saint-Lô but before anyone could do anything, the planes came. We saw them flying over the chateau and heard the explosions and every hour it got worse. Claudine's sister said she would go get her and Aunt Julia and bring them back to the farm. That's what she did."

"How old was she then?" Frank asked through the translator.

"Claudine? Almost eighteen. Géraldine was home during her novice break from the convent. She didn't hesitate, just pulled on a cloak and walked all the way to Saint-Lô, passed through the line at Pont-Hébert, and found them. They were living in caves like a bunch of rats, under the city walls. All the houses were blown up. The whole city had been bombed to rocks and ashes and airplanes coming over every hour. Have you ever tried smoking? I never was one for cigarettes; nasty little things, but these are pretty good."

"In the army. Not cigars." He decided not to say 'just joints.' "I didn't take to it, so, no thanks."

She shrugged and resumed.

"So, that night it started to rain and there was a halt in the bombing. The next morning she found a way out of the tunnels and led them back to Pont-Hébert. The Germans had closed the bridge by then so they found their way back through the farms until they got to Le Dérvesoir."

She stubbed out her cigar and tossed the end into the mulch at the base of the garden wall, then stood up and led them back to the visitors' parlor. Her card partners found excuses to come in, look at Frank, and make themselves part of the reunion.

Morning light shone directly onto the fake Louis XIV love seat where the two of them huddled side by side, looking at each other with expressions of uncertain comfort. Jeremy did his best to keep up. Frank wanted to know how his father had met Claudine.

"I'm getting there. Your mother was a beautiful girl, Francois, very smart, not a bit afraid of the Germans. Isn't that true, Cocotte?" She patted Madame Lavois' hand and waited for her to agree. "I knew you'd come back. I thought every day, what does Francois look like? Will he know me? Will he have her face? Her hands? Short or tall? I never gave up hoping."

"It's true," Madame Lavois added. "But we thought you would look more like Robert Redford."

"Paul Newman."

"JR Ewing."

"Americans don't all look like movie stars; we're just ordinary people."

"Except for the teeth. Americans all have nice teeth."

"When Emil told me," Cocotte added, "that he had found you, I thought you'd look English, all red and round and with bad teeth, but you're not at all like that." Madame Lavois believed that all English-speaking men looked like Winston Churchill. "You're more like, I don't know."

"Like your father," Madame Dupré rescued her. "So, when they got to Le Dérvesoir they hid in a barn, and Aunt Julia exploded. Well, she didn't blow up. The Germans had booby-trapped a barn gate. That's what blew up. Julia was cut up like a sausage. That's how we met your father. Didn't he ever tell you about it?"

"No. He never talked about the war, none of it." Sometime between the first reunion and the second, between the newspaper story and telling Eleanor that he had found her, it occurred to him that they knew as little about him as he did of them, but not why. "The truth is, I'm just now learning about you and my mother. I want to know everything, so tell me everything."

"The Americans had put a surgery up in the old apple barn in Sainte Marie. Your father sewed Julia up from top to bottom and the girls finally made it home and told us what had happened. My other cousin, Doctor Genet, knocked on our kitchen door and told us the Americans had let him look at Julia and what they did for her was impossible, even for a doctor. Then he showed us a drawing. It was Julia, her face, but with stitches and scars everywhere and rubber tubes coming out of her. I never saw anything like it. That's what Genet said—he never did either. It was a miracle, what your father did."

"How far away was your farm?"

"Chateau Dupré? A kilometer? Two? It's just across the river from Saint Marie. Emil didn't tell you? But there wasn't a bridge then so if you wanted to go by road it was a long way, all the way to Saint-Lô and then up the other side. We just took a row boat and crossed over at the laundry house, there on the river."

"Is this what it looked like?" Frank took out Will's drawing of the Sainte Marie laundry house on the banks of the Vire.

"That's it. Your father drew all the time. We used to have a lot of his drawings, all sorts of things. The laundry house is gone now but the barn is still there. Did your father give this to you?"

"Sort of. I found it in his papers. Actually, my wife found it."

"Your wife? You have a wife?"

"I do. She... I don't know what to tell you. She's from England, but she teaches in America. Literature."

"A teacher, and you a journalist. I thought you would be a doctor, or a soldier. Do I have any grandbabies? Great-grandbabies?"

"No, I'm afraid not. Eleanor is the only thing I've done right in my whole life. As for babies, we haven't, well, not yet. What's the church in the drawing?" Frank pointed to the spires, across the river, faintly visible beyond the trees on the riverbank.

"It's the monastery. To get to Saint Marie we walked across the meadow to the monastery, then down to the river, untied the rowboat, and rowed over to the laundry house. It's been abandoned since the war."

"I did all my wash there until my husband bought a machine," Madame Lavois added. "We all did. We didn't get the clothes very clean, but if we wanted to know what was happening in Saint Marie, that's where we went."

"And you didn't find out everything, *Potin*." Gossip. "I'm afraid it's not a very nice story, Francois. My daughter thought your father was a *plouc*. How do you explain *plouc*? He looked like a common soldier and she thought that's all he was, maybe someone who emptied the bedpans. A janitor. He tried to explain what happened and she told him she didn't want to talk to him, she wanted to talk to the surgeon! I suspect she was pretty blunt about it. Then Genet whispered to her that he was the surgeon. That's how they met. I made her go back the next day and apologize. And then, after that, well, somehow, we learned that my daughter and your father began to find ways to see each other. We didn't believe it—it was in the middle of the war! Impossible, but true." She waited while Coco shook her head and while Frank gazed at her with a look of satisfaction, an, 'Ah, there it is' moment. "Now, I want to know about and your father. Genet loved him as much as my daughter did."

She was walking a very fine line, but no one else sensed it.

ii.

"About my father. I don't know where to start."

The starting place in telling his new grandmother about Will depended on Frank correctly guessing what she already knew about Will, whether Will had told them that he already had a family. He concluded that Will hadn't said any more to them about his American family than he had said to Frank about his French one, and waded in.

"Father never talked about the war. When I got drafted into the army the only thing he said to me was, 'Don't try to not get killed; if you do you'll spend all your time looking over your shoulder. That's when you'll get killed.' That and to never salute an officer you respect. Nothing about courage or fear. I mean, I knew he had been in D-Day and that after the war he was supposed to be sent to Japan, but then they dropped the atomic bomb so they sent him back to Europe. That wasn't anything he ever talked about either. My friend Tog, his father was in the war, and the mayor, and a lot of the men where I grew up, but they just didn't talk about it. So, I'm afraid I don't know anything about the time my father was here."

The women nodded, as if they had suspected it.

"First, I need to tell you this, my father died this summer. He was retired from being a doctor. My brother persuaded him to move close to where he lived, in Colorado." No longer any need to point fingers at Peter. "He went out for a walk one morning, and died." The mental image of Will, bouncing off the hood of an army truck on Interstate 25, was planted in Frank's mind so firmly that he saw it when he ate and slept and walked around France looking for hamlets that began with the letter 'B.' "One day he was fine, and then, one day he died."

She rescued him.

"You were tiny when you went to America, Francois, a little thing. Do you remember the day we took you to Dr. Genet's house with your blankets and things? It broke our hearts."

He shook his head. Frank didn't remember that or anything else. His first fleeting memories were of Peter jumping out of dark closets to scare him, and wetting the bed, and riding in the backseat of a very old Ford coupe, and having mumps, but that was about it.

"No, I was too little. We lived in a small town, bigger than Sainte Marie, maybe, but very small. That's where they raised us, just normal." *Shouldn't have said 'they' or 'us.' Does she know anything about Mother?* "An ordinary house. School and church. Summer jobs. Dad was the town doctor until he retired in 1983. He had a little clinic. Broken arms and babies. He knew everyone."

"They?"

"Yes, they. My mother and.... Dad was married."

"Of course he was. He should have been married. I worried about him all those years. He needed a wife."

I tried, he thought. *Maybe she knew; maybe she didn't.*

The stiff visitors' room, the interpreter, the old ladies wandering in and out to peek at Frank, all conspired to make the conversation awkward. It was like strangers talking in a Greyhound bus station to find out if they had ever lived in the same city or been in Vietnam at the same time or had anything in common just so they could keep on talking.

"It was just home. All of my father's friends were there. He delivered most of them when they were babies, went to all their football games and Christmas pageants at the school and things. But Dad was restless, too, always on the go. When I was a boy he would come home and say, 'Everybody into the car,' and away we'd go, driving for hours, up to the mountains. We'd sleep in tents and hike around and build campfires. I mostly just played in the trees. Then we'd pack up and drive back home and I'd go back to school. And summer jobs. They always made me get a job in the summers. Mostly I worked on farms, it was that kind of town, plowing and stacking hay and trying to save enough money to buy a car."

"That's perfect. Did you like working on the farm?"

"Not very much." He thought it was true, but it wasn't. He got through long days alone, sitting on a tractor and making up songs, planning to run away with Tog and become surfers.

"Can you milk cows?"

"Not really."

"Have you tended apples?"

"I eat apples. That's about it."

"You have a lot to learn. Did you buy your car?"

"No. My friend and I were going to buy one and go to California but things changed. So, after school, I went to university, and the army, and after that I got a job for a newspaper."

"A newspaper?"

"I'm not exactly a foreign correspondent for *Newsweek*." He was afraid he already had disappointed her. "I write for a newspaper. Local news. Trials, interviews, that sort of thing."

"Important stories? Is that what you do with your life?"

"Do?" He considered the question. He hadn't invaded Normandy, or integrated the South, or even lifted a finger to criticize Thatcher's and Reagan's attack on Libya. "Stories about bad school teachers are important. And that's how I met my wife, when I was becoming a journalist."

"Of course, dear."

"Then one day, about three years ago, Dad called on the telephone and said 'We're moving up to Del Sur.' That's a little town in the mountains. It's where he liked to fish."

Madame Dupré nodded with a knowing smile, as if she'd been waiting to hear that Will was a fishing man, then turned to look at the other women as if to say 'so there!'

"And that was just out of the blue." The translator was stuck on that for a moment. "A surprise. His retirement was a surprise to me, especially that they were moving away. But Dad was fine. My... his wife..."

"Did you know you were born here?"

"No. My brother teased me about being a war baby, but no one paid any attention to it. I didn't believe him." *Well, I sort of believed him.*

"Then your father's wife was your mother. It's all right. You should have a mother."

"My mother, yes, her name is Virginia. She raised us, me and my brother, but by the time Dad said he was going to retire, she was beginning to lose her memory. She has aphasia, a kind of Alzheimer's disease. I didn't understand it then but now I think Dad felt like he should take care of her after all those years of taking care of everybody else. And then...."

The sunlight on the loveseat shifted and began to play on the floor of the sitting room. It was a concocted room, contrived so that Autumn Leaves could show people who were about to consign their ancient parents to a nursing home that here, this very room, this was a place where they could come every week to visit, just like at home. There were high ceilings and damask drapes to give the impression that it was the salon of a great Parisian home in the Sixteenth, but everybody involved knew it was a charade. The families who dropped off their parents to die at *Feuilles d'Automne* rarely came.

Frank tried to match the features of Madame Dupré's lined face to the gentle face in Will's drawing, smooth cheeks and uneven lips and a hint of hair beneath her scarf, but could not. He always had been bad at seeing resemblances; when someone said, 'he looks just like his father (or mother)' or, 'she takes after her mother's (or father's) side of the family,' Frank never saw anything at all. The girl in the drawing and the grandmother who patted his wrist didn't seem to look much like each other in any detail. He didn't want to tell her that the intrepid young American soldier her daughter had loved had died forty years later because Frank hadn't stopped Peter from dumping him in a place just like Autumn Leaves.

They sat quietly for a few minutes. Madame Lavois and the interpreter squirmed in their seats. Madame Dupré didn't move at all, just nodded and waited for Frank to continue because, even though she knew she was supposed to be telling Frank about his mother and his ancestors and her family history, it was much easier for her when she made Frank do all the talking.

"Was it his heart? He was hurt so badly that we thought he had been killed. When he came back, after they let him out of the hospital, he was pale and all bones. I was always afraid his heart wouldn't hold out."

"You knew he was wounded? My father?"

"Oh, yes, of course." She realized as soon as she said it that she would have to explain it. "He was shot in the back, at the chateau. His army unit had been there about a week and then the Germans attacked. My daughter helped to get him into the house and stop his bleeding. I have no idea how he stayed alive until they got him to a hospital. I was even more amazed when he came back."

"When he came back for me?"

Frank had reconstructed the events in his mind: Will discovered that he had left a baby behind in Normandy, a baby boy, and that when they dropped the atomic bomb on Japan, Will had finagled his way back to France for the sole purpose of finding Francois to bring him home. Learning that Claudine had died in childbirth was all the proof Frank needed to confirm that version: there was a baby, it had no mother, Will would do the right thing, he had come for Frank and, coincidentally, Will loved him best. Who knew why Virginia went along with it? It didn't matter; apart from that, this version explained everything.

"No, after he was out of the hospital. This was long before the war was over. We thought maybe he was dead. Then one day he appeared right out of the woods and knocked on the door. We had no idea how he found us, but he was very good at that sort of thing, always going around in the country on his own. That's when we realized that he and our daughter were more than just, you know, that they cared about each other. Romantically."

The mood in the room became awkward. Frank misunderstood Madame Dupré's tone of voice and measured words to be uncertainty about the indelicate topic of her daughter having gotten pregnant by an American soldier.

"Do you have a picture of her? My mother?"

"Of Claudine? Of course I do. Would you like me to bring it? It's in my room."

"Yes, I'd like that very much."

"Coco, ask the warden to make some tea for Francois." She turned to Frank and patted him on the hand. "I'll be right back. You look like you could use some tea. Coco will go for it."

By the time she got back with the photograph, the card ladies were hovering over Frank and cross-examining his life in Texas.

"Do you have a horse?" Madame Dubois asked.

"A horse? No. I have a Volvo," he admitted.

"A six-shooter? Is it very hard to shoot a six-shooter?"

"I don't have a six-shooter, either. I had a rifle when I was in the army but I never actually fired it, not even when in Vietnam."

"How can you live in Texas without a horse and a six-shooter? And cross the desert?"

"Are there Indians where you live?"

"Yes. There are wild Indians, mostly Comanche and Apaches. They hide behind the cactus with their bows and arrows. After dark they sneak into town and try to steal our horses and womenfolk, which they could do if they weren't addicted to firewater."

"Qu'est-ce la firewater?"

289

"Firewater is whiskey."

"In fact, my wife is Indian, but very civilized. She likes white man's ways."

"Are you very good at poker?"

"Not very. We played hearts in the army, hearts and spades." He had not been very good at hearts or spades, either.

"You can sit in with us if you like. We'll teach you how to play. The ante is usually just one of the little pink ones. Do you have any of the little pink pills? " Madame Lefèvre had not followed the questions very clearly until the matter of cards came up. "I have a new bottle of Darvocets."

"Shh, Leffy. Stop it," Coco hissed at her. Madame Lefèvre frowned and turned away.

Madame Lavois asked another question, a more pertinent question, just as Madame Dupré returned with the photograph.

"I'm sorry, I don't," Frank was saying. "She asked me if I remembered when she found me drowning in the river."

"He doesn't remember anything," Madame Lavois shrugged. "Not when he was floating down the river in the apple crate, or when you took him to the Irish Hospital to pump your stomach or the time he wandered off into the meadow when we didn't even know he could walk!" She stopped and poured a cup of tea. "Here, Francois, brewed, not stewed. Or is it the other way around?" She took the tea strainer from the cup and handed it to him. "I saved your life. Are you sure you don't remember me?"

"To tell you the truth, I don't have any memories at all, not of here. The only memory I have of drowning was on a camping trip. Peter held me under the water until I turned blue. He's my brother."

"Yes, your brother. I want to know about him, too. Heavens, you know more about us than we do about you. First, here is the picture."

From her bosom Madame Dupré unfolded her arms to reveal an old black-and-white family portrait in a paper frame.

"And this is Claudine. *Voila!*"

She held her breath while Frank took the paper frame and studied it.

"She's the little one, with the curls. That's me, of course, and my husband. The plain one is her sister." She glanced back and forth from the photograph to Frank's face. "It was a long time ago."

He turned the photograph over; on the back was written in faded ink *'Pére, Moi, Géraldine 7 ans, Claudine 3 ans.'* Madame Dupré looked away to avoid seeing Frank's disappointment. She did see Madame Lavois' raised eyebrow, and ignored it.

"What was she like, please? My mother?"

"Claudine? Oh, my. She was beautiful. Happy, always laughing and running and jumping around, not at all like her sister. And music? She always played music, and sang. She liked to dance, but there wasn't much dancing on the farm. The truth is that Claudine wasn't much for the farm. She couldn't wait to leave to school in Saint-Lô. Julia never married; she inherited a house from my uncle where Claudine and Géraldine lived when they went to the cathedral school. Claudine was in her last year when the bombing began, when Géraldine went back for them."

"Did she look like this?" Frank showed Madame Dupré Will's drawing; she looked at it, then handed it back to him.

"Not very much. She was a slender girl, very petite, and very good with clothes. All the boys thought she was as beautiful as any movie star. Now, tell me more about Captain Hastings, about your younger brother, your wife, all of it."

Frank did not correct her about Peter being the younger brother. What difference did it make? Everyone who should have been hurt by Will having neglected to mention that he already was married and had a baby, they all were dead now, Claudine, Will, even Peter.

"Peter was the smart one."

"Not if he held your head under water. That's not very smart."

"We fought a lot. I'll be honest with you, I wasn't much of anything. Peter was the one who was good in sports, handsome, and always had girl-friends." For a fleeting instant Frank thought that Peter sounded more like Claudine, except that there was no question about who Peter was. Even the fat woman from Tierra who spoke at his memorial service knew Peter from the moment he was born. "We fought all the time and I got in trouble for it quite a bit. I wasn't a very good brother."

"You don't have to talk about your brother if you don't want to. I want to know about you. You grew up in a small town and went to school. Then what?"

"I went to a public university. I didn't work very hard at it. I studied journalism and then the army drafted me for two years. When I got back from the army, I moved away to get a job at a newspaper in Austin, and that's where I met my wife."

"His wife's an Indian, you know." Madame Lefèvre crossed her arms and smiled.

iii.

The *cherie* volunteer interrupted at eleven o'clock with offers of Jell-O. Madame Lefèvre wavered, asked what colors were available, was told red and green, with bits of pear, and left for the dining hall. Madame Dubois was interrupted to take her tamoxifen dose. Madame Lavois had become restless. It was time to drive to the cemetery.

"They never let us out except to go to the doctor and church, but no one goes to church. We do get to go to school concerts; they're awful. Sign me out."

It was his first act as a grandson. They walked to the reception desk, opened up the guest binder, and she filled out her name, the time, and wrote that she was going out with her grandson. Frank signed it, first as Frank, then as Francois, and within three minutes they were navigating back to Sainte Marie du Vire.

"Did I really drown?" he asked. Jeremy sat in the back and translated as Frank jerked the car around the city walls and through roundabouts.

"Yes, and you were poisoned, too. That's where the Irish hospital was." She pointed to a dull brick elementary school; they weren't three blocks from Frank's hotel. "Coco says that literature students come here from all over because of a translator they had. Your father knew him. I thought there was a plaque."

"Beckett. He was a writer. He won the Nobel Prize."

"I don't know anything about that, but he and Captain Hastings got on together. Back then the hospital was wooden buildings. The rest of this neighborhood was just rocks and dirt, from the bombs. There's nothing of it left here but that school. Come on."

"Beckett gave my father a set of all his books. That's where my wife found the drawings, inside Beckett's books."

They drove past faded houses and disco bars and through narrow streets in the center of St.-Lô. The road climbed and eventually the spires of the cathedral emerged above the rooftops.

"This," Madame Dupré pointed to a house, "was where Claudine lived with Julia. It was a beautiful brick home. She let the ground floor for a piano studio and rented rooms for the girls who were at the cathedral school. Claudine said that the very next day after the Germans moved them into the tunnels a bomb destroyed half the house."

"Where was her school?"

"It's gone too. It was in a building alongside the cathedral, not far from the tunnels. We'll walk by there."

The gothic cathedral had been rebuilt too, but in a way that left no doubt it had been destroyed. Only one spire now stood, more or less; the other had been topped off at the height that remained after it had been blasted in two. The front of the cathedral, between the spires, had been rebuilt with dark green concrete blocks. The medieval stonework of the spires and portal ran along the structure to the edges, then stopped at the green bricks, then resumed at the north tower. It seemed vacant; no one entered, or left. It now was just a vestige cathedral.

"The brick building with the slate roof is where the school was. They wore black dresses with white blouses and black jumpers in school. The girls who decided to stay and take vows moved into the convent and studied under the Clares for a year, as novices."

"What are Clares?"

"A very old order of nuns. They're all gone to Ireland now. Most of the monks and the nuns and all the priests ran away in the bombing, even the bishop. The priests came back to rebuild the cathedral but the nuns never returned." She paused to catch her breath. The bombing had been very hard on St. Lô. "They went to Ireland and then the Irish Red Cross came here with the hospital. This way."

They twisted and turned along another half-dozen narrow lanes and arrived at a cliff. A stone tower flanked hard granite walls that had been the ramparts of the city until the war. Madame Dupré walked past it, found a path that cut through the wall, and led them down the face of the cliff to the main road that ran alongside the river. She turned and pointed upward. Suddenly, a few blocks from where a skeptical beat cop had suspected Frank of looking for a children's playground, they stood before the very scene that Will had sketched: a hill, a path, a dark building at the top, a row of people making their way up.

"That was the old mental hospital. It was the only building left standing for a hospital. Claudine told me that your father was assigned there to help the local doctors treat patients. She went there to see him while he was working, but the French doctors told her to go away. She lived for a while in the rough, in what was left of Julia's house, but it was just a couple of crumbling walls and a stair and a lot of mangy dogs. Do you remember Emil?" She waited. "The mayor? He is Madame Lavois' son. They came here one night because Emil was very sick. Claudine didn't understand what happened but Genet told me that your father stole a jeep full of medicine and took it to him and it cured Emil. He was just a little boy. That was the last time Claudine saw your father."

Chapter Twenty-Six

i.

Cher Eleanor: I went to the cemetery yesterday, in Saint-Marie. I felt like a stranger. There are a lot of graves in the churchyard, most so old that the names and years are too faded to read. Mother's grave is in the middle of a family group next to her father, buried in the middle of other Duprés who I assume are ancestors. There weren't any flowers until I brought some, and the stone is out of alignment, like it had been sinking into the dirt.

This was very hard. The only picture I've seen of my mother was when she was three years old, and I couldn't imagine that child ever being grown-up, certainly not being a mother. *Grand-mère* was very quiet and sad and spent time saying a rosary. An ancient priest in a black top coat and a wide black hat came out of the back of the church, walked through the cemetery, looked at us, and walked back into the church. It all made me feel like an intruder, although I doubt anyone intended it that way...

He had sensed that Madame Dupré was agitated, especially when the priest came. They had spent only a few more minutes in the cemetery and made their way across the town square to a bistro. She had been quiet while they found a table, ignored the waiter, almost didn't look at the menu.

"A lesson, Francois: Always go to the bars closest to the church. Priests know where to find a drink." The *Brasserie de l'Eglise was* a nondescript bar with a green awning whose chief feature appeared to be that it was almost completely full of people having lunch. "Do you have a photograph of your father?" she asked.

"I'm sorry, I don't."

"Your mother? *Votre mère?*"

He also did not have a picture of Virginia. He wondered, first, what kind of son he was that didn't carry pictures of his family and, second, if she would ask anything else about Peter. She didn't. He worked his billfold out of his hip pocket and opened it to reveal a wallet picture.

"Eleanor. My wife."

"Eleanor. A beautiful name. She's very dark."

"She's Indian. On her mother's side. Not American Indian." She ordered a glass of Calvados and another for Frank. "Not for you," she said to Jeremy. "You're not old enough. And you have to get the words right. Coca-Cola for you. *Santé.*"

"*Santé.*"

That night he sent a fax to Eleanor.

...We went for a sandwich in the café at Sainte Marie. When Grand-Mere left us alone for a moment Jeremy apologized to me. He said the day that his uncle and the policeman tried to arrest me for looking at Doctor Genet's house, when they called him to translate, he didn't really believe I was anyone's lost son. He was embarrassed about it and to make it up he gave me a cassette tape of somebody called the Wrang Buggas and invited me to go look at his computers at the apple barn in Saint Marie. I won't, because after I see Chateau Dupré I'm going to check with Air France about getting a flight home Sunday. I've found what I came to find.

Eleanor answered right away:

Yes, Dearest, please, come home. I've always known who you are but selfish me had to struggle with wife me to be patient while you found out for yourself. I don't mean to be disrespectful of Peter, but I don't think I can forgive him for making you believe all your life that you were nobody. I need you, more than you know, and I do very much want you to come home, now.

Love,
Eleanor.

PS: Just as I finished, Candace called. Something may be happing about getting Peter's remains brought home.

PS: PS: Judge Leatherman brought this by for you. I think you should read it right away."

The fax cover sheet gave way to a second message, and a thick stack of more faxed pages:

Dear Mr. Hastings: I was able to get the army to send me the summary of the court martial that you and I talked about in my office some time ago. It may be hard to read, they never made a full transcript, but you'll see what happened. I hope that it helps you.

Sincerely,
Richard Leatherman, Judge (Retired)

ii.

The first page was similar to the military record that Frank had shown to Emil and Prudhomme in Saint Marie du Vire, except that it was written by a prosecutor and the prosecutor had been Judge Leatherman. Frank began to read.

Summary Notes:

General Court Martial of Curtiss, George, Corporal,

29th Infantry Division

Date: *October 11, 1944*

Location: *Temporary Courtroom 4th Infantry Division HQ, Command, Cherbourg*

Charge:*Art. 92, murder of Major Halliburton while on TDY at Chateau Dupre; Art. 58, desertion; Art. 75, endangering post*

Witnesses: *Capt. Deere, Inf., 2d/ 116th / 29th Infantry*

Pvt. Rogers, Inf., 2d/ 116th Infantry

Capt. Hastings, Med. Officer, 261st Field Hospital

The pages appeared to be Judge Leatherman's official notes of a court martial. It began with a summary of the first witness, Captain Deere, who said he had left a medical detachment at Chateau Dupré to study it as a possible forward hospital. Deere returned after a radio reported a German attack and found eleven men had been killed.

Capt. Hastings was unconscious on the floor in the front room, lost a lot of blood, bandage on chest. Deere went up to the second floor, found Major Halliburton dead, one bullet hole in back of head. Corporal Curtiss was not found at Chateau Dupre.

So, there it was: Will was wounded in an attack at Chateau Dupré and a Major Halliburton was killed. Frank folded the fax paper to protect it from smudging, then left his room and went to the bar of the Hotel de Selles.

"Beer, *s'il vous plait.*"

"*Oui, Monsieur Hastings. Nous avons 1664, Stella Artois, Heineken...*"

Frank began to order a Heineken, then remembered: *Beer? I'm in France.*

"*Vin, s'il vous plait.*"

"*D'accord. Blanc ou rouge.*"

"*Rouge.*" It didn't sound very French, not the way Frank said it, but the bartender smiled and brought him a large stem of very red wine. Frank went to an empty corner of the mostly empty bar and resumed.

The second witness was a private named Rogers. He said that the command post was demolished and the platoon leader was dead, so he ran to the main house to look for help.

> Rogers found Captain Hastings on the floor, in bad shape, and Corporal Curtiss cursing at Major Halliburton. Then Halliburton ran upstairs, Curtiss ran upstairs, and Private Rogers heard a shot. Rogers ran upstairs, found Halliburton in a bedroom, shot through head. Curtiss was not in the room and Rogers never saw Curtiss again.

Bad shape? Frank thought. *Deere said Dad was unconscious and bleeding. He was nearly dead.*

He continued to read. Rogers said on cross examination that when the battle started he had been knocked out when a shell hit the barn. He did not see when Captain Hastings was shot.

> Rogers was having trouble hearing and ears ringing because of being knocked out. 'I was shocked up pretty good.' Rogers knows that morphine is what medics use when someone is shot. Question: 'Major Halliburton was a medical officer. What would a medical officer have that a badly wounded man like Captain Hastings might need? Morphine? Yes. So what

you really heard Curtiss screaming at Halliburton was not curs-ing, not 'motherfucker,' but...? Answer: Morphine. And Major Halliburton didn't give his morphine to Capt. Hastings; he just turned and ran.

Frank ordered a second glass of red wine. He was ready to curse Halliburton too. The waiter brought the wine and Frank began to feel the effects of the grape. He turned a page and, suddenly, his father was the next witness.

When battle started Captain Hastings ran to the barn, roof caved in, beams down, men in bad shape. Lt. Campbell had been killed and the other medic, Antsley, was dead too.

Frank remembered the grave of Micah Antsley in the cemetery at Colleville. Names were becoming people.

Then Hastings was shot in the back, hit really hard 'like a bolt of electricity,' in chateau's courtyard. Lost a lot of blood, soak-ing through his field jacket, someone lifted and dragged him to the main house. Hastings was bleeding heavily, getting faint. Halliburton and Curtiss shouting at each other, Halliburton ran up the stairs, Curtiss ran after him. Hastings heard the gunshot upstairs.

So, Frank thought, *Dad was shot in the back, he was dying on the floor, Halliburton wouldn't give him morphine and ran away? No wonder Curtiss shot him.* Leatherman's notes continued with Will's cross-examination.

Hastings wrote a series of notes while in hospital because hav-ing trouble getting his voice back. 'One note seems to say ma-chine-gun fire from chateau at Germans was first thing that happened.'

'No, the first thing that happened was Halliburton ordered Lt. to shoot at the Germans up on the road above the apple orchard, told Lt. to have some guts and act like a man. Then Major Halliburton broke radio silence.'

A question from the judge:

'Did Major Halliburton breaking radio silence have anything to do with what happened with Curtiss and Halliburton after the battle?' Hastings answers Halliburton took the unit radio, tried to call Capt. Deere, and more Germans appeared on ridge above the orchard. Halliburton then ran to a dovecote, took over a machine gun and fired a burst toward Germans, but instead he shot the last American GI scout up in the orchard.' That's when battle started!

Frank was stunned. Whoever Halliburton was, he broke every rule of soldiering, then shot his own scout and fled. Frank remembered when Judge Leatherman said in the interview, 'You would call it fragging. Isn't that what you said in Vietnam, 'fragging an officer?'

Dad went before me, he thought. *Everything I did and saw and thought about in Vietnam*, he realized, *was something Dad did or saw or thought before I was born.*

After the battle Captain Hastings was lying in the courtyard, saw Halliburton run toward front door of main house. Later, in the house, after Halliburton was shot, Curtiss came back into front room, cleaned Hastings' wound, applied sulfa and morphine, and left. Hastings did not see Curtiss ever again.

Question: 'Until today?' 'No, never. This man isn't Corporal Curtiss. This is a man named Douglas.' Captain Hastings says the man on trial is *not* Corporal Curtiss. Hastings knew Douglas in England, he was a clerk in field hospital training school. 'He looks something like Curtiss but I'm pretty sure this is Douglas.'

Frank could only imagine the chaos in the courtroom. According to the record, the judge stopped the trial and brought Deere and Rogers back in; neither could swear with certainty whether the man was or wasn't Curtiss. Then Will had volunteered his own observation:

> Captain Hastings: 'I can tell if it's him or not. Douglas had a medical condition called cryptorchidism. No testicles.' Hastings had examined Douglas in England for VD, and 'cryptorchidism is a very obvious condition, he couldn't hide it.' Judge: You mean this clerk, Douglas, had no balls? Hastings: Yes. Hastings never examined Curtiss, but Private Rogers said Curtiss had two sons. If Curtiss had children, then Curtiss must have testicles. If this man on trial has no testicles, he's not Curtiss.

The notes ended. Frank finished the wine and gathered the pages, then went up to bed. At midnight he woke up with the wine horrors and went to the bathroom to puke it all out. He checked his bureau to be sure that the story hadn't been a nightmare, too. The fax was still there, just where he had left it.

He tried to imagine the scene, his father lying on the floor, Major Halliburton arguing over morphine as Will bled to death. Halliburton needed fragging, Frank decided, for shooting his own men and running away. *And could it have been Halliburton who shot Dad in the back? Why would he? It's crazy.* The more Frank knew about Will's life, the less he knew.

He tossed and turned until two in the morning, when it occurred to him that maybe Judge Halliburton had sent Frank the notes not only so that he would know what had happened to his father but also maybe to guide him to Chateau Dupré. He wondered if Judge Leatherman understood that the court martial against Artemis Washington had been a case of mistaken identity, just like the case against Corporal Curtiss, a case of someone not being who people believed he was.

He slept again, restlessly, but at five in the morning something woke him again. He turned on his light and reached for the notes, then read them until he found the line that had come back to him in his sleep.

> ... blood soaking through his field jacket, someone lifted and dragged him to the main house.

Who? Who lifted and dragged him to the main house?

He left for the nursing home before eight in the morning, hoping his grandmother would be ready to go.

Chapter Twenty-Seven

i.

As the Renault passed beyond the last sunken lane and hedgerow and came out into sunshine above the apple trees, it became apparent why Frank had never found it: Chateau Dupré was not on the way to anywhere, or from anywhere, an enclave sheltered by a jumble of other farms and lanes that hid it well behind the main roads on a gentle slope that led down to the Vire in the distance. The apple orchard grew down the hillside between the narrow road and the walls of the chateau.

From the lane, it was easy to look down into the chateau walls and see exactly what Will had sketched: the massive barn at one end, the chateau house on the other end, separated by a large farmyard filled with crumbling dovecotes and sheds built into the walls. A sign nailed to a tree by the two-wheel rutted lane that led down to the gates warned of a vicious dog.

"*Rouge. Duret, tres douce.*"

"She says they are Rouge Duret, the apples to make Calvados." Jeremy sat in the front next to Frank and both translated and explained. "All the farms have orchards. This one needs work; the trees should be picked by now."

The orchard was a patchwork blanket of reds and greens, fruit and leaves, the gnarled trunks of hundreds of apple trees. The aroma of apples, sweet, rotting, fermenting on the ground, filled the air. Flies buzzed above exposed roots and birds pecked at the fruit. Weeds grew at the bases of the trees and wooden limb spreaders were cracked and broken, letting the branches sag almost to the ground. Voles skittered around the roots.

"She says it's a disgrace, *Monsieur*, that Jean-Claude hasn't kept it in order. She says he's not a faithful tenant, and to not pay attention to anything he says."

"Who is Jean-Claude?"

"She says you will see."

The gate in the wall was not locked; Madame Dupré banged on it with a stick and, when Jean-Claude didn't answer, she told Jeremy to give the gate a push. It opened, to reveal a farmyard inside the walls that was as ill kept as the orchard above.

"*Bienvenue aux Chateau Dupré, Francois. Nous sommes ici!*" She walked into the middle of the farmyard and motioned for Frank to drive the car in and park it, then walk around with her. "This, Francois, is home. This is where Claudine grew up, and her sister. This is where Monsieur Dupré and I tended our orchards. We farmed those fields behind the chateau and raised our dairy cows. I want you to see everything and think how it was, not how it looks today. We have all the time in the world. Where do you want to start?"

"Who keeps it now?" Frank thought it didn't look like it was kept by anyone. "Jean-Claude? Is he here?"

"Let's walk and I'll explain it to you. See that shed by the wall? There used to be here a little house where the men stayed during the harvest. The nephew of my husband's cousin from Saint Pellerin came now and then to help in the harvest; he stayed in that house. Then my husband's cousin gave him the idea that if he married one of my daughters, this would become his chateau. It would never happen; he was older than them, they didn't like him, it never got to that. When the Germans came he disappeared. That is Jean-Claude. He comes for what he wants, disappears, and hides so he can come back when it's safe. He's a coward."

They walked toward the barn, Frank trying to see everything and look out for the fierce dog.

"One day an American soldier came here, drove right up where we're standing, and told my husband he wanted to put a dozen soldiers here for a week, just to rest. By then the war had moved on and we couldn't say no so they came to stay. Two or three of them moved in to the little house where the shed is now; the others slept in the barn. Your father was one of them. It was the first time we met him. My daughter told us that here's the man who did the surgery on Julia and we hardly believed it—he looked like a boy, thin, very quiet. Then we noticed how she looked at him and we suspected."

She let the story hang in the air, long enough for Frank to imagine the scene for himself.

"After that she got up in the mornings, did her jobs, milking the cattle, leading them out to the pasture, kitchen work, never a word, but still we saw. She would cut a few bits of bread, put a bit of cheese into a cloth, maybe some cider, and we'd look up and she'd be outside the walls, walking toward the monastery."

"Where is it?"

"Behind the walls."

"May I see it?"

"You'll see everything. There's a gate behind the kitchen garden. It's a few hundred meters away, toward the river." She pointed, he nodded, and she continued. "An hour later we would see the two of them, walking back across the meadow, from the monastery, and we knew. But, never did we have any reason to believe that either one of them acted improperly. We weren't even sure that they were anything more than just friendly. We never saw them touch, certainly no kissing, no hugging, nothing like that, nothing more than she might take his arm the way she would do with her own father, or me, when they walked outside. Then one day a troublemaker came."

"A troublemaker?"

"A troublemaker. A man who makes trouble for everybody. He was another American, an officer of some kind, and he strutted around like a little general, ordering everyone to do this and that. He demanded to stay in the chateau, told us he had the right, and he bossed the other Americans around something ugly. Your father spoke to him inside our house, we don't know what they said, it was all English, but they looked like they were going to fight. Then they left the house, arguing, and came back out here. A few minutes later, a soldier came and told us to get out of sight and take cover, that there was a German army up above the orchard. We hid downstairs, where servants used to sleep. The next thing we knew, there was machine-gun fire and a cannon shot knocked down our walls. It blew up the house where the officers were living, and demolished the barn."

"And my father was shot."

"Yes. When we came upstairs my daughter and some soldiers were on the floor of the salon, bent over your father. I have to tell you, I thought he was dead. Then they started arguing, right over him, and the troublemaker ran up the stairs. Another soldier chased him up the stairs, and...."

"He shot the troublemaker."

"Yes. He shot the troublemaker. How did you know that?"

Frank told her that Judge Leatherman had sent him a summary of the court martial.

"The Judge? You know him?"

"He was a judge where I live. He wasn't the judge in the court martial. The record was the first time in my life I knew anything about how my father was wounded. To tell you the truth, when I read the summary about the battle, I believe he thought my father lied about who shot Major Halliburton."

"The troublemaker. Yes, Halliburton. What did your father say? To the army?'

"He only said that the army had accused the wrong man. He knew because of some medical question."

The barn was as ill tended as everything else. Unused apple crates stood in piles in a corner. The cattle stalls hadn't been mucked in days; the open gates that led outside suggested that the dairy cows had not been brought in from pasture the night before or milked this morning. Chickens flew around in the rafters. Rakes and tools were scattered on the floor. Madame Dupré seemed relieved to stop talking about the battle.

"Let's go to the house, if you like."

"I would like that, if we're not in the way."

"It's my house. I can go anywhere I want," she said, and led them back across the farmyard, past rusting wagons and piles of abandoned tires and abandoned spring plows, to the chateau.

It was a classical French farm home, stone, with a slate roof. Tall windows ran in rows along the front wall and a broad porch capped wide steps. Columns supported a small balcony above the front door. If the cracked stones had been repaired and the missing roof tiles replaced, the windows washed, it would have been a beautiful home. Madame Dupré banged on the door and yelled:

"Jean-Claude! Come out here! Open the door!"

They waited for Jean-Claude to open the door; he did not.

Frank studied the area surrounding the house. An unassembled aluminum television antennae was propped against a wall. A weed-choked garden was visible around the side of the house and climbing vines choked a faded wooden gate in the garden wall. An assortment of fertilizer bags, garden hoses, buckets, and an abandoned privy toilet filled the near landscape. The wind rustled the vines and, for just a moment, Frank saw the tip of a spire in the distance beyond the wall. Madame Dupré led them around the back of the house, between the wall and the garden.

"*Hercule* always waited at that gate."

"*Hercule?*"

"The vicious dog. He was an old dog, the girls had it from when they were babies, but *Hercule* took to your father. It followed him everywhere. Very sweet dog. Your father used to bring you down to the garden and play ball with *Hercule*. This is his grave. We're going in."

He heard a wooden "pop" and looked up to see Madame Dupré pushing open the kitchen door next to the garden.

Apart from sneaking in and out of the Grumman house with Tog, and breaking into the school gym to shoot baskets on weekends, Frank hadn't committed many burglaries. He understood that the chateau belonged to Madame Dupré; he assumed that she had the right to come and go in her own home, particularly when she had a heavy key to unlock the kitchen door. Still, he felt like an intruder in Jean-Claude's kitchen.

The false décor of the nursing home and the dank kitchen of the chateau could not have been more different. Generations of Duprés had cooked in that room, pumped water by hand, boiled pots and cut up herbs for tisane, slaughtered small animals and sliced up garden vegetables. Now it was a wreck.

New and apparently unused electronic gadgets cluttered the floor. A can opener, a toaster oven, an electric mixer stood beside an upright vacuum cleaner, their unplugged wires snaking toward the door. Faded cabinet doors stood ajar underneath stone counters. Dirty pots and stained cups filled a ceramic sink that was served by a brass water spigot protruding from the wall. A blackened cast iron stove with an exposed gas pipe led to several gas rings on top and, Frank was certain, to a lethally explosive oven. Every surface was covered with macaroni and cheese boxes, soup cans, jam jars, instant potato mixes, dried vegetables, canned milk, breakfast cereal, and tins of ground coffee. The refrigerator stood open and appeared empty. Crusts of uncertain breads lay on the table next to a dirty plate and jam-crusted knife. The black murk of boiled coffee grounds were pooled inside a rusted sauce pan. A new Mr. Coffee, its warranty papers inside the pot, perched on a stool.

"This was our kitchen. Jean-Claude is disgusting. I've quit coming since his wife died."

She picked her way out of the kitchen, into the hallway beyond, where the Minitel and telephone stood. Beyond the staircase was a large salon, tall windows on either side, a knotted carpet on the stone floor, but otherwise unfurnished. A stone fireplace occupied the far wall, its hearth not swept since the last winter. To the left there was the wide, wooden, front door of Chateau Dupré. They were in the main salon of the house.

Will's ghost had not visited Frank at the remnants of the laundry house, nor as he walked through Sainte Marie du Vire, nor even while he stood in the cemetery and placed flowers at Claudine's grave. It did visit Frank now, a gentle visit, calm but sad, helping him sag to the floor in the same place where Will had nearly bled to death more than forty years before. It was a silent ghost, just a whisper to explain that it was for this reason that Frank had been made to work so hard before finding Madame Dupré, and why he had been made to look foolish in front of Jeremy and Emil and the policeman in Saint-Lô. Frank had had to earn it.

"It was here, wasn't it?" He asked.

"Yes, exactly there."

He traced his fingers on the stone floor, wondering whether if he lifted the rug there would be blood stains on the floor. He closed his eyes and tried to see his father, his mother, soldiers arguing, Major Halliburton running up the stairs and Curtiss chasing him while Will almost bled to death.

"Would you like to see the rest of the home?"

He felt, inexplicably, that he did not. If the house had a soul, Frank was in it. Touring Jean-Claude's bedroom, peeping into the chamber where Major Halliburton was murdered, wondering whether anyone had installed a toilet and shower, asking if there were old boxes filled with his mother's things in the attic, all seemed prurient.

"Of course."

There was nothing much upstairs. Jean-Claude's daughter had taken over the room where Claudine and Géraldine had slept. The murder room was empty, nothing to see except a chunk of plaster dug out of the west wall.

Frank smiled and nodded when it was pointed out that as a baby he had rolled an American baseball in one room, had eaten Spam in another, had been rocked to sleep in yet another. The ghost had slipped away.

"May we go back outside?"

"Of course. I ask you this question. Francois, when you worked on the farms did you do things like painting, trimming the branches, repairing the chicken houses?"

"Eleanor and I painted our house. It's a tiny house, just a few rooms all in a row. There are a dozen houses just like it, all along a creek at the bottom of a cliff. They call it The Sisters."

"Sisters?"

"Rich families lived up on the cliff. They built the row houses at the bottom for their servants."

"Were they slaves?"

"No, it was after slavery, but poor. Supposedly the first houses there belonged to girls who were sisters. We painted our home the color of peach blossoms, not leaving it the way others thought of it, but warm, you know? There are peach trees at the creek, by a swimming pool. And trees, mostly oak. So, I guess yes, to painting. And we trim out the dead branches in the spring. But I don't really care much for chicken houses."

"Ah."

"I'd like to see the meadow, if I can."

"Of course."

ii.

He walked alone to the monastery, wading through tall grass and wildflowers, circling the buildings twice before pushing on the door and entering the quiet courtyard. The bell tower had become dirty with decades of smog and inattention and the arched windows were filled with sparrows' nests. Large doors that separated the monastery from the meadow had rotted from its hinges and were in danger of collapsing. A dozen monks' cells lined the inside of the cloister, a large kitchen and storehouse filled the corners on either side of the chapel and refectory. The emptied chapel was a warren for pigeons. It was in the monks' dining hall that the ghost returned.

It was a warm ghost, a comforting one. Frank sat on a broken table and folded his arms and sensed kindly breaths caressing his neck and unseen hands touching his. When he closed his eyes he saw Will, impossibly young, skinny, a too-large army uniform burying him in its folds, sitting with someone in the room, napping, eating bits of bread and hard cheese. The moment passed, only to return when Frank walked back to sit on a stone bench in the cloister, near the overgrown garden.

It was the closest Frank would come to feeling that he belonged. For that half hour he was happy, in France.

iii.

"*Monsieur?*"

"*Oui?*"

"*Madame* Dupré is waiting for us."

He and Jeremy walked back through the tall meadow, making a path through wet meadow grass like Indian scouts, like explorers.

"*Monsieur?*"

"*Oui?*"

"May I ask a question? About soldiers?"

"I wasn't a very good soldier. But, yes. Why?"

"I hope to earn my *bac* next year, and apply for CPGE." Jeremy could see that Frank didn't know the terms. "A *grand ecole.* I'm thinking of the army."

"All right."

"So, when I heard you say to Madame that your father told you to not salute, I wasn't sure I understood."

"He said never salute an officer you respect. I forgot about it, until I was in Vietnam. No one saluted officers in Vietnam. We were ordered to not salute."

"Why?"

"Because snipers shoot officers. If you saluted someone in the field, they usually got shot."

Jeremy considered the idea as they walked, then asked another question.

"*Monsieur?*"

"*Oui?*"

"It isn't my business, but I think there is a better picture of your mother." He waited to see Frank's reaction; it was not his business; he was only the interpreter. "Her *carte d'identité*. We all have them."

They stopped. Jeremy took out a leather passbook, then opened it and showed it to Frank. His identity card listed his name, Jeremy Brissot, and where he was born, his parents' names, occupation, height and weight, and his photograph. He had signed it.

"Your driver's license?"

"*Non.* I am not permitted yet. It is my identity card. Everyone has one. Your mother would have one."

"That was forty years ago. How could we find her identity card from forty years ago?"

"There will be one. It would be registered at the *mairie* of her domicile. She could not enter school without her card. She could not even leave home without it. The Germans were very strict about that, *Monsieur.*"

"Thank you."

"It wasn't my business. I thought maybe it was an idea you might to consider."

"Thank you."

iv.

"I think you better tell me."

Madame Dupré had watched them walk back across the meadow. Frank's look of contentment, first in the salon and now, after he sat in the monastery, that look on his face was what she had waited for. When he now told her that he felt a great peace, she quietly replied that it was time for him to know the rest of the story, beginning with Jean-Claude, who she hated with every bone in her body.

"Where to start? I already told you he tried to insinuate himself, with my daughters, with no luck. He came back after the battle like a maggot to a wound. I don't think I can tell you how hard it was then. The chateau was wrecked and then the Americans tore it apart, barns, houses, everything, trying to find the man who murdered the troublemaker." She caught her breath; Frank tried to imagine the chateau wrecked in a battle.

"Then Jean-Claude took us away," she continued, "first to relatives in Saint-Pellerin. That's where we were when your father found us after he came out of the hospital. Then Jean-Claude demanded we move to another relative at Brix. Claudine ran away, but he found her living rough in Saint-Lô and brought her back to Brix. That's when we discovered she was expecting. From that moment Jean-Claude treated her like she was a dog, lower than a dog." Jeremy did his best to keep up.

"Then she had her baby. It broke my husband's heart, that she wasn't married. To tell you the truth, my husband was never the same after she died. We brought you from the house where you were born, to the church for her funeral, and then back here. The war had moved to Germany. We didn't have anything here at Chateau Dupré, no food, the house torn apart and left open, but this was home. I don't have words to say how terrible that time was. I took you in my arms and Jean-Claude said it was time to go back to Brix, and I said 'No! Why? What more can they do to us?' He said to be safe, but I said 'No, I'm staying here.' Then he said he was going to stay with us, that we needed him to manage the orchard and the harvest. He said he took care of us when the Americans destroyed our home and he would take care of us now, and he moved in. We were too broken to argue. Then Monsieur Dupré had a stroke. They put him in a hospital, I had no help."

"The Irish hospital?"

"The Irish were gone. The medical society ran the Irish out. My husband never came home and Jean-Claude never left." She waited to be sure that Frank understood, then continued. "Then, as soon they moved my husband into the convalescent home, you began to have accidents."

"Accidents?"

"First, here. Right here. You disappeared. Vanished. We found you here in the meadow, sitting in the grass. It was raining."

"I learned to walk?"

"That's what Jean-Claude said, and I thought, well, maybe you did learn to walk. Then you fell off the barn. I locked you up. Then he poisoned you."

"Poisoned me?"

"Do you know what DD-T is?"

Of course he did. DD-T was wonderful fog. In Bridle they drove a truck up and down the streets spraying DD-T into the air. He and Tog and every kid he knew ran along behind the truck, playing hide and seek in the fog. It was like the pipeline, using smoke to cover your movements, except that in Bridle no one was firing a mortar at you.

"Some prisoners of war got into it at one of the other orchards. A few of them died so the prefect outlawed it. A few weeks after you fell off the barn you were sick again, vomiting, couldn't keep anything down. Genet couldn't do anything but the Irish figured it out. They had a laboratory. You had enough DD-T in you to kill a pony."

"Was it proved? That Jean-Claude did anything?"

"No. But I knew."

"Why? Why would he try to kill a baby?"

"Why? *La réserve légale.*"

"I don't understand. Can you translate it?"

"Réserve légale is... the *reserve legale.*" Jeremy tried.

"Then he tried to drown you," she continued. Her soft face had hardened and she gripped Frank's hand. "In the river. In an apple crate. For one harvest only, the harvest you were a baby, Jean-Claude didn't use the cooperative at Saint Marie. He took the apples to the cooperative at Pont-Hébert instead. 'It's closer,' he said, better shares, he had an arrangement, la di da, and then you disappeared. Madame Lavois found you covered up in an apple crate, floating to the sea. The Irish hospital in Saint-Lô pumped out a liter of bug spray and apple bits. I knew then that he would never quit until he killed you. Mr. Beckett told your father what happened. That's when I agreed that he should take you to America."

They sat for a while, looking out at the grass toward the tree line of the Vire. She was visibly angry; Jeremy was shocked. Frank tried hard to remember.

"Did he go to prison?"

"Just for a few months. They opened an investigation but they couldn't prove anything. No one saw anything, no witnesses, and you were gone. The parish priest never recorded your birth certificate. They couldn't even prove there was a baby."

"You knew I was born. And Madame Lavois, and the Irish doctors. You knew I was real."

"It wasn't enough proof. For murder, they said there must be a body and a birth certificate. For everything else, no proof. Jean-Claude was released and he came right back to Chateau Dupré. He has lived here ever since."

"Why didn't you throw him out?"

The faint traces of a smile lifted her mouth. "He claimed the *réserve légale* as the heir on my husband's side. With no baby and no birth certificate, I couldn't prove that he wasn't. I lived in my corner of the house, he fixed up a room in the barn, and we didn't speak for almost seventeen years. He rebuilt the farm and the orchard, harvested the apples and started the dairy back up. He married, had children, his wife died...."

Frank had the gnawing sense that he was missing something. Becky's note, ice on Main Street, Bar Cielo with moments quite.

"Why didn't you speak for seventeen years?"

"Because of you. Captain Hastings was raising you but I knew that you would come home. I waited for your eighteenth birthday...."

On my eighteenth birthday I was burning chicken shit napalm into the letter 'S' on the Bridle football field.

"I waited that summer and the rest of the year. You didn't come home. I waited a few more years, then gave up and moved into Autumn Leaves." She considered saying 'I wanted to die,' but decided it was more than necessary; he was paying close attention to her.

She led them back out of the meadow and through the kitchen gate. The sad garden was full of weeds, the rows flattened by rain and time, the rabbit wire torn and sagging. The wooden steps and the kitchen door looked like a monster's jaw, a black hole.

"But now you're back. Do you understand what this means, that you're back?" He didn't. "Francois, this is yours. All of it. The house, the orchard, the meadow. The barns, the fields, the dairy, even the monastery. Every apple tree, chicken, and cow, all of it. You are the heir. This is your chateau."

The ghost whispered, very gently, and Frank forgot that there was something he had forgotten.

"Francois, it's time for you to come home. Your wife can teach here, easy. I saved enough money for you to fix up the farm." She paused. "You can do something with your life now, something important."

315

He sat on the steps and tried to breathe, the heady air of being wanted, needed even. The love of a grandmother, a landed man with a fine chateau, apples to grow and a dairy to operate, even a chapel where he could go thank the Lord for his fortune, not five hundred yards away.

"Francois?" she declared. "This is your home."

Chapter Twenty-Eight

The phone call was mercifully brief.

Eleanor had been resting on the sofa, a blanket tucked around her for warmth, trying to focus on index cards that listed the traits shared by Emily ("The Knight's Tale") and Dorigen ("The Franklin's Tale"), when the ringing telephone startled her. Frank had said, "*Bonsoir, ma cher femme,*" and she had said, "Are you alright?" Frank then had told her that they were rich. She had asked what he meant.

As he spoke of inheriting a chateau, of a grandmother who would pay for everything, of a clean break and a fresh start, she remembered the other time that she had had something to say but had remained silent. All that Eleanor would have had to do to save Eldred Pott's life while he prattled on about pick hammers and the new Sainsbury's would have been to interrupt him and say 'Eldred, it's over,' but she had not. She interrupted now.

"No, dear."

"No?"

"No. It's not who I am. It's not who we are. You have to decide if it's who you are."

Her tummy had burned. She had been glad to be alone so that if she began to spot or bleed he wouldn't see her. Now she wasn't so sure, but she had to stand her ground.

"It's a chance to have a clean break, a fresh start, dear. To do something with my life."

Silence.

Silence.

Silence.

Silence.

"Hello?" he continued. "Eleanor? Are you there?"

"Yes."

"Can we talk about it?"

"Yes."

"Then say something."

"Alright. I don't understand what you mean when you say you could do something with your life. Inheriting a farm in France sounds like someone else doing something with your life, not you doing something with it."

"Really? What have I done with my life?"

"Dear, that isn't you asking. That's Peter, or Tog."

She wanted to tell him but knew that telling would be unfair. She was obliged to play fair. He had to find what he was looking for by himself. She continued.

"Are you going to just exchange the statue of you that Peter chiseled out of his marble for a different statue of you that Grandmother Dupré is carving out of her marble?" she asked.

He hadn't understood.

"Michelangelo. He said he didn't carve the *David*, that it was always in the stone and he just removed the part that wasn't the *David*. You are not in their stones. You are you, not what others want to make of you."

The tinny hum of the international telephone connection bored into her hearing. She wondered if he had listened.

"Peter made you think you were what's left of a big slab of rock that Peter chipped away with a hammer and said was you. You even let Tog tell you that; he said you failed him, and you believed him. What did Tog ever do for you? Or Peter? Nothing. And now you ask me to say I agree when a woman you didn't even know a week ago wishes to turn you into an apple farmer? Is that who you are?"

Silence.

Silence.

He changed the subject. He was learning how to do things in France, making friends. He knew how to get a picture of his mother. Jeremy would help him get a copy of Claudine's identity card from Emil. Jeremy also said that he would like to help Will at the chateau, restoring the orchard, repairing the buildings. He did not tell her that Jeremy proposed inviting the Wrang Buggas to have a concert in the monastery. Things would turn out.

He then said he had to see Madame Dupré again tomorrow.

"Dear, it's more complicated than just that. We go out every day, for a Calvados so she can smoke a cigar. We walk through town and she teaches me words. More than anything, there's this man who tried to murder me when I was a baby. When I was a boy. Dad brought me to America to save my life. She's waited forty years to get rid of him, but until now she couldn't even prove I existed. If I don't inherit her farm, he will. I owe her that much, don't I?"

"He didn't murder you."

"She even had the chateau deeds transferred. It's called a *compromis du vente*. It takes effect now. It is our chateau."

She had said it was more complicated at home, too. The Volvo needed two new tires. The hot water heater had stopped heating. Birds were nesting in the eaves and she couldn't get up on a ladder to clear them.

"And what about Artemis Washington? Wasn't he something you were doing with your life, proving that they had the wrong man? Are you going to let him die in prison now that Madame Dupré has the right man?"

There had been another silence, concluded by his asking what she wanted him to do. She had answered by saying that he had to decide for himself. He asked if she would consider coming, just to see, and she had said she could not.

Be faithful to your promises, she remembered. Chaucer said that fidelity was the essence of marriage, more important even than the vows themselves, but neither Dorigen nor Emily seemed to have got it quite right. *There has to be a middle ground between telling him what he doesn't know to coerce him to come home and not telling him what he doesn't know because, when he does learn, he might stay. What does playing fair mean, anyway?*

"Do you remember the funeral home envelope?" she had asked. He didn't. "It was in the trunk of the Volvo. Your father's things that he had with him when he, you know, they were inside it. I found it when the man at the gas station showed me the bad spot on the spare tire." He began to remember. "Did you know a man named Fondren?"

"No, why?"

"There was a note in Will's things, from a man named Fondren. He was asking Will about a D-Day reunion. The note was three years old."

"Why," Frank had said to her, "would Dad have a three-year-old note with him when he died?"

"I don't know," she answered him, although she suspected that she did know. "I'll send it to you, if you like."

He had not told her yes, or no, and they had ended the call, neither of them able either to take back what had been said.

She returned to her index cards but *The Canterbury Tales* were beyond her ability to concentrate. After fifteen minutes, she put Dorigen and Emily aside and started a kettle for tea. *The Road to An Khe* was still piled on the lamp table where Frank had left it. She picked it up and held it, wondering if she, too, was about to become another woman in a village, frantically trying to stop a fire.

I am not just your laundry lady, Frank, just going along with you until you set fire to my roof and say oh, well, sorry, but can you still wash my uniforms and sleep with me?

She drank from her cup and settled back against the cushion, knowing that she had to send Mr. Fondren's note to Frank. It was more complicated than winterizing their home or being unable to sleep.

She also didn't want to set fire to Frank's roof. He was not just her laundry boy, either, and there was more to it than whether he took care of the hot water heater and flat tires and slept with her. She cried for a while, unsure if her marriage was over or if she was hormonal or was being unfair or overgenerous, but the next morning she took the note that Fondren had written to 'Will and Geraldine' and gave it to the departmental secretary. She copied it and sent it to Frank by fax at the Hotel de Selles in Saint-Lô, so that when Frank read it he could make the decision for himself.

That was being fair.

Chapter Twenty-Nine

i.

P hilippe put Monsieur Trichet's legal folders in a brief case, latched it, and handed it to the advocate. Trichet, in turn, adjusted his necktie, buttoned his suit jacket, and led them to the reception room where Jean-Claude waited with an ancient priest.

Of all the electronic presents that Jean-Claude's children had given him, he hated the Minitel the most. His children never sent a message to him. As a consequence, it stood, silent, in the hallway that led to the old servants' stairs in Chateau Dupré, the green cursor on its dark screen winking at him, a reminder that he was alone and unwanted. Then, yesterday, the Minitel had rung three times, winked once, and spat out a message:

```
☐Jean-Claude Martel, 36 11 Chateau Dupré: At
ten tomorrow morning I will bring my grandson
to Chateau Dupré. Mme. Marie-France Dupré @ 39
11 Feuilles de Automne S-LF☐
```

The message had kept him awake all night. He had lost his appetite and skipped breakfast, tried to drink cold coffee in the dark at six o'clock, then copied the message onto a scrap of paper. He had been waiting for Trichet when the lawyer arrived in his chambers. Trichet had smiled and told him that when the imposter came to the chateau with Madame Dupré, he would accompany Jean-Claude and they would settle the matter.

"And the priest, Jean-Claude?" he had said. "You say that he knows something of the history?" Jean-Claude assured him that he did. "Bring him as well."

Thus, this morning, the pilgrimage assembled at the lawyer's office, bound for Chateau Dupré and, Philippe observed, to trap the prey in the web.

"Gentlemen? We are ready."

Jean-Claude and the old priest, Father Jean, nodded. They followed Trichet outside, watched Trichet get into his Citroen sedan, start the engine, and drive cautiously onto the street. They got into Jean-Claude's dilapidated Fourgonette and ground the starter until the motor kicked into a congested and smoke-filled wheeze. By fits and starts Jean-Claude then led Trichet out of Saint-Lô, onto the *Voie de la Liberté*, across the bridge at Pont-Hébert, then into the back lanes and hedgerows that bordered the River Vire. A half-hour later, they ground to a halt in the dusty courtyard of Chateau Dupré.

"Right through the front door, Jean-Claude," Trichet directed. The men formed a queue and marched up the front steps. Jean-Claude lifted a hand to knock, but Trichet stopped him. "Do not knock, Jean-Claude. Never act like you are a visitor; act only like you are the owner. You have the right."

Jean-Claude opened the front door, led the priest and lawyer across the threshold, and marched into the kitchen. It was upon entering the kitchen that Trichet began to second-guess his plan.

"You!" Madame Dupré hissed at him. "I told you I never want to see you again, ever."

"Ah, Madame, you have the advantage of me," he replied. "I understood you to say you did not want to see me again, ever, in *Feuilles d'Automne*. *Desoleé*. Please accept my courtesies." He bowed stiffly from the waist and stepped to one side. "And, of course, you know well my client, Jean-Claude Martel. And Father Jean, from Sainte Marie du Vire. We're very happy to see you this morning to resolve this unfortunate unpleasantness. May I ask to meet your party?" He beamed at Frank, who was not beaming, and nodded politely at Jeremy, who in the face of such bristling disagreeableness was rethinking whether he wanted a military life. "May I begin?"

"No. You may end, lawyer. We have no business to discuss with you. Jean-Claude has been told to leave. This is not his home. It is not his farm. All of you, leave. Jean-Claude, you may pack your kitchen gadgets and your junk and put it in your truck. Anything here after this afternoon will be taken out in front of the barn and burned. Good day."

Jeremy could not keep up, indeed was so startled at the confrontation that he made no attempt to translate at all. Frank understood a few key words, '*non*,' and '*resolve*' and '*allez*' but, like Jeremy, understood chiefly that instead of a calm discussion about Madame Dupré's plan to transition him in and transition Jean-Claude out, a battle was unfolding.

"Madame, please. Hear me out. I left you with a *compromris de vente*. Have you not read it? It will save you a great deal on taxes and, more than anything, save a dispute in the courts. You don't want this lovely farm eaten by legal expenses, do you?"

"I do not. That's why I signed it."

"Signed it?"

"Certainly," she said. "With a few changes, but I signed it. Mademoiselle Garnier arranged the proof of signature with her notary. The original has been delivered to the records office at Saint Marie."

"Then all is solved." Trichet beamed, then replayed what he just heard. "What changes?"

"Every place in the *compromis* that had the words 'Jean-Claude Martel', I drew a line through with a pen and inserted the name 'Francois Dupré,' and initialed the changes. The notary said it was quite legal."

The lawyer reasoned that if the chatelaine of Chateau Dupré had waited for a mysterious grandchild to appear before trying to throw Jean-Claude out, all the legal reasons he had advanced why she should sign the place over to Jean-Claude were even better reasons, from her point of view, to sign it over to her grandchild. Trichet regrouped. "Ah, Madame, you forget. Article 721. The *réserve légale*."

"Jean-Claude is not my heir. He has no *réserve légale*."

"Do you deny he is the only male nephew of your husband's cousin?"

"I don't care if Jean-Claude is the Sultan of Syria, but he is not my heir. My grandson is my heir, directly."

"Not until it is proved, Madame. Until then, Jean-Claude has the right of *réserve légale*. You cannot throw him off the land. You cannot disinherit him. You cannot sell the land to anyone else."

"No, lawyer," she snapped. "He tried to get the inheritance by murdering a baby. No court in France would let Jean-Claude Martel inherit so much as a can of dirt."

"Accusations of which he was cleared, Madame."

"For which the charges were dropped, lawyer, not cleared. No one said that he was innocent."

"That this man next to you claims to be your grandson is proof enough that Jean-Claude did not murder the child, Madame."

"What are they talking about, Jeremy?" Frank asked.

"I'm not sure," Jeremy whispered back. "Some of it has to do with her signing a deed to you. The lawyer says the *réserve légale* protects Jean-Claude from her giving you the chateau because he cannot be deprived of his inheritance. But I don't understand how he could be her heir because you are her heir, except that she says that he murdered you, except that you're alive."

"Not me, Madame," Jean-Claude growled. "I did not try to kill this man when he was a child. I swear it."

"Someone tried to drown him and poison him! That was you, Jean-Claude!" she hissed.

Jean-Claude was quiet, for a very long time. He then hung his head and confessed to another man's crime.

"It was not me, Madame. It was the prefect, Marat, who tried to kill Claudine's baby. He knew your husband's condition and wanted part of the chateau for himself. Here's what happened." Jean-Claude ran a boney hand across his face, his glazed eyes caste downward. "It was a terrible time. Claudine was dead. Your husband had a stroke. It was impossible for me to get in the harvest by myself, *Madame*. So, I made an arrangement with Marat. He would get me some POWs to labor in your orchards but I had to give him half the harvest. I agreed. When I took the apples to the co-op, the POWs took the child and dumped him in the river."

"Ah, forty years after the crime you blame a dead man. And why the prefect? And POWs? Why not blame De Gaulle? Or my husband? You're a liar, Jean-Claude. You put DD-T in the child's bottle!"

"No, Madame. Marat brought the DD-T to your farm, Madame. He tried to poison the child. Not me," Jean-Claude declared. "I had nothing to do with it, I swear." He looked Madame Dupré in the face, like a movie actor denying his guilt. "The child was alive when you took him to the Irish hospital. He disappeared after that, not before. My conscience is clean, *Madame*. I made my confessions this morning." He glanced at Father Jean, who nodded his assent that Jean-Claude had in fact confessed those very facts.

"And he confessed them to me as well, *Madame*." Trichet took a document from his briefcase. "Here is his declaration under oath, in legal form. You may read it. When the child disappeared, Jean-Claude believed that Marat had succeeded in killing him. This man has tried for forty years to preserve your farm for you, and you have wronged him. You might turn him out, but you have to win your case first, *Madame*."

"My case?"

"As far as the law is concerned, even if you prove that Jean-Claude is not your heir, he is your tenant." Trichet brought out yet another article of the French legal code. "He has the right to at least six months' notice before you can end his tenancy. And even then, in the end, you will have to prove in court that he is not your heir or he will inherit this farm."

"Francois is my heir. Jean-Claude is not. There! I proved it. The same way you proved Marat was the criminal, not Jean-Claude. With my word."

Trichet opened the briefcase and brought out his secret weapon.

"You say this American is your heir, *Madame*? Of your blood?"

"Of course he's the heir of my blood. He's my daughter's child."

"Then you will have no difficulty proving your case, *Madame*, but with science, new science. It is called DNA. It seems that such proof is indisputable."

Trichet's secret weapon looked very much like a photocopy of an article titled 'Forensic Application of DNA Fingerprints,' translated from the journal *Nature*. Trichet handed the English version to Frank, who read it aloud.

"'Many highly polymorphic multisatellite loci.... Bzzz bzzz bzzz ... DNA of high molecular mass.... Bzzz bzzz bzzz...,'" Frank read aloud, "'will revolutionize forensic biology, particularly with identification of rape suspects.' Jeremy, please tell the lawyer that Madame Dupré is not dealing with a rape suspect."

Jeremy did so.

Trichet smiled.

"I believe this new science may have more application to the case at hand than you understand, Monsieur. There is this." He gave Frank the last item from his briefcase, the real bomb, an article in the Shepherd's Bush Hammersmith Legal Gazette:

"Using the genetic fingerprint in blood cells from mother and son, scientist Alec Jeffreys has detected from DNA to a degree of certainty of one

325

in thirty million that a Ghanan child is the child by birth of an immigrant to England who claimed to be his mother, even though she had not seen him in fifteen years."

Trichet beamed.

"That which science can prove with certainty, Madame, also can be disproved with certainty. Blood tests of your DNA and his DNA will prove that this man is a fake. Jean-Claude is the heir to this chateau."

Father Jean continued to sit with his hands on his knees. Jean-Claude looked at his lawyer with a degree of ignorant admiration. Jeremy translated the article to Madame Dupré as best he could, and she in turn looked at Frank with an equal degree of uncertainty. Frank looked at the boxes of toasters and blenders, the microwaves and cheap radios, and considered his answer.

"We have a saying in Texas, lawyer: 'This is the line in the sand.' It means that once you cross this line, there's no going back."

Trichet waited for Jeremy to translate, then replied. "We too have a saying, Monsieur. It is that you are an imposter. Blood samples will prove it. I don't even need that much proof."

"Because?"

"Because Father Jean says you are an imposter." Trichet turned to the priest, who understood that it was his cue to speak.

"You are not the child of Claudine Dupré. You're too ugly." The priest gathered his sagging shoulders and bony hands and bared his decayed teeth. "I knew Claudine Dupré from the day she was born until the day she died. I knew her baby, a beautiful baby. I gave the birth details to the prefect myself; Marat never recorded them. And you, sir, you are not that baby." He glared at Frank, just as he had done in the cemetery.

So that, she thought, *is why the magistrate could not prove that there ever was a baby.* Madame Dupré would have slapped the priest if Frank hadn't taken her by the arm.

"*Grandmere?* Come with me." Frank stood and helped her to her feet. "It's all right. Let's walk a little. It may even be time for a cigar." He turned to the priest, the lawyer, and the thief. "Gentlemen, we're going outside for a while, to talk. You may go or stay. When we come back, if you're still here, I'll give you my answer."

He led her to the kitchen door and opened it, then turned back to the men in the kitchen.

326

"While we're gone, you're welcome to make yourself some coffee. It's very easy to make, you know. Goodbye."

They walked to the postern gate, opened it, and left.

"And he's too fat, too," the priest muttered, as the gate closed behind them.

iii.

"This may be the loveliest place I've ever been," Frank said. He helped Madame Dupré sit on one of the stone benches of the monastery garden. Pigeons wheeled overhead and dived back toward the broken chapel windows. "I felt a special connection here when we first came a few days ago. I thought you might like to sit here to collect your thoughts."

"He's a liar, Francois."

"Yes, I think so." He took her hand and sat quietly, gazing across the garden and out through the wide gate. "You told me that my father liked to come here. I sat in that room, over there, and had the most calm feeling come over me, as if he was in there with me. I hope you feel it."

"They did try to kill you."

One of the cows that had made its way from the barn to the meadow grazed outside the monastery gates in the soft, thick grass. Frank wondered whether history would repeat itself, whether the cow might explode, if bovine heads and haunches and bags of teats might rain down on them.

"It doesn't matter." He waited to be sure she had understood. "I'm leaving on Sunday. I have to go home."

"Leaving? Getting on your horse and riding off into the sunset when there's trouble? You let a trumped-up lawyer and a crooked priest call you an imposter and you run away? Is that the kind of grandson I have?" She turned her back on him. Jeremy looked away.

Frank took out a note with a sentence he had composed with the help of his Larousse, read it once more, and handed it to her:

"How long have you known?" the note read.

"Known what?"

She handed the note back to him. He handed her another note, one that he had suspected he would need.

"That I'm not Francois," it read.

"I don't know what you're talking about," she replied.

He reached inside his jacket pocket, withdrew a couple of sheets of paper, and handed to her a photocopy of Claudine's *carte d'identité*:

Nom: *Dupré*

Prenom: *Claudine Grâce*

Profession: *étudiante*

Fils/ fille de: *Albert Dupré*

Et de: *Marie-France Dupré*

Né le: *25 mai 1927*

á: *Sainte Marie du Vire, château connu*

Départmente: *Manche*

Domicile: *chez parents*

It was dated January, 1944.

Jeremy had gotten it from the *mairie*. Frank, in a burst of hope, had opened the envelope, imagining a picture of his parents gazing into each other's eyes in a field hospital, walking arm in arm through battlefields, falling in love in the monastery and, in less vivid detail, finding each other in ways that resulted in him. The *carte d'identité* instead proved what had actually happened.

Claudine's face was the shape of a heart, her chin a gentle and clean point that ended above a schoolgirl's white collar and blue sweater. Her skin was so perfectly clear that when Frank first saw the copy of her identity card he believed that the original photograph must have been touched up. Fair hair was parted just to one side of the middle of her high, wide forehead, falling away in perfect harmony on either side of her face. Her eyes, widely open and with lovely brows and lashes, stared with such poise as to make anyone who saw it deceive himself into believing that she was eager to see you. Wide cheekbones framed a slender nose that was perfectly proportioned, pert, balanced, nostrils slightly flaring. Her mouth, lips barely parted to form a lovely W, revealed perfectly even teeth. Claudine was beautiful, a Boticelli *Flora* but very alive. Frank had no trouble remembering a face exactly like it.

"I should have known, *Grandmére*, but I didn't want to know. The only photograph that you had of Claudine was of a three-year-old child. You didn't have any of her dresses or even so much as a doll or a school dress in a trunk in the attic. Then, when I asked about Claudine and my father you always answered 'my daughter.' We drank brandy and you smoked cigars and told me stories about the battle but almost nothing about Claudine. I heard what I wanted to hear." He studied her face to see if she denied it or was angry. She knew. "And the priest is right about one thing—I'm too ugly to be her son."

They stared at the arcade in the monastery, the graceful and evenly spaced archways that divided the places of work and worship from the gardens and paths, he hoping that the soothing air that had whispered to him before would return to tell him what else to say, she hoping that he would change his mind.

"I still want you to have the chateau, Frank. I want my affairs settled. I don't want him to have it."

"I can't, *Grandmère*," he answered. "It's not mine. But he won't have it. I'll see to that,"

"Does the blood thing matter?"

"I don't think so."

"I've read stories where they prove things by blood in courts."

"I know. Those are the kinds of stories I write for the *Gazette*, police stories. Don't worry; I know what to do."

"What am I supposed to do?" she asked, maybe to him, maybe to no one.

He waited to see if she was listening.

"Let me tell you a story. I was about eleven years old and one day I took a snake home, to scare Peter," he went on. "I put it in his bed but he didn't go to his room, not right away. That night we went straight to dinner."

"What are you talking about?"

"How hard it is to get rid of a snake. Mother asked if anyone wanted seconds, more biscuits, more gravy, more iced tea, and we all said yes, even my father. She got up from the table and went to the stove to pour more gravy and when she looked up my snake was staring back at her from over the back of the stove, eyes open, tongue flicking around. She shouted and would have beaten it to death with the gravy pot if she hadn't scared it so much. It jerked up and slithered away and disappeared through a gap in the floorboards beneath the sink. We hunted for it all night with flashlights, garden tools, and baseball bats, but we didn't find it."

"Did you ever get rid of it?"

"Yes. It kept popping up in the back yard. I tried to kill it with a hoe, fed it poisoned mice and crickets and sicced Hercules on it. I couldn't get rid of it. Then one day I went out and got a better snake to drive it away. That's what we're going to do, Grandmère."

"I don't understand."

"Jean-Claude's a snake. The priest is a snake. I'm just going to get you a better snake. You'll see."

She didn't seem very satisfied.

"Are you leaving me?"

"Yes."

"Are you ever coming back?"

"I don't know. I would like that, but I can't see that far into the future."

"I do want you to be my grandson, Frank. I'm sorry I tried to trick you."

"I never had a grandmother, either. I wanted you to be my grandmother. I still do. It'll be alright."

"What are you going to tell them?"

iv.

"Jeremy, please try to explain this to them." Jeremy nodded. "This is called a Mr. Coffee. Here's how it works."

Frank took the coffeemaker apart, rinsed the pot, and removed the plastic coffee basket. He took Trichet's paper copy of Article 721, tore it into a circle, and stuffed the *réserve légale* into the basket, then used a spoon to add coffee. He poured water straight into the top, then plugged Mr. Coffee into the wall plug. A red light came on. It soon began to hiss and sputter. Coffee dripped through the legal filter. Frank rinsed out a nasty cup, rinsed it again, poured coffee into it, then drank it.

"I always drink a cup of coffee when I make a decision. It's very good coffee, not like pressed coffee, but like American coffee, if you like that sort of thing. Here's my decision."

The lawyer, the priest, the old man, all of them glared at him and waited for Frank to speak.

"I'm leaving on Sunday. I'm taking the *compromis* with me. Now, first, Monsieur Martel, you may stay here for six months from today if, but only if, you have the orchard harvested, the trees cleaned up, the barn painted and put on a new roof, and you have the house repaired to a new condition, inside and out. You will do this at your own expense. Second, you will leave *Grandmère* Dupré in peace with her friends at *Feuilles d'Automne*, but any time and every time she wants to come here, you will welcome her and let her enjoy being home." He stopped to catch his breath and form his words. "Third. Next week, then again at the first of January, and again every three months, you will send her a statement of accounts for the harvest, the dairy, the planting of the field and mowing the meadow by the monastery, and the expenses. She will send them to me to review. Do you understand me?"

Jean-Claude had the basic terms in his mind; Trichet was busily thinking of difficulties.

"Listen carefully. If you fail in any one of these, you will be thrown off the farm and you, Trichet, can then try to persuade the new prefect that the old prefect attempted to murder me for Jean-Claude's benefit. Fourth, if you don't accept these terms, you will leave today. Immediately. You will gather your clothes and get in your truck and leave." He paused, then turned to face the priest. "Last; Father Jean, you're a liar. I don't know the specifics, but no honest priest would let a man accused of murder live in his victim's home for forty years without a word to the authorities. You're going to die soon; get right with your Boss before you do."

They glared at him.

"Any questions? No? Those are my decisions. This meeting is over."

Trichet was not through.

"You are still an imposter. I will prove it. With science."

"Lawyer, if you want to use this DNA science, the police or a judge can have some of my blood very soon, but not today. I'm leaving Sunday. I doubt that there's enough time before then for you to even find Professor Jeffreys in England, much less persuade him to forget about all the rape cases and immigrants from Ghana and turn his microscope on me. Don't fret; you will have your chance, but not before Sunday. But, listen carefully: this is my line in the sand. If you do get these DNA tests done and they're wrong, then Jean-Claude is going to pay the price for your crossing my line. It will be a heavy price. I know something about handling bullies and you, all of you, are through bullying Madame Dupré."

331

"Jean-Claude did not try to murder you. He did nothing to you."

"I don't care."

"Then why?"

"Because he did try to destroy my family. He very nearly succeeded. That's why. Goodbye."

The accusers walked out to watch Frank and Madame Dupré and Jeremy walk toward Frank's rented car. Just as they opened the car doors a *whoomp!* erupted near the chicken coop. A flash of fire and noxious smoke rose from the bare ground. Then, just as quickly, it subsided into a stinking mess of diesel and poultry leavings, scorching the letter 'T' into the barren ground.

By the time Jean-Claude found a hose to quench it, Frank and Madame Dupré and Jeremy were driving away through the orchard.

V.

Frank stopped at Autumn Leaves to say goodbye. Madame Dupré said he could change his mind, even that he could keep a horse at the chateau because, even if he was not Claudine's child, he was the kind of child she wished that Claudine had had. She hoped that he would consider. He said that he would. She kissed him on both cheeks, and he kissed her, and said thank you.

He drove to Sainte Marie to say goodbye to Jeremy and Emil.

Officer Prudhomme stood in the town square near the water fountain, hoping that Frank would park illegally, but Frank left the Renault near the apple barn. He knocked on Jeremy's door, thanked him and shook his hand, and said goodbye. Jeremy gave him a cassette of *Poshgirlsshaggin'* and told him that he might want to buy a personal computer with something called a modem.

Frank walked up the rutted path to the center of town but the *mairie* was locked and Emil was nowhere in sight. He took a few photographs of Dr. Genet's faded windows, of the church, the *mairie*, and the Calvados barn, so that he could better explain to Eleanor where he had been.

His last stop was the cemetery. He looked out for Father Jean but the old priest stayed away. He did not photograph Claudine's grave but did concentrate on it so that he would remember it for the rest of his life.

He drove away from Saint Marie, around the *calvaire* at the traffic circle, and out past the Champion mini-store on the Saint-Lô road. He pointed the Renault toward Paris, and the airport, where he could send a fax to Eleanor to tell her thank you before his flight.

Chapter Thirty

"Please sirs, to take your seats. The general will be with you very soon."

The men nodded and took their seats at the conference table.

Khan, Foreign Affairs, nodded politely to Khan, Defense, and to Khan, Internal Security. None of them nodded at Farman Ali, Intelligence. Ali assumed control of most meetings of the core ministers; that he instead was seated alongside them meant that the meeting would proceed as General Zia wanted it to proceed.

The Khans, the Law, the Foreign and Defense and Internal Affairs, each wondered whether they might be about to see video clips of themselves on closed circuit televisions or read carefully-typed excerpts of careless statements that they had made while speaking to someone on the telephone. In just such a meeting, Salik, Media, had seen a film of himself taken by closed circuit television, speaking with an American in a parking lot near the consulate in Karachi, and then been demoted to Salik, local news broadcaster. Ali, Intelligence, had supplied the video. Each squirmed and wondered whether Ali himself might be in General Zia's sights.

The aide opened a panel in the wall. The ministers turned, expecting to greet General Zia but instead took in their collective breaths and scrambled to attention. General Rahman himself marched through the opening, went directly to a seat at the head of the conference table, and faced them.

"Akhtar Abdur Rahman, Gentlemen. Inter-Services Intelligence." The silent chill that had reached them through hundreds of miles of telephone lines at the meeting the month before was now a verbal chill that went right down their spines. "Be seated. Praise be to Allah."

"Allahu Akbar."

"Gentlemen," Rahman instructed them, "open the folders before you. On the first page you will see that there is a photograph. Study it."

334

The photograph showed the SS *Antares* riding at anchor. In the background there could be seen a manmade jetty. In the distance port cranes serviced cargo ships in dock.

"The next page, gentlemen."

The second photograph also showed the SS *Antares*, but much closer. Its American flag, the bridge, its working decks, even some of the sailors on deck were visible.

"Thank you, ministers. You have unique responsibilities. General Zia values your advice. I value your advice. What do you see in the photographs?"

Khan, Foreign Affairs, saw an American naval vessel entering the Port of Karachi.

Khan, Defense, saw an American naval vessel that was not entering the Port of Karachi. General Rahman agreed with him.

Khan, Internal Security, saw the American naval vessel maintaining a distance from the breakwater at the entrance of the harbor. Although not visible in the photograph, each of them knew that Masroor Air Force Base was situated just beyond the port, close enough to dispatch aircraft to intercept any vessel that attempted to breach the harbor without permission.

"And our Brother Intelligence? What do you see?" General Rahman asked.

"An American naval vessel that, in the morning, had a large container on its deck but in the afternoon does not have a container on its deck. And it is turned one hundred eighty degrees, as if leaving the port rather than arriving."

"Precisely. Gentlemen. I will not insult your intelligence of the English language but I must ask you a question of English. American English, to be precise. Do you know the expression 'nuts?'"

"Nuts?"

"Precisely. Nuts."

"Nuts are to be eaten, sir. Such as cashews, sir. In America there are pea nuts. The President Carter was a man of pea nuts."

"Very good. What is the expression 'a man is nuts?'"

"Ah," said Khan, Foreign Affairs. "I should have considered it. For a man to be nuts he is considered to be a deranged man. 'See that man? He is nuts.'"

"Yes, that is also true. But there is something else," said Rahman. They then understood that Inter-Service Intelligence already had the answer; it was not a quiz. "When a person likes something very much, what do they say? In America?"

"Very good, sir. They say a man who is besotted by a woman, such a man is nuts about the woman."

"Or," added Khan, Foreign Affairs, "when a man is devoted to something to an excessive degree. Like our Brother Bin Laden." He waited for the others to wonder who was their brother Bin Laden. "He is training the men in Afghanistan. The Americans say he is a radical Islamist nut."

"How do you know that, Khan?"

The cold voice startled them. Khan, Foreign Affairs, clamped a hand over his own leg to prevent it from shaking. Khan, Defense, gulped audibly.

"How, Khan, do you know about our brother Bin Laden, training men in Afghanistan?"

"Bin Laden has requested the Ministry of Defense to provide equipment for his camps, General. For training. His fighters. In Afghanistan. Sir."

The temperature in the room became very cold. They waited to see if Khan, Defense, disappeared. He did not.

"That is not true," Rahman said at length. "You will forget, Khan, the mistake of thinking there was such a request. There was not. Do you understand?"

Khan, Defense, understood. The others understood as well.

"Do not be concerned with Brother Khan, please, ministers." Rahman let his words hang in the air. "The American General Casey has proposed a very ambitious schedule to establish training camps. They are very important, the training camps. Our friend President Reagan is very enthusiastic about the training camps. The camps are not your concern, ministers." He paused to be clearly understood. "And we know nothing of a Bin Laden in Afghanistan. "

The men squirmed. Khan, Defense, wondered to which hellhole in the desert he would be transferred, where his sons would go to school, whether his wife would become an outcast.

"Nuts," Rahman resumed. "I believe that what our Brother Khan was describing was that a person who is a zealot is said to be a nut. So, then," he continued. "What, gentlemen, is a Jesus nut?"

The men let their breath out.

"Ah, sir, you have tricked us. Very good. A Jesus nut is an American who is a Christian zealot."

"They appear very much on television, Sir. I believe in the south of America. Many people watch them."

"They believe in serpents."

"And money."

"They are very famous, Sir."

Rahman laughed, a forced laugh, the laugh of a prison guard making sport of frightened men.

"Ah, ministers. Ah, ah. You have made me laugh. It is not an American Christian. It is an airplane part. It is called the Jesus nut." He laughed again. "It is on top of the helicopter. It holds the entire helicopter to the rotor blades, all of its weight, everything. American pilots say that when that nut breaks, the only thing a pilot can do is pray to Jesus? Ha, ah ha. Pray to Jesus to not fall out of the sky!"

Apostate dogs.

Blasphemers.

Ignorant whoresons.

The ministers then did laugh at the image of a floundering pilot, stars and stripes on his shoulder patch, hands in prayer, begging a bolt for salvation, fluttering to his death.

"So that is where the name comes from; it is the Jesus nut. Turn to the next page of your folders."

A line ink drawing with fifteen labeled items showed the principal components of a helicopter rotor system. In the absence of a helicopter to let their eyes match up the items in the drawing, the diagram looked to the ministers more like a devilish toy assembly, an erector set. As they read the part labels and imagined how they might fit together, an aide quietly opened the door and led into the room another man who walked forward to place a small box on the table. He opened it, took out a red grease cloth, then placed on the cloth a splined metal block with a threaded core.

"Gentlemen? This is Airman Parvaez Suleman. Airman: tell the ministers what this is."

"Yes sir. It is a Jesus nut, sir."

"What is important about this specific nut, Airman?"

"It is cracked, sir."

Each of the men looked at the Jesus nut. There was a very fine, very faint crack on the spline.

"Airman? What happens when one of those nuts cracks?"

The air force shoots the helicopter mechanic, he thought. However, what he said was, "The helicopter crashes, sir."

"What do you do when you discover such a crack?"

"We write a red X on the log book. The helicopter is grounded until the nut is replaced with a new nut."

"How many of our helicopters are grounded at the moment, Airman?"

"Fifteen of the American ones, sir. For replacement of the Jesus nuts. Some also for hot sections, too. I don't know how many more Jesus nuts will come apart on the next inspection, but a dozen more engines with hot section overhauls are coming up soon. And there are other parts on order, Sir."

"Do we have Jesus nuts on standby, Airman? Can you repair the helicopters with what is in your supplies?"

"No, sir. But we should be able to repair them soon, sir. They were requested some months ago."

"I see. Thank you, Airman. Go."

The aide led the mechanic out of the room. When the door closed behind him, General Rahman resumed.

"Look again at the American vessel near our port, my ministers. Brother Intelligence? Tell us what you think is in that container on the deck of the American vessel."

"Jesus nuts, General," said Farman Ali.

"Jesus nuts, yes. Many other things as well, but in particular, Jesus nuts. They are listed in an American military delivery document, Export License 5735-1986. If you look very carefully at the container on the deck of the *Antares*, you will see those very numbers painted on the side. But still, the *Antares* rides at anchor instead of signaling to enter the port to unload. Tell me, Ministers, should we ask the Americans for them?"

"If we need them, sir." Khan, Defense, knew he was being singled out; he grasped for a straw. "Perhaps our Brother Khan, Internal Affairs, knows whether we can obtain them elsewhere. Or manufacture our own."

Khan, Internal Affairs, was being singled out as well. He knew that there was not a metallurgical factory in Pakistan, or within a zillion miles of Pakistan, that could make such a high-grade precision-cut piece of alloyed metal before every helicopter in South East Asia quit flying. He limited his answer to saying that he would inquire.

"The container is no longer on the deck of the SS *Antares*, Ministers. It has been put back inside the cargo section of the ship. Tomorrow the *Antares* will weigh anchor and sail back to Washington. I must instruct you, Brother Khan, Foreign Affairs, or you, Brother Khan, Defense, to speak with your American liaison about the container that was exhibited to us in plain view on the deck of that boat. What instruction shall that be?"

"That we would like to have delivery of our... Jesus nuts, sir?"

"So say you all?"

All voted yes.

"Good. Brother Khan, and you, Brother Khan, you will please instruct the American military attaché at the embassy, and the port liaison at the consulate in Karachi, that we wish to have our goods delivered. The meeting is concluded. Praise be to Allah."

"*Allahu Akbar.*"

"You may go. Good day, gentlemen."

The men stood. The men began to file out.

"Brother Ali," Rahman interrupted them. The harsh voice spoke in even tones, the chill even more raw than usual. "Please wait. There is another matter. For you."

Ali stopped, clenched his jaw, and waited until the aide closed the door. The others fled. The door closed behind them. The conference room became very quiet.

"Of course, General," Ali, Intelligence, replied. "I am your servant."

Rahman's servant Ali had no doubt that the meeting was called for the sole purpose of demonstrating to the core ministers that Rahman was watching him and, most likely, that the Prime Minister was watching Rahman. Ali didn't care; Rahman watched everyone. He returned to his chair and waited.

"My Brother Intelligence," Rahman continued. "Disregard the little theater with the Ministers Khan."

"I am at your command, General. If you wish for me to observe the Khans shitting themselves in their tailored suits over a bolt, I will observe them. If you wish me to disregard them, I saw nothing." Ali was not shitting

339

himself, but he did understand that the theater was not over.

"Thank you for the photographs of the *Antares*, Farman. Very good photographs. A thousand words, each." Rahman used Ali's first name to indicate that he was not out of favor; the minister understood Ali's dilemma. "But, to the point: why, Brother Intelligence, has the American navy not delivered our Jesus nuts?"

Ali, Intelligence, considered engaging in double-speak, of the pilferage of arms between the Port of Karachi, where American arms arrived, and Afghanistan, where they were delivered to Bin Laden's training camps. He considered mentioning the rumblings that America was exploring some kind of trade with Iran for an American kidnapped in Beirut and might make a few demands of Pakistan in the process. There were a few other possible smokescreens for which Ali could blame the Americans, but he knew better, and decided no. He would say what he believed.

"They are annoyed, General."

"Yes. They are annoyed. They are not belligerent. They are not making threats. They do not send little weasels around from the embassy to demand an end to pilfering or to whisper about our spies in Beirut, or even about Bin Laden. They play the larger game, my Brother Ali, the more patient game. But with their Jesus nuts they are telling me that they are annoyed with us. In fact, they are telling me that they are annoyed with you."

He placed one more document on the table. It consisted of one page of the American export license listing the helicopter mast retention assemblies, the Jesus nuts, stapled to a single page of the Consular Certificate of Transport of Human Remains. The name '*Peter Hastings*,' and the profession, '*Pilot*,' and circumstances, '*September 5, 1986 – Pan Am 73 [Abu Nidal hijacking Karachi]*' had been typed into the certificate. The signature was blank.

"Farman, do you see that they are connected, the question of their pilot and the Jesus nuts?" He waited for Ali to nod. "In short, Farman, they want their pilot back."

Farman Ali knew that America wanted him back; he didn't care. The time had not come for him to unleash the pecking of crows, the desiccation of bodies, the bleaching of bones and rotting of coffins. Farman Ali shook his head, no.

"No, my General. There is nothing to return." They both knew that he

340

was lying, but there were no witnesses.

"I know what you feel, Brother," Rahman answered. His voice had not softened but by speaking slowly and in quiet tones Rahman, Inter-Services Intelligence, gave Farman Ali, Intelligence, the illusion that he cared what Ali felt. He showed Ali another photograph, of Pakistani helicopters aligned outside a hangar, none with rotor blades. "An American satellite took this photograph of our grounded helicopters. In a few days, American television networks may broadcast this photograph and announce that Pakistan's fleet is grounded because we cannot repair these aircraft, which they will say were generous gifts from America to its Asia friend. Every government on earth, and Abu Nidal, and Hezbollah and Hamas and Ghadafi and everyone else will be told that we, Pakistan, cannot defend ourselves without, I hate to say the words, America's Jesus nuts. So, I regret to go against your personal wishes in this matter, but we send the Pan American pilot back to America."

"Shuja, sir. He was my family. Please don't ask this."

"I am sorry. This time you must yield."

Ali knew the decision already had been made. Ali's private vengeance could not be the cause of holding the nation up to global embarrassment for want of Jesus nuts. There would be no loss of face.

"And the vengeance you feel, Brother, we shall direct it to Abu Nidal himself," Rahman continued.

It might be true. It might not be true. Abu Nidal was a Palestinian zealot.

The enemy of my enemy is my zealot.

"Every blow and insult you intended to inflict on behalf of the death of Shuja, you will inflict on Abu Nidal, Brother Farman. This is my word."

It was no longer a matter of Rahman permitting Ali to save face. It was a matter of Rahman telling Ali things, without witnesses.

"When must I give him up?" Ali asked. His hidden prison, his intelligence jailers, his methodical secrecy, those chosen few who knew, they would have to be told in private that General Rahman had intervened, that Farman Ali's plans had been taken from them. He would have to tell them that Rahman would visit them.

He was too late.

"God has already willed it, my Brother Ali. It is done. I am sorry."

Rahman opened his coat and removed a final photograph. The

container had been returned to the *Antares'* deck. A Pakistani helicopter, nose down and main rotor pitched to climb, flew away from the ship. On deck, in front of the container, three American sailors attended to a simple wooden coffin. It was done. Rahman already had visited Ali's secret prison and secret jailers.

The body was in American custody. Jesus nuts for Pakistani helicopters would be delivered within hours.

"I am your servant, General Rahman," Ali put his hands together and bowed.

"Praise be to Allah."

"*Allahu Akbar*, my General."

Chapter Thirty-One

i.

Then, suddenly, he found her.

ii.

Géraldine found a bright red apple on her reading table. Underneath the apple there was a note. 'A man is at the gatehouse,' it read. 'He wants to see you.'

The nuns had been given dispensation to cross over the stream to the cathedral for contemplative prayers on All Saints Day; she had felt a need to attend. During the nuns' service the chapel was closed to visitors, but the cathedral was not. The hushed footsteps of a few country tourists, some students from across the canal, the deacon, had padded along outside the chapel while she prayed and made concentrating difficult. She had tried to focus on the soul of Sister Margaret, their late sacristan, and President Kennedy, a sort of customary prayer introduced into the convent when he visited Galway shortly before the Cathedral was dedicated and even more shortly before he was assassinated. It had not been satisfying; her prayers had seemed memorized rather than heartfelt. Some days were better than others, even for prayers. Then, while they quietly made their way out of the chapel, across the footbridge, and back to Nun's Island, she had sensed that she was being watched. She had drawn her habit about her shoulders and hurried back to the convent.

Thus, the note had not surprised her. The apple had.

The younger nuns had picked the last of her apples more than two weeks before. They had romped around in the garden, sung to the crows, waved brooms, and stood on benches to pluck what they could. It had been a small harvest, not more than two bushels, and many of the apples had been small themselves. The consensus was that they were too sweet; the nuns had promptly chomped them into pulp to boil for jam.

This was not one of her apples, not from the convent trees. It was new and fresh and large. She drew her robes back on, straightened her wimple, and found a cloak, then changed her mind.

'What kind of man?' she wrote on the note. 'And now?'

She took the note to the chapter room to find the postulate. Conversation was permitted, technically, after six-thirty and until Compline, but she didn't want to draw attention to herself or the note. She gave it to Sister Brenda, who read the note and shrugged, she didn't know what kind of man.

Géraldine nodded in the direction of the hallway to suggest that they go out there to talk.

"I don't know, Sister. A man. Not so old, and not from here. American, maybe?"

"And the apple?" she asked.

"He gave it to me, Sister, and said I was to give it to you. I told him that we weren't teachers but he said to give it to you anyway, that you would understand."

"That I would understand."

"Yes, that is what he told me to do. Have I not done the right thing?"

"No, Sister, I think you do the right thing. You may go back."

Géraldine put the cloak on again. She left the main house through the garden door and made her way under a flat evening sky across the convent's great lawn to the gatehouse. She entered the rear door, used by the nuns and postulates so that they didn't have to leave the convent grounds. The visiting cell inside the gatehouse was to one side of this door. Géraldine knocked on the gatehouse porter's hallway door to alert him that she was there and, after a few moments, the porter spoke to her through a panel. He, too, could not say anything more about the man except that, yes, he was a man, and yes, he was waiting.

The porter said that it was highly unusual, it being of a Saturday and almost dark and all; she only nodded and entered the cell. She indicated that she would go into the nuns' visiting cell and, once the man was shown into the visitor's side of the screen, she then would decide whether to allow the visit.

It was a sad room, even for Galway. The nun's side was no more than five or six feet square, with nothing to distinguish it except a crucifix on the wall above the grille screen. The light was intentionally dim and the walls painted dark grey to make it less likely that visitors could easily see the nuns' faces through the grille.

Géraldine drew near the grille, sat, and waited.

When the light on the visitor's side was switched on, and Frank came in to take his seat, and she saw who had come for her, she had to grip the side of her chair to keep from sliding to the floor. Forty years of contemplative silence were the only experience she had in controlling her breathing, yet even so, she knew that he could hear her.

"It's a Rouge Duret," he said. "The apple." He waited for her to reply but, understanding that she might not, he continued. "I learned about them from Jeremy Bissot. He's a student at the Institute Saint-Lô. He wants to be an army officer. A very nice boy."

She studied his forehead, his sandy hair and eyes. This much of Will, at least, had been passed on to his son.

"Jeremy explained the trees to me in the orchard at Chateau Dupré. That's how I knew you were here, from your apple trees by the garden wall, between the cathedral and the convent. Rouge Duret trees."

Géraldine knew that he must have watched her praying and as she left the cathedral. She still wasn't able to speak to him, or even decide whether to speak to him, and waited.

"Your mother is well. I've seen her. She's not happy, but she is well. She has her friends in Saint-Lô. They live in a place named Autumn Leaves. *Feuilles d'Atomne*, I can't say it very well. They play cards and take walks and she smokes cigars. It's not too far from the Irish Red Cross hospital, where it used to be, in Saint-Lô. They thought I was a cowboy. Do you know very much about cowboys?"

Géraldine found it hard to concentrate. He looked like Will would have looked, she was sure, at the same age, but mostly in his forehead, and maybe his eyes. He was American, but she wasn't sure how to think of it, a *modern* American. His face was clear, his teeth even and white. His hair was longer than Will's hair had been. He was larger than she had imagined he would be and seemed older than she had imagined. His voice was more nasal than she remembered Will's voice having been. She thought every day of Will's voice; his son didn't sound like him or sound like his medic or his friend. Will had never said so many words to her in such a rush. She was accustomed to Irish English, schoolgirl Irish, priest Irish, abbess Irish, but Will's son spoke a lazy American language; she had to struggle to stop looking at him to hear what he was saying. She wanted to reach through the grille to touch him.

Bless us Oh Lord in this moment of need and help me I pray in the name of the ....

"Do you know who I am?" Frank asked. She heard him, and knew that he must be was waiting for her to say something. "I'm Frank. Hastings. I've come to find you."

She moved her chair very slightly forward, close to the grille, and turned so that what little light came through would fall on her face. She nodded, yes, she knew who he was. He saw her, faintly through the grille, but it was enough. He knew that it was her.

Géraldine was not beautiful, certainly not in the way that Claudine had been beautiful, but there was no doubt that when she had been twenty or twenty-one she had been pretty, in a clean and simple farm girl way. There was a trace of a slight, gentle smile. Her eyes, no longer as clear as when Will drew them, were set gently into her face, her skin no longer as young. A faint wisp of hair, almost white, escaped beneath the upper fringe of her wimple, at her forehead.

Frank took from his jacket a copy of the drawing Will had made of her. He rolled it tightly and pushed it through the grille.

"At last I've found you."

Silence.

Silence.

Silence.

"Can we talk?"

'Can we talk?' she thought. *What do you expect me to say, Frank Hastings, if we talk? What do you want? Why are you here? Now your father is died and I have gave forty years to Jesus, you find me here and give me this drawing and ask can we talk?*

She closed her eyes and remembered rising from their bed. She remembered how she had felt when she removed her night shift and then put on her underclothes, a skirt, a blouse, a thin jumper, tied her scarf around her head and tucked her hair into it, looking at Will the whole time. It had felt so natural.

All I wanted in life was your father. He looked at me and touched me. He drew me and said he would never leave me. Why did you come here now Frank Hastings? she asked herself. Then, *Dear God help me because I cannot do this.*

She said nothing.

"Is the man outside listening to us?" Frank asked

She edged as close to the grille as she dared and shrugged. *I don't know.*

"I've looked for a long time to find you," he said. "I had to find you."

He waited.

He waited.

"I..." He paused. "My father is Will Hastings. He passed away this summer. Do you know that my father is dead?"

She knew. No one had told her, not exactly, but she'd known the moment he died. Géraldine had been anxious all through July, and without any particular reason. It had been a good July at the convent, sun and not much rain. The students from Mercy school had visited with them. They had gardened. They had sewn. They had taken baked bread onto the lawn for nun picnics behind the walls. There had been a day in the city, her annual medical examination, and a day of communion with the nuns at Sacred Heart.

But every day of the month she had felt an increasingly crushing weight in her chest. On the last day of July it had been so heavy that she hadn't left her bed. Then, the following day, the weight was lifted. She knew that Will had died, even though his package didn't arrive until the middle of August.

There had been her attempt at confessing; she had found nothing new to confess, certainly not to the new priest, nor had she had the courage to admit anything old to him. She had requested permission to go to the cathedral to pray alone and the abbess had told her of course. She had prayed for the soul of Will and for their child and had cried uncontrollably, then returned to the convent and resumed her life. Frank only confirmed what she knew.

She nodded.

"My father was a very kind man, all his life. I love him very much. I didn't understand it until he died but he was kind to me when I was a boy, I think kinder to me than to my brother, and he was a good man. I think you would like to know that. He raised us, with Virginia, in a good way, but he never told me anything about you. I didn't know about you, not even the fact of you, nothing, before he died."

It had been agreed that Will would not say anything to his family about her, and he had kept the agreement.

"My brother used to be hateful to me," Frank continued. "We fought a lot when we were boys. When he didn't know how else to fight, he would say mean things about me. Mostly he said that I was an illegitimate child. He used to tell me that my father brought me home from the war, but I didn't think anything about it. Brothers say mean things to brothers, even at funerals."

He paused. She knew that he was struggling to talk to her.

He says he has looked a long time for me. He's found me; I can listen.

"I'm sorry, it's probably not the right way to tell you all this, but I've tried so hard to find you and now I don't know what to say. After my father died, my wife found this drawing of you, hidden in one of my father's books. Then we found some letters, hidden letters that my father wrote when I was a baby, and it all made sense. For the first time in my life I realized who I really was, am. I understood that my brother was right, that I came from a different mother. That's when I started to look for you, because I had to find you. That's why I'm here, to find you."

She moved her chair back from the screen so that he couldn't see her as easily. It had been a mistake. She wanted him to go. She wanted to go.

"Can you say anything? Please, anything?"

It became clear that she would not. She sensed his frustration, but he had no right to come into her life. That Frank Hastings had looked for her a long time, maybe as long as three months, did not absolve her forty years of marriage to Jesus. Jesus still was a jealous husband. He had been furious when she chose Will and He reminded her that she was already promised to Him. Will's son had no right to come into her home forty years later and expect her to break her vows.

"My father loved you, even until he died." Frank waited again. "I'm certain of it. He had this letter with him when he was found."

Frank took Eleanor's fax and rolled it very tightly, then pushed it through the grille. It snagged on the small square wires; she pulled them through to her side.

Eleanor had addressed the fax cover sheet to Frank at the Hotel de Selles in Saint-Lô, four days previous. It consisted of a single sentence:

Dearest: Whither thou goest. - Eleanor.

The second page of the fax was a faded handwritten note, addressed to
Will:

> 5/30/1983 — Doc and Geraldine, I hope you'll join
> us – I can't believe it's been forty years.

She knew that he must have heard her deep intake of breath through
the grille. She knew that he waited again to see if she would say anything, or
if she had fainted, or if she had had a heart attack or a stroke. She sobbed,
but very quietly, and after another long pause he continued.

"It was sent to him by a man named Fondren. I don't know Mr.
Fondren. I'd never even heard of him but he wrote this note to Dad three
years ago and sent it to him with a pamphlet about an army reunion they
were going to have in Normandy in 1984, to celebrate D-Day. The old army
buddies were going to go back to where they waded ashore. But Mr. Fondren
wrote it to 'Doc and Geraldine,' not 'Doc and Virginia.'"

Pause.

"Dad never mentioned the reunion to me, or Mr. Fondren, but then
he might not have. I live hundreds of miles away and he didn't go to the
reunion, so why mention it? He probably would have called me to say if he
was going to go, but not to say he wasn't going. It would have been a very big
trip for them, for Dad and Virginia, because they never traveled anywhere
except the mountains."

Living in silence is not the same as living with the constant noise of radio,
television, telephone, movies, schools, jobs, or even the noise of attending Mass.
It was a lot to understand, even if she had been living in Ireland for forty years.

"Dad had this note with him when he died. Why? A three-year-old
letter from a man asking him and Geraldine to meet in France, after forty
years? He had never talked about a Geraldine, and Virginia didn't know
anyone named Geraldine. So why would Dad keep this in his billfold? And,
I didn't think about it until just now, but within a few weeks of getting the
letter, Dad retired. He and Virginia suddenly left everything and moved
away, to a cabin in Colorado." He finished by asking again: "Why?"

He waited again. Nothing.

"He lived his entire grown up life married to Virginia, but—the hidden drawing of you? Hidden letters about bringing me home from France? And a note from someone who knew about you forty years ago and still thought my father was married to Geraldine?"

A bell rang, a very soft bell, one chime only. There still was no sound from Géraldine's side of the grille, nor any other sound until the door behind Frank opened.

"Compline, sir," the gatehouse porter said to him.

"Compline?"

"Evening prayers. It's time." The porter was polite, but insistent.

"Just a few more minutes, please." There was a slight rustling from the other side of the grille.

"Sorry, sir. They must keep their rules, the Clares. Visitors don't always know, but it's my job. Time."

"May I ask her?" Frank replied. The porter watched Frank turn to face the grille and ask if Sister Géraldine would extend the visit.

She would not. Her side of the cell was empty; the door closed behind her as she left.

"They do keep their rules, sir," the man said again. "Prayers and quiet, sir, prayers and quiet. I'll be helping you find your way out, sir. It'll be dark outside." He opened the door for Frank to leave. "And your paper, sir."

"My paper?" Frank stood, turned, then noticed that the fax had been shoved back through the grille. "Yes, thanks." He picked it up, stuffed it in his jacket, and followed the porter out to the little road that would lead him back to Bridge Street. Her looked at the paper under the porch lamp.

Géraldine had written her own note on it.

"Excuse me, sir," he asked the porter. "Delia Lydon?"

She had written 'Delia Lydon, 9.'

"Delia Lydon? Across the river, sir. In the lanes. You'll find 'er, easy." He walked Frank out of the gatehouse and nudged him into the dark passage that led to the bridge to the center of Galway. "Good night, sir."

iii.

Delia Lydon was not a 'er but a place.

From Frank's view, the porter at the gatehouse had been right; he found 'er easy. He had walked toward the bridge, noticed the Mill Street police station, and gone there to ask if they might help him find her. "Why are ye wanting to go there, for the love of Jesus? It's a pub, you Gom. Right manky dive." The desk sergeant had cross-examined him closely about seeking prostitutes, looking for drugs, and wanting to get in a pub brawl; only his hotel reservation, his passport, and an airline ticket from Shannon to Dallas persuaded them that Frank was the ignorant American he claimed to be. He then had walked back to his hotel, fully aware he was being shadowed by a cop. He sneaked back out an hour later, waded through a mob of drunks and sailors and prostitutes and found Delia Lydon on Quay Street near the docks, where he drank Guinness with his back against a wall until eleven o'clock at night before realizing that '9' meant nine in the morning, not twenty-one in the evening. He was back waiting at the pub when the doors opened and the beer trucks began deliveries early the next morning, wondering if he had been had.

From Géraldine's view the Delia Lydon was the one place in Galway where no one would look for a nun. She had been awake, praying, when the knocker came for her at matins, and still had not slept when the call came again for lauds. She had asked the abbess for a visiting day; the abbess had granted it without asking who had called on her the evening before. Géraldine was not a problem Clare.

She was, however, a troubled Clare. The decision to lie had been an easy one to make; novices did it all the time, postulates often enough, and never in forty years had Géraldine seen any of them suffer much for it. As for her own lying, apart from not having fully confessed to anyone, not from the day that Jean-Claude and Father Jean had dragged her out of her room and handed her over to the bishop in Saint-Lô and until now, she hadn't had much practice at it. Actual lies still seemed to be more complicated than mere misleading, and she planned to try that first. She hoped that by meeting Frank at the Delia Lydon she wouldn't have to do either. No one questioned a nun, not even Americans and publicans, and especially no one questioned a Poor Clare, not in Galway.

This view of her circumstance was more or less reinforced when she waited outside the back service door. The Guinness truck stopped and the beer man rolled a barrel in the back door on a handcart; she slipped into the pub behind him. The publican almost fainted at the sight of a nun behind his bar.

"Jesus, Sister, what are you doing here? You give a man a fright, you do," the bartender quivered. She gazed toward the mostly-empty tables.

"Counseling a soul, sir," she answered. He almost dropped an empty beer keg on his foot. "I've come to help that troubled man sitting there, if you please. The soul can be comforted anywhere."

Frank had been waiting, as she had suspected he would be, at a front table where he could watch the street and the door. She studied him from the bar and thought about leaving, of hurrying back to the convent and going no further.

Bless us Oh Father in this my hour of weakness and guide me as Your will commands, I pray You...

She wanted to touch him, to see if his skin was Will's skin, if the curve between his shoulder and his neck was Will's, if his smell was his father's smell. She instead stood behind him for a minute, studying him, while he looked for her through a cluster of hung-over sailors and Garda and shop-keepers who were rinsing the cobblestones in front of their doors. When Frank looked in the glass and saw her reflection he turned so quickly that he spilled coffee on her clothes, then on his.

"Good Lord, I mean damn, I mean I'm sorry." He began to wipe her skirt, then realized that would be more offensive than saying good Lord or damn, then wiped the damp spot on his crotch which, all in all, would have been even more offensive than the others if she hadn't laughed and told him to calm himself.

"I sit with you?" she asked. "You say you look for me and when you find me, well, was you finding me just to put tea on my clothes?" She smiled and brushed at the damp spot on her habit, then wiped her hands on her sleeves. "Or is coffee?"

"It's coffee. Sit, yes, sit, of course. Bartender, a towel? No, coffee. Wait, do you drink coffee? Or tea? Do nuns drink anything?"

"Sometimes. Not now. Is while I am supposed to be having cleaning up, with the postulates. After breakfast. I have had."

She spoke so rarely, particularly to anyone not a Clare, that she was flustered herself. Will had always had that effect on her, she remembered, and it was nice in a small way that his son had the same effect on her. She calmed herself; there would be less to deal with if she let him do most of the talking.

"So, you have found me. You are like your father," she said. "Will Hastings is always looking too. *Was* always looking. The first time I know him he is looking at soldiers in the hospital. Then he is looking for his brother, his brother's airplane is crashed. Then he is looking for Germans. Then he is looking for a place for the hospital. And after he is being wounded, then he is looking for me. I don't know how he finds me, but he did. Now, so do you." She smiled at him, in a nervous way, and wondered why she had said so much if her plan was for him to do the talking. "You say can we talk. For a little, yes. What does you want to talk with me, *do* you want to talk with me? I don't talk so much."

Frank wanted to go right to the heart of the matter but didn't know where to begin. Drivel about Drouet apples and cowboys, of proving who he was, had wasted the night before in talking about things that didn't matter. But she could have stayed behind the convent walls and he would never have seen her again, yet here she was, in a bar, waiting for him to say something.

"Is that how you met my father, when he was looking for something?" It was a place to start.

"I meet him in the barn at Saint Marie, where he is doing the surgery on my aunt. I thought he was a janitor; I was not so nice to him. My uncle makes me apologize to him. Then I see him walking across our field in the night and someone tells me he is always searching for his brother."

He loved the way she said 'de' for 'the' and 'loo'ing' for 'looking.' He wanted to sound like her.

"Can you tell me about that, him looking for his brother? My father never talked about having a brother."

"Never?" Finding his brother had been the only thing Will had cared about until he cared about her, and he hadn't talked very much about it to her, either. It occurred to Géraldine that, possibly, the less Will had said about anything to anyone, ever, the less she would have to explain. "His brother is flying a plane on the day of the landings, D-Day, J-Jour, and he disappeared. So when I first know Will Hastings he is going out from Saint Marie at night and walking around in the farms to find his brother. He's very sad, then; it is his only family. I don't think he finds his brother, ever."

Frank looked out the window again. A Garda policeman led a few sailors toward the docks. Shopkeepers washed the windows of green and pink storefronts. A shoe shop, a chip shop, a few schoolgirls in their plaid skirts carrying their books, men stopping at Kenny's for a newspaper. It could have been Saint-Lô or, in a pinch, Saint Marie, or Brix, or Cherbourg, or any of a dozen places that weren't Bridle. He seemed lost.

"You're the only person who ever told me that my father had a brother," Frank said at last. "I'm afraid that I found him." He tried to remember the details, but so much had already happened since then. "I was at the military cemetery, at Colleville. I was going to give up and go home. I hadn't found you, not your name, not Chateau Dupré, nothing. I was going to leave France but then I found a grave, Peter Hastings." She waited while he collected his thoughts. "The employee at the cemetery found his record. He was the only Hastings buried in Normandy. He was from Texas. And my brother's name is Peter, too." Was. "It was too much of a coincidence. That night I read the letters again and it was like, well, who is Peter Hastings? I don't understand anything."

"What letters?"

In morning light through a bar window she thought that Frank looked like Will but also that he did not, not exactly. He was pleasing to look at, at least not unpleasing, in an American way, in his blue denim jeans and loafers, a button-collar shirt and worn blazer. His hair needed cutting and he seemed a bit lost but then, she was lost too, on new ground. She watched him sip what was left of his coffee. When she said, 'What letters?' he seemed to like her soft French voice.

"They were hidden somewhere in the cellar of our house. My father wrote them, some from England, some from France. The name Peter was in this one:

> '20 June Isigny France: I told the army to put Peter's things in a box and ship it to me in Tierra in care of you. I don't have anywhere else to send things. If I make it back I'll come to Tierra for it. Thank you – Will.

"I didn't pay much attention to it the first time I read it," he contin-ued. "I thought Peter must have been a friend. Dad was sending his friend's things home. Now I'm sure it was his brother. The things he sent back were his brother's things. Then they named my brother Peter." None of it was very clear, even now, after reading the letter and finding the grave and listening to Géraldine talk about his father looking for a brother. "But they never talked about him, neither my father nor Virginia. It's all new to me."

"I'm sorry you don't know about your uncle."

"He's older than me, Peter. My brother. Did you know that?"

It slipped out.

That there was a Peter before there had been a Frank meant that Dad had already been married to Virginia. The thought had lodged in the back of Frank's mind from the moment that he first calculated that his father had fallen for a seventeen-year-old schoolgirl in France while Virginia was back home with Peter. He had decided to leave it in the back of his mind because it was a fact beyond hurting anyone, with Claudine and Will dead and Virginia in a state of aphasia. *Even Peter's dead.* The fact didn't un-lodge when he realized that it had not been Claudine. *Dad did the honorable thing; he brought me home, Virginia knew, even if I didn't. What difference does it make now?* he had concluded. Until now, when it slipped out. He knew it had hurt her.

Géraldine glared at him.

"Is this why you find me?" It had gone from the back of his mind to the front of his mouth. She glared; for Peter to be older meant that Frank was accusing her of adultery. "You don't know me, Frank Hastings. You don't know anything."

Her eyes bored into him. She gathered up her habit and he was afraid she was going to leave.

"I'm sorry. No, I didn't come here to accuse you of anything. It's plain that my father loved you, apparently he always loved you, and I love my father. I just came to find you, that's all. I have to know you. I have to know who I am." He watched. She settled into her chair again, and stopped gathering her robes. "When I learned that I was, I don't know how to say it, not an orphan, that Virginia isn't my real mother, I had to find you. What difference does it make if, you know, if you and my father loved each other? I came for you."

He spoke quietly. She knew he was sincere. She wouldn't have to lie, perhaps.

He wanted her to say it again, '*mother*', her *t-h* sound that she couldn't pronounce and that came out as '*moder.*' He thought she was beautiful, even under a nun's bonnet and robes. He was afraid she was about to stand up to leave.

"Because my brother always called me names, said that I wasn't really his brother. I don't look like him or Virginia. Then I found that my birth certificate was changed. '1945' was changed to read '1948.' Brix was changed to Bridle. And then, this:"

He gave her the telegram.

> The baby and I made it out of France, now in New York, leave for Tierra, arrive Sunday on the 3:15 train. Now Peter will have a playmate.
>
> Love, Will and Francois

It was addressed to Virginia, at Tierra, in October, 1946. The paper had yellowed, the teletype faded, the words as clear to Géraldine as they could be. She studied it for a while, then gave it back.

She softened. She wanted to know Frank, too. It was why she had come.

"My mother asks if you are a cowboy? I've never known a cowboy. Are you one?"

"No, not really," he answered. "Bridle was a cowboy kind of town, where I grew up. People had horses and some cattle, but I was a town boy. I worked at gas stations."

"Your father worked in the doctor office, when he was a school boy."

"You knew that? About my father?"

"Yes. We tell each other everything. And he draw me pictures of things where he lived."

"Like what?"

"Where he goes to school. The house where he lives. A friend, those things. He was so funny. He made me a drawing of a nurse with a bedpan because when we meet I mistake him for the nurse with the bedpan. He knew what I was thinking, always."

"Do you still have them, the drawings?"

"No, I lose them when I come to the convent."

It was true, it wasn't true. The drawings had been in the servant's room where she and Will had lived for two weeks, under the kitchen, when Father Jean first found her. Later, Dr. Genet offered to find the drawings for her but she had said no, to please keep them, because her vows required her to give up her earthly goods. Genet had loved Will almost as much as she did. Everyone loved Will, nearly.

"Did you love my father?" Frank asked. "I'm sorry, I shouldn't ask that but I...took the drawing I gave you yesterday, and some other drawings, to Sainte Marie to look for you. That's how I finally found your mother. She told me that I was her grandson. Everything she said matched everything that I already knew, the drawings, the dates. But then she said I was your sister's baby, Claudine's. She knew I wasn't."

"Do you know why she says that to you?"

"Yes. She wanted me to inherit your farm. So that a man named Jean-Claude would not inherit it. She says she hates him."

"Yes."

"Yes what?"

"Yes. I love your father." *Still.*

"Then what happened?"

She didn't understand.

"What happened? You loved my father. He loved you. I am born. You're here. Your mother wants me to be her grandchild. What happened?"

"What happened?"

"Why did you let me go?" He finally asked what he had come to ask. "I feel this, I don't know, like a hole in my life, like I don't belong. Peter told me I was a bastard, a French baby my father brought home from the war. Virginia always preferred Peter. She was good to me, she never treated me badly, but I grew up like I was living in someone else's home. I don't know what it's like to be in a convent but I do know what it's like to live your life thinking you're a bastard, believing that even your own mother doesn't want you. Why did you let me go? Was I a bad baby? An ugly baby? An embarrassment?" He paused and gathered his thoughts. "I want to know why you entered a convent instead of keeping me. That's why I'm here. I want to know why you didn't want me enough."

He had taken her wrath and now, he believed, she should take his. For the first time he looked not at her soft face and gentle features but directly into her eyes. He wanted her to know that her turning him away had hurt.

"Shh, Frank Hastings," she whispered. "Shh. Don't think those things. I love your father, but I wasn't free to be with him." She had planned to lie as much as necessary, before she understood that Frank knew absolutely nothing. She instead told the truth, though only as much as needed. "Frank, I wasn't free to be your mother. I was already promised."

"Promised?"

"Yes."

"To Jean-Claude?"

"No. Jean-Claude wanted Claudine, but everybody wanted Claudine. But no, I was never promised to him."

"Then who?"

"To Jesus. I already make my vow, Frank. I could not be your mother. I was promised to marry Jesus."

The bar man asked if he would like more coffee, if she would like some tea. Would Frank like a Guinness, or a glass? Were they ready for the bill? It wasn't going as she thought it would go, but she wasn't through.

"How do you find me, Frank Hastings?"

"I found you when I stopped looking for you."

The only things that had been in France were the clues. The monastery, where Géraldine loved to spend time with the monks. The disappearance of the monks. The destruction of the cathedral and the convent. That Géraldine rescued Claudine and Aunt Julia when she was home on a break from her novitiate. The reappearance of priests to rebuild the cathedral, and the disappearance of the nuns. The appearance of the Irish to build a hospital. That Madame Dupré never mentioned Géraldine again, not after the battle at the chateau.

"When your mother told me stories she always said 'my daughter' instead of 'Claudine.' Your mother showed me where my father was shot, inside the chateau, in the battle. I sat on the floor where he nearly bled to death and I swear, I felt him there, like he was with me. But when your mother told me the story she said 'my daughter' instead of 'Claudine.' It was *my mother* bent over my father, nursing him when he was bleeding to death on the floor. Nurses weren't schoolgirls; they were nuns. And more than

Children of a Good War

anything, my father didn't draw Claudine. He drew you."

The barman brought more coffee to Frank and thought his soul looked more troubled than before the nun came in. He wanted them to leave because nuns are bad for business and by mid-morning the Murphy brothers would be stopping by for first pints. Géraldine asked for a pot of tea. They stirred.

"It was hard for me to believe a seventeen-year-old girl was my mother but I wanted to believe it, I really wanted it. Then I saw Claudine's picture and knew right then who my mother was *not*. But I also realized who my mother must be because by then I knew everything about you except where you were. Even that wasn't very hard to figure out. My father drew a sketch of the Irish hospital in Saint-Lô. Why? To tell me something. The Poor Clares disappeared from Saint-Lô about when the Irish came. The missing Poor Clares were found here Ireland. Did you want to marry Jesus that badly?" He was still immature. He wanted not just to prove how he had discovered the truth, but also to make her feel guilty for running off with Jesus. He failed.

"No. I didn't want to marry Jesus that badly. I wanted your father to live that badly."

She hadn't expected Frank to be so logical. He had understood so little and found out so much. Lying probably would have been easier.

"What really happened to my father? How was he wounded?"

History is no more than what people agree it is, the best memories of people who were there. *Did Halliburton shoot Will*, she asked herself again. Maybe. She believed that he did. Will's friend believed that he did. But she did not actually see Halliburton shoot Will. She only saw Will fall in the courtyard, a hole in his back, the light going out of his eyes, and Halliburton with a pistol running past him and up the steps into the house. Had a German bullet found its way over the chateau wall and hit Will Hastings? Would knowing the truth make any difference?

"I don't know. He was running across the farmyard when somebody shoots him. We carry him into the chateau and I pray to God that your father does not die." She thought that Frank had a right to know the bargain she made with her Father-in-Law. "He was white, and not pulsing. The wound hole in his back comes out of his chest. He has lost all his blood and he wasn't making any sound. I pray for him very hard. I say 'God? If you let Will Hastings live I will come back to the church. I promise.' When they

359

take him away I thought he would not live."

She looked down to the leaves settling in her teacup, to the saucer, the spoon, the wooden table, and closed her eyes. God remembered her bargain, and God collected.

"And then you left him?"

That was the question, one of the questions, which had to be answered. She didn't answer it.

"Then Jean-Claude takes us away. He has the little house on a farm of his relatives in Saint-Pellerin. We live in the up-part of the house over the main room, where you have to go up and down a ladder, and he keeps us hiding there. I thought your father is dead. We just stay there. Every day Jean-Claude tells us the American soldiers is still at Chateau Dupré, they are digging in the walls and the barn and the house. Then one day Jean-Claude tells us that the Americans have found the soldier who killed their officer in the chateau. They are going to have a case in court and then shoot him. It is your father's friend."

"I don't understand. Who was my father's friend?"

"The soldier the Americans are to shoot. He was your father's friend. He was at Chateau Dupré that week with the other soldiers when they are looking for a place to make a new soldier hospital, until the battle. He helps me carry your father into the house when your father was shot, and take care of him. He gives him some morphine and bandages and ran away. Then the army say he has murdered Officer Halliburton in the house."

"Was his friend's name Curtiss? My father's friend?"

"Maybe."

"Or Douglas?"

"I don't know. It's a long time. He was a friend of your father at Chateau Dupré. The man he has murdered was a very hateful man. He hated your father. So, the Americans are going to shoot him, your father's friend, that is what we are hearing. It is not possible to find us where Jean-Claude hides us, but one day Jean-Claude is in the room below shouting to a man to go away and I hear it is your father has come into the house and is talking loud. I think, 'He's alive!' I thank God he has come to find me. That night I hide away from Jean-Claude and walk all the way home to Chateau Dupré, and your father is waiting for me. Then I know what your father truly feels for me. And I break my promise to God."

The barman brought them a roll of paper towels, and the bill, and stood over them. They ignored him.

"I stay there with your father every day, Frank Hastings, every day. We live together like we are married, and we agree we never leave each other. It is true. But then after some weeks the American army takes him back to the war. God comes to find me. He takes me back to Jesus."

She looked away from Frank, at the men drinking pints at other tables, at a dartboard on the wall, at the till, at the sign painted on the Delia Lydon window. She saw Jean-Claude and Father Jean in their room below the kitchen.

"I don't understand what happened."

She looked at Frank across the nasty table, his grimy coffee cup, her tin pot of tea, his long face. She had to tell him something.

"There was a priest in Saint Marie. He had sponsored me in Saint-Lô when I finish school, to enter the convent. I am a novice when the Germans come to Saint-Lô but I have gone home for a period of contemplating when there is the allied landings. When the cathedral is destroyed in the bombs, I don't go back. Then later, when your father and I are together, I love your father and again, I don't go back to the church. When Father Jean knows I am living with your father he waits."

She closed her eyes and remembered walking with Claudine in the night across the meadow, beyond the convent. They slip through the trees and down to the rowboat, cross the Vire, and walk past the Calvados barn to Saint Marie and knock on Dr. Genet's door. He opens the door and takes them in. She remembered the cold examining table, the boiling water, the sterile cloths, the candles, the soothing voice, the crying, the labor. Three days later, after dark, they leave. Claudine, miserable and sick herself, helps her and they row back to Chateau Dupré.

"After your father is taken to the war in Belgium, Father Jean tells me I am coming back to the church; I have promised God I will be a nun, and broke my promise. I don't answer but I know I promised God if He lets your father live, that is all, I will go back and I am breaking that promise too."

Father Jean pushed Claudine away, wrapped Géraldine in a robe and trundled her up the stairs. The last view she had of her family was Claudine, in the hallway, running.

"They takes me to the bishop. He sends me here, with the Irish nuns."

"Who brought you to the bishop? I don't understand. Who?"

"Father Jean. The priest. And Jean-Claude. I am put in the truck of Jean-Claude and held until we are at the bishop, in Saint-Lô. I am there some nights, and then I am brought to here. They don't let me to come back home. I knows later from my mother about Claudine, and about your father."

She had said enough. Frank had lowered his face to his chest; she understood that he realized that she made a promise but not a choice.

"That's when my father brought me home."

She didn't answer.

"Didn't you want me?"

"I wanted you. Yes, very much. But this time God tells me I made a bargain with Him for your father, and He makes me keep it. When your father comes back to France I am already here, in the convent."

It was only a small lie, an omission, really. No one needed to be hurt by a fact long buried, certainly not Frank. It was a fact for her to keep, and she did.

"And my father brought me home with him," Frank concluded.

"It is what the telegram says," she answered. Another small omission, by avoidance.

It was time for her to go back to the Poor Clares. Being with Frank Hastings was hard. She was tired and needed to pray.

The first of the morning's alcoholics stumbled into Delia Lydon. Even the worst of them saw Géraldine in her habit and stopped in the doorway. The best of them backed out of the pub, looked up over the door to check the sign, and wondered if he was in the right place.

"Fokin' nun's 'avin' a pint."

"Peckin' 'at poor foker, more likely,"

"Either way I ain't steppin' foot in a place wi' a fokin' nun."

That was enough for the bartender.

"I 'ate to be a bother," he announced to Frank with a glance at Géraldine, "but 'is is a place 'o commerce. Yeh needs to order a round or its time yeh go."

Géraldine stood, flapped her habit, and for the first time since landing in France, Frank experienced real panic. He had looked and not found her, not looked and found her, and for want of ordering a Guinness was about to lose her again.

"Will you come home with me?" he asked her. "Please?"

He surprised himself. Even before he said it out loud, he understood that he wanted to take her home for the sole purpose of not letting her disappear again. He had searched for her, that's all, just to know who his real mother was and hear her say why she hadn't kept him. He had no other plan for her, no idea of what he would do with her. He had no idea what Eleanor would say.

"Time's up. Out yeh go." The bartender pulled out her chair, glanced at Frank, and led them to the door. "Come back anytime," he added, ushering them onto Quay Street as fast as he could. He stood aside for the Murphy brothers and the real drunks to get through the door.

For the first time, Frank touched her. He took her arm in his arm and led her down the rat-dirty street, stepping around puddles, carts, discarded beer bottles, police, and a few derelict souls poking in rubbish bins. To his surprise, she took his arm as well, reaching with her free hand to pat him on the hand that held her arm. He loved her touch; when he looked at her he saw a glimpse of the same smile that Will had seen when he sketched her in their bedroom, more than forty years before.

They walked to The Long Walk near the docks, then across the river to a wharf where small, open fishing boats bobbed in the water. They sat on a stone bench facing the Corrib where it opened into the bay, where she untangled her arm from his but took his hand and held it.

She shook her head no.

"This is the Claddagh," she said. "Before there is houses here, for the fishermen families. They take the little boats and goes out to the bay, sometimes the ocean. It's all changed now; everything is gone. The fishermen. The houses. Here they make rings."

"Rings."

"Is rings made for the fingers, of two hands with the fingers together, like this." She took his hand and wove her fingers though his, then gently separated them so that the fingertips touched, forming a cradle. "Is the rings that touch with a heart in the middle. When you have it on this hand, the right one, you are together but not married, and if is on this hand, it means you are married." She pushed an imaginary ring on the third finger of his right hand, then on the same finger of his left. "The fishers who lived here, they wear it when they go to sea. The man and his wife twine their fingers and they keep the ring to always be connected together. If the man doesn't come home from the sea, he is drowned, his life and his wife, her life, still are connected. This ring is named the Claddagh too."

She sat quietly, looking across the Corrib and out to the bay, remembering the rings that she and Will had woven in the monastery from stems of grass.

"No. I don't come with you, but our fingers is like the Claddagh. I cannot be your mother, but I always am with you."

The boats weaved back and forth against the current, tethered by lines to the dock. Across the water, on The Long Walk, cranes and cement trucks lined the waterfront. Dozens of laborers swarmed a construction site. New apartments, flats, shops rose up from the shore. Frank wondered what the Claddagh had been like when it was a fishing village and what the working docks had been like before being repurposed for tourists and yuppies.

"Will you tell me another thing, Frank, before I go?"

He said that he would.

"About Virginia. I want to know about her. I think she is a good mother to raise you to be like your father."

There was a hint of infidelity to the question. Was he being faithless to the woman who raised him by talking about her to his mother? Or faithless to his mother by telling her that Virginia had been a good mother and a good wife? He considered what she was asking and what he should tell her.

"I thought she was an unfair mother. Peter was handsome, athletic. He got new clothes, new footballs and tennis shoes. He was popular and she held parties for him. He was smart and she helped him get into a better college. I wasn't any of those things, and she didn't do them for me."

A solitary man, covered in oilskins and a bucket hat, removed a line from a cleat on the dock and began to row one of the open boats out into the current. Even that, Frank thought, was not for fishing, not that late in the morning, but was just for show.

"I didn't understand it when I was a boy. Not until I met Eleanor did I figure out that Virginia had raised me to not depend on anyone else, to be on my own when I grew up. I don't have much now but I have everything I need. Peter always had more, and it was never enough." He had never said that before, not clearly, but it was true. "Virginia was a good woman. She was a good mother."

Géraldine understood.

"Where is your brother now?" She asked in such a way that Frank believed that somehow, hidden in a cloister away from newspapers, televisions, movies, that somehow she knew where Peter was. He was wrong.

"He's dead."

"I'm sorry, Frank. I thought you would say he is in a big company or something."

"He was. Peter loved flying. He became a pilot, for Pan Am. His plane was taken by hijackers, in Pakistan. He was shot."

She didn't know. Frank gripped her hand more tightly, then less tightly, and she heard him breathing quietly. He felt and sounded the way Sister Margaret had sounded after her brother was murdered in Roscommon. They were quiet for a few minutes.

"Were you friends? Your brother, after you are men?"

"No. We still argued, even at Dad's funeral. Peter sent me a letter telling me to never talk to him any again. That was a few days before he was killed."

"I'm sorry, Frank. It is not so long ago, is it?"

It was, he knew, part of why he needed to find a mother. He needed to tell a mother that he had written a hateful letter to Peter, not spoken to him again before Peter went to Karachi, and that he wished he had not. He needed to tell Virginia that he loved her and didn't blame her for preferring Peter, but Virginia wasn't there to tell. He needed to know that he was forgiven for fighting with Peter. He had not said goodbye to Will; he needed a mother so that he could do it better, the next time.

"No, it was only a few weeks or so."

"Can I see the letter please? The letter asking your father to meet his army friends?"

He gave her the fax from Fondren. She put Eleanor's cover sheet on top of it and read it again.

"You are happy with your wife, Frank. Is it true?" He said yes, he was very happy. "I think she has to be a kind woman, and loves you. Go home, Frank. It is what I'm asking you, to not be my son, but be your wife's husband. It is time to stop looking for something. You know all there is to know. Now, just be you."

The air on the water was more cold than warm, a chill wind blowing toward where they sat. Gulls flew above, swooped down on the fishing boats, then over the rock embankment, crying as they dived for mullets, rising, flying again. A tug whistled across the harbor as it began to pilot a freight-laden boat toward the ocean. Sunlight peeked through the overcast and sent rays of light down onto the Corrib.

"She says to you whither thou goest. It is the story of Ruth, that Ruth tells her mother-in-law that where she goes, Ruth will go, and her people will be Ruth's people. That is a beautiful thing for a wife to say." As Will had been just before he died, Géraldine was concerned for Frank but knew that he would be all right.

"Eleanor said that when she agreed to marry me. 'Whither thou goest I will go. Thy people will be my people, and thy ways will be my ways.' I can't tell you how I felt when she said that to me. We say it now, still, when things go haywire."

"And whither you go, does she go?"

"Yes."

He considered saying no, that he had asked Eleanor to leave with him to Saint Marie when Madame Dupré offered him the chateau. But Eleanor had said no, he knew, because the Frank who asked Eleanor to follow him was not the Frank whom Eleanor had married. The people who he told her would become her people were not his people. He wondered if Eleanor had known that when she said no. It didn't matter. She had sent him Fondren's letter when she could have kept it, when keeping it might have meant Frank would come home sooner. Her promise to be fair when he looked for his mother was still her promise. He knew that he had not been fair to her.

"Do you love her?" It was clear that he did; his declaration was unnecessary. "Then whither she goest, you have to go there too, Frank Hastings. She is your people. It is time for you to stop looking for something that is past. Everything that was, it's all changed, your father, me, the world, everything. I wish the past is different, but it is only the past. I cannot have you for my son. Go home, Frank, and be a husband to your wife. Be a son to Virginia."

She removed her wimple to kiss him. He saw that her hair was almost gone, thin, cut short for her headdress. The lovely face of Will's enamored youth was going away with it; there remained the warm and caring look that he would remember.

She turned his face to hers and kissed him on the cheek, fully and with as much love as she dared. He was Will's son and his skin was Will's skin. His lips would have been Will's lips as well. She kissed only his cheek, though, because she was a married woman, and her Husband was a jealous Husband. Then she left.

iv.

He found her package on his bed, apparently having been placed there sometime after he had left for the Delia Lydon. It was a large manila envelope, addressed in Dr. Hastings' neat handwriting to Sister Géraldine Dupré, Society of Poor Clares, Nuns Island, Galway, Republic of Ireland. There was no return address on the envelope and the green customs declaration ticket stapled onto it next to the stamps almost obscured the postmark. By careful study Frank made out that it had been posted from Colorado Springs on July 31, 1986.

If Will had included a letter to Géraldine she had kept it or disposed of it. The only message inside was a tiny handwritten note from her to Frank that said simply 'I think it is better for you to have these now.'

Inside the envelope there were two bits of cloth wrapped in plain white paper. The larger one was a faded scarf made of rough homespun fabric, a few once-chestnut wisps of hair clinging to it. There was folded into it a square of blood-soaked cloth that had been torn from a bed sheet and ripped into a bandage. The blood was very faded, even where it had been trapped in the cloth's wadded creases. He was sure that Géraldine had used it to try to stop Will from the bleeding to death, then kept it.

He searched carefully inside the envelope, in the rest of the hotel room and in his bags and clothes, but there was nothing else, no other note, no more envelopes or packages or relics. The scarf and the bandage were the only physical proof that Will and Géraldine had ever been together.

Frank tried to imagine, at the airport, on the airplane, in passing through customs and immigration in Dallas and again on the connecting flight to Austin, his father, keeping the scarf for forty years, hidden somewhere in his bags or books or in the cellar, then sending it back to Géraldine when he sensed that he was going to die. *Did he keep it with the photograph of Mother on the porch?*

Frank would never know.

V.

Eleanor, watching the passengers spill like so many ants from the jet bridge, saw him well before he found her across the crowded waiting room. She saw his face light up and saw his eyes twinkle and knew that he was home, truly home, and that her moments quite at Bar Cielo were over.

They kissed like teenagers while waiting for his bags to arrive. When they came up for air he said, simply, "I have so much to tell you."

"And I," she answered, "I have something to tell you."

Chapter Thirty-Two

The moving company had been in the house all day, not to move them but to size up the boxes of china and towels and videotapes, the stove, the refrigerator, the beds and chairs and tables and closets full of clothes and Pan Am uniforms, and the garage full of tools that Peter had bought to keep the Corvette in perfect condition. Candace watched the blinking light on the video recorder, its green digital numbers flashing 12:00, *blink blink*, 12:00, *blink blink*, 12:00, *blink blink*, in the dark bedroom. She didn't know what time it was; the recorder had been unplugged and packed into the moving boxes, then unpacked and plugged back in without resetting after Jeff pleaded for the fortieth time to watch *The Muppets take Manhattan* because, he insisted, there would be no Muppets wherever it was they were moving to. She had put Tiffany and Jeff to bed at somewhere between seven o'clock and nine o'clock, she was pretty sure, and then gone to her bedroom and put on three layers of clothes and climbed into the bed, where she wrapped herself in a duvet and two blankets to keep from freezing to death in case she slept.

She closed her eyes and tried to see Peter's face but saw only Dr. Young, the psychiatrist whom Pan Am arranged for her to see. She had filled out his intake form:

Reason for consultation: *My husband was murdered by hijackers in Pakistan*

Dr. Young had read the form out loud while she sat on a soft armchair, then looked over his desk and said how sorry he was and asked what she would like for him to do for her. She had thought to herself that, if he didn't know, how was she supposed to know, that she didn't know because no one had ever murdered her husband before, that it was his job to help her, that the only reason she was there was because Pan Am had paid for three sessions and Rocky had driven down from Denver to make sure that she went to the first one. But she hadn't answered him.

"It's all right to be angry," he counseled her. She had not asked permission to be angry and would have continued to be angry, even if he had counseled her that it was a bad thing. "They did a terrible thing to you, Candace. Yell at them. Scream." She hadn't yelled or screamed, not in his office. "And don't worry if you're not crying. There is no one way to grieve. You have to grieve the way that you feel like grieving. Not everyone cries."

Dr. Young spent fifty-five minutes telling her that it was normal for her to lose twenty pounds but that she should try to eat, that she should be sure to have support around her, such as her parents or co-workers or friends from church, that she should not feel guilty just because she couldn't remember what Peter had told her in the driveway just before he had climbed into his Corvette before his last flight, that it was normal to feel disbelief over what had happened, to deny it even, and that she didn't have to be strong for the children because they were going through the same thing. (He did suggest they come in for three sessions, too.) He assured her that it was normal for there to be a lot of red tape in getting her husband's body home, but the government sure owed her a lot better than what they had done about it so far. He prescribed Valium for her, three times per day, and asked her if she would not schedule her follow-up appointment until the following Tuesday because he and his wife had planned a long weekend getaway. "Just about any other day is okay." She had not gone back.

Now when she closed her eyes she saw Dr. Young's face, his fake neutral expression, his phony sympathy, his know-it-all dismissiveness of her ignorance about how to grieve over the death of her husband. She wished Dr. Young had been on the plane with Peter and closed her eyes harder because that, too, was probably a normal response to the sudden death of a loved one. A loved one, as if Peter was a tired old parent, or a faithful dog. It was cold because she hadn't paid the natural gas bill since the first of October.

She also had disconnected the telephone, not from failure to pay the bill but by physically unplugging the wall cord. She couldn't take any more intrusive phone calls:

"Yes, Ma'am, KSPG television. We're sorry for your loss. Can you tell us more about what Congressman Ashburton is doing to get your husband's body home?"

"Mrs. Hastings? We're from the White Doves, at Second Baptist? Would you like us to come by?"

"Candace? Mr. Alger, from Pike Elementary. Just asking about Tiffany and Jeff; they haven't been to school since…"

"Ma'am? This is Bill Harper, at Front Range Savings and Loan. I'm real sorry to bother you, but I think there's some confusion about your house payment. It's normal at a time like this. So, can you…."

"Candy? This is Mom."

Candace disconnected the telephone after her mother had called to say that Loving Arms Nursing Home had telephoned her because no one answered the phone at Candace's house.

"Dear? Are you all right?" her mother had asked.

"I'm fine, Mother." *I'm not fine. I'm terrible. The kids are eating boxes of macaroni and cheese and drinking Kool-Aide and I haven't done laundry in a week and the bill collectors are sending hate mail about the house payments and the television and the stereo and the microwave and ….* "Why did they call you?"

"It's Virginia. She's…"

"No, Mother. I can't take any more." She settled her nerves for a moment, then apologized. "I'm sorry. It's all right. What about Virginia? Has something happened? What?"

Candace had added the guilt of not going to see Virginia at Loving Arms to the guilt of being a bad wife and mother, but there was only so much incapacity to help others that she could tolerate.

"I don't know, not exactly. They called to say that Virginia…she said something. Words. Well, not words exactly, but that she was singing. Like a song."

Candace had decided that it was a dream, that she had to wake up to stop it. She looked around the living room, saw the boxes, the moving blankets over the television and stereo, the empty kitchen counters on the other side of the breakfast island, Tiffany curled up in a corner with a book, Jeff picking his nose. It wasn't a dream.

"Singing?"

"That's what they said on the phone. 'Mrs. Hastings is singing. She put on that red dress she likes and some nice shoes and walked down to the dining room and started humming. Then she sang.' That's what they told me. Do you want to go over there and check on her?'"

Candace had said yes, she would go, but when she hung up the telephone she disconnected the phone wire from the wall socket and hadn't left the house since. She thought that, when morning came, maybe she would get some Valium after all. The green light blinked again, and again, but she huddled in her cocoon and almost didn't hear Tiffany in the dark.

"Mommy?"

She just wants to climb into bed with me. Don't answer. Don't move. She'll be all right. She'll go back to sleep. The bedroom door opened. A hall light cracked the darkness and landed on her face.

"Mommy?"

"What is it, Tiffany?"

"There's someone on the porch."

"No there isn't, Sweetie. Go back to bed." Tiffany, more than Jeff, had nightmares about the man on the porch.

"No, Mommy, there really is a man on the porch."

"Shhh, Sweetie. It's just a bad dream."

"Mommy, he's knocking on the door. I looked out the window and there's a car in the street. I'm scared."

"There's nothing to be afraid of, Sweetie." Candace unwrapped her cocoon of tracksuits and blankets and reached her arms out to hold Tiffany. "Climb in, Sweetie. You can sleep with me."

Then Candace heard the knocking.

"Stay here, Tiffany. Don't make a sound. Don't turn on the light."

Candace wrapped a blanket around her tracksuit and walked as quietly as she could to the front of the house and peeked out Tiffany's bedroom window. The car on the street was nondescript, not a police car, not a shiny car, not an old car, but a plain car without a bit of chrome or ornamentation, even on the wheels.

She waited to see if the car would drive away. It did not so, after a few minutes, she tip-toed back into the front room, avoiding the boxes, to the kitchen where she was pretty sure she could find a telephone to plug in to call 9-1-1. There was another tap on the door. She tripped on a box.

"It's me," came the voice through the door. "It's me."

No it wasn't.

"I'm home."

It wasn't true. It was another nightmare, a trick of memory. She walked softly to the door and looked through the peephole.

Her first thought was that there was a homeless wretch on her front porch. He was unrecognizable at first, the wild beard and wretched hair, his face sunken and contorted. He was bundled under a navy pea coat and his arms were crossed, hands stuck into the sleeves for warmth.

Her second thought was to fling open the door and jump onto him with what strength she had, and to yell.

"You're alive," she screamed. "It's you! Oh, my God, you're alive."

Peter took his hands from his sleeves and wrapped his arms around her as best he could, and began to cry. She kissed his pocked and leathered face, touched his forehead and smelled his foul hair, and kissed him again, before pulling him inside the door and shouting for the children.

"Tiffany! Jeff! Wake up. It's your father. He's here. He's alive."

Children of a Good War

Part Three

Chapter Thirty-Three

S troke, kick, stroke, kick, turn, breathe, stroke, kick.
Eleanor saw without seeing the lane marker below and to her left and counted without counting the seconds before it would bend upward at pool's end.

Stroke, kick, stroke, flip, turn, touch, push, glide, stroke, kick. Mr. Patterson was gone. Stroke, kick, breathe. Mr. Patterson had always ordered fresh cardamom and ginger for her. She had never considered that he might leave, even when she saw the hand-printed poster in the store window, beneath the poster that said

Lettuce 19¢ head
Farm Eggs 89¢.
Closing March 1.

There was very little call for lettuces or farm eggs in Eleanor's cooking so she hadn't paid much attention to the sign. In fact, she thought Mr. Patterson was the owner so when she walked to the Fresh Plus for lentils and turmeric, and he wasn't there, she had asked if was ill.

"No, Ma'am, he's quit."

"Quit? Why? He can't quit. I need him." Fresh Plus was a store where the old customers spoke to the employees like that. "Where did he go?"

"Safeway, maybe. Or HEB, down on Oltorf. I don't know. Why? We're all quitting. He just didn't wait for the rest of us."

Thus Eleanor had learned that her grocery store was being razed, a new Schlotzsky's to be built on its ashes. Stroke, kick, stroke, breathe, kick. There already was a Schlotzsky's on Congress, a little one, not much more than a trailer. Eleanor had never eaten at Schlotzsky's but had noticed the queue at its door from time to time, composed mostly, she had assumed, of people waiting for the Continental Club to open. The Continental Club had been a surprise, too. Stroke, stroke, she felt hot, even in the cold water, a hot flash, stroke, stroke, oops, stroke, kick, turn, breathe, stroke, kick. So, had the Continental Club driven Schlotszky's away with loud bands and suddenly overcrowded parking?

Eleanor had not taken kindly to the Continental Club. Geographical quirks in the atmosphere carried thumping bass guitars and clashing drum-beats down a winding side street, past ancient oak trees and across the creek to The Sisters, then into her kitchen table. It upset the quiet she needed if Dorigen and Emily were going to become a dissertation. She neared the pool's end and began to duck her head to enter the flip turn, then paused.

Is this safe, she asked herself? *Should I be doing flip turns?* She glided to the pool's edge and rested her elbows on the coping, then tried to think whether anything in a flip turn, anything anatomical, or positional, or even psychological would possibly hurt the baby. *I don't know. It's so strange*, she reflected. *I have swum thousands of yards every day since I was fourteen, fifteen. How many flip turns? Hundreds of thousands? Probably. But if my head drops below my heart and I rotate my legs and knees up and flip and then stretch my body out and hold my breath, that can't be good for the baby. Can it?* Another hot flash.

Being fair with Frank had been very hard on Eleanor. She had missed him terribly and wanted to call a hundred times to ask him to come home. Being fair, however, had meant that she had to let him look for his mother until he found her or they ran out of money. If Madame Dupré had of-fered the chateau to Frank just one day earlier Eleanor would have packed her winter clothes and followed him to France and offered herself up as some kind of post-medieval chatelaine to a broken-down farm; but Madame Dupré had not offered it to Frank the day before Eleanor had gone to see Dr. Gaines for her recurring bleeding fibroid and learned that the fibroid was a baby.

After that, being fair with Frank had meant not asking him to come home because she was pregnant or, a few days later, because she had stum-bled across the name 'Geraldine' in the trunk of their old Volvo. Everything had changed, then, and Frank would have to come home because he was ready to come home, not because she had told him something coercive or withheld something that might have kept him away longer, which it did. Being fair had been harder, but it had been the right thing to do. She pushed away from the coping and began to swim, gently, higher in the water, more breathing turns, toward the other end.

He was so happy, she remembered. *I was afraid he would be disappointed, or unhappy, or think I tricked him. We talk about everything but after the first two d and c's we never talked about a baby.* "When?" *he asked.* "Mid to late April," *I answered. Then I understood he meant 'when?' and I thought, it had to have been when we got home from Bridle. After we got the letters, after Tog gave us those damnable letters. He felt so alone, then, and we held each other all night. So,* "After Peter's memorial service." *And he remembered and said* "Sure, of course."

They had looked at baby beds and rocking chairs and discovered not only how expensive a baby could be but also how much room they didn't have. For the first time they went to a big box store, a Target, and decided they could afford a baby bed and rocker but couldn't squeeze them into their house. Without saying anything, each had noticed the other looking at the real estate section of the Sunday paper. Another change.

Forbede us a thing, and that desiren we,
Preesse on us faste and thane wol we flee.

Who said that? The wife of Bath? I think so, stroke, kick, stroke. Or Emily? No, Emily did not wish to marry; I wish little else. Certainly not Dorigen. Did we not want a baby because we thought it was forbidden? Perhaps.

She had told Frank the minute he came home, even before they left the airport, again being fair, in case *thane wol he flee,* but he wanted only to be with her.

"Oh, my," he said. "Are you sure?" he asked.

That same night she had said he didn't have to be afraid, Dr. Gaines had advised her it was safe, and they were not afraid, no more so than the night of their wedding. Frank had slept for hours with his hand low on her tummy and she had cried, she was so happy. Now she had to sleep on her back, another change, to go with enlarging nipples and darkening areola and the need to pee a lot.

Should we take it to church? My God, am I really asking myself that?

Turn kick stroke kick stroke breathe.

They weren't a churchgoing couple. Eleanor had been raised Church of England, Frank Protestant. She had not been to a service on her own since Eldred Potts' family had told her to stay away from his funeral. Frank had not gone to church since Vietnam. Reverend Altgelt had conducted their wedding in Will's and Virginia's living room. They associated churches with funerals, and guilt.

But we did learn right from wrong, lying from telling the truth, stealing from buying. How are we going to teach it not to lie or steal or do drugs? What if it's a thief, or grows up to become a drug addict? What if I'm sixty and it—it's not an it, stroke, kick, breathe, elbows on coping, turn, glide—*it's a her, or a him,* she wanted a her, but only just a little more than a him, *and it's in jail for something horrible and it asks me why didn't I raise it to go to church because then it wouldn't be in jail? How are we going to do this?*

Glide.

She pulled herself out of the pool and drew a heavy coat around her against the mild winter chill. Even that was a change. Last year she would have pulled a dry towel around her and slipped on her jogging shoes, then trotted home. This year she walked.

Am I still me? she wondered as she strolled. She counted the changes in her life: the baby, her changing body, the annoyance over music and the sleeping on her back, not wanting to eat tandoori chicken because it upset her stomach; having to drive rather than walk to a grocery store because her town was changing too; finding a church; and no longer being sure of the importance of writing a dissertation on two imaginary medieval women on the road to Canterbury.

If you change one part of me for something new that is exactly the same as the part changed, and then you change another, and that part looks like me too, and you keep on until one day everything I was has been changed but I still look like me, I sound like me, I act like me and I care about the same things, about my husband and Chaucer and my ginger and turmeric and swimming...

Am I still Eleanor?

She smiled and walked to their home, reflecting that none of who she was, or would become, had to do with her biological parents.

To ask the question was to answer the question. We are who we are.

ii

Failure of Local Bank is Tip of Iceberg

A *Gazette* special report, by Frank Hastings

The failure of City Federal Savings and Loan may be only the first of many. Bank examiners became concerned when local homebuilder CP-N declared bankruptcy in December, stranding hundreds of construction workers, subcontractors, and would-be buyers. The largest segment of its unfinished work is a defunct condominium project on the north side of the city, named I-35 Condominiums, now nothing more than steel and concrete skeletons surrounded by chain link fences and disfigured by graffiti, and littered by construction material that the bankruptcy receiver has refused to release to the cheated subcontractors.

More than two hundred lawsuits were filed during the past year against borrowers who obtained loans from City Federal Savings that had been secured by mortgages on the I-35 Condominiums. The loans ranged from $1,000,000 to over $4,200,000.

The story went on to describe how letting the banks regulate themselves led to City Federal's failure and would surely lead to more. The story also had a big red stamp on it, marked REJECTED - DO NOT PUBLISH. Frank stood before his editor, furious.

"Goddammit, Marty! We've got to run this story!"

"Goddammit, Frank! Who do you think we are? *The New York Times?*" Burman tossed the story back across his desk. It skidded off and landed on the floor, at Frank's feet. "You think we should go around causing a run on the banks? Is that it? You want to wake up tomorrow and see lines around the block of every bank in town? This isn't the Great Depression, for crying out loud. This isn't 1929. We have a duty to this town."

It was a point Frank had not considered. Of course, he hadn't considered it because he and Eleanor had spent two hours standing in a line at City Federal Savings and Loan trying to get their savings out after the federal regulators announced that their own bank had failed. It had not been a problem, other than their having spent a sleepless night upon learning that City Federal was, as Pat C. Oh described it, "tits up," and then having to stand in the line, only to be told that their own savings and deposit accounts had such small balances that they wouldn't lose a penny. He was angry, not wounded, and inquisitive rather than presidential. His good, his and Eleanor's and their growing baby's, was not necessarily the same as the public good.

"But it's true, Marty. It's accurate. Us playing ostrich with what's about to happen isn't going to stop it from happening. We can't tell subscribers that the world is rosy just because the Longhorns look good in spring training and hide from them that their banks may collapse tomorrow. That's not what newspapers are for."

"No. Leave the fear-mongering about banks and whatnot to the East Coast liberals. It's spiked." Burman crossed his arms and glared across the desk. "Christ, Frank; you've got the story of the century. Go write that."

"Can I at least shop it to the magazines? Texas Monthly? Freelance?"

"Not if you want to stay on the payroll. You know the rules; you want to freelance, pitch it to me first, not after you write it. Ah, come on, Frank. You'll be okay. Lots of people buy a house on a reporter's salary. You and Eleanor sell that little slave cabin you're in and use it for a down payment. It'll work out. She going to keep on teaching after the baby comes?"

They hadn't decided. After ten years, Eleanor was within months of getting Chaucer's theory of courtly women to her doctoral adviser. "I can finish it before she comes," she had said. "What if she's a he?" "Before *he* comes. Or *they*. Then revise faculty adviser critiques, defend my dissertation, and Presto! I'm Doctor Herald. I won't be out of action for long, dear," she had said.

"So, back to the classroom and he, or she, goes to day care," he had argued.

"Or, you can be a home husband. Finish *An Khe*." She knew how to argue as well.

"Right. We can live off the proceeds of *An Khe*." Even Frank knew sarcasm when it appeared.

"Or, I can stay home and we live off the royalties of *The Real Canterbury Women*. And the movie rights."

It was hard to decide.

"We haven't decided," he answered to Marty. "She's still swimming every morning. It's hard to imagine her slowing down."

"So, buy a house with a pool."

"Right. Actually, that's what led me to write the piece. We were house hunting and went out to look at some condominiums. Then our bank failed." Eleanor had received the certified letter from the bank receiver, opened it, and thought the bank failure was because of Frank's credit card bill from France. "We thought we had lost our house. Apart from a dying Volvo, that's all we own."

"If you want to write a blockbuster," Burman picked up, "you know what you can write. It's there in front of you. It would write itself. What exactly is your brother doing, now?"

Frank had always hated writing stories with a source "who remained anonymous because he was not authorized to speak publicly." He knew Burman would hate it too.

"We're off the record, Martin. No comment. Okay?" Burman clenched his jaw. "He's flying crop dusters in Amarillo. Gets a charter flight now and then. That's all I know."

"That's crazy. Your brother's a hero. If the public knew what the Pakistanis did to him they'd knock down the White House gates to demand war."

"I think that's why the public doesn't know what happened to him. In fact, I think that's why the public doesn't know he's alive. Privately, his wife told Eleanor that he couldn't pass his flight physical for Pan Am. They wouldn't let him near an airplane."

"What's the real story?"

"Eleanor hasn't told me. I think that means Peter's wife hasn't told her. The official word from his camp is that I'm a bastard for running off to France and leaving Mother in a nursing home while he was stuffed into a hole somewhere in Pakistan. He wants nothing to do with me." Still. Again. Both. "So, I couldn't write his story if I wanted to, because he won't talk to me."

"You must have really pissed him off."

"I think he's been through a lot. And I think the savings and loans are about to have a crisis that will cost you and me and every one of us millions of dollars. That's the story we need to tell, something that matters. In the big scheme of things, Peter's alive."

"Nope. No can do. What else have you got on the burner?"

"Nothing." Almost nothing. Maybe something. "A science story, maybe."

"God help us. Get back to the city beat, Frank. And don't worry; it'll all work out. Eleanor, the baby, the house. Just quit trying to set the town on fire, okay? No more racist schoolteachers, no more shuttering the teller windows. Find a couple of embezzlers, okay? A drug dealer murder. Write those. That's what readers want. Bye."

iii

Peter saw it differently.

"What do you mean, Rocky? I gave my life for this airline." Rocky and the Denver station manager had asked Peter to come to the airport after they received his flight physical. "I passed every single test he threw at me, even the psych test. I can fly any airplane in the fleet."

"It came from upstairs, Peter," the station manager said. "If you want to move into operations, take a go at flight training for the new pilots, we can do something. But you can't fly anymore, not for Pan Am. It's too risky."

"What risky? Look at this!" Peter laid his check rides on the table, one at a time like a stack of cards. "Perfect. CAT I zero zero. Perfect. Loss of two engines. Perfect. Upset during descent. Perfect. There's not one thing I can't do in a 747 and do it better and safer than any other pilot in the company."

"Listen, Peter, we think you're a hero. New York thinks you're a hero. But ... no."

He and Rocky left the station manager's office and walked to a new coffee shop in the passenger concourse, a Starbucks. Skiers in bundled clothes, lawyers in winter coats, endless rows of salesmen flying to Rapid City and Billings stood in a queue to order lattes and three-dollar hot chocolates with a shot. Two men in business suits raised their voices to talk into bulky mobile phones that looked like black bricks with rubber antennae.

They found a corner table.

"What's going on, Rocky? This is bullshit and you know it."

Rocky had tried for three weeks to find a way to tell Peter Hastings that he was poison, hoping that Peter would fail his flight physical exam so that he would not have to say a thing. Peter called daily to say he was sick of convalescing and needed to get back to flying. When the doctor's report came in he knew their friendship was probably over. He took it to the Denver station manager who said he could keep Peter on the payroll only if New York signed off. New York eventually Peter offered a management job, non-flying, at less salary. Rocky ordered a small latte with a shot of cinnamon and took a deep breath.

"You had a gun on the plane, Peter. That is absolutely verboten." He realized where he was and looked around to see if anyone had overheard two men in Pan Am uniforms talking about carrying guns on planes. No one had.

"I've carried my service pistol with me for ten years. There's not a vet in this company who doesn't carry a sidearm with him. You carried a sidearm when you flew." Peter looked at Rocky's briefcase. "I'm willing to bet there's a sidearm in your bag now, Rocky. That's a cover-up."

"Peter, there's also not a military veteran in this company who ever pulled a gun out and started shooting people, either." *Pause, deep breath.* "You should have run for the terminal, Peter. You could have escaped. You would have escaped. Billy."

"Billy?"

"The goat. The Academy. Poncho Pete the escape and evade artist. You could have gotten away on the other side of the plane. You didn't have to shoot that guy."

Rocky had watched the videotape a hundred times. In his mind's eye he saw Peter slither down the front landing gear, creep along beneath the fuselage, and hide behind the main landing gear struts. On the near side, the emergency slide filled with screaming passengers, their saris and shalwars and business suits billowing in the night. The tarmac on the far side of the airplane was dark and empty. Rocky could close his eyes and count the passengers, count their steps as they fled the plane, count the seconds ticking away on the videotape, and count every step Peter had taken after he jumped out from behind the landing gear to where he stopped, lifted his service pistol, gripped it in both hands, and blew off the back of Shuja's head.

"Do you have any idea how many televisions there are in the Middle East?"

Peter stirred his coffee. He looked at the loudmouths on their cellular brick telephones. He wondered what a shot for coffee might be. He wanted to fly airplanes.

"Two hundred million, Peter. Do you know how many of them have seen you shoot that man on television?" It was the first time in his life that Rocky had told Peter that he was wrong, really wrong. He loved Peter and he loved Peter's wife and kids and he loved sitting around on off days and talking about flying gunships and stealing goats and getting drunk, but this time Peter was really, really wrong. "As best we can tell, half of them already hate us anyway, without you shooting one of them in the back of the head."

"He was a terrorist, for God's sake. They were murdering our passengers. Of course I shot the son of a bitch."

The crowded queue thinned. Moon boots and thick socks and rolling bags slid past their table on the way to the concourse to board ordinary flights to ordinary places, to sell insurance policies, go to hospitals where loved ones were having babies and getting chemotherapy, to where ordinary people lived and worked.

They didn't tell him, Rocky realized. *They dropped him in a hole and starved him on rotten food with contaminated water until his teeth turned black and the cut where they hit him on the back of his head got infected and who knows what else, and no one told him why.*

"Peter, he was their son of a bitch. The man you shot. He wasn't a terrorist. He was a Pakistani security agent. He was on the plane because they had a warning about Abu Nidal wanting to take another 747. And two hundred million Arabs watched you shoot him."

The concourse speakers announced that the door to Flight 1481 to Grand Junction would be closed in three minutes, that passengers on Flight 1481 to Grand Junction must get to gate C 23 or the plane would depart without them. A child wanted to go to the bathroom. A teenager raced past Starbucks after stealing a *Playboy* from the Hudson's Bookstore next door. Three flight attendants rolled their bags toward the baggage carousel.

A security agent. Jesus Christ.

"It's worse than that, Peter. This guy's brother-in-law is the head of

Pakistani Intelligence. It was his group that snatched you out of the hospital and took you wherever they took you and then put out the story that you were dead. If the State Department hadn't gotten a spy in there somewhere you would have been dead, sooner or later. I really don't know the details but part of their deal to get you back was that you not sit in a cockpit, any-where." Rocky looked Peter in the face; Peter looked away. "This is a good deal, Peter. Being alive is a good deal."

It was not so much a part of the deal as a parting threat. Abdur Rahman had not put it in writing. He had not even said the words, not as such. But when the State Department dangled a box full of Jesus nuts at him with a photograph of a dozen disabled Pakistani helicopters, Abdur Rahman had suggested to the American negotiator that it would be very difficult in the future for him to protect any airliner with Farman Ali's prisoner on the controls. "Crew manifests, immigration agents, airport operations employ-ees, there are many, many people...," he had said to the diplomat who told him that it was in everyone's interest to turn Peter Hastings back over to the United States, "...there are many people who tell people things they should not tell." Just as someone in Farman Ali's secret jail had told someone in Abdur Rahman's employ that Ali had the American in his grip. Just as someone in the Americans' pay had told the CIA. "If Peter Hastings ever flies another Pan American airplane, my friend, I fear greatly that someone who knows about it will tell someone who should not know about it. Who? Abu Nidal? Hamas? Ghaddafi? I don't know, but I could not guarantee the safety of that airplane," Abdur Rahman had said. "I'm only mentioning it."

No one had told Rocky, but no one had needed to tell Rocky. It wasn't Pan Am's first hijacking.

"If those crazy bastards ever find a plane with you at the controls, Peter, they will blow that plane to kingdom come. No one is going to let you fly another 747, ever."

"I can still fly a DC-9. A 727." His captain's uniform hung limply on his frame, making him look like a schoolboy dressed in his father's blue suit. His swollen knuckles stood out as he wrung his hands and gripped the table. Even Peter's teeth had withered inside the hole of his jail cell, making his face seem skeletal.

"No, Peter. Not even a 727, or a DC-9, or anything else that Pan Am flies, or anyone else. I'm sorry. You shot first and asked questions later.

It's over."

Rocky waited patiently in hopes that a look of acceptance would come over Peter's face. Peter could learn operations. He could learn to be a chief pilot in charge of training. He could be something other than what he wanted to be. The look didn't come.

"Fuck them. I've got rights. I'm a union pilot. Fuck them, Rocky, and fuck you too. I did this for them. They can kiss my ass." He stood up, bumping the table with his knees, and tried to go. Rocky held his arm.

"Peter, stop. You came back from the dead. Do you understand that? I drove your family to Bridle to your funeral. I told a church full of people who love you that you could walk on water, change water to wine, feed a thousand of them with a loaf of bread, because I believed you were larger than life. Do you know how many people prayed for you, how many of us believed you were dead and that we'd never see you again? How many of us pestered the State Department and volunteered to go to Karachi to get your body and even fly your plane home? We care about you, Peter. We care for Candace and Jeff and Tiffany. We want you in the family, Peter. But you can't fly anymore. It's not safe."

Peter shook his hand off and walked away.

iv.

"They betrayed me, Candace," he told his wife. "The bastards let me rot in a hellhole and then stabbed me in the back." He omitted only a few facts. "They're afraid if I'm flying and some terrorist gets wind of it, they'll try to go after the plane."

Even that had been enough for Candace. "I'd rather you work in a gas station than fly, if that's what they're going to do."

"You don't know what it was like, sitting in that hole, drinking slop out of a bucket and listening."

The listening had been hard. Down the corridor steel doors opened, men were hauled out, footsteps dragged men away, then silence. Sometimes the footsteps came back and the steel doors opened and a man was tossed back in. Sometimes a trap door was sprung in a floor above him, or a volley of shots, and the footsteps didn't come back to that steel door. Otherwise, it was silent. It had been very hard.

"You don't know what it was like here, without you, without news of you. I thought you were dead!"

"I'm not dead."

Candace asked him to try becoming a manager for a while. He said no. She said they were about to lose the house. He said fuck the house. She said why not talk to Frank.

"Do you know what Frank did while I sat in that hellhole waiting for them to hang me? The bastard took off for France. Did he do one single thing for you? For Mother? She needed him and he turned his back on her. I wouldn't talk to him if he was the last person alive."

Thus, within two months, Peter's accumulated sick pay and vacation pay ran out. TWA, American, United, and Delta all politely said that they weren't hiring any 747 pilots just then. His union representative said that Pan Am would fight his grievance every step of the way. Bill Harper at Front Range Savings and Loan repossessed their home for six months of arrears in payments. Peter and Candace moved to Bridle, where he became a crop duster pilot. He refused to sell the Corvette because something would come through for them.

It didn't.

Then Shirley Carter called him on the telephone, personally, from Tierra Savings and Loan, to say:

"Peter, I'm sorry, real sorry, but I can't give you all a loan against Will and Virginia's little house, not even with your power of attorney. It seems that, well, there's a problem with the title."

Chapter Thirty-Four

Mr. Cheatham sat deeply in his leather chair, rocking back and forth while he read.

"Um, hmmm." He held the paper closer to his face and squinted. "Um, hmm." He read a few more lines and put on a superior smile, then laid the article on his desk.

"So tell me, Mr. ...."

"Hastings."

"Yes, sorry, Mr. Hastings. So, what do you think I'm supposed to do with this, this, what is it?"

"DNA."

"DNA. What am I supposed to do with this DNA? 'Halt the presses! Call England! We want some DNA.'" He was not a geneticist, or even much of a scientist. He made a steeple with his hands and fingers and waited for a reply to his quip.

"It's in the last sentence. Listen. '...will revolutionize forensic biology, particularly with identification of rape suspects.'" It was so obvious, so clear. Cheatham had a client who was a rape suspect, indeed a client who had been convicted of rape. "Miss Vines changed her story to identify Artemis Washington in court. If you submit their DNA for tests, it will clear him."

Cheatham smiled again. He picked up the *Nature* article, scanned it again, put it back down on his cluttered desk. There was no money in the case, not any more. He had got all there was to be got. It continued to be, however, interesting.

"She did, did she? Interesting. Why do you say that, Mr. Hastings?"

Frank withdrew the police composite drawing from a manila folder and handed it to Mr. Cheatham, exactly as he had done months before, after Washington's trial. Cheatham studied it and handed it back. He was

390

enjoying the visit with Mr. Hastings considerably more than he had enjoyed their first meeting.

"The police made this drawing of the suspect long before Artemis Washington was arrested. They gave a copy to another reporter at the *Gazette*. This is your rapist." He handed it to Mr. Cheatham, again, and was relieved that Mr. Cheatham studied it this time.

Cheatham scratched his chin.

"So, Mr. Hastings, how would this DNA thing work? We write off to England, tell this professor what we want, and then what?" Cheatham's smile was unnerving. He rocked in his chair, back and forth, willing to let Frank make a fool of himself but also willing to learn a bit more about DNA. "Sounds like a long-shot to me."

Frank had prepared for this. He pulled out another manila folder, opened it, and took out the one-page letter from GeneTech Laboratories in Boston.

Dear Mr. Hastings: Enclosed is the complete laboratory analysis of the blood samples you sent to our laboratory. In summary, there is a 99.9999% probability that the donor of Sample A is the father of the donor of Sample B. All fifteen genetic markers matched. Even though Sample B was drawn within the last month and Sample A was reputedly recovered from a piece of stained cloth reported to be forty years old the genetic markers do not degrade....

"They teach genetics at UT, Mr. Cheatham. Dr. Haralson there referred me to GeneTech in Boston. GeneTech said it would attempt to do the study based on Dr. Jeffrey's method. This is the result." Frank had it all figured out, but he could tell that Mr. Cheatham was skeptical, leaving an atmosphere of uncertainty in the office. Frank had the eerie feeling that he was back in the third grade at the Bridle school auditorium, auditioning for the role of playing a grape in the elementary school celebration of spring. Mrs. Frost hadn't liked his interpretation of being a grape. "So, it seems all you have to do is get the sheets or panties or whatever from the DA, Mrs.

Vines' sheets that were in evidence at the trial. Get a sample of Artemis Washington's blood and send them in."

Cheatham chuckled, not in a good way.

"Just pick up the phone? Call the DA? 'Can you lend us Miss Vines' bloodstained underthings for an experiment?'"

Frank would have been a good grape, hopping around on stage in purple-stained long johns with artificial leaves glued to his head. Tog was an apple. Frank was not chosen to be a grape; he was relegated to the wheat field, dull brown, anonymous sticks hidden quietly in the corner of the stage while spring was celebrated in dance and song.

"Yes, something like that. I guess you'd have to file a motion or something, I don't know how it works. And get a doctor to go to the penitentiary to get a blood sample from your client."

"He's not my client any more, Mr. Hastings. He hasn't had the energy to pursue an appeal, and told me to drop it." Cheatham was perplexed how anyone could be a newspaper reporter and know so little about the news. "You don't know what's happened, do you? To Artemis Washington." He studied Frank's face for a long time, his serious demeanor and eager ideas. He decided that Frank was not an idiot, or lazy, or even a do-gooder who would blame Cheatham for not using the police composite drawing to exonerate an innocent man. He concluded that Frank didn't know. "Have you been out of town, Mr. Hastings?"

Cheatham called his secretary into the office, asked for a couple of cups of coffee and the Washington file. They talked about Longhorn spring football practice, about work on the police desk at the newspaper, about the pictures of children on Cheatham's wall. She brought the coffee and the file.

He rummaged around in the folders and papers and found a medical report of his own. He handed it to Frank.

"Artemis is a dead man, Mr. Hastings. He's got AIDS."

Frank felt sick. He had never known anyone with AIDS. He didn't think he even knew anyone who knew anyone who had AIDS. He thought of Eleanor and the peanut growing in her womb and tried to remember what he had touched in the courtroom. Had he shaken hands with Artemis? Had Artemis spit on him in the bailiff's anteroom? And Cheatham himself? Could he have AIDS from all the times he spent sitting next to his client?

Frank closed his eyes and thought of the water pitchers on the counsel tables in the courtroom. Cheatham and Artemis Washington must have drunk the same water. He scooted his chair back, not wanting even to touch the report.

"You're safe, unless you're a gay and somewhere along the way Artemis stuck it to you. You don't get AIDS shaking hands. Here's how it works, at least in Artemis Washington's case. The jury says life and the sheriff takes you back out of the courtroom. They put you in a holding cell and sooner or later you pull the chain. That's when the penitentiary sends a bus to the jail and all the prisoners headed to the pen are chained together and put on the bus. When you get to the pen you go to a diagnostic center for the wardens to sort out where to put you. Are you with me?"

Frank was with him, so far.

"So Artemis is in the prison diagnostic center and he gets sick. Not surprising; a lot of convicts get sick when they look up and see themselves being processed like a bunch of Milk Duds while some angry white guy with a big belly and a big gun and a short haircut decides where they're going to spend the next sixty years. Artemis is sick in the processing center. He loses weight, gets a fever, gets scared, they send him to a prison in Beaumont. Artemis goes out on the prison farm and chops cotton or sugar cane or whatever they do on the farm and he collapses. Sores all over him, shaking. Prison hospital sends him to Galveston where a real doctor takes one look at him and says he's got full-blown AIDS. They run a blood test and, sure enough. Artemis Washington, my friend, is going to die before summer. It's safe to drink the coffee."

Frank didn't know what to say. He looked around the room, the cluttered desk and the cheap brass scales of justice on Mr. Cheatham's bookcase and the *Nature* article and decided that maybe he wouldn't have been such a good grape, or a tight end, or a lieutenant or any of the other things he had toyed with in life and not succeeded. The coffee was bitter.

"So, no blood tests from Artemis," Frank sighed. Cheatham nodded in quiet agreement. "He'll die an innocent man. Well, innocent in the rape sense. I guess if you get AIDS you're not innocent of everything." He tucked his own paternity test back in its folder and began to gather his other things.

"But, what about this? The police sketch? We can still make a push to clear his name. Shouldn't we do that? For his family?" Frank remembered the hostile woman who had answered his knock at Artemis' address and demanded that he leave. She would feel better in her old age if her son was proved innocent. It would comfort her. "The misidentification. By Miss Vines."

Cheatham had spent twenty years practicing law before he fully grasped the basics of criminal cases: Your client has a lot of reasons to lie; you will spend more time chasing down the missing truth of their stories than you will ever spend looking for nuggets in the investigative report or for novel questions of constitutional rights; the police weren't kindly, but they are good at what they do. He shook his head.

"Read this."

"Eloy Tucker, 32, services at Mount Olive to be held Tuesday, 9-2-82."

It was an obituary for some man who died almost five years before.

"And this."

"'Eloy Tucker, APD Number 82-744099, arrested 6-22-82.'"

A full facial photograph and a side profile photograph were attached, a fingerprint card at the bottom. The mug shot of Eloy Tucker, charged with one count of sexual assault, matched the police composite sketch as skillfully and accurately as Will Hastings' sketch matched Géraldine Dupré.

"Miss Vines didn't misidentify Artemis, Mr. Hastings. Artemis did. He's the one who described a man he saw breaking into an apartment and reported it to police. It might have worked if he had kept up with his family. He didn't and the rest, they say, is history. If I had put that sketch into evidence at the trial a whole file cabinet of worse evidence would have come into the case. First, that Artemis, not the rape victims, is the one who told police what to draw. Second, that Eloy Tucker was his half-brother. Third, that Eloy Tucker was killed before five of the six Bluff Springs rapes that Artemis was accused of ever happened. Do you understand what that means, Mr. Hastings?"

It meant, Frank realized, that the strongest evidence against Artemis Washington would no longer be that the Bluff Springs rapes stopped after he was arrested. The strongest evidence would be that the Bluff Springs rapes continued for a long time after Eloy Tucker was dead and that Artemis had tried to blame him. Artemis apparently did not keep up with his family.

"No, that isn't the strongest bit of evidence that would come in. Oh, maybe it is, how do you decide that kind of thing? No matter. The strongest bit of new evidence that the jury never heard was that Eloy Tucker's blood didn't match a single bit of blood on any of the sheets or bath towels or carpet samples or dish cloths that the police recovered from any of the six. Sort of like your DNA tests, it would prove conclusively that Eloy Tucker was not the Bluff Springs rapist. I did my best to persuade the jury with what I had to work with, Mr. Hastings." He sat deeply into his chair and made another hand cathedral. "The last time you came here I ran you off because I had no idea that Artemis Washington had AIDS. You're going about making a news story out of that drawing would have led to an insurance trial. The DA would have dragged him back from the pokey and tried him for another rape just in case I won the appeal on the Vines case. As it happens, you didn't and, well, now it doesn't matter. In the army we called it OBE."

"OBE. Overcome by events." *The RPG shot up from behind the hill and hit the helicopter in the fuel tank. The search for booby traps was overcome by events.*

"In a nutshell. Overcome by events. I'm just waiting to hear if one more bombshell blows up." He paused and waited, amused at the *danse macabre* that he had to watch. "It'll make a good story, Mr. Hastings, and I promise to call you first if it happens. That'll be your big exclusive story out of the Artemis Washington case."

Frank was dazed at the signs and turns he had seen and missed. *What else could there be?* Cheatham told him.

"The DA told Miss Vines to go in for testing. Now we're waiting to see if she has AIDS too. Amazing what advances they're making these days, this blood stuff. Well, we'll see. Time will tell. Good to see you, Mr. Hastings. It's always good to see you."

Frank stood up to go, hesitant to prolong what already was an uncomfortable meeting. Unfortunately, he didn't know who else to ask.

"Mr. Cheatham? Doesn't your firm handle real estate and deeds too?" He knew from the I-35 Condominium files at the courthouse that it did. He probably would have gotten a better answer, he thought, if he had gone to find Mr. Dean, the lawyer who sued on all of the I-35 loan defaults. "Can I ask a question about a real estate document?"

Cheatham smelled more legal business and told Frank that of course he could. He waited while Frank dug back into his pile of papers for the last time, then took what was handed to him and read it.

"This looks like a loan agreement from an outfit called Tierra Savings and Loan. The letter tells you to sign the deed of trust and send it back so that her bank, this Mrs. Carter, can loan money against your property up in Bridle. It doesn't say who to, or how much. How much are you borrowing? That should go in here somewhere. And what happens if the loan isn't paid back is kind of lopsided; if you sign this the way it is, if you're late five minutes with a loan payment, the bank gets clear title to your land. It's a very one-sided deal. Do you want me to send you over to one of my partners to fix it up for you?"

Frank hesitated, then asked.

"Can I tell you a story?"

Chapter Thirty-Five

i.

The highway into Tierra was both intriguing and challenging, at least for Eleanor.

She was something of a specialist on Texas towns, at least the towns she had seen in driving back and forth to Bridle. She thought that all of them had been laid out by the same town planner: Highway into town. Gasoline station. General Motors dealer. Grain elevator. Barbeque shack. Dairy Queen. Town square. Courthouse on square (with minor variations: Victorian red brick courthouse with clock towers; neo-classical courthouses with white columns that evoked plantation architecture; square brick courthouse with uniform rows of large glass windows set within aluminum frames; and, ugly courthouses that blended castle turrets with the steps and gothic windows of a Baptist church). Barbershop. Beauty shop. Drugstore. Water tower. Lumberyard. Houses on uniformly square streets, shaded by gasping elm trees. Church steeples visible above the elm trees. Older houses on the opposite end of the town from the newer houses. Grocery store. Ford dealer. Competing gasoline station. Highway out of town. John Deere dealer. Cemetery.

Tierra was many of those things, yet different. The grain elevator was, in Tierra's case, a large metal cotton gin with a row of drying houses and clusters of cotton trailers in the yard. The barbeque shack was an ancient sideboard building named Nona's. The drugstore was closed. The houses on the poorer side of Tierra tended toward crumbling stucco. But, more than anything, Eleanor was intrigued by the town's new houses, a big city suburb sprung up from the cotton fields on the edge of Tierra in a subdivision named Tierra Heights.

"Tierra must be a rather large town," she said. "Tierra Heights. Designer homes from the $100,000s. Close to work and play." A billboard portrayed a happy family holding hands as they walked along a sidewalk in front of a happy brick home with flowerbeds and a veritable forest of trees. A few deer peeked out in the distance. There were no particular heights. "I don't know why, but I had the impression that Tierra was like Bridle, only without your family. This is quite impressive."

The large stone entrance to Tierra Heights appeared on the left hand side of the Lubbock Highway.

"This must be very new. The trees aren't quite so verdant as the advertising board, are they?" A gaze beyond the gate revealed a dozen new homes, no deer, no trees, no flowerbeds, no happy family holding hands on the sidewalk. There were, however, fifteen or twenty concrete slabs with plumbing pipes poking upward. Some slabs had framing studs in place. Others bore unroofed rafters, rough electrical stubs, some piles of building material, and chain link fences. There didn't seem to be much work taking place. "Oh, my. Another building site in distress, by the look of it."

Frank smiled and drove past the GM dealer and the cotton gin, then turned off the highway at Nona's, in search of the Tierra Savings and Loan. He assumed the town square would be near the faded water tower that rose up through the elm trees. He avoided the potholes and ignored the cluttered vacant lots and entered the town where his parents had grown up.

Eleanor's confidence in small towns was restored when they found the square. Men in their pickup trucks waved to them. Women in front of the beauty shop smiled and watched them drive by. The courthouse itself filled the center of the town square, and it was a safe gamble that the bank would be nearby. However, before they found the bank, Frank saw Sandy Clayton standing in front of a barber's pole; he steered the Volvo into an angled parking space, then rolled down his car window and waved. Sandy waved back and walked over.

"Hello. What can I do for you?" Sandy chirped. His right hand was already reaching through the car window to shake Frank's hand, his face slightly puzzled at who it was. When he saw Eleanor in the passenger seat he put back in place the memory of Peter Hastings' memorial service. "You're...." He grinned.

"Frank, and my wife Eleanor, Hastings. I'm Peter's brother. We met you at his funeral. The memorial service. How are you? I wasn't sure you'd remember me." That was not exactly true; he had seen Sandy's face relax when he saw Eleanor, whom no one forgot. There weren't a lot of more-or-less black and white couples in Texas, certainly not in Tierra. "We've got some business in town. Saw you and wanted to say hi."

Sandy was good at saying hi. He put his hand on the car roof and leaned in through the window.

"Boy, that was some deal about your brother, eh? Him getting out of there. What's the story on that? We heard it through the grapevine, not a word about it in the news. That's the way it is—somebody gets killed, big story, somebody comes home, not a word. Anyway, what's the story?"

"They had him. They let him go. That's all we know; very hush deal. I think it's supposed to be kept quiet."

"Right. Well, why don't you'll come in?" Sandy pointed to the barbershop. It was late morning on a Thursday, not a busy time. "Sit a spell? I've got some coffee made up. You'll drive all the way up here this morning?" He was infectious.

"We need to get on over to the bank. You know," meaning that Frank already had said he had business. "See Mrs. Carter. Where is the bank?"

A cloud came over Sandy's face, his eyebrows furrowed, he squinted. Maybe it was the sun. He lifted his hand off the car roof and used it to tuck his empty shirtsleeve back inside his waist band.

"Over there. See the courthouse? There on the corner's the memorial. Just around that corner, there's the bank." He stood back from the car, stiffly, as if he regretted having stopped to talk to them. "She know you're coming?"

"I think so. We called her and said we wanted to stop by on the way to Tierra. She sent us some papers and we need to talk about that. That's all."

"Um," Sandy nodded. "Um. Well, nice to see ya'll. If you decide you've got time for coffee, come on back." He waved to the Volvo more than to Frank. "Or a haircut. Won't take a sec." He grinned again. Frank grinned.

The Volvo backed away and headed off around the courthouse, past the war memorial monument, and right into the front parking spaces of the Tierra Savings and Loan. Shirley saw them get out of the car and bounced and jiggled to meet them at the front door.

ii.

The loan difficulty was quite simple, they learned. It would have been straightforward had either Frank or Eleanor known anything about it in advance.

"They left you the house," Shirley explained. "Well, I guess not *left* it to you. They deeded it to you. Here. Here's a copy the title company gave me."

The deed was dated July 1, 1986.

> Woodrow Wilson Hastings and wife, Virginia Sullivan Hastings, grant, convey, transfer, and remit to Franklin R. Hastings and wife, Eleanor Hastings, all right, title, and interest...

It had been file-stamped for recording with the Bridle County clerk on July 7, right after the holiday.

"So, when Peter needed the loan I thought everything was fine and dandy. I needed the deed to secure the loan so he sent me that power of attorney. That's when the title company figured out that Peter didn't own that little house up in Bridle. You do! It's so good Peter's safe and sound. You must be real happy. But his power of attorney over your momma isn't any good, not unless Peter has the deed too. Or you sign the loan for him with the deed in your name." She smiled at both of them. It was so simple.

The power of attorney was dated June 29, 1986. It gave Peter the power to "do any act or thing that Woodrow Wilson Hastings or Virginia Sullivan Hastings, or either of them, could do as if they did the thing personally."

"So, we've drawn up a deed of trust for the loan. Frank, if you and Eleanor can just sign it, I'll get a notary over here and fix it up and that's that."

"How much did Peter want to borrow, ma'am?"

"Just ten thousand dollars," Shirley beamed. It wasn't much of a loan, not compared to the loans she made for Tierra Heights. "The house is appraised at $35,000, with the lot and all. It's a nice house, for Bridle."

"Can I have copies?" he asked.

"Sure you can. Let's get them signed first, and make copies with your signatures. That's the way we usually do it." Shirley smiled at Frank and Eleanor, as if they were family. She beamed at Eleanor, asked her if that long car ride made her tired, and said Frank was just a spitting image of his daddy. "I'll get the notary."

"Well, we can't sign it yet, not today."

Shirley sat back down.

"Is there a problem?" The once-beaming round face and swollen eye sockets faded to a round and cloudy face with clenched jaws underneath a parchment smile.

In fact, Eleanor thought, Shirley's face now looked a lot like the stone entry to the Tierra Heights subdivision.

"If there's a problem I can get Mr. Farley at the title company over here," Shirley continued. "He can explain it better than I can. Or Mr. Doggins. He does our paperwork if there's a legal problem." She beamed again.

Frank beamed back.

"No, ma'am. No problem at all. It's just that, well, with all the things going on, with Peter being in Pakistan and all, this was all put off until now. Probate."

"Probate?"

"Yes, ma'am," Frank went on. He thought Shirley Carter's face looked like a traffic light, signaling stop or go or yield, whatever she felt at the moment. At this moment it was a bit yellow. He entered her intersection. "No one probated Dad's estate after he died. That's why we're on the way to Bridle. There's a probate hearing tomorrow up there at the county court-house. To probate Dad's estate. This will clear up everything pretty fast, I think." He reached away from his padded visitor's chair toward Eleanor, sitting in her padded visitor's chair, and took his wife's hand. "I think it'll all be straightened out this week. Tell me, Mrs. Carter—how well did you know Dad and Mother? I really didn't get a chance to talk with you very much at Peter's service. I seem to remember you were their best friends."

Shirley's traffic signal face began to waver between red and amber.

"Taking care of Peter and all when Dad was away at the war," he continued. "I was struck by your memories."

"Oh, yes," the now green light proceeded. Shirley had loved Peter.

"It was hard back then. We had been on food rationing for years and then all the soldiers were coming home and there weren't jobs for anybody, not here. Your daddy was sent back to the service after the war was actually over so Virginia was having a tough time of it by herself. We took care of that little boy whenever she would let us. That's because we were best friends. We all grew up together, Hoyt and me and your parents. It was hard, but those were good times when you look back on it. I'll get your copies."

Frank and Eleanor looked around the lobby of the Tierra Savings and Loan. It was not significantly different than City Federal, smaller but with the same carpeted floors, the same stained wood tables with pads of checks and deposit slips for customers to use when they came inside, a half-dozen teller windows with marble shelves. There was only one teller at work. A secretary at a desk just beyond Mrs. Carter's desk could be heard telling two men in work clothes that she would process their construction draw as soon as Mrs. Carter was free. Shirley returned.

"Here you go, Frank. It was so good to see you. And you too...."

"Eleanor."

"Eleanor, yes, of course. Well, you two drive safe on the way up to Bridle, hear? And I'll wait to hear from you next week."

She jiggled and bounced up from her chair to shake hands. Frank and Eleanor shook hands with her and rose to go, then stopped.

"Ma'am, could I just ask one more thing?" He waited. "Can you tell me why Mother and Dad left Tierra?"

She didn't remember the details; it was so long ago.

There was a pickup truck parked next to the Volvo, in front of the bank. When Frank opened the car door for Eleanor he heard a delighted voice:

"Look, Dad. It's Jesus of Lord's family! They're here!" Sonny was delighted. He opened the pickup door and sprang out, rushing up to stand in front of Frank and Eleanor and radiate joy.

"Hello, Sonny," Eleanor said back, smiling at how seeing Sonny could bring her such pleasure. "Hello, Mr. Carter."

"Hello to you," Hoyt said. He got out of the pickup and walked to where Frank still held the open door. "Listen, Frank. Can we go somewhere to talk? I..." Hoyt paused and measured his words. "I... There's something I need to tell you."

Chapter Thirty-Six

i.

The courthouse in Bridle was in a style category of its own: 'new brick elementary school with flat roof.' Bridle didn't need much of a courthouse. Speeding tickets, car titles, voter registration cards, and local taxes were all paid or dispensed, as the case might be, from a single office near the front door. Deeds were recorded, marriages were licensed, and births were filed in a slightly larger room across the hallway.

The courtroom itself was almost an afterthought; no one sued anyone in Bridle County and anyone foolish enough to commit a crime wasn't foolish enough to choose the longer sentence that invariably came from denying it and having a trial. Except for Judge Altgelt's bench and an adjacent desk for the county clerk to handle his court files, it would have looked not so much like a courtroom as a public auditorium where the volunteer fire department met and county livestock agents demonstrated progressive methods of screwworm control.

"Estate of Hastings?" Judge Altgelt announced from the bench. He looked out over the room, assembled now as a courtroom with two wooden tables placed before him for the parties and their lawyers. The clerk handed him the file. "I have the application of Peter Hastings to be appointed the representative of the Estate of Doctor Woodrow Wilson Hastings. Is that right?"

"Yes, your Honor." Peter and his lawyer nodded vigorously from the bench on Judge Altgelt's right hand side.

"And I also have the application of Peter Hastings to rescind a deed that Dr. Hastings signed just before he died, if I understand the papers." Peter and his lawyer nodded again. "So, then we have the papers from Frank

Hastings, opposing." He looked up. Frank and Mr. Cheatham sat at the table facing Judge Altgelt's left hand side. "Who are you?"

"Daniel Cheatham, Your Honor, for Frank Hastings. Yes, we oppose."

"Did you really come all the way up here from Austin for this, Mr. Cheatham? Did they strike oil under Dr. Hastings' house?" The clerk tittered. Frank cringed. He had worried about agreeing to let Mr. Cheatham's son be his lawyer but, as Cheatham said, "He needs the experience. Besides, the whole story's too good to be true." Frank had agreed to pay his airfare. "You two men come up here."

The lawyers walked up to Judge Altgelt's bench.

"And Virginia?" the judge continued. "My goodness, how are you?" He looked beyond the tables to the rows of padded frame chairs that had been arranged for an audience. Virginia sat on the front row, between Eleanor and Candace. "You look awfully nice. It's good to see you."

Candace whispered in Virginia's ear. Virginia smiled. The judge turned to the lawyers.

"What the hell is going on here, you two? Are you really telling your clients to get into a suit over that house? It can't be worth more than what two high-powered lawyers would charge for arguing about it." He glared. Peter's lawyer started to speak up but Judge Altgelt jerked his head at him, a sure sign that the judge didn't want to be answered. Cheatham took the cue and waited. "Okay, you. What's this about?"

"Doctor Hastings died last summer, Your Honor, without a will. He did sign a power of attorney in favor of his son, Peter, to do everything Doctor Hastings could do. At the time he died, they lived a few miles apart. And, I'm sure you know, Mrs. Hastings isn't able to handle her own affairs, so she can't administer his estate. She couldn't really have known she was signing a deed to her house over to Frank Hastings."

"Is there anything," the judge asked, "to administer? Other than this house? It's been empty ever since they moved to Colorado." The lawyers said there was not. "Okay, Mr. Cheatham. Do you get a lot of comments about your name?"

Cheatham didn't get it. He plowed in.

"Doctor and Mrs. Hastings did sign a power of attorney to Peter Hastings exactly two days before they signed the deed, but Peter didn't do anything with it until *after* they deeded the house to Frank Hastings and his wife, Eleanor. If Mrs. Virginia Hastings was competent to sign a power of attorney, she was competent to sign the deed. Peter shouldn't run her affairs by being appointed to administer a house that Frank owns."

"Is that about it?" the judge asked. "Is that the whole fight?" It was. "Well, we're not going to fight about that. Do you hear me?" Neither lawyer was sure what Judge Altgelt meant, but neither lawyer was prepared to argue with him. "Not in my court. Not in public. You two go sit down. Send your clients up here. I'm going to talk to them." Cheatham started to protest; Altgelt held up his hand. "Off the record. Do it."

Cheatham backed away from the bench, toward the table where Frank sat, keeping an eye on Judge Altgelt as if he thought the man was going to pull a lever and drop a trapdoor out from under him.

"You don't have to do this," Cheatham whispered to Frank. "It's irregular." He watched Frank stand up and begin to walk to the bench. "Don't let him tell you have to do something. That's what I'm for."

Peter had played football with Judge Altgelt's son; he walked right up the judge, smiling.

"How are you two boys doing? Peter, good to have you back in town. Not often I get to tell someone you had a great turnout for your funeral." Peter was doing fine. "Kids settling in at school?" They were. "And your mother? She looks good. But I'll tell you, Peter, we all knew before your folks ever moved up to Colorado that she wasn't, you know... She coming home?"

"I guess that depends on how this comes out, Your Honor."

"Sure it does. What's she doing here in court, then?"

"Frank set it up. His lawyer filed a notice that he was bringing her, since it might affect her estate, and they paid for it. She's with us at the house right now, though." Talking with Judge Altgelt wasn't that hard. Peter relaxed.

"And you?" He turned to Frank. "Do they still call you Nitro? You can still see that big old letter S on the football field." He smiled at Frank as well. The reason Frank hadn't been hauled into court over burning chicken coop napalm onto the football field was because Judge Altgelt and most of the rest of Doc's friends thought it was funny, if not repeated. "You can plead the fifth. How are you?" Frank was doing fine. He was keenly aware that Judge Altgelt was looking over his shoulder at Virginia and, most likely, at Eleanor. "Well, here's what we're going to do. Listen to me."

They listened.

"You two are going to go sit in that little room over there. It's the jury room. Cleanest room in the building, just needs to be used now and then. And you two are going to stay in there and talk to each other until you two sort this out. Do you understand?"

"Sir?" Peter asked.

"Do I need to say it again, Peter? You and Frank are going to go by yourselves into that room and sit at the table and talk to each other until this is settled. Period. You aren't going to prove to me that you're the best person to administer your father's estate and that your mother isn't capable of taking care of it. And you, Frank, are not going to parade your mother on the stand as some kind of proof that this power of attorney is no good because she didn't have the mental capacity to sign it. Besides, if that's true, and I don't care if it is or it isn't, that deed wouldn't be any good either, so you need to think twice before asking me for something because if push came to shove, I might have to give it to you. Understand?"

"Yes, sir."

"So that's it. Go. Frank, if you need to send your high-powered lawyer friend home, send him. There isn't going to be any trial today. Believe me, if there's a trial, you'll know it, you and him both. Go."

Young Cheatham sputtered. Judge Altgelt told him not to worry. If Cheatham had learned anything from his father it was to not make things worse. He stopped sputtering.

The judge watched from the bench as the two brothers walked back into the jury room, turned to see if he was watching them, and closed the door. He announced that there was no other business that day but he would stick around in case either of the boys needed anything. The lawyers left. He walked up to Virginia and asked her how she was. She stood and looked confused, but smiled, and Candace took her hand and held it until the judge said goodbye. Then, Virginia, Candace, and Eleanor sat down to wait.

ii.

Peter looked at Frank. It was the first time he had seen him since Will's funeral. He expected Frank to have aged, or gotten fat, or changed in some way as Peter had done, and was disappointed when Frank looked the way he always did.

From his perspective, however, Frank's view of Peter was troubling. He was skinny. His knuckles were so knobby that Frank believed he had arthritis. A slight cleft in one cheek made him suspect that Peter had lost some teeth on that side. His hair was thin. Only his eyes had that same confident look, the one that had scored touchdowns and won track and field ribbons and marched Becky Collins to the middle of the football field, knowing that the town was there to see him more than her. That look reminded Frank that Peter really was back.

"I met the Carters. They were friends of Mother and Dad growing up, until they moved here. They came up here for your funeral. She's the one you asked for the loan." Peter stared at him. "I guess they're not really a couple any more. Mr. Carter lives in town with their boy, Sonny. He's handicapped."

"So?" Peter was not happy with Mrs. Carter; if she had sent him the money he wouldn't have been stuck in the room with Frank. "What's his handicap?"

"Sonny only sees the good in people. He says to tell you he's real glad you're not dead. He liked your funeral."

Peter had already had enough.

"It's not your house, Frank. It's Mother's. All you're doing is hurting her. It's her nest egg."

"Maybe so, Peter. I'm not sure that borrowing ten thousand dollars against her nest egg is the best way to take care of her. What's the money supposed to be for?"

Peter didn't believe he owed Frank an explanation of finances, and said so.

"Besides," Peter added, "you didn't care one dot about Mother, you never did, not until now. Now you want a bigger house for whatever kind of kid you and your... wife... are going to produce, and suddenly you want a piece of property you never knew you owned. Supposedly owned. In fact, if you cared about Mother, you would have been there with her while I was in that rat-infested pit in the desert. What'd you do? Run off to France. By the way, did you find your mother?"

Frank watched Peter mouth the word 'bastard,' presumably in silence in case Judge Altgelt was listening at the keyhole. It had taken less time than he had expected it would, since this time he had something Peter wanted, but Peter had come right to the point. Frank decided that nothing was to be gained by putting things off.

"I did." He waited. "I've brought something for you to sign. If you sign it, you can have the house."

"Sign something?" Peter's mind raced. What on earth did he have that Frank wanted badly enough that he would turn over the house for it? "What?"

"A letter. Here it is." He passed a typewritten letter to Peter, and a ballpoint pen. Peter read it.

> Dear Tiffany and Jeff: Your uncle Frank had a dog named Hercules, that he loved very much. It's buried in the backyard of Grandma and Granddad's house. Hercules died because I murdered him, with drain cleaning poison.

Peter read the letter and laughed, not in a kind way.

"Fuck you, Frank. Fuck you and the dog you rode in on. You'll spend every dime that you ever make before I sign that letter or anything like it." He put his elbows on the table and crossed his arms. "Fuck you."

"It was the day I destroyed your airplanes, Peter," Frank answered. He was surprised at how calm he was, so far. "I found Hercules in the backyard. His mouth was foaming, and he started convulsing. I thought he had rabies but he wasn't attacking me or running around in circles or spitting, just burning inside his mouth. There was Drain-O in his water dish and in his dog food, but he hadn't touched them. The only way to get Drain-O into Hercules' mouth was to hold the can to his mouth and pour it in, just like a stopped-up sink. He let me hold his head in my lap while he howled. He died in about fifteen minutes. I would have killed you but you weren't home. Then I went into your room and destroyed every model airplane I could get my hands on. They locked me up in my room that night and the next day Tog and I ran away from home. You know why you killed my dog, Peter? Because Dad gave Hercules to me, and you hated it."

Frank spoke with a lot more authority than he felt. He had never before taken charge of a conversation with Peter. He held his hands under the table where Peter couldn't see them, in case they were shaking.

"You can't prove it." Peter snarled and wadded the letter up, then threw it in the trashcan. He began to flip the ballpoint pen between his fingers, like a baton.

"No," Frank answered. "Not unless you sign the letter, I really can't. You told Tiffany and Jeff that I destroyed your planes, but you didn't tell them why. Are you sure you won't sign it?"

Peter laughed at that.

"Okay, you won't sign it. That would have gotten us out of this room in ten minutes, but there it is. Let's talk about the deed and the power of attorney. That's what Judge Altgelt sent us in to talk about. I thought he made a very good point; if Mother wasn't competent to sign the deed she wasn't competent to sign the power of attorney. But if she was competent to sign one, she was competent to sign the other and the deed is good. It's not heads-I-win tails-you-lose. It looks like Dad had the deed notarized and mailed it here, to Bridle, for filing. What did you do with the power of attorney?"

Peter looked at him like he was demented; the power of attorney was in a lockbox at the house. He used it whenever he needed to do something on Mother's behalf.

"Here's what you did with it. On the same day the clerk here filed the house deed, you used the power of attorney to sell Mother and Dad's house in Del Sur. Then you flew to Dallas, met me in the airport, and as a perk of being a pilot's family, we flew to the Bahamas. Brothers. Buddy trip. A little skin diving. Remember?" Peter's eyes narrowed; the *fait accompli* was about to be on the table for discussion. "So, we go for a swim, a few drinks, and we talk about Mother and Dad. You say she's doing worse, maybe they ought to go to a nursing home. I say Dad's a doctor, he can take care of her better than anyone. Remember?"

Peter remembered. He would have gladly flown them to South America, but he didn't have enough crew benefits for a hotel in South America.

"I had to move them, Frank. It was what was best for her. She'd have died spending another winter up in that cabin in the mountains." Peter had told himself that. He had told Candace that. He had said it so often that he believed it himself.

"And you said, 'Frank, enjoy yourself. Have a beer, there's lots of time to think this over, to come up with all the pros and cons. We'll make a decision at breakfast." Frank was getting more and more angry. He hadn't told anyone except Eleanor what Peter had done in the Bahamas, and she had soothed him. Now it was bubbling back up. "Somehow, during that entire trip, you forgot to mention that you had already sold their house in Del Sur and booked them a slot in that awful nursing home. Do you think you forgot to mention it because when I came down for breakfast the next morning, you weren't there?"

He realized he almost was shouting, and checked himself. Peter seemed to be enjoying it. Frank looked out the jury room window. The tree limbs swayed in the breeze. Sparrows flew to the electric lines. A grain truck rumbled past the courthouse.

"Let me ask you, Peter: when you called me out at Dad's funeral, and when you wrote me to look at the alterations in my birth certificate because I wasn't just a bastard but a dumb bastard, were you thinking what I must have looked like in the lobby of that expensive hotel when I came down for breakfast the next day and they said you had checked out? You left me with the bill and cleaned out our hotel safe so I had no money. No credit cards. No airline tickets. No way home. It took Eleanor three days to get enough documents and money together to get me out of the Bahamas and on a bus from Miami to Austin. By then you and Candace were already in Del Sur, moving Mother and Dad out of their little cabin and into Loving Arms. You didn't just kill my dog, Peter. You killed my father. Why do you think he jumped off the highway bridge?"

"You can't prove that either, Frank." Peter was a little less assured, less cocky. He was afraid that Frank brought a big-city lawyer to Bridle, that he probably could prove exactly that. He now understood that this was not a fight over a ten-thousand-dollar loan.

"When you were in the hellhole, why didn't you just call the Pakistanis and tell them to put you in a nursing home? You couldn't survive there two weeks, Peter, not without your Corvette and your Walkman and your big new television. I don't know why you thought Dad could."

Peter was ready to leave. He not only wasn't getting what he wanted, he didn't want to have to listen to any more of Frank's accusations. Not even Judge Altgelt would make him sit through that. He had two crop duster jobs lined up for Thursday and had bid on a couple of others, and a charter flight from Amarillo to Arkansas. If they paid in cash, he could...

"How dare you call me a bastard, Peter? You're the bastard."

Peter walked to the door. Frank blocked it.

"I'm nearly through, but you're not leaving until I finish. Then, if you want it, I'll flip you for the house. Heads or tails. You never let me win at heads or tails, so what's to lose? And I don't care if I lose; you spent my first eighteen years telling me it wasn't my house, so why would I want it? You bent the spokes in my bike. You burned my biology paper and put sulfur in my chemistry experiment. You told the coach I was a queer. Remember that? Any idea how hard it is to be on a team when the guys have all been told you're a homosexual? And Kathy Tarper—remember her?"

"Who?"

"Kathy Tarper. I finally got a girlfriend. I had to go to Sundown to get one, but I had Kathy Tarper. Wrote letters back and forth, drove over to the movies on Saturday nights. Good girl. Until the Sundown rodeo. Then you took Kathy Tarper, too. My only girlfriend, and, well, you know what you did. Bareback riding?"

"That why you married Eleanor? Couldn't get another white girl to go out with you?" Frank made the mistake, Peter felt, of practically giving the house to Peter with a coin flip. Frank always crumbled in the end. He was crumbling now. Peter could say anything he liked.

"No, I married Eleanor because we went out a dozen times before I even noticed she was black, as you call it. I never saw her skin or color or anything else because I was listening to her voice and hearing about how wrong it was to take advantage of mine workers and shipbuilders until one day I was so in love with her that I would have asked her to marry me if she weighed three hundred pounds and had the skin of a hippopotamus. That's the same Eleanor who you told the waiters at your wedding rehearsal dinner to not let come in the room, that it was a private party. You always told people I was a bastard, but then you would go and act like one."

Peter started to push past the door. Frank grabbed his arm.

"These are for you, Peter. They'll only take a minute and then I'll go out myself and tell Judge Altgelt we're all done. Look at this." He then handed Peter a copy of the letter that George Grumman had written. It seemed years ago, and Frank hadn't been sure he could find it. He had used a yellow highlighter on one particular sentence.

> ...It was like something about the picture did set your mother off and maybe if you look at it you will figure out what it was. That should settle Peter down. I'm sorry...

It was paper-clipped to a print copy of the snapshot of Will and Virginia, standing on Poppy Sullivan's porch.

"You bastard," Peter hissed. "This is the picture that upset Mother at Father's wedding. I don't know where you got this, but I'll never, ever let you use it to hurt her again." He began to tear it up.

"So, I finally looked at the picture, like Mr. Grumman said. I've got another copy. Here. Look." He handed a magnifying glass to Peter. "Look closely, Peter." He waited. "Look at the uniform. In fact, look at the collar."

The branch insignia on Will's uniform collar, the caduceus of the army medical corps, was not a caduceus. It was the wings of a glider pilot. Peter didn't understand.

"Mr. Grumman was right, Peter. Look closely at the picture. That's not Dad there with Mother. At least, it's not my dad. Didn't you ever wonder where you got your love of flying?"

Peter sat back down at the desk. He had never thought, not for a minute, that there was someone else on the planet that his mother might have been with on Poppy Sullivan's porch. He didn't understand who was standing next to his mother, not even when Frank handed him a picture frame.

In the frame was a yellowed copy of Poppy Sullivan's announcement in the *Tierra Times*, the Easter edition of 1944, reporting Will and Virginia's elopement. Next to it in the frame was a fading copy of Peter's birth certificate. There was a third space in the frame for another document, but it was empty.

"Hoyt Carter gave this to me, yesterday. He said it had been in his closet for over forty years. I asked him what it was. He told me that Mrs. Carter had been making up a special surprise for Dad for when he came home from the army for good. It was indeed a surprise. Mrs. Carter never did give it to them. Instead, they ran Mother out of Tierra. Mother and you. Before Dad even made it home."

Peter looked at him blankly. Dim images floated across his mind, thoughts of playing the license plate game with Mother in the seat of a very old car. A train station. Dad with a monkey on the platform. Nothing good was coming, not from his point of view.

"Mrs. Carter hated Mother for marrying Dad and for having you. She hated her more when she found out that Mother had you but had *not* married Dad." Frank paused to be sure that Peter heard what he had said, then continued. "That blank place in the frame was meant to hold Mother and Dad's wedding license from the elopement. It's blank because there was no elopement. Not to a justice of the peace in Clovis, New Mexico, anyway. They don't even have justices of the peace in Clovis. Do you understand what this means? Do you get it, Peter?"

Peter was ready for the facts to change, but not the history.

"It just means they got married somewhere else."

"Maybe. Probably. But they didn't get married in Clovis, or Tierra, or Lubbock, not in 1943, or 1944. That's all the county clerks I could get to before the day ended and we had to come here. They probably did get married somewhere, someday, but not before you were born. Why? Because that man you're looking at is not my father. He's yours. I'm not a bastard, Peter. You are."

iii.

Peter was still sitting in the jury room when Frank came back in. Virginia was on Frank's arm, walking, smiling, as Géraldine had done a few months before, but with a vacant look. She saw Peter sitting in the jury room chair and brightened. Frank led her to a seat next to him. She patted Peter on the shoulder and smiled. He laid his hand on her red dress and reached for her hand.

"Mother?" Frank asked. "Mother? Can you hear me?" He waited. "I've found Peter."

She looked at him, a quizzical look in her eyes.

"Peter. Father's brother. I've found him."

She looked at him very carefully, and the smile dissolved from her face.

"He died in the war, Mother. He's buried in the army cemetery, in France." He paused to see if she had any sign of recognition. "I took a picture

413

of his grave at Colleville-sur-Mer. Do you see the tombstone? Lieutenant Peter Hastings, Texas, June 1944."

She took the photograph of Peter's grave and held it. Tears began to slip down her cheeks. She nodded.

"He was a hero, Mother. He landed his glider in a field surrounded by Germans. One of the men on his glider broke his leg. Peter was trying to carry him to safety when they were killed. Peter was a hero. He's someone we should be proud of."

Virginia looked at Frank, carefully, studying his eyes and his face. He gave her the photograph of her standing with Peter Hastings on Poppy's porch. She held it with the photograph of Peter's grave and began to quietly weep.

"It's all right mother. It's all right. I know you loved him. I understand now." He took her hands in hers and smiled at her, sadly, her sitting next to Peter but focusing on what he was saying. "It must have been so hard, not knowing, all those years."

Virginia got to her feet and put her arms around Frank's neck, then hugged him. She heaved against him, trying to breathe, nodding, and her chin pressed three or four times into his shoulder. He kissed her on the forehead. He looked out the window again. The wind had stopped. The truck had passed. The sun beamed through the window in rays, as beautiful as those he had seen in the windows of the cathedral In Galway, and in the garden of the monastery behind Chateau Dupré.

"Thank you, Frank." Virginia had to work to find her lost voice, then to form the words and pronounce them. "Yes, yes, it was very hard."

Chapter Thirty-Seven

A bare patch of dirt at the back of the Grumman's yard stood out against the scrub grass and Lucille's vegetable garden, silent evidence that Tog's Bambi had been wheeled away and left nothing alive in its place. A 220-volt cable that had been plugged into the Bambi was neatly coiled and hung on the utility pole. A custom-fitted plastic pipe capped off where it had once served Tog's miniscule bathroom. Frank knocked on the screen door. Lucille opened it.

"Heard you were in town, Frank." She stood blocking him from her kitchen door. "How's Virginia?"

Frank had not remembered Lucille being so small or weathered. Her hair had gone gray and hung limply on her neck. She wore a dark blue cotton tracksuit that was too large for her.

"She's fine, Mrs. Grumman. We went to the cemetery this morning. Becky Grey brought some folding chairs and she sat there with my wife and Peter's wife, studying Dad's grave. Right now there's just the little steel plate marker, and I think she was pretty sad about that. Peter and I are going to put up a real headstone, soon. She's at the house now. You might want to go see her."

"Tog's not here," Lucille said back. She crossed her arms and might have added 'mmmphhh' to her sentence. She still blamed Frank for losing Tog's football scholarship and for everything else that had gone downhill since.

"Yes, ma'am. I saw Tog yesterday, out at Bump's. After Judge Altgelt finished up. I thought he might have told you I wanted to stop by and say hello." She didn't unfold her arms or stand aside for him to come into her kitchen. "I was hoping to talk to Mr. Grumman for a few minutes. Is he home?"

He was home, Frank was sure. As best he could learn from Marshall, George still worked the late shift at the nuclear bomb factory. George's pickup, parked in the driveway, implied that he was home and would have an hour or so before he left to drive to work. She said that she would see.

"Hey, Frank," George said from inside the kitchen. "Lucille, let the boy in. He said he wanted to talk for few minutes. I suppose he does." He turned his attention to Frank. "How are you, Frank? What are you doing with yourself these days?"

"Hey, sir," Frank said back. They sat at the kitchen table. "I'm fine. Doing? Oh, still at the paper. I'm working on a couple of stories. Just a heads up – if you've got your retirement in a savings and loan, you might want to get it out. I think we're headed for a run on the banks."

George laughed. He didn't have a retirement account in a savings and loan. He hoped he could stay in one piece long enough to draw social security.

"Do you remember the Carters? They came up from Tierra, for Peter's funeral. I saw them Thursday. They're going to lose everything when her bank goes under. Probably within a couple of weeks."

George remembered the Carters. The man who claimed he had been Doc's best friend didn't know much about Doc; the woman claimed to know everything. George figured they deserved whatever they got. He asked Frank, "You still settin' fires?" George laughed. He agreed with Judge Altgelt; nobody had forgotten Frank's napalm burn on the football field.

"Yes, sir," Frank smiled. "I set one a couple of months ago, on some-body's farm. You can always find a little bit of chicken shit, pardon me, ma'am, and some diesel. Burns right into the dirt. It'll still be there."

"Understand you and Peter had a little set-to yesterday," George nudged. He wanted to know where this was going. He knew that the fight over the house had come to nothing; Judge Altgelt had told him over coffee early that morning that it had been high time the two brothers acted like grownups and he would have kept them there until kingdom came to make sure they did. "Everything all right? You okay?"

"Yes sir. I'm fine. We were just wrapping up some things to do with Dad. In fact, that's why I came to see you, to talk about Dad. You were his best friend. I thought you could tell me some things I don't really know about him."

George shifted in his chair. Frank seemed to be there just for a visit. He asked what it was that Frank had in mind.

"Do you know how he got wounded? In the army?"

George shifted again. He folded his hands, unfolded them, said he understood that Will had been wounded in a skirmish of some kind.

"Did you know him then?"

"Know Will? When he was wounded?"

"Yes, sir. I know you were in the army too, Mr. Grumman, but none of you men ever talked about it, not you, or Dad, or Judge Altgelt. So I thought you could tell me how Dad got shot."

George understood then that Frank had not come to chat. Frank had come to find out details of things that, George now suspected, Frank already knew. Lucille, however, did not understand that, and asked:

"Why do you think George and Doc knew each other in the army?" She thought she could stop the visit right then and put Frank Hastings in his place.

"Because I met somebody who knew Mr. Grumman and Dad when they were in the army. Before Dad was wounded." He waited to see if George would answer, but George just folded his hands, and unfolded them. "I thought maybe you knew if a man named Major Halliburton shot my father in the back."

George stood up from the table. He considered asking Lucille to make some coffee but he needed a minute to get his thoughts in order so he made the coffee himself. He found a Folger's can in the pantry and scooped out ten scoops. He put them into a filter in the Mr. Coffee that he had bought Lucille for Christmas. He poured in a pitcher of water and pushed the button to get it started. He took out coffee cups, saucers, and three spoons. He didn't know if Frank used sugar or milk but decided to put them out anyway, rather than break the silence. When Mr. Coffee had dripped its last drop into the pot, he poured coffee for each of them and sat back down.

"I think he did. I couldn't prove it." He stared at his coffee cup instead of looking at Frank. It wasn't something he had talked about in a very long time. Frank would not stop with that, he was sure, and thought maybe he should tell Lucille to leave, to go to the grocery store, or go see Virginia. There would be things, little things, which might come out that she didn't really know.

417

"What happened, Mr. Grumman?"

"We were in this old farm, just resting and staying out of the way. We'd been in the line for over two months. We'd crawled on our stomachs under machine-gun fire and climbed up a cliff to fight those sons of bitches in the barbed wire. They fought us day and night across a bunch of canals and then these hedgerows. We didn't know what we were doing, there were solid trees lining these sunken roads, made us sitting ducks in the pitch dark, and the Germans hid in every one of them and shot us up like a bunch of Girl Scouts. And it stunk. There were bodies everywhere. Germans. Us. Cows. Goats. Horses. We finally got out of the hedgerows and busted into a city, Saint-Lô. It was a wreck. Houses all knocked down. Church destroyed. Hand-to-hand fighting. And then my unit got pulled out of the line and sent up to this old farm for a week. That's where I met Doc. He was already there, doing a recon for a new field hospital. It was out of the way, quiet, six or seven miles to Saint-Lô, but behind the lines. Then one day this little German patrol shows up and we get into a skirmish."

George stirred his coffee. Lucille wanted him to maneuver away from the hard parts.

"The Germans fired down on us from up on a road. Nothing but an anti-tank gun, but they blew us to pieces. It knocked the barn door in and blew up our command post. Men everywhere dead and bleeding on the ground. Your father was running all over doctoring men when he got shot in the back."

He waited to see if Frank would ask another question. Frank did not.

"By then, the skirmish was over and we were trying to pick up the pieces when I saw him get hit and knocked to the ground. By the time I got to him this girl from the farm was on the ground helping him and then Major Halliburton ran past us and into the house. We dragged your father into the house and laid him out on the floor. There was a hole in his back and this farm girl was trying to stop the bleeding, but Halliburton just stood there. He had a web belt on, some bandages and morphine. I tried to get them off him and he took off running up the stairs."

George was surprised at how little his telling the story upset him. He was the only one alive, he knew, that could know what actually happened, but he was glad of what actually happened. Frank could ask anything; he would tell him.

"You said that's where you met my father. Did you mean 'meet up'? Didn't you already know him, in England?"

George looked at Lucille, and shrugged. He wasn't going to volunteer, but he wasn't going to lie.

"Why do you think I knew your father in England?"

"Because the court martial summary says Dad testified that the man they had on trial was a man he knew when he was training in England."

Lucille knew about the court martial. She didn't know about the summary. She didn't want Frank Hastings in her kitchen, and told him to leave. George shook his head, no, that Frank could stay. He drank deeply into the coffee cup, then set it down.

"How did you know it was me, Frank?"

"I met the farm girl, the girl who ran to him when he was shot and cradled him on the floor of her farmhouse and tried to keep him from bleeding to death. She told me the same story, except that she couldn't remember your name, just that you were Dad's friend. The army record says they court martialed Corporal Curtiss, an airplane name. Dad testified that the man they had on trial wasn't Corporal Curtiss, it was Private Douglas, another airplane name." He waited to see if George would admit it. "But I know that his best friend is Mr. Grumman. Another airplane name. How many names did you use in the war, Mr. Grumman?"

"Just those three."

"Why would Major Halliburton try to kill my father? My father wouldn't harm a flea. Why?"

George almost couldn't remember. They had been friends, the three of them. He had been Douglas then, in England, before they ever invaded France. Being Douglas training as a medical clerk in England was a lot safer than being Grumman in the infantry had been in Sicily, so he just forged a new personnel file and got some dog tags, cut himself some orders, and went to Shrivenham.

"We were at this training school, in England, and we just hit it off, all three of us. Your father and me, and Halliburton. I don't know why. Guys do. We did all this field hospital training together, went on passes together, and then one day went into this town, to a club. All the soldiers were hitting on the local girls, you know? It was just the way things were. And the girls were hitting on the soldiers. So we're having a beer and Halliburton has this girl cornered and he's about to get her to put out for him and your dad tells him he's got to use a rubber. We called them French letters. Imagine that. And he didn't have one. Hell, rubbers were everywhere, but it was reg. If you showed up with the clap, VD, you got court martialed. But Halliburton couldn't find one and then the girl sort of sobers up and wanders off with another guy, and that's that. Halliburton went over the top. Furious. Men laughing at him in the club. He couldn't take it. So, the next thing we know, Halliburton blames your dad. We get back to the camp and Halliburton is duty officer and he makes your dad do short arm inspections. You know what that is? Drip checks, for VD. He humiliated Doc in front of the men at midnight. Every night. Every GI."

"And the men, in front of him."

"You can say that again. But your dad was just going to let it go. Then one night, right before we shipped out, we got this pass to go to London. Your dad's brother was supposed to meet Doc in a club there, said there was something he really wanted to talk about. We go there and Will's brother doesn't show up but Halliburton does, and he's drunk. And mean. He starts pulling Will around by his service tie, dragging him up to the prostitutes out on the street, yelling about rubbers and all, and well, enough was enough. I'm not saying what I did to him but after that I wasn't Douglas any more. I got some unit patches and was working on making me a new personnel file when I showed up at the replacement depo as Curtiss. They put me in the 116th. I landed on the beach in the first wave. Two months later, I look up and there's your father, in this chateau. Three days later, Halliburton shows up. He keeps clear of me but he starts in again on Doc. Harasses your father in front of the men. In front of the girl. In front of her family. And then the skirmish starts."

George was surprised at how easily it all came back to him. It was easier when it wasn't necessary to lie, or fudge the truth, or leave parts out.

"We all knew Halliburton was after the girl's sister. Christ, she was gorgeous, but just a kid. I don't know how we found out what Halliburton did to her, maybe your father told me. They would have told him, so maybe that's it. We were all thinking about cutting off his dick anyway for raping that girl but then we look up and there's this German patrol sitting up there on the road. We let it sit. It wasn't bothering us; we didn't bother it. Then Halliburton comes running out of the command post like something was after him. He gets up on the wall and lets fly at the Germans with a machine gun. The battle didn't last ten minutes. We were like the barrel of fish that was being shot into."

"Halliburton fired the first shots?"

"He did. And the Germans pretty much fired all the rest. They wiped us out and then left. There was your dad, running from man to man, patching them up, digging up bandages and scissors and medical stuff and trying to keep them alive. He ran up to Halliburton and asked him to give him his medical belt. Halliburton took a swing at him, all those men bleeding to death and Halliburton wouldn't even hand over his medical pouch. And that's what nearly got your father killed."

"What nearly got him killed?"

"When Halliburton tried to punch him your father stepped back and came to attention, then saluted him. Within a second, a shot whizzed by Halliburton's head and buried in the wall behind them."

Frank had to smile. No one had to frag an officer they hated. All they had to do was salute them in a combat zone; some sharpshooter would put a round in him.

"Every single man in that unit hated Halliburton. But whoever took a shot at him missed. Then your father was shot in the back. You bet, I think Halliburton shot him. No, I couldn't prove it."

"And they court martialed you for shooting Halliburton instead."

"My body. Another soldier's name. Yes, they court martialed me."

"And Dad testified for you. Something medical."

"Your dad saved my life, Frank, with his medical jargon. He said I wasn't Corporal Curtiss because Corporal Curtiss had kids and that I was someone else, a guy he knew in England who couldn't have kids because..." George Grumman stopped talking, whether from having a bad memory or from embarrassment or both.

"Because you had no testicles," Frank said, very matter-of-factly. "It's in the court martial notes."

George hung his head. Lucille would have slapped Frank if George hadn't put a hand on her leg.

"And the judge had you examined and..." Frank went on.

"I have balls, Frank," George snapped. "They just never dropped. Your father knew that from short arm inspections back in England. He had a medical word for it. But I guarantee you when the court martial judge had them examine me, I sucked 'em up inside me like my life depended on it, and they bought it." George paused, mortified, short of breath. "Listen, Frank; if Doc hadn't been there they'd have shot me, no question about it. My goose was cooked. I was a dead man."

Frank tried to look away. Mrs. Grumman glared at him from across the table. Behind her there was an old Kelvinator refrigerator, a wall of hand-built cabinets over the gas range. To his left, the kitchen sink stood beneath a window with curtains made from flowery print, a mirage to help her smile as she watched her beans and tomatoes wither in the Texas summer heat. He tried to imagine what would have become of her if the army had shot George Grumman. She would have been bitter, a widow, no pension from a soldier convicted of murdering his superior officer, or desertion, or any number of other crimes. No little house in Bridle. No man to raise Ronald and Albert. No one to hold her when it was cold, or in the dark. No Tog.

"So you killed him. For shooting Dad in the back." Frank waited for George to answer.

"I didn't shoot him, no sir." George was surprised. He thought Frank had figured it all out. "I took his medical pouch off him and took it down-stairs so your mother could save your father's life. But I didn't shoot him."

Lucille looked moderately triumphant. George had put Frank in his place. George was innocent and Frank was still a bastard.

Frank was going to be patient.

"Then who did shoot him, Mr. Grumman? And why did you run? Why not stay and prove you didn't do it?"

"Because I knew sitting right there on the floor, watching Doc bleed, that if he came to he would believe I shot Halliburton. He did believe it, for the rest of his life. It looked like I shot the son of a bitch, though, so I ran. I had to. I think it made it easier for Doc, later, to do what he did, believing I killed the man. Sort of a life for a life kind of thing."

They drank coffee for a while. Frank asked George if he remembered French coffee. George didn't; all he had was GI coffee, or jail coffee. Did he have any brandy, or cigars? Or cheese? George had some cigars and, maybe, some cheese, there at Chateau Dupré, before the battle. Then George asked Frank:

"How did you figure all this out?"

"You made me. You and Tog." Frank paused to put his thoughts in order. "Peter and I had this spat at the funeral, he called me a bastard again, you heard it. He said that sort of thing to me all my life. You wrote me a letter, after Dad's funeral, and said you had never heard the story of my being a war *orphan*. Then, after Peter's funeral, Tog handed me all these letters about Dad bringing Baby Francois home from the war. Francois, Franklin. It was right there on paper: I was a bastard. But I wasn't an orphan. There was a lot more just like it but that was enough, so off I went to France to find my mother."

"And you found your mother."

"Yes."

"Your father really loved that girl, Frank. It's nothing to be ashamed of. She was a fine girl. I'm glad you found her." George knew all about Géraldine. He had told Lucille everything he knew. It all fitted together. "I'm not saying anything against Virginia, but I think Doc always remembered that girl. I'm glad you found her."

"Oh, you're talking about Géraldine. I did find her. It was hard work. You know what France is like, but I found her. And, yes, I'm sure that Dad loved her." He almost added, *'Just like Virginia loved Dad's brother,'* but there was no reason he could think of to tell Lucille about Peter. George probably knew; he knew about the man who was really on the porch with Virginia, but Lucille didn't need to know. "But Géraldine Dupré is not my mother. Virginia is. Always has been. You know that. I was born on your farm. In 1948. Judge Altgelt says he remembers it like it was yesterday." He let it sink in, then added: "He said Dad was so shook up delivering me that he messed up my birth certificate."

They stared at each other over the wooden table and the chipped cups. Harsh sunlight came through the window. Frank knew what was coming next; George knew what was coming soon.

Frank took a copy of Claudine's identity card from his jacket pocket and handed it to George. George stared at it for a long time, and nodded. He passed it to Lucille.

Lucille had never seen a picture of Claudine. She had never liked Frank, not even when he was born. She had wanted to build this very house that they were sitting in now, like friends, because she never again wanted to set foot in their farmhouse where Virginia was visiting when she went into labor with Frank. She had been as dismayed as Peter when Tog began to play with Frank as soon as the child was old enough to waddle around the house. She was even more dismayed when Tog completely forgot about Peter and became Frank's best friend. She catalogued the list of evils Frank had brought on Tog: the running away from home, the near-drowning in a fifty-five-gallon oil barrel submarine in a shallow lake behind the school, the broken leg on the ice sheet on Main Street, the botched football scholarship and now, for Tog to be living in a travel trailer behind Bump's farmhouse without a penny to his name. She could, and did, blame Frank Hastings for every one of these crimes, and more. Claudine was, even to Lucille and even now in a photocopy of a faded schoolgirl identity card picture taken by a besotted German photographer, the most beautiful girl she had ever seen. Tog looked exactly like her.

"Is this who shot Halliburton?"

George shivered and gripped the side of the kitchen table to keep from knocking his coffee cup over. At length he answered.

"I chased Halliburton into a bedroom upstairs. She wasn't in there, that's true, but her father was, and it startled me. He grabbed my rifle and put a bullet right through Halliburton's head. Then he handed it back to me, sort of bowed his head like he was saying, 'There, that's done," and then disappeared somewhere inside the house."

Frank saw it now. He hadn't seen it before. Claudine's father hadn't had to run up the main stairs or run back down them. He had disappeared through one of those wooden panels in the hallway that was really a maid's stairs and come out downstairs, by the kitchen door, where Jean-Claude had put up his Minitel. Frank should have figured that out without believing the worst in Mr. Grumman. He was Dad's best friend.

"You ran and that saved their lives. Dad saved yours. I think it was a pretty easy decision for him."

"I loved your dad, Frank. He was the kind of man you loved. He didn't care if you were rich or poor, smart or dumb, officer or GI – if you were his friend, he'd do anything for you. He was a good man."

George waited while Lucille sorted out what had happened. It was going to be hard on her, but it had gone on a lot longer than anyone thought it would, a lot longer than she had thought it would. They would be all right.

"Does Tog know?" he asked.

"Yes. I told him yesterday. He didn't believe me at first. He thought I was coming up with a story so he would stop calling me a bastard."

"I guess that picture did it, even for Tog."

"It took him a while to see it, but yes. He knows."

"And the family?"

"That's why Dad brought Tog home. France was a wreck. His mother was dead. His grandfather had a stroke. His grandmother was alone on a big farm, fighting off starvation and a man who was trying to steal their farm. You owed somebody your life and Tog needed someone to raise him, so Dad brought him to you. You adopted him. A life for a life."

George nodded. Frank was sad, the bearer not of news but of facts that didn't want telling.

"Get out of my house," Lucille hissed. "You've never done anything but cause trouble. You were hard on Virginia. You were hard on Tog. Now he's going to turn on me, because of you. Get out." She jerked up from her chair and almost knocked the table over trying to get to the kitchen door. "He was my baby and you always took him away from me. Your stupid submarines and dogs and firecrackers and running away. Who do you think you are, wrecking lives like that? Get!"

Frank was ready to go. He understood why George had let the lie go on for forty years. Doc believed George had taken a life, and owed one, so it was George's duty to raise Tog. But Lucille had no right to make Frank feel guilty for uncovering her secret, no matter how much she still adored the man-child she had raised.

"Me? I'm just someone who always wanted to know why things happened the way they did." He put his hand on the screen door and opened it. "Part of me is part of everyone I've ever known, ma'am. Of everywhere I've been. Everything I've done and the things people did to me. But in the end, I'm just me."

"You're nobody is who you are. You hear me? Nobody," Lucille spat back at him. "You're damned sure not who you want us to think you are."

"No, ma'am. No one is."

He stepped onto the porch.

"Tog's not yours to lose, ma'am. You and Peter and Tog, and even you, Mr. Grumman, you let me believe I was someone else until I had to go off to find out who I really am. Now Tog has to find out who he really is. It's not a bad thing." *Tog'll be a lot better off in Chateau Dupré than he is now*, Frank thought, *rotting in that godforsaken travel trailer next to Bump Burford's caved-in chicken house, daydreaming about Becky Grey and touchdowns.* "Goodbye Mr. Grumman. Goodbye, Mrs. Grumman."

He walked back to the Hastings house, which would again become Virginia's house and then, after she passed away, would become Jeff and Tiffany's house. All of that was in the future, he knew, and he couldn't tell what the future would bring. Trying to understand what had happened in the past had been hard enough.

Bridle had changed some since the day he had graduated from high school and vowed to never return. As he walked toward home, he noticed that the electric wires that had always cluttered the view of the clear blue sky still cluttered the view, but on the utility poles there now were cable boxes with coaxial wire running in all directions; people in Bridle could watch the same twenty channels of televangelists and reruns of *I Love Lucy* that dull people watched in Austin, or New York. Men he had known all his life still parked their pickup trucks to drink coffee at The Corral but their sons who played for the Broncos had lost their grip; they lost the Homecoming game the night of Peter's funeral and every game after. Elizabeth Grey and the Bronco girls were running track in the state meet. The Bridle Grocery still had lettuce and farm eggs on sale but it also had a special on croissants and hummus. *Who*, he wondered, *had introduced Bridle to croissants and hummus?*

He crossed the street to walk by the locked door of Will's medical clinic. A paper sign listed the schedule of the new doctor who came from Amarillo to see patients, Tuesdays and Fridays, from ten until three. A cinder block garage housed a new ambulance that stood by to drive Bridle's pregnant and broken to a regional medical center in Amarillo. The spire of the old St. Mary's Catholic Church cast almost no shadow in the noon day sun but, beyond it, Frank saw where Bridle had spent money and sweat to build new playing fields on a vacant lot. A girls' soccer game was underway, all skinny legs and shorts and empty white goal nets.

Only the Grumman's little frame house seemed to have changed not at all.

Eleanor was standing in the yard when he turned the last corner to home.

"Was it hard?" she asked. She walked out to the street to meet him, her barely visible tummy detectable underneath the thin dress that was blown against her by the constant wind. He and Eleanor had made their marriage agreement so much better than the one his father must have made, and the one his mother must have accepted. He thought Eleanor was the most beautiful black pregnant Indian English woman he could imagine, and took her hand in his.

"It was hard, and sad. The facts didn't change but history did. That's never easy on anyone."

She looped her arm into his elbow and walked in step with him back to the house to collect their things. She could feel his sense of his own history being reformed in the sound of his voice. It hadn't been easy on him, either. They stopped on the kitchen porch and she tilted his face toward her to kiss him before going inside to say goodbye to his family. Through the screen door they could see Candace and Jeff and Tiffany making sandwiches. Virginia was sitting at the kitchen table, watching them.

"I love you, Frank Hastings," Eleanor said, and smiled. "Let's go home."

She entwined their fingers until their fingertips made a heart. Their Claddagh rings nested into one another.

"I love you Eleanor Herald. Yes, let's go home. Moments quite, with someone special."

Chapter Thirty-Eight

i.

Tranquility was rare in their tiny home.

Ruth napped in her crib. Eleanor had gone for a swim. The mailman opened the metal slot in the door, dropped the mail through, and stepped off the porch. The compact disc player was, thankfully, switched off. *An Khe* lay spread out on the living room floor, hundreds of sheets of paper, all red lines and strikeouts, Hood quite unable to bring himself to frag Major Liddy. The only sound that could be heard inside the house was a blue jay attacking the neighbor's cat on the bank of the dry creek, twenty yards away, outside the open window.

The idea—how to finish *An Khe* properly—had come to Frank two weeks before during their rushed trip back to Bridle, but he had had no time to himself since then. He now gathered up the pages, turned them this way and that to align them, and gave them a good look. Frank wondered if he should ask Miss Barkley to keep an eye on Ruth, just in case he became distracted, but decided it wasn't necessary. He had only a half-hour, at most, and Ruth always napped longer than that. She was, he knew, quite a good baby.

Outside the house, along the path to the swimming pool, a stand of mountain laurel grew at the base of the cliff where the dry creek formed a moat around the little neighborhood park. Sycamore leaves floated gently down to land in drifts along the path and, as Eleanor walked toward the swimming pool, she thought about the day that she had followed Eldred Potts as he led Mr. Barkus' cow back to its pasture. There was nothing on the footpath between their little home in The Sisters and the neighborhood swimming pool that even remotely resembled Faversham—no ancient inn for travelers, no new Sainsbury's or a queue of patients waiting at the new medical clinic. What had brought Faversham back to her thoughts was the article in her alumni newspaper. "Students return to dig," the headline had read. She left her towel and terrycloth robe alongside the pool and dived into the cool water.

It was only Eleanor's fourth or fifth venture to the pool since Ruth's birth. During the early months, when Ruth looked up at her from the crib they had jammed into the bedroom, or nursed, or slept, or gripped Frank by the finger, Eleanor had not had a single thought of swimming. In the months that followed she had juggled motherhood with finishing her dissertation while teaching a section on 'Malory to Marlowe.' Winter came, such as it was, wet but warm, and by the time she defended her dissertation and applied for her degree, most of a year had gone by without her swimming a single lap. She was surprised, now, to find that she had missed it, especially missed the quiet freedom that it gave her to think and contemplate how her life had become completely different than she had expected it would.

I did so want to dig, she thought, stroke stroke stroke. The story, which she had read to Frank in the car on the way to Bridle, went on to say that "... Professor Graves will lead the first group of students to investigate the ruins of Faversham Abbey since the tragic death of a student in an explosion there some years ago." It appeared that UXB squads, ground radar teams, historians of the Luftwaffe all had scoured the ruins for years, looking for more buried bombs, and found none. Stroke stroke flip, touch, kick, stroke. *It would have been quite nice to know that I dug up just one important thing in my life.*

It had been an impromptu trip. Virginia hadn't been well enough to come to Austin to meet her new grandbaby, and besides, if she had, there was no place for anyone to sleep in their tiny house. So, when the university posted Eleanor's name on the degree list, they had celebrated by driving nine hours to Bridle to introduce Ruth to her grandmother and cousins.

Marshall Grey had brought Becky and Elizabeth to the house to see the baby. Candace and Tiffany and Becky and Elizabeth had held Ruth and rocked her, changed her nappies and fed her, and Virginia had gazed quietly into Ruth's deep almond eyes and caressed her tawny skin. The women and girls had dressed her in jumpers and dresses, put little socks on her feet, and tied a very becoming ribbon in her thick black hair and asked why didn't Frank and Eleanor move to Bridle. Jeff then had drowned out their cooing with the blast of crashing machinery, overlaid by cymbals and off-scale human shouting.

"What is that?" Becky had shouted.

"The Wrang Buggas," Jeff had shouted back.

Ruth had perked up immediately, nodding her head in rhythm with the sounds of unsynchronized road graders smashing into one another.

"Turn it off," Candace ordered Jeff, explaining somewhat defensively that, technically, it was not Jeff's compact disc player but Peter's. Eleanor discovered, halfway back to Austin, that the compact disc player had been stashed under a pile of baby quilts on the back seat of the Volvo. It was giftwrapped with a note that said, 'Baby gift. Graduation present. Take it. Keep it. - Candace.'

And now Eleanor had a baby who would take a nap only when she could rock in her crib to the racket of the Wrang Buggas.

Stroke stroke stroke.

It was about that time on the road when Frank had asked Eleanor a question that, at the moment, seemed like a bomb.

"Do you ever think about what would have happened if I hadn't asked you to marry me?" he had asked.

"Yes, of course I do. I would have waited another week, then asked you. Why?"

"I was, well, to be honest, I was wondering if you ever wondered about, you know." She denied knowing. "Do you ever wish you had gone back to England? You were going to use picks and toothbrushes to dig things up." He waited. She had smiled but said nothing. "The lost world of the Anglo-Saxons?"

Stroke stroke glide, touch, flip, push, stroke.

"The article about Faversham. Do you ever wish you had gone back to do that?"

She had almost stopped breathing.

"Never. Not for a moment. It's never occurred to me." *Everything I have and everything I care about is in this car*, she added, to herself. *Everything.*

Nothing more was said about it, then or after, but when they unpacked and she sorted Ruth out and held Frank close to her at night, Eleanor listened to his voice for sounds of doubt. She feared that while she had everything she had ever wanted, Frank did not.

A low point had come when she read Frank's feature in the following week's *Gazette*, a series of three articles titled, '*Chickens: Free range, cage, or genetically bred.*' They weren't very interesting articles. Free range chickens were sort of the earth mothers of the poultry kingdom, pecking at grass and grubs. Broilers and layers, however, were stuffed into cages and force-fed until they could be eaten or made to lay eggs, and they were cheap. Genetically bred super chickens, Frank had written, were larger, produced even more, and were cheaper in every way, except that they were full of BT toxins and caused test rats to become sterile. Writing about chickens was a steep drop from writing about the collapse of banks and home builders, or about the Bluff Springs rapist.

She swam for fifteen minutes before the connection between Frank asking her about the past and Frank writing articles about super chickens struck her. She flailed to the pool ladder as fast as she could, yanked herself out and ran, pulling her robe, flip-flops, and towel with her. Just as she jogged across the Barkleys' yard toward her own front porch, she heard it.

WHUMP!

Smoke plumed up behind their home, a thin, dark, noxious vapor, rising straight into the harsh sunlight. Eleanor stood still in her own front yard and watched, shading her eyes, shocked. She then ran inside to make sure that Ruth was alright.

While Eleanor and Candace and Virginia showed off Ruth, Marshall Grey had taken Frank to The Corral for a hamburger. Bump Burford had walked in. Bump had no idea who Frank was.

"I was Tog's friend," Frank had ventured. "Tog Grumman. He was doing something with cable television wires out at your farm last year."

"That piss ant? Is it true he went off to France? Craziest thing I ever heard." Bump then had asked if Frank was the piss ant who had burned that 'S' onto Bridle's football field.

Frank had grinned but kept his mouth shut.

"Ask him what his nickname was, Bump." Marshall had gouged Frank in the arm. "Nitro. That's what we called him. Nitro. But it wasn't nitro. It was diesel fuel stirred into chicken shit, Bump. Your chicken shit, to be precise."

"Burnt damn good, I'll say that for it. Stain's still there. That must have been over twenty years ago."

That's when Frank began to think how long ago it had been when he had indeed been Nitro and, not quite that far back, when Eleanor had day-dreamed of digging up ruins. He asked her about it on the long drive home.

Eleanor had genuinely not cared for one second that she had forgotten all about archeology and Faversham Abbey and the life she might have had if Frank had not been the fork in her road, and he wished he had been as wise as she. After they got home, it took him almost a week to find a poultry farmer to not only explain the esoterica of chicken management but also to give him enough chicken excrement to compose a reasonable amount of nitrogen and ammonia which, when mixed with some diesel that he drained from the Volvo, would do the job.

When Ruth was fully asleep, he went out back to the old brick barbeque grille. There, in the hot, still afternoon, he said goodbye to Vietnam, to Major Liddy, to Thuy Phuoc and particularly to the pathetic hero-victim of that sorry story. With the words, "Goodbye, Hood," Frank flicked a Bic lighter at the mess and jerked his hand back. *An Khe* exploded in a frenzy of immolated pages and smoldering grudges that had outlived their usefulness.

"FRANK!" He turned to find Eleanor running out the kitchen door, shouting at him. "STOP!"

But it was too late. She pounded her fists on him for a moment, and said he was a fool, and demanded to know what if it had caught the house on fire and what about Ruth. He held her and told her that, as fire-starters go, he had always been a very good one, burning exactly what he intended to burn and nothing more.

"Why did you do it?" she fussed at him, bewildered but knowing exactly why. "You spent years writing it. It was good. It was...."

"It was awful. It wasn't true, not exactly, and it was time for me to let it go. I don't want to live in the past anymore."

Ruth slept through it all.

ii.

A week later Eleanor heard the mailman stuff the mail through the slot in the door. There was the assortment of envelopes that threatened to overwhelm them, balance bills from Eleanor's obstetrician and from Ruth's pediatrician, a notice from the hospital that it had filed for payment with *The Gazette's* insurance company but had not actually received payment. There also were the messages that neither of them had ever contemplated, photography studios that guaranteed pictures of their new baby that would be treasured for generations, life insurance proposals from companies that would be their rock of strength if any of them died, free trial copies of *Parent Magazine* and *Modern Mother*. There were the expected bills as well—the mortgage payment, the gas and electric bills, a bill from Floyd for the Volvo's new tires, the telephone bill, a printer's bill for Eleanor's dissertation.

There was also a thick padded envelope, from France, with a hand-printed letter enclosed. Eleanor lifted Ruth from Frank's arms so that he could open it.

Dear Frank, Eleanor, and Ruth: Grandmère and the ladies of Autumn Leaves send their love. Emil and Prudhomme say *salut*. I won't tell you what Jean-Claude says.

Jeremy is still trying to get the Wrang Buggas to do a concert in the monastery. Their tour starts in October. Here's the CD.

The package is from Aunt Géraldine. I don't know why she didn't just mail it to you but I'm sending it on. Enjoy the pictures.

Francois Georges Dupré

Underneath, he signed it "Tog."

The CD was 'Missing Monks,' titled over a cover photograph of the monastery behind Chateau Dupré. The scene, shot in the evening in the cloisters and upward through the gothic tracery of the vacant window embrasures, gave a ghostly effect to the once-tranquil courtyard where Frank had told Madame Dupré that he knew that he was not Claudine's baby. He could only imagine Jeremy and Tog and the Wrang Buggas setting up amplifiers and crisscrossing the garden with thick electric cables to blast their sound across the countryside. Ruth would love it.

The pictures were more soothing. There was a snapshot of Madame Dupré, Madame Lavois, Madame Lefèvre, and Coco Dubois, standing with Dr. Ben Khetta. Each of them held a glass of brandy and a cigar. Another showed the forecourt of Chateau Dupré, where Will had been shot. One picture included the barn, whose new roof shaded a poultry coop, a hint that Jean-Claude had kept his end of the bargain.

"This is the orchard. Rouge Druets, for Calvados."

"What are the bottles?"

The orchard glittered with hundreds of glass bottles stuck onto the tree branches. Tog had come up with a scheme to grow apple seedlings inside wine bottles and then fill the bottles with cheap Calvados, with an apple inside, to sell to tourists.

There were two photographs of the cemetery. Tog had written the word 'Mother' on the backside of a picture of Claudine's grave. The other showed Dr. Genet's tomb.

"Dr. Genet got me arrested," Frank told her. "I was looking inside the windows of his house when Emil's policeman hauled me away."

Tog had clipped a note to the picture. "Dr. Genet gave your father his old wicker fishing creel. He smuggled me out of France in it."

"One more mystery solved." Frank smiled at the thought of Will crossing the Atlantic with a squalling baby hidden inside the creel, that one photograph of Virginia and Peter tucked inside the lining where it would remain for almost forty years. The creel had done its work.

"Open the package," Eleanor nudged him.

The package was postmarked from Galway, Ireland, but without a return address. It was directed to M. et Mme. Frank et Eleanor Hastings et Mlle. Ruth Hastings aux soins de Mme. Marie-France Dupré, chateau connu, Sainte Marie du Vire, La Manche, France.

Géraldine had embroidered a christening blanket for Ruth. On it she had stitched in white linen "Où tu vas, Je vais avec tu."

"Whither thou goest, I go with you," Eleanor said aloud.

Géraldine also had written a card in her lovely language, saying only "Is true always. - G.D."

Inside a tiny paper box she had put two rings, woven from the straw of grass stems.

Ruth began to stir. Eleanor gently released herself from her husband

and took the blanket and the rings to show to the baby. Frank sagged back on the sofa and stared blankly at the monitor. An hour passed before Eleanor could shower and change, before they had tea, and until Eleanor took Ruth to nurse. It was a special day.

iii.

It was not until almost midnight that Eleanor realized that Frank was awake.

"Are you alright?" she whispered. The room was so small that it was difficult to get in or out of bed without bumping Ruth's crib; she slept quietly.

"I missed something," he answered. "I saw something, without seeing it. I missed it." His eyes were wide open, staring in the dark at the ceiling. It might have been the tea, the manuscript, the sheer joy of finding himself in his home with his wife and his daughter. It wasn't any of those.

"What are you talking about?" she whispered again. "Go back to sleep."

He lay quietly for another fifteen minutes. When Eleanor made sounds of deeper sleep and Ruth sighed the cooing burr of an uncluttered mind, he inched his way out of the bed and into the living room where he could study the blanket, Géraldine's note, the rings. All were as free of guile as Géraldine was herself. He pored over them carefully and turned her envelope inside out; they were exactly what they appeared to be, and no more. He read the note again – all the *Feuilles D'Automne* ladies were present and, as best he could tell, accounted for.

It was there in front of him, on the picture of Dr. Genet's tomb. In the sweet sadness of imagining his father and Dr. Genet spiriting Tog away, Frank had missed the small flagstone next to the doctor's grave.

Enfant Américain. Né et mort, 1945

He felt Eleanor's hand on his shoulder.

"What are you doing up?" she whispered.

He showed her the photograph of the baby's grave in the churchyard of Ste. Marie. It was not that the child had been buried next to Dr. Genet, but that Dr. Genet had been buried next to the child.

"When I found Géraldine I was certain that she was my mother. But I wanted to know why she entered a convent instead of keeping me. 'Was I a bad baby? An ugly baby? An embarrassment?'"

"What did she tell you?" Eleanor took his hand.

"She said 'Shh, Frank Hastings, don't think those things.'" He sighed. "Then she told me about being kidnapped. She said she was already in the convent when Dad came back for her. So I asked her if that was when Dad brought me home, but she didn't answer me, not exactly. What she said was, 'That is what the telegram says.' Then I asked her 'Didn't you want me?'"

Frank touched the photograph very lightly with his finger, running it along the edges of the tiny grave.

"'I wanted you,' she told me. 'Yes, very much.' And that was when I began to think that she might not be my mother. I wanted her to be, very much, and she wanted me to be her baby, very much, but I had this sense that neither one of us quite got what we wanted."

Eleanor sat quietly as he worked out the rest of it.

"She didn't lie to me; she just didn't tell me that the baby she wanted, she had already lost. Or that the mother I wanted, I already had."

Frank had thought about it, whether his father should not have married his mother because he loved Géraldine, or if his mother shouldn't have married his father because she had been in love with his father's brother.

Even the details of their deception had consumed his thoughts. Shouldn't they have told him and his brother, Peter, what had happened during the war? Had his father kept Géraldine's scarf hidden somewhere and mailed it back to her on the day he died, or had Géraldine kept it until she gave it to Frank? Where had the picture of Virginia standing on the porch in Tierra with Peter, Will's brother, been hidden for decades before Frank dug it out of his father's fishing creel? Had Virginia stopped talking because of that stupid letter inviting Will and 'Geraldine' back to an army reunion, and was that why they suddenly left Bridle to move up to Colorado?

In the end, he had decided none of it was important. His father and his mother each had lost the ones they wanted and married the ones the ones they loved enough. They had agreed to raise Peter, his brother, as their own and to have Frank, and questions of whether they married wisely were long settled.

"We don't know everything."

"No, but we know all that matters," Eleanor answered.

The earliest bit of dawn began to filter light through the window. Ruth was stirring in her crib. Eleanor picked their baby up and Frank gazed into her deep, dark eyes.

"Look at her," he whispered. "She's so beautiful." He wanted to keep her from all of the harm that he knew would come with life. "The one thing we do know is who our baby is."

"Yes," Eleanor whispered back. "But she doesn't."

"No," Frank answered, and sighed. "Not yet. But who she is, that's something Ruth will have to decide for herself."

About the Author

Jack Woodville London studied the craft of fiction at the Academy of Fiction, St. Céré, France and at Oxford University. He was the first Author of the Year of the Military Writers Society of America.

His **French Letters** novels are widely praised for their portrayal of America in the 1940s, both at home and in the Second World War, and as Americans evolved from the experience of that war into the consumer society of the baby boom generation. *Children of a Good War* is the third book in that series. The first book, *Virginia's War,* was a Finalist for Best Novel of the South and the Dear Author 'Novel with a Romantic Element' contest. The second volume, *Engaged in War,* won the silver medal for general fiction at the London Book Festival, among other awards.

His craft book, *A Novel Approach,* a short and light-hearted work on the conventions of writing, is designed to help writers who are setting out on the path to write their first book. *A Novel Approach* won the E-Lit Gold Medal for non-fiction in 2015. Jack also is the author of several published articles on the craft of writing and on early 20th century history.

His work in progress is *Shades of the Deep Blue Sea,* a mystery-adventure novel about two sailors and a girl, set on a Pacific island World War II.

He lives in Austin, Texas. Visit him at jwlbooks.com or contact him at jack@jackwlondon.com.

CPSIA information can be obtained
at www.ICGtesting.com
Printed in the USA
FFHW02n2246150818
47838380-51530FF